To Debbie

SEAGULLS OVER WESTMINSTER

RICHARD WADE

Best wishes
Richard Wade
5/19

'We just need to get you elected and then it will all fall into place'

Prologue

'I guess you must be feeling pretty stupid right now' said Lionel, shaking his head.

The idiot dressed from head to foot in a seagull costume slowly nodded his beak. Only his two eyes and sweating forehead were visible through a small viewing hole in the seagull's neck, but his embarrassment was still clear to see. Lionel did feel slightly sorry for him. It wasn't *his* fault that things had turned out the way they had tonight.

'Well, shake a tail feather and let's get it over with.' He turned to the others, who were all waiting patiently in a group, and shouted 'OK, everyone, it's showtime!'

He climbed the four steep steps up to the temporary stage and they all followed obediently behind him. The costumed idiot clumsily waddled along at the back, struggling with the yellow diving flippers that were doubling as the seagull's feet. The outfit was clearly not designed for climbing stairs.

As he reached the top, Lionel could feel the heat from a vast bank of TV arc lights pointing towards the stage. Word had spread rapidly around the hall that his announcement was imminent, so the large crowd were already subdued. A hundred or more camera shutters chattered like rapid machine gun fire as he stepped into the light and some of the more fanatical supporters briefly began to whoop and cheer. But it was all very half-hearted and quickly died down. Even *they* must be thinking that it isn't appropriate any more. Not tonight.

The expectant hush quickly returned as Lionel reached the small wooden lectern at the front of the stage. He waited until everyone was in position behind him, cleared his throat and then leaned forward into the microphone. He took a deep breath and began to carefully read out loud:

'I LIONEL MONTAGUE, as Acting Returning Officer, hereby give notice that the total number of votes given for each candidate at the by-election held on Thursday 8th May 2025 is as follows....'

Bradley

MONDAY 6 MAY 2024

One Year Earlier

Bradley Deakin stared out of the taxi as it swung around London's Hyde Park Corner. The sun reflected on his instantly recognisable swept-back grey hair, catching him squarely on his good side. Unusually - and largely because he was alone in a driverless Robo-Taxi - he wasn't giving much thought to how he looked, as his mind was distracted elsewhere.

He'd been invited to meet the Chairman of the Opposition Party, Peter Wilkinson, and Bradley had initially assumed it was to discuss an interview for his talk show *'Speakin' to Deakin'*. But, unusually, Peter had asked him to meet at his house in Victoria, rather than at the party's main offices. He had also insisted that no-one be told about the meeting, so Bradley was therefore intrigued.

It had been a bad week for the Opposition Party, especially their leader, Matthew Draper. Last week, they had lost a by-election - almost unheard of against an increasingly weak government that was now twelve months into power.

Bradley had first met the Chairman back in 2010 when he had himself become an MP. At the time, Peter was already a senior figure in the party and only became Chairman in May 2023. That was just after the General Election that had dumped the party back into opposition once again. Bradley had often visited the Chairman's house socially, but not for some time. Surprisingly, Peter was there to meet him at the front door even before he had emerged from the taxi.

'Bradley, so good to see you again, my friend' he said warmly. 'How are Emma and little Stephen? Not so little now, I guess.'

'Yes, he's growing up fast' Bradley replied, equally warmly. 'Thirteen, would you believe?' He deliberately hadn't mentioned Emma, who had thrown him out of the house last week and not spoken a word to him since. It was all too complicated to explain and could wait for another time.

Bradley had liked Peter from day one. The Parliamentary veteran had immediately taken the promising new boy under his wing and they had remained friends ever since, even after Bradley unexpectedly lost his seat in 2015.

'So, what's all this about?' asked Bradley, as they walked into Peter's comfortable lounge. 'I didn't think cloak and dagger meetings were really your style?'

'No, sorry about this' Peter replied, slightly embarrassed. 'But I thought complete privacy was probably best on this occasion.'

'So, I assume this isn't about coming on my show, then?'

'No, it isn't' said Peter, sitting down on the couch and gesturing that Bradley should help himself to coffee. 'I'll get straight to the point. You're aware of the current dire situation with the party's leadership, especially after last week's car crash of a by-election. Bloody disappointing to say the least.'

'Yes, it was' said Bradley 'but not entirely unexpected.'

Being host of a popular talk show, where he interviewed senior politicians as well as A-List celebrities, Bradley always displayed impartiality on screen. But, in his heart, he had never lost his allegiance to the party, and never would. 'Matthew does seem to be under a lot of pressure' he added, trying to be diplomatic.

'You could say that' replied Peter with a wry smile. 'But even when we chose him last year, he was only ever going to be a caretaker leader. You'll remember the awful set of candidates we had to choose from at the time. As I recall, you were pretty harsh about them on that show of yours...'

Bradley had indeed described it as *'like trying to choose a new village idiot when none of the candidates are remotely qualified for the job'*. Draper was chosen as the best of a very bad bunch but, at seventy-one years old and keen to retire, he was never going to inspire a new generation of voters.

'Yes, I'm not ashamed to say I was' Bradley replied. 'And I haven't changed my view since. If Matthew went tomorrow, God knows which faceless loser you'd find to replace him. Err, sorry Peter, I didn't mean to be quite so . . .'

'. . . honest? No, not at all' said Peter. 'My thoughts entirely. And a sentiment shared by most of your former colleagues on our side of the House too, I'm afraid. The only blessing is that the government are in the same sorry state as us in terms of rubbish leadership, so it's a bit of a race to the bottom. But that's been the case for over ten years now. It's no wonder we're stuck with this endless run of hung Parliaments.'

Bradley was about to comment but Peter hadn't finished.

'Britain needs someone the whole country can unite behind and really want to vote for. I don't mean the die-hard loyalists who would vote for a trained chimp as long as it was wearing their party's rosette. No, I mean the swing voters in the middle. *They're* the ones who can really deliver the sweeping majority that any successful government needs. People want a leader with charisma. Say what you like about Thatcher and Blair, but they both had it in spades. Yes, they lost the plot by the end, but they were able to inspire - or maybe fool – people into thinking they were the start of a brave new dawn in British politics. We need someone like that now. Throw in a weak leader on the other side – like our current Prime Minister - and suddenly we've won a massive majority and a good ten years or more in power.'

Bradley could see Peter's point. The country was bored to death with the current crop of insipid politicians and constant General Elections - one almost every two years since 2015.

'So how can I help?' he said, still bemused at why he was there. 'I suppose I could ask the BBC to commission a new talent show for you? Last one voted off becomes Prime Minister, how does that sound? The contestants could give the judges a rousing policy speech whilst baking chocolate brownies. What do you think?'

'Probably not, but it's a thought I suppose' said Peter, with only the slightest smile. 'But, seriously, we've got a much better idea. Perhaps even more radical than that, if it's possible.'

'Which is what?'

'We want you.'

2

Harvey

MONDAY 6 MAY 2024

'There's a letter for you on the kitchen table' shouted Claire from upstairs as Harvey removed his jacket in the hall. 'Looks important.'

'OK, thanks' he shouted back. He wandered towards the kitchen, largely unconcerned about the mystery letter. Harvey Britten had just walked the two miles back from the BBC Radio studios in Brighton and was in dire need of a sit down and a cup of tea.

He had retired just over a year ago on reaching his sixtieth birthday, having worked for the Southern Savings and Investment Bank for forty-two years, ever since he left school. For the last two decades he had been an SS&I branch manager but, by the end, couldn't wait to call it a day. Luckily, the bank was just as keen to see the back of him too and offered him a very generous retirement package to encourage him to throw in the towel.

Harvey had enjoyed every minute of the last twelve months. There were only three things that were important in his life - his family, his football team and the city of his birth - Brighton. Even when the bank had sometimes moved him to other branches around Sussex during his managerial career, he had always managed to commute back home every night to his wife, Claire, and their beautiful daughter, Samantha. She was now twenty-eight and living in Tunbridge Wells with her husband Piers, a successful city fund manager. Three years ago, they had presented Harvey and Claire's with a precious little grand-daughter, Phoebe, who was now the light of both their lives.

Retirement had also allowed Harvey far more time to support his beloved football team, Brighton and Hove Albion, known affectionately as the Seagulls. He had supported the Albion – as they were otherwise known – ever since his father first took him to a match at the age of six. Indeed, his vast knowledge and enthusiasm for the team had led directly to his regular appearances on Radio Brighton, a wholly unexpected career change.

Last September, the producer of the Radio Brighton Breakfast Show, Ashley Parker, came up with a new idea for the Friday programme, whereby 'real' Seagulls fans would come in to preview the weekend's football matches. Finding himself with time on his hands, Harvey had applied and was amazed to be chosen for a trial. He was articulate, quick witted and utterly relaxed on the air, but whilst that clearly played a major part in him being chosen, it was his instant rapport with the host, Dale Glover, that was actually the deciding factor. Their comical on-air banter immediately appealed to the listeners and, within a couple of months, the other fans were shown the red card. Harvey's role was later extended to include a review of the daily newspapers as well. His natural flair for broadcasting was as much a surprise to him as anyone else, but Claire said it was because he had the perfect face for radio.

He put the kettle on and turned his attention to the cream coloured envelope on the kitchen table. It had a distinctive, green portcullis logo in the corner with the words '*House of Commons*' printed underneath.

'Looks official, who's it from?' said Claire, having walked in behind him. She delivered a kiss on his cheek - something she did whenever he arrived home - and he gently stroked her arm in return.

'Looks like it's from the government' he said, looking concerned. That can never mean good news.'

'Is it your knighthood come through at last?' joked Claire.

'About time, if it is' he replied, carefully unfolding the letter. 'Hmmm, interesting. It's from Sarah Billingham. She's our MP, isn't she?'

Harvey knew very well who Sarah was, having voting for her in the last election. It was not the first time he'd voted for her party, but he had not told Claire that. She was far more committed to supporting the current Opposition Party than Harvey ever was, and had been a card-carrying member from way back in her university days. She still attended local meetings but no longer helped out during elections, distributing leaflets or otherwise drumming up support. Her arthritic knees had sadly put paid to that level of commitment.

Harvey generally supported the party too, but only to show solidarity to Claire as it helped avoid family arguments during stressful election campaigns. But he had been known to secretly vote for the other side now and again. Certainly, what with Brexit and all the other nonsense over the last ten years, he had become increasingly disillusioned with politicians on all sides. In his view, they were all just as bad as one another nowadays and even Claire was beginning to reach the same sad conclusion.

It was telling that they didn't even use their old party names anymore. The *Anonymised Naming Regime* came into force just before the last General Election in 2023. It now meant that, whoever was in power at a given time, was obliged to call themselves the 'Party of Government' - or POG. The other side then became the 'Opposition Party,' or OP. There had been a realignment of parties in the fall-out from Brexit and it essentially left just two main parties after various mergers and annexations. The anonymising approach was supposed to make it easier for younger people to understand politics, giving them a straight choice between government or opposition. Harvey was never sure how that helped and, if anything, thought it actually made things more confusing. But a national vote on the idea was held via social media and the verdict came back strongly in favour. It seems that partisan flag waving was now seen as 'non-inclusive' by the younger generation, so that was that. The public had spoken and - as always, in Harvey's view – had made a complete mess of the decision.

Either way, he had backed the winner last time round and Sarah Billingham was now the POG MP for Brighton and Hove. He had only really done so because she was born and raised in Brighton, like him, and claimed to support the Seagulls. To Harvey, that was the only thing setting her apart from her cocky young rival who had only looked about twelve anyway. Claire had backed him none-theless, despite having her own reservations about his abilities - but such is party loyalty.

Harvey felt he had actually made the right choice in voting for Sarah, despite the government itself now being weak and direction-less. She was making something of a name for herself in Parliament and was seen as a future high flyer. She was also building a good local reputation as well, but Claire would never accept that she was doing a good job. In her eyes, at least, any politician associated with the POG just couldn't ever be trusted.

Harvey began reading the letter out loud:

'*DEAR MR BRITTEN, I'd be delighted if you and your wife, Claire, would join me at a constituency dinner at the House of Commons on Tuesday June 4th 2024. I do hope you will be able to come.*'

'WHAT US?' said Claire, in disbelief. 'She cannot be serious, surely?'

3

Bradley

MONDAY 6 MAY 2024

Sorry?' said Bradley, thinking he must have misheard.

'I said, we think the best man to lead the party back to government is you.' Peter stared Bradley full in the eyes as he told him, presumably to gauge his reaction.

'And who are *we*, exactly?'

'Senior people in the OP' Peter replied, grandly. 'I'm here on their behalf, but fully support the idea myself, of course. I know it sounds a bit random, but just think about it for a minute. You've got everything it takes. You were a bloody good MP with great prospects. Everyone said so. It wasn't your fault you lost your seat — you were just a victim of national party voting. You've got huge charisma and, let's be honest, you're a good-looking bastard and the camera adores you.'

'I didn't know you cared' said Bradley, dryly.

'Well, you're not just some glossy celebrity without any political credentials, are you? Not like Donald Trump was at the start. You're clever and articulate and, on your talk show, I've seen you wipe the floor with even the most experienced politicians - including me, sometimes! But most of all, the public love and trust you. I just know you could win support from the middle ground very easily.'

Bradley was genuinely lost for words - a rare experience – and his heart was racing. Whilst it had been his lifelong dream to be Prime Minister, the very same electorate who now supposedly adored him had cruelly shattered that ambition nine years ago when he lost his seat.

'I'm flattered, obviously' he said 'but. . . *seriously?*'

'Very much so' said Peter. 'Look, with a majority of just four, we all know that the government will be lucky to survive another two years, at most. But we're not making any headway against them because the public think we're just as bad as them - if not worse - especially with Matthew in charge. But if we could just find an inspiring leader with popular appeal, at a time when the POG has no-one like it to compete, then I know we could really win big next time round.'

'It's a very nice idea' said Bradley, 'but it's the stuff of fantasy, surely? Our MPs wouldn't just accept me swanning in and taking over as easy as that. Nor would the wider OP membership for that matter. Would they?'

'Look, this isn't something we just thought up over a drunken dinner one night' said Peter. 'We've been conducting secret polling and focus groups for months, asking people who they would *really* like to see as Prime Minister. Someone they would truly vote for in a *real* General Election - not just a hypothetical one in a survey. We included the usual suspects from both parties, of course, but also a few more radical choices like you and some other credible characters - serious broadcasters, industry leaders and so on. For balance, we then threw in some more lightweight celebrities - popular comedians, singers and such like - to ensure it wasn't just the idea of celebrity in itself that might attract people.'

'And the judges' verdict was . . . ?' asked Bradley, not really taking it seriously.

'Surprisingly, the celebrities didn't do as well you might expect when people thought about it seriously. Politicians didn't fare too well either, of course, and Matthew was right near the bottom. But that's not a surprise either, I fear.'

'Was the PM in there too?'

'Of course, mid-table finish' said Peter. 'But people already see him in that role anyway, although it does highlight the gulf between him and Matthew at the moment.'

'I suppose I must ask,' said Bradley. 'Where did I finish in this table? Just out of interest.' He tried to appear nonchalant about it but was actually desperate to know.

'Top of the heap' said Peter, excitedly. 'Every single person scored you highest and said you had everything they want to see in a Prime Minister. Take out all the frivolous reasons that some people gave - about you being a sex god and all that - and most of them gave the same reasons as I just told you - they like, respect and trust you. Believe me, Bradley, this is a serious and reliable piece of research. It proves you could *really* swing an election for us.'

Bradley said nothing, trying to decide what to do. He had reluctantly put his political ambitions behind him when he joined the BBC, seven years ago, and was now loving everything about his TV career - the power, the fame and, oh yes, the money.

'Again, it's all very interesting and flattering' he said, finally. 'Of course it is. But - and forgive me if I'm being a bit crass here - I've just signed a new two-year contract for way more than both the PM and Leader of the Opposition earn between them. Why would I give all that up for the slim possibility - not guarantee – of being Prime Minister one day? It's quite a leap of faith.'

'Because the chances aren't slim and it's not just about the money with you is it?' said Peter. 'I remember your drive and ambition when you first became an MP. It's what I immediately liked about you and I nurtured your potential as best I could. I was devastated when you lost your seat – devastated! If only you'd hung on to your dreams just a wee bit longer and tried to get back in again, two years later. I told you we would find you a safe seat somewhere.'

'Yes, well,' said Bradley. 'Who knew General Elections would start coming around as often as my gas bill. The next one wasn't supposed to be for five years and I really couldn't afford to wait around that long. I had a wife and toddler to support.'

Not trying to get back into Parliament during the unexpected snap election in 2017 was actually one of Bradley's biggest regrets.

But it was not just the shiny new BBC contract that had stopped him from trying again so soon after his defeat. The bitter humiliation of that loss had badly bruised his ego and briefly dampened his enthusiasm for a political career.

And I did *want* to be PM at the time' he continued. 'But times change. I'd be risking everything that I've built up in my TV career since then.'

'Look' said Peter. 'When you get to be PM . .'

'. . . *If* I get to be PM.'

'*When* you get to be PM' continued Peter unabated, 'money is the last thing to worry about. Have you ever seen a poor former Prime Minister?'

'Well, no' said Bradley, realising he may have appeared a bit mercenary. 'But let's not get too far ahead of ourselves, shall we? Even if I agreed, there's the tiny matter of me not actually being an MP anymore.'

'Of course,' said Peter 'We need our leader in Parliament, so you would have to win a by-election first. The sooner the better too and I'm hoping we can find you one of our safe seats to inherit. Trust me, Bradley, you have a lot of friends in the OP who see the sense in all this. Even Matthew says he would go quietly if you were lined up to succeed him. But he's hanging on by a thread at the moment so we don't have much time. There's always some idiot wanting to put their own leadership ambitions above the party's best interests. But leave all that to me, for now. I just need you to agree to the idea in principle.'

'OK, look' said Bradley. 'I'll have to think long and hard about this, but I really am grateful for the offer.'

'You deserve it Bradley,' said Peter. 'And clearly, you'll need to speak to Emma as well. It's a very big decision for her too, I know that.'

Bradley didn't reply. The recent break up could not have come at a worse time, but hopefully he could repair things with his wife before anyone else needed to know.

'Right' said Peter. 'You have a good chat with the family but please keep it confidential for now. It needs to stay under wraps until we're ready to go.'

'Will do' said Bradley, standing up to leave.

'But please let me know by next week if you possibly can' Peter continued. 'Trust me, Bradley, this is your time. You could be one of the most successful leaders we've ever had. I really believe that. We just need to get you elected and then it will all fall into place.'

BRADLEY SAT in the RoboTaxi on the way home, wondering what to do for the best. There were so many variables to consider. He would be giving up - risking - so much. What if it wasn't as effortless as Peter said? He would then look a failure - an experience he never wished to repeat after losing his seat. Standing up there on stage that night as they announced his defeat had scarred him for life.

Bradley Deakin saw himself as a winner - exactly what he now was in his TV career. But, if he turned down this golden opportunity, how would he feel at the next General Election when he might perhaps have been right there – standing on the steps of 10 Downing Street? Would he be haunted by 'what ifs' for the rest of his days, all because he took the safe option?

The horn sounded in the driverless taxi and it suddenly braked, shattering his concentration. The cab had automatically hooted at a van jumping a red light. *Bloody hell, these things even have road-rage built into their circuits!*

It brought his mind back to a more pressing issue: Emma. Before doing anything else, he first had to resolve things with her and - to do that - she needed to start returning his calls.

Harvey

MONDAY 6 MAY 2024

'Hi Dale, its Harvey.'

'Hello H, nice surprise. Shouldn't you be having your mid-morning nap by now?'

Like all good relationships, no-one really knew why Dale and Harvey hit it off so well, both on and off the air. Their radio partnership had thrived in the eight months that they had worked together and, during that time, they had also become firm friends.

'Silly question' said Harvey 'but has Sarah Billingham invited you to some dinner or other next month? We've got an invite but I'm not entirely sure why.'

'Well yes, she did. But I thought it was only for A-listers' joked Dale. 'Has she got as far down the bottom of the barrel as you?'

'Yeah, yeah' said Harvey. 'Seriously, why would she invite us?'

'Because you know *me*, I expect' Dale replied flamboyantly. 'I went to school with her. She's an absolute sweetheart and we're still really good friends, even now she's an MP. Hasn't changed her a bit. She's a Seagulls fan too, of course, and, for some reason, finds you amusing. Can't think why.'

Harvey was surprised. 'Really? I never knew you had friends in high places. So, what *is* this dinner, then?'

'Local MPs have them all the time, H. Gives them a chance to butter up their party workers. In exchange, they get a mediocre meal and a tour of Parliament. But Sarah often invites a few local celebs along too, just to give it a bit of glitz. Me, obviously, just to make it *really* fabulous, but I suggested that, this time, she might like to invite you along too. Only to make up the numbers obviously, but she's actually looking forward to meeting you. And I thought Claire might enjoy being shown around the Big House too - party allegiances aside.'

'Gosh' said Harvey, spotting the kindness hidden behind his friend's banter. 'Well, thank you. We'll look forward to it. I think.'

Harvey hung up. It would indeed be nice to have the guided tour but, to do so, Claire would need to have dinner with an MP for the party she had despised all her life. Not something she would normally do – unless or until Hell suffered an unexpected cold snap.

Bradley

TUESDAY 7 MAY 2024

Bradley waited for the electronic gates to open before turning his Lamborghini into the driveway. The gravel crunched reassuringly as he parked alongside Emma's Audi. He always left the car in that spot but, tonight, felt strangely like a visitor to their Hampstead home.

Emma had still not spoken to him since their argument. Thankfully, their son, Stephen, rarely took sides and had spoken to his father every night since. They hadn't discussed exactly *why* Bradley was not living at home at the moment, but the boy wasn't stupid. Sadly, there had been an increasing number of arguments in recent years.

Stephen had passed on Bradley's request about needing to urgently discuss something really important with Emma. It took her until 10 a.m. this morning to finally respond by text, instructing him to come over at seven. He felt unusually anxious, like a naughty schoolboy summoned to the Headmaster's office. He used his house key to get in and was relieved to find that Emma had at least not changed the locks. He wondered whether he should actually have rung the doorbell instead. He didn't know the correct etiquette for husbands who had been thrown out of the family home.

'Hi, Ems, it's me!' he shouted from the hall, trying to sound as normal as possible. 'Where are you?'

Their home was a very large, seven-bedroomed house bought in 2020 after Bradley's BBC contract was first renewed for an eye watering salary. It meant things were finally looking up and they'd both enthusiastically collected the trappings of wealth ever since. The house was certainly modern and flashy and some might even call it tacky and decadent. It certainly smelt of money and success – but that was the whole idea. To Bradley, life was not just about *being* powerful and successful, it was also about being *seen* to be so.

'In here' murmured Emma from the lounge. She had a mournful tone, the sort of voice people put on when ringing into work, pretending to be sick. He found her slouched on the sofa sipping a glass of white wine. She was dressed in an expensive designer tracksuit but looked unusually dishevelled. She was still an attractive woman, slim with long bleached-blond hair, but tended to wear too much make up nowadays for Bradley's liking. She wasn't wearing *any* tonight, though, and was not looking her best. She had red eyes, suggesting she had been crying, and Bradley guessed she had already drunk too much of the near empty bottle of wine on the coffee table. This was not going to be easy, but he never expected it would.

'Our son is at a friend's house for the night, in case you were wondering' she said without looking up. 'I thought it best.'

Bradley was disappointed but didn't think it worth starting an argument over. 'You're probably right' he said, deciding on the diplomatic approach.

'So, what do you want to talk about first?' said Emma, finally looking him in the eye but with utter contempt in her face. 'Your adultery with that little tart or this important 'thing' you so desperately need to discuss?'

'Um . . .well, I haven't exactly prepared a written agenda' said Bradley. 'But it goes without saying that I'm desperately sorry about . . . well, you know.'

'So, let's start with that, then, shall we? Since you brought it up. Keep the suspense going on the other little *thing* for a while.' Emma took another slow sip of wine. She was slurring her words and clearly putting all her effort into keeping it together. 'Tell me about little Dixie bloody Chandler' she said, injecting venom into each word.

Last week, she received a call from someone in the BBC make-up department who she had met once at a party. The snitch had told her about Bradley's fling with Dixie, a young actress from ITV's medical soap drama '*Crash Team*' in which she played a nurse. Last December, Dixie had been a guest on Bradley's show to discuss the new series. It wasn't the first time he had slept with a pretty young actress and he hadn't intended it to be the last. He wrongly believed the unwritten rule that '*what happens at the BBC stays at the BBC*', but Emma's new 'friend' had dispelled that little myth. She had not taken it well.

'Look, it's like I told you last week' he said, having rehearsed his defence on the way over. 'Whatever she told you was exaggerated. It was just a one-off bit of fun . . . not an affair. I've never done anything like that before and I promise it'll never happen again. You know I love you, Ems. It was just . . . the situation. We'd all had a few drinks after the show, you know how it is.'

'No, how is it?'

'Well, she . . . fancied me, I guess. And it was her who made all the moves, I swear. But I'd had too much to drink, she is a very attractive girl and, since I was staying over in the flat, I guess I . . .'

'Ah, yes, now I see! *You wished you were in Dixie, hooray, hooray*'' sang Emma, sarcastically. She had probably thought up the line earlier and been waiting for a chance to use it. But, all the same, Bradley secretly thought it was quite amusing. He made a mental note to use it on Dixie next time he saw her.

'Look, I was a fool' he said. 'I wanted to tell you at the time but, well, because it meant nothing, it didn't seem worth hurting you over. I've learned my lesson, so please forgive me, Ems. I really don't want to lose you over this and, I swear, I haven't seen or heard a word from her since. It's *you* that means . . . *everything* to me. You do know that, don't you?'

Emma gave a long, slow sigh and unsteadily put the wine glass down, saying nothing. He felt like a fallen Roman gladiator, waiting for the Emperor to give the thumbs up or down to spare his life.

'So, what is this big *thing* you need to discuss?' she said finally. Bradley was surprised by the suddenly change of subject. Did it mean he was forgiven? Highly unlikely. The judge had simply adjourned the court to consider her verdict. But he was pleased to move on to discuss the main purpose for his visit.

'It's big, Ems. *Really* big' he said. 'The party want *me* as their leader. They think I could lead them back to power and . . . you know, I think I probably could too. But it would mean giving up the BBC show and going back to politics. The salary would go as well and I'd have to win a by-election, but Peter doesn't see that as a problem. Sweetheart, if it happens, we could all be going to Downing Street!'

He was garbling his words and knew he was talking too quickly. But he was unusually nervous and way too excited. Emma initially looked surprised but then sat back on the couch in silent thought.

'It would mean a big change of life for us' he went on, having calmed himself down. 'A *huge* change. So, we really need to be strong and stick together. God knows, you've seen me through all the ups and downs in my life this far. Good and bad times. And you know I couldn't have done *any* of it without you. We're so much bigger than one silly mistake, you and me - we're a team. So, please don't throw it all away just because I've been a complete bloody idiot.'

'Are you asking me or telling me that this is going to happen, Mr Prime Minister Deakin?' Emma finally looked him in straight in the eyes but there was still a hint of sarcasm there.

'Neither' said Bradley. 'There's so much for us to think about. That's why I needed to talk to you first. If *you* decide that we shouldn't do it - if *you* don't think it's best for all of us, as a family - then I won't. I'll call Peter and tell him. You *both* come first in my life, always have done, always will. Nothing is more important than my family, you know that.'

He secretly prayed that she would agree, but knew it was going to happen anyway - with or without her. It would just be so much easier with her there beside him. He tried his best to look sincere, but needn't have worried. She was staring into the unlit fireplace – anywhere than at his face.

'It *was* what we always wanted' she said after a few moments. 'What we were always working towards.'

Bradley felt the fishing line jerk. She was on the hook.

'It is. And you were – you *are* – an essential part of it. I need you right there beside me - you are my rock. We could have it *all*, Ems - both of us, just as we always planned. What do you say? Can you forgive me, please? I know things haven't been all they should over the last few years. That's my fault, and I'm truly sorry. But I do love you so much, Ems. So, shall we do this? You and me, together against the world?'

Still silence. 'And you swear on your life that it was a one off with this . . . Dixie?' she said finally.

'I swear on Stephen's life.'

She sighed again. A long, deep sigh. 'OK. I'm not promising anything but come home tomorrow and we'll give it a go. But this is your *last* chance. I promise you, Bradley Deakin - I SWEAR - that if you EVER look at another woman, or if I EVER find out you've lied to me, I'll divorce you in a heartbeat and you won't see Stephen or me again. Do you understand?' There was anger in her voice, but also a sad resolve. As if she was being practical rather than following her heart. 'Now, tell me you love me again and bugger off.'

There was only the slightest hint of a smile on her face, but it was enough. Bradley was home.

HE DROVE BACK to his small rented flat in Kensington. He normally only used it to stay overnight before and after recording his show but, reluctantly, it had instead been his home for the last week or so. After tonight's lucky escape, he had decided to stop seeing Dixie after all. It wasn't serious, just sex, and they had only hooked up a few times since the drunken encounter he described to Emma. But it wasn't worth the risk of either a political scandal or Emma leaving him for good. He knew she had meant what she said.

There had been many such flings over the years. Initially at party conferences, with assorted interns and researchers, and countless other opportunities since then at the BBC. None of them meant anything to him and all involved understood the rules of engagement. But, as of now, he needed to be extra careful and act like he was the perfect family man. Voters expected to see a loving husband and father - not a serial womaniser with a broken marriage. He could fake that easily enough, at least for now.

He called Peter from the car but, annoyingly, it went to voicemail, so he left a message:

'Peter? Bradley Deakin. You know that new reality show we were talking about? Just wanted to tell you - it's a 'yes' from me.'

6

Claire

TUESDAY 4 JUNE 2024

A tour of the Houses of Parliament was an exciting prospect for Claire, despite large parts of the building still being encased in scaffolding after years of renovation. She had been in two minds about 'sleeping with the enemy' tonight, though - having dinner with a POG MP and her loving disciples from Brighton. It wasn't that she actually hated them personally. Indeed, she actually had many friends who were POG supporters. But she disagreed with them so passionately on a political level that she worried about embarrassing Harvey by getting into a heated argument. This was really *his* night.

Claire was still getting used to the idea of her husband being a minor local celebrity – just as Harvey was himself. He'd been invited tonight so the guests could mingle with a few famous faces alongside their darling MP. Harvey and Dale were being joined by Giselle, a fellow Brightonian and the current big name in rock music. She, too, was an old school friend of Sarah Billingham and Claire was a big fan of her songs. So, it was the chance to meet *her* that had ultimately persuaded Claire to come. She decided to therefore be polite, bite her tongue and keep her political views to herself - just for tonight - and enjoy the wider experience.

They walked through to the central lobby and checked in at the desk, admiring the ornate surroundings whilst they waited. Suddenly, they heard a gentle, but friendly, voice from behind them.

'Hello, I'm Sarah, welcome.'

They turned to see Sarah Billingham MP greeting them with a warm smile. Harvey had *Googled* her earlier and discovered that she was thirty-four years old, but she actually looked younger in the flesh. Petite, pretty and dressed in a smart two-piece suit, she was - as Claire's mother would have described her - 'instantly likeable.'

'You must be Harvey? Oh, I do love listening to you with Dale. You both make me laugh and he says you're the best thing that's happened to his show in years.'

'I'll tell him you said that' said Harvey. 'He'll deny it and probably sue you for slander.'

Sarah gave an infectious giggle. 'And *you* must be Claire? Wonderful to meet you. I hear you're a doting grandmother to the dearest little girl?'

Claire was amazed that Sarah knew about Phoebe, but assumed Dale had filled her in with their background story beforehand.

'I hope she isn't as much trouble as my little terror' Sarah went on, chatting like an old friend. 'Charlie, he's five. How old is Phoebe?'

'Three' said Claire, even more impressed that the MP even knew her granddaughter's name.

'I bet she's gorgeous. We'll talk children later. And football. But thank you both so much for coming.' Sarah smiled and walked over to welcome another group of guests with equal gusto.

'See? She doesn't bite, does she?' smiled Harvey. 'Really nice lady, actually.'

'Yes' Claire agreed. 'Well prepared too, I'll give her that.'

Unsurprisingly, there was a lot of banter about football over dinner, with Sarah and her guests expressing strong views. Harvey was impressed with Sarah's knowledge and her passion for the Seagulls was clearly on a par with his own.

Dale was sitting way down the table as Sarah had presumably distributed the handful of celebrities sparingly amongst the guests. Thankfully, Giselle was seated nearby so Claire had plenty of time to talk to her too. She tried very hard not to like Sarah, but struggled as the evening went on. Being seated opposite her at dinner, they had spoken at length. Baby talk dominated and, thankfully, party politics never really came up. Claire was particularly keen to know how Sarah juggled life as both a young mother *and* a politician.

'It's not easy' Sarah explained. 'But my husband, Dan, is a diamond. He's an IT project manager and works from home a lot, which helps when I'm at Westminster so much. And both sets of grandparents fight for babysitting rights so it's not as bad as it could be. But I miss both of them so much when I'm away. It's hard not being there at Charlie's bedtime.'

'So, what on earth made you want to become an MP in the first place?' asked Harvey.

'It certainly wasn't my life's ambition, that's for sure' Sarah replied. 'People encouraged me to stand but, really, I owe *everything* to that man at the end of the table - Alistair Buckland, he's my absolute hero. Have you heard of him? He took me under his wing when I was first elected as a Councillor and was meant to be our candidate in the election last year but stood aside for *me*. Can you believe that?'

'Sorry?' said Claire. 'Why on earth would he do that, if you don't mind me asking?'

'Because he is a kind, generous and truly selfless man who put the party before his own ambitions. There aren't many people who would do that, I can tell you. I must introduce you later, you'll love him.'

Claire stared at the apparent saint sitting at the far end of the table. He was in his sixties with a slightly bloated face and thinning grey hair. Overweight for sure, and with a slightly grumpy expression, he was not engaging in the conversation around him and actually seemed a bit bored.

After dinner, Sarah was good to her word and introduced him to Claire and Harvey.

'Here he is' she gushed. 'My Brighton rock! Alistair - this is

Harvey and Claire Britten. Harvey's on the radio with Dale – does the football review I was telling you about.'

Claire could not have been more disappointed. Having built him up to be something special, Alistair was mono-syllabic and unsmiling - if not borderline rude. He clearly wasn't remotely interested in meeting them and Sarah looked embarrassed. She quickly introduced them to a couple of other guests instead, who were big Seagulls fans and keen to meet Harvey.

Claire kept an eye on Alistair Buckland whilst Harvey charmed the two giggling guests. After a while, he disappeared, presumably to go home early. In Claire's book, it was no great loss. Typical POG.

At the end of the evening, Claire felt like she had made a new friend in Sarah, despite the MP's making everyone feel the same way. But they appeared to have made a real connection and even exchanged phone numbers - something Sarah didn't do with anyone else.

IN THE TAXI back to Victoria Station, they reflected on a lovely evening.

'Well, you were getting on very well with Sarah, weren't you?' said Harvey. 'So much for party loyalty. Traitor!'

'She's lovely – for a POG' said Claire, knowing she was being teased.

'So, I assume you have switched sides and will now be voting for *her* next time round?'

Claire thought about it. 'Sadly no' she said - and meant it. Whilst she liked Sarah personally, nothing – but nothing – would ever make her vote POG. 'How about you?'

'Without a doubt, yes' said Harvey. Claire suspected he had actually done so last time. She knew her husband was far less partisan than she was, but didn't mind as much as he thought she did. His ability to judge people on their own merit was one of the things she loved about him.

'My only concession is that I now wouldn't be *too* upset if she won' said Claire. 'And I concede that she *is* a very good local MP. At least she cares about Brighton - even if she is horribly misguided in her politics.'

'I guess that's the closest POG will ever get to your vote' laughed Harvey. 'A moral victory at least. Maybe you'll be persuaded when the time comes, but, personally . . . I think she's terrific.'

'Yes, she most definitely is.'

7

Alistair

THURSDAY 6 JUNE 2024

Alistair Buckland took another sip of whisky as he gazed over the English Channel from his penthouse apartment on Hove seafront. The sun was setting and the magnificent view helped to calm his nerves - as did the whisky.

He had just called Sarah to apologise for being such a miserable old sod at the dinner on Tuesday. She hadn't been impressed. It was only because he loved his occasional one-to-one dinners with Sarah in Westminster and had thought the last-minute text invitation was therefore for just such an occasion. But, in fact, he had only been invited because one of Sarah's other guests had dropped out. Not only did he find himself sharing her company with twenty over-excited constituents but, worse still, he was seated far away from her at dinner. He also had a vicious migraine that night - the after effects of a hangover - so got into a bit of a huff and wrongly let his feelings show.

He knew he'd been completely unprofessional and Sarah had told him as much during the call. He apologised profusely and blamed it on the migraine which, thankfully, she accepted. The last thing he ever wanted to do was upset or disappoint Sarah.

She was doing so well. Only this morning, the *Daily News* had listed her as *'one to watch'* which made Alistair feel like a proud parent. He had guided her career since she was first elected as a Councillor back in 2015, at the age of just twenty-five. At the time, Alistair had just been elected for his third term and was very pleased to show her the ropes. There was something captivating about her zest for life and compassion for everyone and everything. Perhaps there was also a physical attraction on Alistair's part too, despite her being nearly thirty years his junior. Either way, they hit it off immediately and he was now her close friend and mentor.

His affection for Sarah had certainly cost him personally. He had been the almost certain choice for POG candidate last year, after previously missing out more times than he cared to remember. But that was until the OP announced their own candidate for the election, a bright young buck who greatly worried the POG grandees. They felt he was better placed to attract the vital youth vote in what was expected to be a very close contest.

Alistair was highly respected and rarely made enemies. But some in the POG were concerned that his age - sixty-one at the time - might deter younger voters when placed up against such a youthful adversary. Sarah was herself young, attractive and an equally vibrant prospect. So, the former care worker was persuaded to throw her hat into the ring too, placing her in direct competition with Alistair.

He could have fought her for the candidacy and, quite possibly, would still have been selected. But part of him agreed that Sarah stood a much better chance of winning the seat. Their friendship also meant a great deal to him and he didn't want to fight her for the candidacy. So, after much soul searching, he instead stepped aside, putting party and friendship above his own ambition. The ultimate show of loyalty to his protégée.

Sarah had duly won the seat, albeit with the tiniest majority in the country – just 173 votes. But she was now blooming as an MP and clearly there to stay. That, at least, reassured Alistair that both he and the POG had made the right choice. But it had been difficult for him, one of the hardest decisions of his life, as he was unlikely to ever get the chance to stand again. Even if Sarah lost the next election - which looked increasingly unlikely - it could be years before he had another shot at the title himself. By then, he would most likely be pushing seventy so, in reality, he knew his chance had now gone. He would instead have to see out his political career working as a local Councillor.

It was not a complete waste of his talents. He had held some very responsible roles in his time and each was rewarding in its own way. For example, he was currently chairing a committee looking at ways to cull the seagull population in Brighton. New laws had recently been introduced to address a growing national problem by removing the birds' protected status. It opened the door for a more radical solution than just neutralising eggs. A major cull of live birds was therefore now being proposed in Brighton as well. Alistair knew it would be controversial and would doubtless face severe criticism from the many animal rights activists that flourished in the city.

But even such an important project as this could not compare to the responsibility of being a *real* decision maker in Parliament. A prospect that had forever slipped through his grasp. So, he took another sip of whisky, watched the sunset, and reflected on what might have been. Then he poured himself another glass.

8

Bradley

THURSDAY 6 JUNE 2024

'So, how are we looking?' said Bradley.

It was the first meeting of the task force that Peter Wilkinson had formed to handle Bradley's leadership quest and they were both in attendance. Alongside them were the OP's Chief Whip, Trevor Wilson, and a Public Relations cum media consultant called Rod Archer - a life-long OP activist.

First off, Bradley needed to get himself elected and, for that, he needed a by-election. Waiting for the next General Election would be too late. If Bradley wasn't leading the party by then, the POG would be up against Matthew instead. He was currently so weak that they could end up retaining power for another five years. That would obviously be a tragedy for the party but, on a personal level, Bradley wasn't doing this just to become Leader of the Opposition for the next few years – he wanted to be in Downing Street.

'I'm working through a list of our own MPs who are getting past their sell-by date' said Trevor. 'We're still trying to persuade one of them to step down for the greater good. But it's a struggle. They're not exactly queuing up.'

Bradley frowned. 'You know, the more I think about it, the more trying to force a by-election worries me. It's a dangerous approach.

The public only tolerate elections when it's absolutely necessary. So, how will it look if we bribe some old lag to step aside, in exchange for a peerage or a dodgy knighthood, just to manufacture a by-election for me?'

'I agree it's a big risk' said Rod. 'But it's even more of a risk if we instead wait for a by-election to trigger naturally. Essentially, for that to happen, an MP has to either die, contract a terminal illness or be unseated in disgrace. And it's then in the lap of the Gods whether their seat is winnable. What if it's a POG MP with a huge majority or one of our own MPs with a tiny one? Neither seat would be suitable and it could be months or years before the perfect opportunity falls into our laps. No, we need a safe OP seat with a big fat majority - and we need it now. If a few voters feel miffed at being dragged to the ballot box unnecessarily, then so be it.'

'Quite right' said Peter, nodding enthusiastically.

'Meanwhile, we need to work on your image, Bradley.' Rod went on.

'I thought that was my strong point?'

'Yes, but you're currently seen as a TV star, not a political figure anymore. People have placed you in a box marked *'celebrity.'* So, if a by-election was called tomorrow, it would take the public by surprise when you suddenly stepped forward. They have to get used to the idea of you being a *real* contender as Prime Minister in waiting, not just their fantasy choice in a survey. That's vital, if they're really going to get behind you.'

'OK, I can see that,' said Bradley.

Initially, he hadn't been sure what to make of Rod Archer, who had an intense, slightly sinister, air about him. He usually dressed entirely in black, adding sunglasses and a matching baseball cap whenever he was outside. Bradley wasn't sure whether he just looked super cool or more like a wannabe CIA agent who hadn't passed the physical. He was very much Peter's man. Bradley was vaguely aware of his background in lobbying and as a political journalist on various OP supporting websites, but knew little else about him. There was apparently a dalliance with the military somewhere in his past and he certainly cultivated an aura of mystery about him −

suggesting he 'knew stuff' but was unable to reveal his sources. But Bradley had dealt with hundreds of lobbyists in his time and that was a very common approach. They all gave the impression of having inside information that no-one else knew, usually just to give themselves an edge over their rivals. But Peter spoke very highly of Rod and, so far, he seemed to be talking sense.

'So how do we get our own version of the story out there?' said Trevor.

'We drip feed it' said Rod. 'First, we release the survey that shows Bradley as the people's choice for PM, which will plant the idea in the public's mind. Then we can start them talking about it. Peter, could we get your mate Alan at the *Daily Record* to do a feature article supporting the idea?'

Alan McQueen was editor of the *Daily Record*. As most people now got their news from the internet, print media had dramatically declined in the past ten years. Whilst there was still a big demand for national daily newspapers, the switch to online had taken quite a toll on the industry. Following a succession of closures, consolidations and mergers over the past five years, just two national newspapers of any note now remained. The *Daily Record* was a rabid supporter of the OP whilst the rival *Daily News* was equally loyal to the POG. Together, they dominated the UK press, both in print and online form.

'I think he'd be up for it' said Peter. 'He can't stand Matthew.'

'My sources tell me that, after last month's by-election result, the PM is being pressed to call a General Election whilst Matthew is looking unelectable. But current polling still only puts POG five points ahead, which is not a certain winning position. My bet is he'll wait until the Council elections next May and, if POG gets a good set of results out of it, then he'll go for October 2025. So, we *must* get Bradley a seat long before then so that he can be nicely in place and ready for a General Election whenever it happens.'

'So, basically, if no-one steps aside, we need someone with a winnable seat to conveniently drop dead right about now, is that right?' said Bradley.

'If all else fails, yes' said Rod. 'But we'll keep pushing for a suitable MP to resign. Trevor and I are gathering dirt to help twist a few arms. I can't stress how important it is to get an early by-election. Without it, we're stuffed.'

BRADLEY LEFT the meeting feeling impatient. It was all so near yet so far. Whilst he was waiting for a taxi back to Hampstead, a couple of women passed by and muttered behind their hands, clearly recognising his face. He actually liked people pointing him out in the street or asking for selfies. Especially pretty young tourists. He had done very well there in the past - but not anymore. He'd turned over a new page and was now leading a spotlessly clean life. Emma had forgiven him and things were going just about OK at the moment. He had to keep his nose clean and ensure that the world saw his home life as something straight out of the glossy magazines. He would need Emma and Stephen right there beside him when the time comes - the perfect image of a leader and First Family in waiting. There was no room for secrets in a race to be Prime Minister.

9

Gabrielle

WEDNESDAY 12 JUNE 2024

Gabrielle was thirty-eight years old but still as beautiful as she had always been. In her early twenties, she could easily have made the grade as a fashion model. Tall and slender, with a classic bone structure, long flowing auburn hair and huge brown eyes, she had a natural elegance and sophistication that belied her humble roots, so would probably have excelled in a modelling career. But that would have required some level of self-confidence and self-esteem - both of which had been stolen from her younger self by Tom. He was the only man she had ever given her heart to and, in response, he had shattered it into a thousand pieces. Not once, but twice.

On the second occasion, she was only twenty-one years old and it was the pivotal moment in her life. The day all the romantic dreams of a bright and intelligent young girl were replaced by cynicism, hatred and bitterness. She was not the first - nor would she be the last - young woman to be cruelly duped by the first man she had ever really loved. But, at the time, she had no-one to turn to for support and had instead allowed Tom's rejection to consume her, eating away at her soul as the years progressed. It led her to conclude that men are all bastards who are only after one thing - a 'thing' that she had in abundance, so used to fight back.

Gabrielle did not really see herself as a prostitute. She was not some grubby little whore, selling her body on the streets for the price of a tab of heroin or because some filthy pimp made her do so. No-one ever told *her* who to sleep with and she had never touched drugs in her life. She knew exactly what she was doing and had never been paid less than £500 a time for her expert services. Indeed, back in her real heyday, the price was even higher. She carefully chose and vetted her clients - she never called them 'punters' - and it was always *her* decision whether or not to take them onto her books. Always.

The qualifying criteria was that they be rich, successful, usually married - which largely went without saying - and preferably either famous or a borderline criminal. In at least one case, it was actually both. The aim was to maximise their blackmail potential when the time came to activate the Plan that Sophia had taught her, all those years ago. The Plan had given Gabrielle power and control, something her clients would soon discover to their considerable cost. They all foolishly believed that discretion was her middle name and, to enhance that façade, she never used their real names. She also pretended to have no interest in what they did for a living unless they volunteered the information themselves. They always did, of course, bragging endlessly about what big shots they were - which would prove to be a very costly mistake on their part. In reality, she already knew everything about them before taking them on. It was part of Sophia's Plan. They would soon have to pay to stop their sordid little secrets from going public.

It was not just their marriages that would be at risk if they didn't pay up. For her most bankable clients, it might also be their freedom too. Of course, having paid her a tidy sum to keep quiet, they would inevitably try to find her, probably with the intention of silencing her for good in at least one case. She had some very unpleasant characters on her books. But good luck with that. Gabrielle was not her real name and she would simply disappear without trace to a luxurious retirement in France, leaving them to pick up the pieces of their broken lives. Oh yes, she would still expose them anyway - even after they had paid handsomely for her silence. That would be cruel, of course - a complete betrayal of their trust - but no more than each of them deserved. Her final act before vanishing would be to deal with Tom himself - saving the best 'til last.

In the meantime, she would continue entertaining her few remaining regulars. She had originally intended to launch Judgement Day in two years when she was forty, but had recently decided to bring that forward. To be frank, business was not what it once was and, to make matters worse, it was getting harder to process cash nowadays in an increasingly cashless world. Unsurprisingly, her clients didn't like to pay by credit card. Too many of them were also drifting into the arms of younger, Eastern European girls. But losing business to cheap foreign imports no longer bothered her like it once did. Their betrayal would simply add a disloyalty premium to the price they would eventually have to pay for her silence.

So, everything was clear in her mind about launching the Plan apart from one small dilemma - the rich old man currently taking a shower in the bathroom. He had just enjoyed another night of expensive passion with Gabrielle and she was now lying on the bed waiting for him. He had been a regular for some ten years or so and there was certainly no doubting *his* loyalty. He would never trade her in for a younger model and, unlike most of her other clients, had always been very kind to her. He had even given her advice on setting up her own business as a beautician. Of course, he thought he was helping her make a fresh start when, in reality, she just needed the business as a front to launder cash. But she was grateful, even so. It was an unsolicited act of friendship and Gabrielle didn't get many of those in her life.

FG - as she called him - was clearly in love with her - anyone could see that. But, for some reason, she didn't actually mind. When other clients had said they loved her in the past, it always gave her the creeps. But, with FG, it brought a strange feeling of contentment. Only *he* did that – made her feel relaxed and comfortable in his company. She even looked forward to seeing him, sometimes. So, if it could ever be said that she liked *anyone* in this miserable world – especially a man - then it was probably FG. She just didn't know why.

But that was creating a problem for her. Should she bring him down with all the others come Judgement Day, or give him a free pass for services rendered? It was pointless updating his file if she was going to spare him, but that update was now overdue - and her record-keeping was always meticulous. The Plan demanded it.

When she had first taken him on, he seemed to be different to all the rest. If he had become a serving MP as he'd promised, he would now be her biggest trophy. But that never happened and FG was now, essentially, a nobody - a loser. And losers weren't worth blackmailing. In truth, she should really have dropped him long ago, but somewhere along the line she had become attached to him and he was now something of a charity case. And she saw no harm in having just *one* person in her life that she could talk to and who actually listened to - and even cared about - what she said. But business was business, so she decided to go ahead and update his file today. She could always make a final decision on whether or not to use it against him when the time came.

She heard a clattering in the bathroom as he finished his shower. She had a clear view of the bathroom door from the bed, across which she was lying provocatively. That was all part of the distraction whenever she was collecting evidence. Outwardly, she would appear to be casually browsing through her phone but, in reality, it was set to the camera function with the flash and sound switched off. She would discreetly angle the phone towards the bathroom door, a technique she had used many times before on many unsuspecting clients.

FG duly emerged from the bathroom wearing only his underpants. She silently pressed the camera shutter before effortlessly switching the screen back to her emails in one sleek movement. It was always a dangerous and delicate operation but FG, of all people, wouldn't suspect a thing. None of them ever did. They would only see the compromising images, along with all her other damning records, when they eventually dropped onto their door mat with an extortionate demand for money attached. Yes, that was *real* power and control.

'Nice shower, sweetie?' she said, smiling broadly and looking lovingly into FG's eyes. 'Everything OK?'

'Yes, wonderful, my darling girl' said Alistair. 'Everything is just wonderful, as always.'

10

Harvey

SUNDAY 14 JULY 2024

'Well, I wouldn't vote for him' said Claire, indignantly.

'Really?' said Dale. 'But you're a loyal OP supporter and he's one of your own?'

'No – there's something about him I just don't like. Too good looking for a start.'

'What?!'

Harvey and Claire had invited friends and family over for a barbeque to enjoy the exceptionally warm weather. Dale and his partner David were enjoying Harvey's first batch of cremated offerings whilst talking to their hosts about the current big news story – Bradley Deakin.

'Don't you like good looking men, then?' asked Harvey, with a smile. 'I thought that's what you first saw in me?'

'I mean he fancies himself something wicked' Claire went on, trying to explain herself. 'All that *Silver Fox* nonsense. How old is he anyway? Can't be more than his early forties yet he's got all that luxurious grey hair. Must be dyed. He's one of those blokes who's always looking at themselves in the mirror. *Look at me – aren't I God's gift.* Bet he has manicures too.'

'Well, I like him,' David chipped in, munching on a blackened sausage. 'He makes me laugh. Remember when he did that piece on his show about the anonymised party naming nonsense? What was it he said…*If the Party of Government is POG, then it should be the Party of Opposition too? But that would make them POO, and they don't have the monopoly on poo. POG can sometimes be poo, too. So, you either vote for a poo POG or a poo POO. I don't want to poo-poo the whole stupid idea but, well, I think its poo!* Made me laugh, anyway.'

'He can be funny, yes' said Claire. 'Or, at least, his scriptwriters are. But I just don't see him as Prime Minister material.'

In the last week, Deakin's name had been all over the media. A survey was suggesting that most people in the country were so disillusioned with faceless political leaders that they apparently saw Bradley as the best option to lead them into the promised land. Harvey was not averse to the idea himself, but Claire's views on Deakin were well known to him as she was always tutting or huffing whenever they watched '*Speakin' to Deakin*'. The survey had certainly set the press and social media forums into overdrive. The general consensus was that it wasn't such a bad idea and endless discussions had since ensued about how it could realistically happen. As to where it left the current OP leader was anyone's guess, but Harvey assumed that Matthew Draper was now a dead man walking.

'Our listeners certainly seem to like him, don't they H?' said Dale. 'We didn't have a single negative call on Friday when we were going through all the press coverage.'

'What? Yes, guess so' replied Harvey, who was only half listening as he tried to scrape a burger from the griddle. 'But it's all theoretical isn't it? He's not even an MP and I doubt the BBC would be too happy if he started campaigning for the OP. Whatever happened to impartiality? You'd never see Dale expressing a political opinion, would you?'

'Thank you, H' said Dale, bowing graciously. 'Hmmm, actually… if he *did* pursue the OP leadership, I guess there would be a vacancy to host his show. Perhaps I'll put my name forward….'

'*Gobbing off with Glover?*' said Harvey. 'Not really got the same ring to it, but . . .'

They all laughed as Sarah and Dan Billingham walked over,

leaving Charlie and Phoebe getting on famously in the paddling pool. Since the dinner last month, Claire had spoken to Sarah a few times on the phone and was amazed that she had accepted her invitation to the barbeque.

'Come on, you lot' Sarah joked. 'Harvey's cooking can't be that funny, surely.'

'Pretty laughable from where I'm standing' said Dale, winking at his co-host.

'We were just discussing Bradley Deakin' said David. 'The Man Who Would Be King – apparently. How's it all going down in Westminster?'

'It's been bouncing around for a few weeks now' said Sarah. 'Long before that survey was conveniently published. They're desperate for someone to stand down but there are no takers yet, as I understand. Surprising really. Their MP's all want Deakin as leader but none of them will give up their own seat to let him in.'

'I don't agree with all that anyway' Harvey chipped in. 'I mean, MPs should have ties to the place they represent. Like you Sarah, a Brightonian born and bred - worked here, served on the Council. You know everything about Brighton and Hove and you represent us really well as a result, if I may say so.'

'You may, thank you,' said Sarah.

'But just parachuting someone into a random constituency just to get him a seat doesn't seem right to me, especially as a way to make him leader. Presumably, if a by-election came up tomorrow, he'd be off like a shot, wherever it was – Doncaster, Lewisham, Portsmouth – anywhere. But what would he actually *know* about any of those places or their local problems? And then, as soon as he won the seat, he'd be too busy at Westminster being leader - or even Prime Minister - to worry about his constituents. No, I believe that the place an MP represents should actually *mean* something to them. Not just be chosen by sticking a pin in the map.'

'I do tend to agree with you' said Sarah. 'So, just out of interest, if Deakin was standing against *me* here in Brighton at the next election - who would you all vote for?'

There was a chorus of support, but Claire instead looked thoughtful and said nothing.

'Its OK Claire' said Sarah, playfully. 'I seem to be ahead in the polls here in the garden and a little opposition is always healthy anyway.'

'Sorry,' said Claire 'but it's an interesting question, though. If it *was* down here then, yes, I guess I'd have to vote for Deakin, No offence . .'

'None taken.'

'. . . but it would be with a very heavy heart. I agree with Harvey about him not being local and I think he'd be a lousy local MP.'

'I don't understand' said Dale, looking bemused. 'You're saying you would rather vote for someone who you personally dislike - and think would do a rubbish job - than vote for Saint Sarah here, who is Brighton to her core and a truly fabulous local MP? How does that work?' Claire looked a bit embarrassed.

'She can vote for who she likes' said Sarah, easing the situation. 'But it proves that most people vote for their party rather than the individual. Its why I see so many totally unqualified misfits in the House of Commons. Some of them really do amaze me. Personally, I wouldn't put them in charge of an ice cream kiosk on the pier without supervision, let alone give them a say in national law making. But that's just the way of the world. They are elected simply because they're lucky enough to have a constituency that's fiercely loyal to their party whilst, elsewhere, much better qualified and dedicated local candidates lose out because *they* have the misfortune to live somewhere that strongly supports the other side.'

'Well' said Harvey 'whilst I usually lean towards the OP at elections, I confess that I actually voted for you last time, Sarah. That was solely because I saw you as the better option as our *local* MP. But if you stepped down at the next election, it would depend to a great extent on who the POG replaced you with as to whether or not I'd vote for them again. It also depends on how well the government is doing at the time – which is pretty rubbish at the moment - no offence.'

'. . . none taken, again' said Sarah. 'Well, personally, I'd rather die than see Bradley Deakin take my seat in Brighton and Hove just to further his own naked ambition.'

'Don't say that' chipped in Dale sharply. 'Because, ironically, if you *did* die – that's exactly what *would* happen, given the current situation. He'd be on the first bus down here.'

'Yes' said Harvey. 'Too right he would. So be careful crossing the roads. We're quite happy with you just where you are, thank you very much. Deakin can go dump himself on some other unsuspecting constituency when the time comes.'

'Well, thank you' nodded Sarah. 'But, don't worry, I'm not going anywhere. Now, Harvey, are you going to serve those bloody burgers or should we arrange a ceremony to scatter their ashes off the pier?'

11

Bradley

WEDNESDAY 17 JULY 2024

Bradley was waiting on the phone to be interviewed on BBC Radio 4's *Today* programme. The host, Drew McKinley, was an old friend and they had both worked together on the BBC's last two General Election night programmes. The OP supporting *Daily Record* had printed a lengthy editorial on Monday entitled '*So, is Prime Minister Deakin really such a bad idea?*' Peter had since been doing the rounds of media organisations but this was Bradley's first live interview on the subject himself.

'OK, Mr Deakin, Drew is just doing the introduction' said the researcher. 'Putting you live now.'

Bradley could hear the broadcaster's gruff Scottish drawl coming down the phone and braced himself for the interview.

'Now, you'll doubtless have heard a great deal of noise around some recent research which suggests that a vast number of people, rather remarkably, want none other than the BBC's own Bradley Deakin to be their next Prime Minister. Well, we're lucky enough to have the man himself on the line now. Good morning to you Mr Deakin.'

'Morning Drew, good to talk to you.'

'So, if the current press furore is to be believed, I assume you're already choosing new curtains for Number Ten! Is that right?'

'No not at all, Drew' replied Bradley. 'I've just been enjoying my summer break. This came as a total surprise to me but it's obviously very flattering to be seen that way.'

'Well, I'm sure it is,' said Drew, who's tone suggested he didn't believe a word of it. 'So, what do you think about all this political adulation being heaped on you?'

'Well' answered Bradley, 'If people would rather see the likes of me as PM than either of our current political leaders, then it probably says a lot more about *them* than it does about me.' *Best to show some humility.*

'It does indeed' said Drew. 'But you lost your seat back in 2015, which suggests that the voting public did not see you quite so much as the Messiah back then, did they? Couldn't wait to be shot of you, so it appeared at the time.'

It was a cheap shot but Bradley accepted it. 'Well, no, not really. Of course, it was extremely difficult to give up my political dreams as I felt I still had much more to offer. But as you know, Drew, there are many factors that influence how people vote in elections, so I didn't take the loss of my seat personally.' *Like hell I didn't!*

'Well, some would say you dropped those dreams with indecent haste, did you not?' Drew went on. 'Indeed, hasn't politics always played second fiddle to your life in the TV spotlight? After all, I recall you'd only been an MP for a couple of months before your face was all over the television. What were they called now? Ah yes, the *'Three Amigos'* wasn't it? So, isn't it fair to say that politics isn't really where your heart lies and the public are perhaps misguided if they now see you as Prime Minister? You're a media lovey now, aren't you?'

Drew was being adversarial but Bradley knew he would have to get used to it. He was on the other side of the fence now, and his friend was actually right about his early brush with TV and he had, indeed, loved the celebrity spotlight ever since.

Bradley had become an MP in the 2010 election that gave rise to the first formal coalition government since the Second World War. The public interest around it led BBC producer Aaron Sheldon, (who went on to produce '*Speakin' to Deakin*') to create a panel of MPs to discuss political issues on '*Newsnight*', the BBC's nightly news and politics show on BBC2. The panel was made up of the youngest, and newest, MPs from the three main parties of the day and, at twenty-seven, Bradley was one of the three 'babies of the house' selected.

The panel might have passed unnoticed were it not for the immediate rapport that developed between them. But Bradley shone out as the clear star, with his acid put downs, straight talking and a quick-witted humour that appealed to the TV audience. It was also clear that his good looks, athletic physique and piercing blue eyes played no small part in his popularity. A women's magazine subsequently voted Bradley as '*Westminster's hottest MP*' three years running.

The '*Three Amigos*' - as they became known - were soon moved to the higher profile Sunday morning politics show. His increasing popularity gradually led to guest appearances on other TV shows, including '*Have you Heard the News Then?*' the BBC's long running comedy panel show. It was normally a graveyard for political guests, as most MPs tried too hard to be funny and ended up embarrassing themselves instead. But not Bradley. He more than held his own and was duly invited back on two subsequent occasions. Aaron told him he was wasted as a politician and that a glittering TV career awaited him if he ever wanted it. That was to be a prophetic suggestion.

The media success initially helped Bradley and Emma survive financially after he lost his seat – politics having been his main source of income. There was some limited TV work - mostly reviewing the newspapers - but his big break came as guest host on *Have you Heard the News Then?* for one episode in 2016. It was a great success, and Aaron was able to persuade even the most cynical BBC executives to give Bradley a try-out hosting his own chat show. The rest, as they say, is history.

'Yes, I've very fond memories of the '*Three Amigos*' said Bradley. 'But all this is simply hypothetical, Drew. For now, I'm just looking forward to the new series of '*Speakin' to Deakin'* in September and will let others speculate about the political stuff.'

'But on that point,' asked Drew, 'does it not question *how* you can realistically be impartial whilst also being championed as the next Leader of the Opposition, if not Prime Minister?'

'Not at all' Bradley replied. 'People obviously know my politics as a former MP, and I've never had a problem displaying impartiality. As I say, nothing has changed.'

'But if the OP asked you, I assume you would graciously accept the offer to be their leader?'

'I would seriously consider it, yes, of course' said Bradley. 'But I haven't been formally asked yet.'

'Well, we will doubtless see what happens' said Drew. 'I'm afraid we must leave it there. Thank you for talking to us this morning Mr Deakin. Enjoy your holiday and, well, perhaps I should wish you good luck in finding yourself a by-election. Its seven forty-three and you're listening to the *Today* show with me, Drew McKinley . . .'

Bradley thought the interview had not gone too badly, all things considered. A few minutes later, his phone pinged with a message from Drew. '*Sorry to be such a git. Welcome back to politics!*' Welcome indeed.

12

Alistair

WEDNESDAY 17 JULY 2024

Alistair was on a train to London to attend a Local Government Association conference. He was a willing volunteer, but his enthusiasm was not prompted by the two boring days of debate that lay ahead. It was actually because it gave him an opportunity to see Gabrielle and, better still, to do so on Council expenses.

It was not that he abused his position as a Councillor and, in reality, could very easily afford a two-night stay in a London hotel himself. Indeed, when covering the bill himself, he always chose much better accommodation. But the remuneration for being a local Councillor was tiny compared to the work involved. He therefore had few qualms about seeing Gabrielle at the same time, given that the Council would be paying for the hotel room anyway. Its not as if she would be staying for breakfast.

He hadn't seen Gabrielle for more than a month and it certainly gladdened his heart to have the opportunity tonight. He knew it was an unusual relationship, certainly one that no-one else could possibly understand. But she was the source of his greatest strength and happiness. To his mind, there wasn't actually anything wrong with him seeing her anyway, just because he paid for the sex. He wasn't married or otherwise being unfaithful, so it was nobody else's business what he did with his money or who he slept with. In reality, all his romantic encounters put together would not take up more than half a page in his biography, so Gabrielle was an unconventional solution to the barren wasteland that his love life had become.

It was the only positive thing about him stepping aside for Sarah last year. Had he been elected himself, he would have had little choice but to end it with Gabrielle. As an MP, it would otherwise risk a major scandal as people would inevitably see their relationship as something sordid and grubby. Everything it was not. He'd been touched that Gabrielle had actively encouraged him to stand. She believed in him, saying it was his last big chance to fulfil his potential. And she was actually angry when he had stepped aside, which showed just how much she cared about him– really wanting him to make the best of himself.

Their paths had first crossed at the party conference back in 2015. On the second evening, he had been in a hotel bar just outside the security cordon, making small talk with a group of local Councillors from Southend. It was then that he caught sight of her and it was just as if he had been struck by a thunderbolt.

She was sitting on her own at the bar, sipping a cocktail. Alistair used the pretext of buying another round of drinks to shuffle up beside her. She was wearing diamond earrings, a clearly expensive little black dress and holding an - apparently real - Gucci handbag tucked in closely beside her. She looked like she was in her mid-twenties and, quite simply, was the most beautiful, classy and captivating woman Alistair had ever set eyes on. She casually glanced towards him as he approached and smiled, briefly. He was smitten from that moment on.

'Glad you had more luck getting a drink than me' he said after a few minutes of fruitlessly trying to attract the barman and clumsily trying to start a conversation. It was little better than *do you come here often* but, remarkably, did the trick. She smiled again.

'You probably aren't wearing enough diamonds' she said, speaking with a gentle, home counties accent. He was slightly surprised. Such an exotic creature could easily have originated from anywhere in the world.

'You're probably right' he replied, pleased to get a response. 'But I suspect a beautiful girl like you never waits very long for a barman to notice her.' He was showing unusual boldness and his heart was beating like a sledgehammer. 'Whereas, an old fart like me could be here all night.'

She giggled slightly and his heart melted still more.

'Don't put yourself down' she said. 'Shall I use my feminine charms to get him over here?'

'No, no, thank you' he replied. 'I'm actually enjoying the wait for a change.' *Alistair Buckland, what has got into you?* He was normally a bumbling wreck when faced with flirtatious situations, very rare though they were.

'I'm Alistair Buckland, by the way. Pleased to meet you miss . . . err . . .' *Worth a try.*

'Gabrielle' she replied, omitting any more details. She was staring ahead again, slowly sipping her cocktail. Alistair worried she was losing interest.

'Err . . . I'm a Councillor in Brighton' he said, as if that would suddenly make her fall at his feet. '*Brighton you say? Wow, let's go upstairs right now!*'

'Here for the conference then' she said with no great enthusiasm. 'Although, not an MP.'

'Not yet, no' he said. 'But I expect to be very soon.'

It was not entirely a lie. He'd been promised a chance to stand in the recent election but it had fallen through, yet again. But there was always next time. He was therefore exaggerating his prospects and it seemed to work. She looked vaguely interested again, briefly raising an approving eyebrow. This only encouraged his exaggerations.

'Yes, I've been earmarked to stand in the next General Election. Still five years away, sadly, but you need to start preparing well in advance to win over your would-be constituents.'

'Do you expect to win?' she said, her attention held for the time being.

'Oh yes, very confident' he replied. 'Almost certain. It's been my life's ambition to serve as an MP and I firmly believe that this is finally my time. Can't wait.'

'Hmm. Well, good luck with that' she replied. It went quiet again.

'So, what about you?' he said, trying to keep the momentum going. *What's a nice girl like you doing in a dump like this?' Come on Alistair, you can do better than that.* 'The conference is boring enough for those of us who *have* to be here. I'm assuming you're not a delegate.' *Marginally better.*

'And what makes you think that?' she said sharply, either offended or pretending to be.

'Err . . . sorry' he said. *Oh God, he was sounding patronising, sexist or whatever-ist.* 'I didn't mean you wouldn't be a brilliant Councillor. The best. It's just that. . .well . . . you're not wearing a security pass and, anyway, we can't afford diamonds like those on our salaries. You're also sitting here enjoying a nice cocktail whilst everyone else is desperately trying to network.' She shrugged nonchalantly and took another sip. He seemed to have got away with it.

'Yes, well, I was supposed to meet someone here, but it looks like he's off doing some of that precious *networking* himself.' There was a hint of bitterness in her voice. 'I seem to have been stood up.'

'He must be mad' said Alistair, being a bit forward again, but why not. Unusually, he found himself flirting with a stunningly beautiful girl. What's the worst that could happen? Well, other than the usual – getting nowhere. But onwards and upwards, this was a shot at the Premier League. 'I can't think of *anything* that would be worth standing *you* up for.'

'Well, thank you, kind sir' she said, turning to him again and smiling. 'But not all men are gentlemen, like you.' Again, Alistair felt his legs turn to putty.

'Were you . . . err . . . supposed to have been doing anything nice with him?' he said.

'Dinner' she replied. 'At *Monteprento's.*' Alistair knew it was a very expensive and exclusive restaurant in the city centre.

'Well, if it's still booked . . .' *Come on Alistair, you can do it.* 'I'd be . .

. err . . . honoured to stand in for him. My treat, but only if you'd like to, of course. But it seems a shame to waste the booking. It's lovely, so I hear, and very hard to get a table.'

‚'Expensive' she said, abruptly. 'Very expensive. Are you sure you can afford it on your tiny little Councillor wages? Given that you can't stretch to diamonds?'

'Very much so' he said. *Time to show off again.* 'I wasn't talking personally. I sold off my family farm several years ago for a seven-figure sum so I can afford all the diamonds I need. Or you need.' *Very bold.* Alistair was never one to brag, especially about money, but he was throwing the kitchen sink at this one. He knew he would never get a better chance. She turned her head towards him again, looking him up and down but without being too overt about it.

'OK' she said. 'The table's booked for 7.30.'

And so it began. Over dinner, he spoke a lot about his life whilst she mostly listened. In fact, he knew little more about her by the end of the evening than he did at the start. To his surprise, if not initial shock, he discovered she was an 'escort'. He soon realised that, in fact, she was actually a call girl but, by then, it was too late. Alistair was hooked. He was slightly disappointed that she wasn't sitting there solely because of his charm, good looks and allure, but he was also a realist. Those were actually the *last* reasons she would be sat there with him.

The other object of his affections at the time was Sarah Williams, a hot new Councillor who had just been elected. She clearly liked him - but not in the way he liked her. Instead, she was engaged to a nice young lad called Dan Billingham and only had eyes for him. Back then, Alistair was fifty-three, fat, balding and lacking any of the attributes needed to either lure Sarah away from her hunky fiancé or for a girl like Gabrielle to otherwise give him the time of day. So what did it matter if she charged? She wasn't some cheap tart from under Brighton Pier. She had more class than any woman he'd ever met - although, in truth, he rarely encountered glitzy society girls during his farming days. And the one advantage he had over Dan Billingham - or anyone else, for that matter - was money, lots of it. If a night with Gabrielle was to cost £1000 – as it did - then it would be money well spent.

She was nothing like he expected a call girl to be anyway. She actually refused to sleep with him on that first night. Nor on their next encounter, come to that, when they had dined at another obscenely expensive restaurant, this time in Mayfair. It was as if she really wanted to get to know him first. Just like any woman. Take the financial aspect out of the equation and there was no real difference to any other courtship, at least in Alistair's mind. And when she finally agreed to seal the deal, well, it was a night of unbridled heaven.

The arrangement continued month after month, year after year. He would always book a fine hotel in London where she would then join him for the night. General Elections came and went and, to his disappointment, he was overlooked every time. Gabrielle always seemed as disappointed for him as he was himself. He was sure he would be chosen to stand eventually, but it did not actually happen until last year. It was the first election fought under the new boundary changes which combined all three Brighton and Hove seats into just one. It should have been his big chance but, instead, he had stepped aside for Sarah. Gabrielle was really angry that, in doing so, he was sacrificing his own dreams and ambitions. He found that very endearing.

Although the intimate part of their relationship was based on a price tariff, it never seemed that cold or clinical to him. Handing over money simply became a formality and they then got on with enjoying each other's company. Yes, for him, at least, the sex was incredible. But it was only a few minutes of the whole night together. They always talked and laughed afterwards, discussing everything from politics to mundane everyday issues. Occasionally, he even asked her advice about tricky problems raised by his constituents. He did the same with Sarah too, but Gabrielle was always touched that he asked for, and listened to, her opinions. He suspected that her other clients didn't ask her views on anything.

Oh yes, he knew he was not the only man on her books, but he tried not to think about that. Recently, she let slip that client numbers were beginning to dwindle as she got older. He was pleased. Let them go, all of them. He'd happily be the last man standing and would never desert or betray her. Nor would she him. Gabrielle was the sole of discretion. She nicknamed him '*Farmer Giles*', which she eventually shortened, affectionately, to FG. He liked it. It was as if he became someone else whenever he was with her. All the loneliness, underachievement, frustration, insecurity and sadness went away in her arms. She was all that really mattered and all he really lived for. The best moments for him were not about the sex any more. He loved it when he sometimes woke up in the night and found her hugging him so tightly - her head on his shoulder and her arms wrapped around him - hugging him like a frightened child clinging to their parent. Feeling safe and secure in his strong arms. She was always asleep at the time and probably didn't even know she was doing it, so he never told her - just in case she consciously stopped. But it was a wonderful feeling of love and trust that she could neither hide nor repress in the way she did when awake. Yes, she most definitely cared for him - even if she didn't realise it herself.

And so – nearly ten years on – the relationship was still in place. They were friends, lovers and confidants of sorts. In financial terms, it had cost him dearly over the years. He didn't like to add it all up. But that was the only unusual part and it was worth every penny. He just wished they could run away together. She was the best thing in his life - his lovely, beautiful, enigmatic Gabrielle.

Sarah, the other woman in his life, had married Dan in 2017 and they now had a lovely little boy called Charlie. With her, Alistair's affection had quickly evolved into a form of paternal love, especially after Gabrielle started to fill the other void in his life. He began to truly care about her and her family, greatly valuing her friendship, her trust and the fact that she saw him as a mentor. She and Dan even named him as one of Charlie's Godparents. He had been deeply moved by that.

So, there were two wonderful women in his life. They brought him joy - if not the total fulfilment that he craved - and he loved them both, each in different ways. He could not imagine what his life would be like without one - or both - of them in it.

It would have broken his heart to know that, very soon, he would have to find out.

13

Terry MacDonald

MONDAY 2 SEPTEMBER 2024

Sitting in Brighton Council's media room, Terry MacDonald looked around to see if anyone else that he knew was unlucky enough to also be covering this tedious press conference. Certainly, nobody would be there by choice. You always go where your Editor sends you, good or bad, and this looked like one of the bad ones.

The room was half full of reporters with a few photographers either standing along the sides or crouched down at the front. At the rear, two TV cameras were mounted on tripods and their presence called for bright arc lights, giving the room a sense of drama that, in Terry's eyes at least, the occasion did not merit.

It was his last day as a reporter with the *Brighton Argus* before taking up his new role on the OP supporting *Daily Record* in London. He was actually more of a closet anarchist but always kept his true politics to himself. When being interviewed for the *Daily Record* job, he pretended to be a lifelong OP supporter in the hope of getting his big break. But he would have equally claimed to be a POG supporter if he was going for a job on the *Daily News*. The ploy had worked, even so, and he was starting his new position on the Investigations Team next Monday. Today's miserable little gathering would therefore be one of his last assignments in this dead-beat town.

The press conference had been called to announce the Council's plans to cull the seagull population, which was apparently getting out of control. The spokesman was some fat git called Alistair Buckland, Chairman of the Environmental Committee or some other poncey title. He was rambling on about the high cost of cleaning up seagull crap and so on - as if anyone cared. Terry loved London, where he was born, not Brighton. There were usually a few seagulls down by the Thames, but not enough to get excited about like this old fool was doing.

He studied Buckland, who was sitting in front of a large blue and white backdrop with the words '*Responsible bird management for the next generation*' printed in large letters above his head. It was hardly the snappiest of titles. '*Seagulls - let's kill the annoying little buggers*' would have been Terry's choice. At least that would do what it said on the tin. He assumed the pompous title was Buckland's uninspiring choice. The press handout said he used to be a farmer - but Terry could have guessed that. Despite wearing a suit and tie, the signs of an outdoor life were only too clear in his weather-beaten round face and thinning, unkempt grey hair. Terry couldn't decide if he looked more like a rustic farmer or a salty old sea dog. It was certainly one of the two.

He was already aware of Buckland from previously having covered the Council elections. Terry rarely forgot a face, nor a name, and recognised him when the presentation started some fifteen minutes ago – or was it an hour, it certainly felt like it.

Terry could see his photographer, Jimbo, across the other side of the room. He was snapping away enthusiastically but Terry wondered how many photos of an old fart sitting at a desk were actually necessary. Terry could not wait to leave the likes of Alistair Buckland and all this provincial stuff behind him and start a much more fulfilling career on a big national newspaper. Finally, he had a chance to make a name for himself. All he needed was a major scoop that would then turn him into a *real* player. A scoop that, unknown to him at the time, was currently sitting right there in front of him.

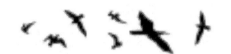

14

Harvey

MONDAY 2 SEPTEMBER 2024

'Harvey! Come quick! Its him!'

Harvey was making two mugs of tea in the kitchen. He had left Claire in front of the television waiting for the local news programme to start, so picked up the mugs and walked briskly back to the lounge. 'Who is?' he said as he entered the room.

'HIM' said Claire, clearly agitated and pointing at the TV.

'Who? Where?' he replied, seeing only the title sequence scrolling across the screen with no sign of anyone likely to cause such a reaction.

'Well, he's gone NOW' she said dejectedly, implying that it was Harvey's fault for not getting back in time. 'He'll be on in a minute, though. It's their main story. Something about seagulls.'

'WHO?' Harvey said in frustration. Claire shushed him to be quiet as the news anchor appeared on screen in front of a live projected shot of Brighton Pier.

'GOOD EVENING. A radical new plan to reduce the number of seagulls in Brighton was announced today as a way to reduce the multi-million-pound annual clean-up bill. The Council said that the birds cause extensive damage to

property and physical attacks on tourists and residents are increasing every year. A three-month consultation was launched this morning to consider ways for bird numbers to be dramatically reduced by some 40% by 2028. Alison Richards reports…'

HARVEY WAS none the wiser but assumed all would shortly be revealed. However, he recalled a proposed seagull cull being discussed on Dale's show a few months ago, so this must be related. The TV report showed stock footage of Brighton with seagulls noisily picking over rubbish bins and generally not being seen in their best light. A few quick interviews with tourists and shopkeepers followed, all complaining about the birds making their lives a misery. The voice-over then returned to the studio.

'WELL, the Chairman of a committee that looked into the problem, and who today unveiled the council's report, is Councillor Alistair Buckland. He joins me now live from Brighton seafront. Good evening, Councillor…'

'SEE? I TOLD YOU. ITS HIM!' shouted Claire as Alistair Buckland's face appeared on screen. The seagulls above him cawed noisily, right on cue.

'Oh, I *see*. The miserable old sod from Sarah's dinner at Westminster,' said Harvey, recognising him instantly. Harvey didn't really agree with the cull and knew it would receive huge opposition in Brighton, which was awash with animal rights campaigners, Vegans and other tree-hugging types. He guessed they would be manning the barricades before the interview had even finished.

When it did, the studio anchor moved on to a round-up of other news, which included a story about the last remaining bank in Brighton announcing its closure next month. It was his old branch of the SS&I in North Street and was not unexpected, but Harvey was still saddened. The branch had not just played a significant part in his working life but there was also a strong sentimental attachment in his home life as well. It was where he had first met Claire.

He was just twenty-one and she was nineteen. By then he was a bank teller, a prestigious role at a time when internet banking was still years away. Claire was working at a local store and had been entrusted with the mundane daily task of banking the takings. It was a sunny day in July when the pretty, confident young girl first appeared at his window and immediately struck up a rapport with the shy bank clerk. Although there was an immediate attraction, the weeks passed with no hint of Harvey bravely asking her out.

She was only working at the shop during the summer break from Cambridge University where she was studying politics, so the clock was therefore ticking before her return. It was Claire who actually made the first move – visiting a local pub with friends where bank staff were known to hang out after work. Enough of a fledgling romance was then kindled to survive Claire's return to university.

They kept in touch but only saw each other when Claire was home visiting her parents. On graduating the following summer, she then took a job in London, much to Harvey's distress. He was desperately in love but didn't know how to tell her. Again, it took Claire to make the decisive move. It was New Year's Eve 1987, and she invited him to a party where the fireworks finally went off. But it was not until Claire moved back to Brighton two years later that the relationship really moved forward, leading to their marriage in 1993. Unsurprisingly, it was Claire who proposed.

Samantha was born two years later and their lives were then complete. They bought a small, unassuming house in the Kemp Town area of Brighton, thanks to a low-rate staff mortgage, and had lived there ever since. Sam grew up and, five years ago, married Piers, a successful fund manager in the City of London. Thanks to Piers being pleasingly wealthy, the Bank of Mum and Dad was able to close its doors and allow Harvey to seriously consider early retirement. Claire was now working part-time as a manager at the local hospital, where she still loved her job.

Harvey adored his family and revelled in the happy, trouble-free home life that they all shared. He had the added pleasure of now working with Dale on the radio and there was nothing on the horizon to upset his pleasant little world - which was exactly how he liked it. Harvey Britten did not like change or uncertainty in his life, which made it all the more remarkable that he would soon be facing a great deal of both.

15

Gabrielle

THURSDAY 12 SEPTEMBER 2024

It was 10 a.m. and Gabrielle was sitting in her bathrobe, but it wasn't because she had got up late. In fact, she'd not long arrived home, having spent the night in a hotel with Ivan Pevlonichic, her most lucrative - and most obnoxious – client.

He was a Russian sleazebag who she called '*Big Red*'. He had dragged himself up from nothing to achieve an obscene level of wealth through corruption, extortion and a degree of good luck. But despite having all the clichéd trappings of wealth - the decadently sized yacht, private jets and garish homes scattered around the globe - he still had no class or manners. Essentially, he was a well-connected gangster, heavily involved in drugs, arms dealing and pornography. People trafficking was probably in there somewhere too, just to complete his deeply unpleasant CV. Even so, Gabrielle had willingly accepted him onto her books as he easily met the qualifying criteria for Sophia's Plan.

Tough guy though he was, *Big Red* made clear that his wife Svetlana must never, ever, find out about their arrangement. It seems she was the daughter of an even bigger - and nastier - gangster who had told Ivan exactly what would happen to him if he was ever unfaithful. Apparently, he would end up looking like a hamster after two crucial parts of his anatomy were ripped off and stuffed into his cheeks. In *Big Red's* seedy world, that was not just an idle threat - it was a promise and the only thing that really scared him. Gabrielle had initially wondered why he therefore took the risk, but having since seen a photo of Svetlana – who resembled a women's shot putter from before the Russian drugs scandal – the reason was pretty clear. Apparently, it was some sort of arranged marriage as part of a deal to win her father's investment.

There was certainly no dilemma about *Big Red* being included in Sophia's Plan. Gabrielle would positively enjoy bringing down the odious Russian thug whose vile tastes she was obliged to fulfil. At least he paid her handsomely for her services. His room safe was invariably overflowing with packets of cash from dubious sources and he handed them out like they meant nothing.

Whilst Gabrielle always put on a great show for her well rewarded efforts, she hated every second. Whenever she got back home in the morning, she spent ten minutes in the shower before a thirty-minute soak in the bath. It helped to ease the light bruising that *Big Red* tended to leave but mostly served to wash her soul clean of the whole filthy experience.

She hugged a comforting pillow to her chest whilst sipping a cup of coffee on the sofa. She had turned on the TV to watch last night's *'Speakin' with Deakin'* on catch-up. She wasn't a fan of Deakin – far from it in fact, finding him arrogant and self-centred, like most men. But he wasn't currently presenting the show and a guest host had taken over for the foreseeable future. Gabrielle had read that the BBC asked – or perhaps told - Deakin to take a break, just until his political ambitions were clearer. That would wipe the smug grin off his face.

She was only watching because one of the guests was Sally-Jane Palmer, a young Z-List English actress. She was there to promote her latest film about the life of a high-class call girl. Whilst naturally interested, Gabrielle knew that it would bear no resemblance to reality. She skipped through the recording until the actress appeared on screen - all teeth, tits and blond hair as she sashayed onto the set. To his credit, the guest host gave her quite a hard time, mostly about the gratuitous nudity throughout the film. The little darling tried to explain how it was essential to the plot or, more likely, essential to getting the film any form of audience.

He also pressed her about glamorising the call girl lifestyle portrayed in the film, whilst suggesting that the lead character – named Monique – was a strong woman, fully in control of her life. The host queried whether that was a good image for impressionable young girls to see. Ms Palmer had no real opinion on the subject, being just an air-head actress who was only there to sell her tacky little skin-flick. She was not qualified for a high-brow discussion on the merits of prostitution in modern society.

It annoyed Gabrielle that high-class prostitutes always had names like Monique anyway. Or Gabrielle for that matter. But she knew the likes of *Big Red* would never book a girl called Deidre or Susan, even if they turned out to be gorgeous. They wanted their whores to sound exotic. Alfredo had explained that sad logic to her when interviewing her at *Acquaintance* eighteen years ago - the escort agency where she had first started in this game. Oddly, he extended it to his own role as manager too, given that his real name was actually Roger.

Gabrielle's real name was Sharon, which definitely had to go. Alfredo tapped into his computer and grandly announced that she would now be known as Gabrielle. Just like that. No debate or right of appeal. It was simply the next name on his alphabetical list. Had the interview taken place an hour earlier she would have been called Francesca - and ten minutes later it would have been Gloriana.

It was not as if Sharon - now Gabrielle –actively sought the life she had ultimately led, unlike the fictional Monique in the film. She'd been raised in a grotty, two bedroomed council flat in Uxbridge, West London, ten floors up in a dated tower block with a lift that rarely worked. Her mother, Teri, was a waste of space who chain-smoked and drank away most of the benefit money intended to raise little Sharon - a child she had deeply resented since birth.

Sharon's father had never been on the scene and she suspected that money had changed hands as part of her conception. Yes, it was true. Her mother was not averse to turning the odd trick herself to pay the rent. At the age of around six, Sharon vaguely recalled being sent to her room and ordered not to come out whilst *'mummy has a friend over'* for half an hour or so. The noises she heard through the paper-thin walls made no sense to the child until very much later. She was never sure whether her mother gave up her little side-line soon afterwards or decided to only open the shop when Sharon was at school. Either way, she could not remember it happening again in later years.

In her defence, Teri did work very hard and - despite it all - kept Sharon fairly well fed and clothed, despite living in near poverty. She worked in bars and clubs every evening, took cleaning jobs by day and otherwise did anything she could that involved payment in cash. She would certainly be classed as a benefits cheat nowadays by those inclined to pass judgement. But, regardless of where the money came from, she was out of the house working for most of the time which meant that Sharon grew up way too quickly. Essentially, she brought herself up - shopping, cooking, cleaning and putting herself to bed. It was a solitary homelife with no relatives or siblings on hand to ease the pain. Teri never spoke of Sharon's grandparents and she assumed there must have been a major falling out some-where down the line. Whatever the reason, no relatives ever featured in Sharon's life, apart from her mother, and she learned to rely on no-one but herself.

She was actually very popular at school, especially from the age of ten when the pretty young girl showed early signs of the beautiful woman she would eventually become. In a mixed-sex school, pre-pubescent boys swarmed around her like moths whilst the girls aspired to her level of early maturity. They tried to acquire it by association and she became the girl they all wanted to be seen with or - for the boys - fantasise about.

The not so orderly queue of boys ready to kill for any form of bodily contact with Sharon grew ever longer as she aged. She did, at times, experiment with sex and, of course, had the pick of would-be suitors. The first lucky soul to go all the way was Steve Matthews and the deed took place in the toilets one night after a school disco. He was a good-looking lad, the star of the school football team and, like Sharon, appeared older than his years. But it was a disappointing introduction to sex and memorable only for starting her lifelong mistrust of the male gender.

Steve somewhat exaggerated the quality of his performance when later boasting in the locker room. Whilst that enhanced his own credentials as some form of rampant stud, the knock-on impact gave Sharon a reputation as an easy lay. When both stories came to her ears she reacted angrily. Across the crowded school canteen one lunchtime, she shouted at Steve for all to hear: '*Oi, tiddler dick! Please tell your mates that thirty miserable seconds does not make you a sex god! Girls — trust me, you'd get more fun out of triple maths than sex with that useless tosser.*'

The place erupted into laughter. Steve became a figure of fun to both sexes whilst Sharon was even more of a hero to the girls. She was clearly not someone to mess with and, unsurprisingly, she then wasted no more time on boys of her own age.

It was not that she was cynical about love or relationships. Far from it. She aspired to falling in love, getting married and having children. She took a Saturday job in a newsagent's and would often browse through the glossy fashion magazines during quiet spells. It gave her a taste of the glamorous lifestyle that she craved and the woman she wanted to be - rich, sophisticated and classy. A million miles from what she actually was and, in reality, ever looked likely to achieve. But it gave her ambition.

By the time she eventually left school at eighteen, Tom had already broken her heart once but she was still on course for a normal life. She trained as a beautician and worked in the make-up and perfume department of a London store. It allowed her to taste the life that she continued to read about in magazines. She sold ridiculously expensive creams and potions to women with more money than sense, learning how to sell them the dream and feel good about themselves. It also taught her the presentational skills that she would later use to good effect in selling *herself*.

It was not a badly paid job, but she knew that, if she was ever to really taste the high life herself, then she desperately needed more money. She therefore took additional part-time jobs in the evenings, usually waitressing in bars or night clubs. She knew it was little different to her mother's approach, except that Sharon had a clearer focus and purpose. She was looking to improve her life, not just pay the bills and buy vodka.

One such job was in a restaurant where she befriended another waitress called Jenny, a pretty young girl herself who asked if Sharon was interested in making some *real* money. Jenny, it seemed, worked on the side for an escort agency. Sharon believed that was just a posh name for 'prostitute' and was surprised that Jenny spoke so enthusiastically about it. But her friend said it wasn't like that at all, at least not at *Acquaintance*. She simply accompanied VIP's to events and functions and, at the end of the evening, the clients were expected to provide a taxi home. There were apparently very strict conditions about not touching the merchandise. She spoke of attending the most glamorous functions, dressing in beautiful - but hired - ball gowns, eating in the finest restaurants and sometimes being driven around in limousines. It all sounded like the world Sharon dreamed of - only not quite the way she wanted to experience it. But she gave it a try even so.

Had her first client been an animal like *Big Red*, then she would probably have ended it very quickly. But he wasn't. He was a polite, amusing Australian businessman visiting the UK for a conference who just wanted company for a boring corporate dinner where he didn't know anyone. It was the most delicate and delicious meal Sharon had ever tasted and took place in luxurious surroundings. She really enjoyed herself and was, indeed, sent home safely in a taxi afterwards without problems.

But as the months went on, a recurring theme gradually developed. More and more of her clients either hinted at - or came right out and asked - if she was interested in any 'overtime'. After initially denying it, Jenny confessed to occasionally providing 'added extras' herself. Sharon was shocked, but also intrigued. Jenny was outwardly very middle class and didn't seem 'that sort of girl' - whatever that was. But Jenny said it was little different to having a one-night stand after a party – except *she* went home with a bundle of cash in the morning rather than the indignity of still wearing the same knickers.

It took a few more weeks before Gabrielle was tempted to test out Jenny's theory, when a good looking young corporate banker from New York asked the inevitable question after a pleasant evening. They were sitting in his hotel bar and Sharon had drunk more than a few glasses of fine wine. She had no real intention of seeing it through but, just out of curiosity, hinted that she might.

'What sort of amount might persuade you?' the banker asked.

'Oh, I don't know, £500 at least' she replied, assuming he'd laugh and the conversation would end there and then.

'Is that all?' he instead replied. 'You're selling yourself cheap there, honey. I've paid way more for much less in the past. *You* are in a different league to the rest.'

She was amazed. 'Well, I didn't say I *would* do it for that' she replied, quick on her feet. 'I said *'at least'*. Probably more like a thousand. But even then, I doubt it.'

'OK. Let's call it £2000 to help ease your doubts. What do you say?'

Whilst Sharon may have been shocked at the idea, in her guise as Gabrielle she decided to see it through. Again, had it been an horrific experience, it would have been the first and last time. But he was not unattractive, the sex was good and she left next morning with £2000 in cash. She felt slightly disgusted with herself but knew it would take months to earn that sort of money in her day job.

Increasingly, she received repeat business and asked regular clients to contact her directly, cutting *Acquaintance* out of the deal. She soon gave up the exhausting bar and restaurant work, realising she could earn far more money lying on her back. She actually refused more offers than she accepted - being selective even then. But she chose them on the basis of looks and personality at the time, rather than the strict qualifying criteria of Sophia's Plan. That came later.

It was all going along very well and her savings were growing rapidly. She was able to move out of the low-rent bedsit in Vauxhall and into a nice two bedroom flat in Acton. Her night work was intended to finance her future life and career, hoping to one day set up her own cosmetic and beautician service. Jenny used *her* extra income to get the deposit together for a flat. It was all controlled, sensible, and no big deal. The mantra was *'if you've got it, use it'* - all just a means to an end.

That end looked like it had arrived when Tom, her childhood sweetheart, walked back into her life when she was twenty-one. Quite by chance, he passed by carrying a bottle of designer perfume that he'd just bought from one of her colleagues in the department store. He looking her up and down as he walked by and appearing to like what he saw. But why wouldn't he? She was now a beautiful woman, tall, slim and capable of turning heads of any age. Then he suddenly stopped and turned around. She, of course, had recognised him immediately.

'Sharon?' he said, walking back. 'Is that you? My God look at you! You look fantastic!'

She didn't of course, caked in the thick warpaint she was obliged to wear on duty. Outside work she wore very little make up at all. Her skin was perfect and she only applied a little mascara to emphasise her stunningly beautiful eyes. They were her best feature by far. A client once told her that her eyes *'didn't just say 'come to bed' - they also turned down the covers and placed a chocolate on the pillow.'*

Tom said he was working in London and had only popped in to buy perfume for his mother's birthday. He was still single and clearly keen on resuming their relationship. She was thrilled to see him and all the old emotions came rushing back. She may as well have gift wrapped her heart in pink tissue paper and placed it in the carrier bag alongside the perfume. She had given it to him before and was now handing it over again, free of charge and with no returns policy.

They were together for eight wonderful months. He was really busy, often working at weekends and evenings, so it was sometimes difficult to see each other, not least because he lived outside of town. But he often stayed over in a hotel for work so they either spent time there or at her flat in Acton.

She stopped accepting work from *Acquaintance* in exchange for a life she assumed would now be with Tom. She said how much she loved him - had always loved him - and he told her the same.

Marriage, kids, a house in the suburbs - it all looked possible. Sharon was confident about the future for the first time in her life. But it was 2007 and someone had just invented the I-phone. Tom was obsessed with new gadgets and bought one almost immediately. One day, late in the summer, he proudly gave Sharon a guided tour, showing her how it could take pictures and send emails and texts. Apps were still in their early days but they could both see the phone's huge potential.

It was a couple of days later that he left her flat in a rush one morning, accidentally leaving his phone on the bedside table. She was still in bed and spotted it almost immediately. She casually turned it on – biometric access and PIN numbers being something for the future – to see, again, what it could do. She wasn't spying on him, nor was she suspicious. She just wanted to explore the magical new phone with the intention of buying one herself.

As she touched the App to view his photo collection, her world immediately collapsed like a house of cards. She saw photos of Tom with a pretty young girl - smiling, cuddling, enjoying time with friends. Clearly, she was his 'significant other' but Sharon refused to believe it until she opened the text App. To her horror, top of the list was a girl's name. It contained multiple messages, all loving, some sexy and some - worst of all – practical, everyday exchanges. The most recent was sent only last night. Nine words that confirmed her worst fears: *'can you get some milk on the way home x.'* He was living with the bitch.

She burst into tears just as the front door opened. It was Tom, who'd quickly realised that he had left his phone behind. Sharon demanded to know who the girl was. He sheepishly mumbled some nonsense about it being over - but the texts had damned him. She threw him out and that was it - finished. He left her door keys on the table and she had neither seen nor spoken to him since.

She became a lost soul, her confidence shattered. Foolishly, she went back to *Acquaintance* and became Gabrielle again. It actually helped to hide behind someone else, to get inside another character - another life. She put on an act, appearing to be her usual vibrant, alluring self when with clients but an emotional wreck back home.

They began throwing money at her again for sex and she gradually became less choosy. If the price was right, she performed - even if they repulsed her physically. The money rolled in but her self-esteem, her sense of purpose and her pride all rolled out in the other direction.

She had one regular client who was a rich Italian businessman called Matteo. He always paid her generously and appeared to be obsessed by her, as they all were. But he was a dubious character - not unlike *Big Red*. One day, he invited her for a weekend on his luxury yacht in Monte Carlo. It was for the 2008 Grand Prix weekend and she was naïve enough to think it would just be the two of them. But, when she arrived, she found she was actually one of ten girls - all there to entertain Matteo's five male guests. She confronted him angrily but he told her she would receive £20,000 for the weekend - so what was the problem? She hated herself, but did it all the same. She was slowly turning into a whore for hire and, worse still, was becoming anaesthetised to it. In her own mind, her life wasn't worth living anyway. So, what the hell. Let them do what they wanted. Thank God Sophia had been there to save her.

Sophia was not one of the other girls - all off-the-peg bimbos with surgically enhanced breasts bulging from their string bikinis. She was different. Older, possibly in her late thirties, but still gorgeous. A classic Italian beauty with long black hair, olive skin, large Dior sunglasses and wearing subtle - but expensive - jewellery. She said little, but Gabrielle felt as if she was always there – watching her. Silently studying from the side-lines.

Early on the last evening, Gabrielle was lying alone on the sun deck. The men were either too pissed or drugged up to want female attention for now, or had not yet returned from watching the Grand Prix. Sophia slowly approached and sat down on the sun lounger beside her.

'*Ciao Bella*' she said in a soft, seductive Italian accent. 'My darling, you seem sad, so sad.'

'It's a sad, sad situation' Gabrielle replied, quoting Elton John for no apparent reason. She didn't know what exactly to make of the woman, who was slightly intimidating, clearly extremely close to

Matteo and set aside from the others. 'Sorry, I'm not sure who you are?'

'Me? I'm Sophia' she replied, removing a cigarette and lighting it with a large, apparently solid gold, lighter. 'I watch you and like what I see, *Bella*. You remind me of me when I was young. Not like these cheap little whores. But I worry for you.'

'But you don't know me' said Gabrielle, unnecessarily harsh in her tone. She was off duty so her façade was down. She hated everyone at such times.

'Oh, I think I do, *Bella*' said Sophia. 'You're better than all of them, *si*? Beautiful, with class. But I think perhaps you are lost like I was.'

Gabrielle looked out to sea, saying nothing, but she was mildly intrigued. Apart from Jenny, she had never spoken to anyone about her second career and was not sure how to proceed.

'Why you do this . . . this life, *Bella*, if I may ask?' said Sophia.

'There are worse ways to earn a living' said Gabrielle, looking around the boat - as if the surroundings somehow made it all worthwhile.

'But you hate it, I think?'

'Hate *them*, yes' said Gabrielle, 'but the money, I like.'

'Ah! the money!' said Sophia, lying back and drawing elegantly from her cigarette. She immediately exhaled a long, slow stream of smoke into the air. 'What we are doing for the money. We sell out bodies but also sell our souls, *si*?'

Gabrielle, again, said nothing.

'You hate them but you hate yourself more, yes? Or you will soon, if not now. I know.'

'Sorry, are you here to cheer me up, or what?' said Gabrielle, sitting up and looking back at the uninvited companion behind her. 'If you are, then . . . well, I'm afraid it isn't working, so . . .'

Sophia shrugged her slender shoulders and continued to draw heavily on the cigarette, causing her cheeks to suck in.

'*Bella*,' she purred gently, whilst slowly sitting up and turning towards her. Her face was an inch away from Gabrielle's and her huge brown eyes were hypnotic. 'I tell you something, please. I am friend *si?* If you want to carry on letting these assholes do whatever they want, just for the money, then go ahead. But it will destroy you inside. Believe me, it did me when I was young. But then I learned to take control. Take the power *myself* - not let them hold it over *me.'*

'And how did you do that exactly?' said Gabrielle, still appearing to be dis-interested but now, actually, fascinated.

Sophia then explained how she had turned her own life around from being an expensive working girl in Milan to someone with a Plan. For her, it required a hidden camera, but she spoke adoringly about the new smart phone now taking the world by storm. How she would have loved one of those little beauties to make life easier.

'The Plan gives me the power' she explained. 'When they're screwing me, I know I can destroy them any time I want. It is, how you say, liberating, *si?'*

'But will you?' asked Gabrielle 'destroy them? Otherwise, what's the point?'

'*Si!* But of course!' she went on. 'You need a Plan *Bella.* Five years, ten years, whatever you like. The time when you decide you'll stop and disappear into the night. I am forty this year. That is my time. It's been twenty long years and I've saved enough to buy the place of my dreams. But it can never be enough. So soon, I launch the Plan. I will show them all the dirt I have on them and tell them they must pay me bigtime or I will expose them. I have chosen them all carefully. They will all pay, they will have no choice. Their marriages, their businesses, their freedom all depend on it. They pay and I send them the evidence. No hard feelings. I just disappear with enough money for the rest of my life. You must decide on where your dream is too, *Bella.* The countryside, the lakes, the sea? Wherever you want. Find it. Work towards it. Keep it safe and secret in your mind - always. Picture it when they are screwing you. Then, one day, you finally launch the Plan too and then . . . you disappear - *phoof.'*

'But they'll find you, surely' said Gabrielle.' No-one can really disappear nowadays.'

'My name is not Sophia, it never was. She will vanish like the night because she never existed. And I will vanish too, forever.'

She explained how to get a false identity, what sort of evidence Gabrielle needed to collect and how to choose the right clients. Rich, married, dodgy dealers, famous, whatever. Anyone who would pay the highest price to buy her silence when the time came.

'So why are you telling me all this?' asked Gabrielle.

'You do not find it interesting? Tempting even?' she replied. 'I hope you do. I look at you - a beautiful girl with her whole life before her, as I was. You are me and I am you. Where is all this taking you? How will you ever stop? I think you can still be saved. I've seen too many girls like us. *Si*, they get rich but they lose everything else. Their being. They turn to drugs or drink to make it all bearable. You'll do that too, *Bella*. I know. Please, either get out now whilst you still can or set yourself a Plan. It will save you. I know this. I want to help you, *si*?'

GABRIELLE WENT BACK to London with Sophia's words echoing around her head. The weekend had been pivotal in many ways. It endorsed her view that all men were scum - but she had come to that conclusion already. They were either liars and cheats, like Tom, or arrogant beasts who believed they could buy anything or anyone. The idea of a Plan made sense. She *did* like the money, it was her only comfort. But Sophia was right. She no longer knew where she was going or wanted to end up. Tom had shattered her hopes, dreams and ambitions and she was now just circling the drain.

So, she would employ Sophia's Plan, but with one big difference. For her, it would not just be a business transaction where everyone went on with their lives afterwards. The pleasure, the comfort − yes, the power − was not just knowing that she *could* expose and destroy them if she wanted to. No, it was the knowledge that she *would*.

She had therefore adapted Sophia's Plan and had stuck to it religiously for fifteen years. But things were moving fast. She had now decided to launch Judgement Day early next year. So, she needed to spend the next couple of months putting the final practicalities into place. Activating the international bank accounts that had all been set up in false names. They would be used to receive the ransom money before making it disappear from the banking system without trace. She had learned how to do that from a dodgy - but besotted – city trader a couple of years ago. She was leaving him out of the Plan to ensure his silence.

Sadly, she had never heard from Sophia again. Nor Matteo for that matter. She assumed he lost his appetite after Sophia hit him with her Plan. Gabrielle truly hoped Sophia was now enjoying a long and happy retirement somewhere nice. Living the life of luxury that she had worked for. Meeting her had certainly changed Gabrielle's life. She owed her everything and hoped that, one day, their paths would cross again and she could then thank her in person.

But, sadly, Gabrielle had been right. No-one can completely disappear nowadays and fugitives are always tracked down, eventually. Three years ago, in 2021, an unidentified female body was discovered in a large trunk recovered from the bottom of Lake Como, Italy. It was weighted down by heavy stones and forensic experts calculated it had been lying there for ten years. When Gabrielle read about it at the time, the thought had never crossed her mind as to exactly who that body had belonged to.

16

Harvey

THURSDAY 19 SEPTEMBER 2024

'It's 7.18 and I'm Dale Glover on the Breakfast Show, here with Harvey Britten looking at today's papers. We've been discussing last night's disastrous match at the Amex Stadium where the Seagulls lost 3-0 to Sunderland in what is their worst start to a season for . . . how many years H?'

'Twenty-eight,'

'Twenty-eight years. Wow, since before I was born' joked Dale. 'Pretty dire stuff. So, let's move on to the big news story of the day – which is OP leader, Matthew Draper, giving his closing speech to the party's conference yesterday in Birmingham. And, by all accounts, H, it was an even worse performance than the Albion last night, if that's possible?'

'It looks that way, Dale' said Harvey. 'I think the political sketch writer in the *Daily News* sums it up nicely by describing it as *the deceased standing over his own grave and reading out his last will and testament before jumping in.* By anyone's standards, it went down like a lead balloon and his future as OP leader now looks even less secure than the Seagull's Manager.'

'And I understand the vultures are now circling?'

'So it seems, yes' Harvey continued. 'The papers all speak of various MPs being out on manoeuvres to gather support for their own possible leadership bids. They seem to be getting impatient waiting for the Messiah, Bradley Deakin, to come and save them. That's despite a National InstaPoll yesterday which gave him an impressive rating of 48% as the public's choice for best PM, compared to just 28% for Prime Minister Pritchard and a rather pathetic 15% for Matthew Draper. So it looks like most of the opposition MP's want to wait a little bit longer in the hope of Deakin finding himself a by-election. Unless someone else steps in first, of course, as they certainly can't go on much longer with a lame duck like Draper at the helm.'

'So, they all want Deakin – that's everyone but you, I think, H. Am I right? I assume you're still opposed to the idea?' Dale knew how to press Harvey's buttons.

'I've nothing against him personally' said Harvey. 'As I've said many times, it's just the idea that he'll go swanning into wherever a by-election is called and expect people to accept him as their local MP. Emphasis on the word *local*. And wherever he ends up, someone local will probably have been putting in the hours for years, working tirelessly to earn their own place as OP candidate next time around. But then - boom! In he'll come and they'll be side-lined by Mr Big Shot. I say again, what can he possibly know about that constituency to justify representing them as MP? He'll probably have to look it up on a map. The whole of society seems to be going that way. Everyone is fast-tracked nowadays. In my day….'

'Oh Gawd, here we go…' teased Dale.

'Well, in my day, people learned on the job. That should go for MPs too. It's like my old branch of SS&I in Brighton, which is sadly closing at the end of this month. Now, I started at the bottom and worked my way up but, nowadays, it's all graduate, fast track area managers coming in and thinking they know best. I don't think there's any substitute for experience and Deakin is a classic example.'

'It's true' said Dale. 'I started on hospital radio and worked my way through the system here at the BBC in Brighton. First as a studio assistant and so on, until I finally got my own show. But, nowadays, we just take people off the street and, next minute, they're co-hosting the show with me!'

Harvey smiled. 'OK, point taken. But you know what I mean.'

'Sure do H. Let us know what you think on the usual number. Until then, here's Giselle with her new song – *'He's not worth it.'*'

Dale faded down the microphones and looked at his friend. They both burst out laughing.

17

Alistair

FRIDAY 20 SEPTEMBER 2024

Alistair lay in bed beside Gabrielle. It was 3.a.m. She was sleeping peacefully, facing away from him with her long, sleek bare back uncovered. He thought about pulling up the sheet to keep her warm, but that was like throwing a blanket over the Venus De'Milo. She was just too beautiful on the eye.

Alistair reached silently for the glass of whisky on the bedside table. He had been drinking it earlier and was sure there was still a mouthful left. It was warm and a bit stale, but would do. His mind wandered to the current political turmoil in both parties and imagined how his life might have been if only he'd followed his intended route into politics as a young man. Might he have been there now, right in the thick of it? Perhaps advising the PM on what best to do in the face of a weak OP? Maybe he'd have been Prime Minister himself? Sadly, either possibility had evaporated many years ago. Instead of having a successful political career behind him, he had spent way too many years working as a bloody farmer.

The Buckland Farm had been in the family for several generations. During that time, it had grown into a vast, sprawling estate, spread across the South Downs of East Sussex. It was primarily a dairy farm, but the family had also swallowed up neighbouring businesses over the years and had ended up harvesting rape seed and various other crops as well.

Alistair never had any interest in farming as a boy. Despite being forced by his parents to muck in – literally, where the cows were concerned – his main instinct had always been to get away. He was a studious child, rarely seen without a book and never happier than when he was at school, learning. He became fascinated by the law and social justice and seemed destined to become either a lawyer or a politician when he grew up. But his ambition to leave the farm inevitably caused friction with his parents. He was an only child and, as such, was expected to, one day, take over the family business, as generations had done before him. But he had no interest whatsoever in doing so.

He went to university to study politics, where his parents hoped he would at least have studied agriculture. When he graduated in 1984, he moved into a flat in Fulham, West London, taking a job with Westminster Council as a graduate manager in social services. By now, his heart was set on being a politician. He'd been active in the party at university and, rightly or wrongly, was told that working for the Council would be 'a good way in'. He worked tirelessly for the party in the hope of first becoming a Councillor and then, hopefully one day, getting the chance to stand for Parliament.

There was constant pressure from his parents to come home but he never saw any reason to do so. They were only in their mid-forties and he was sure they'd be working the farm for at least another twenty years or more. Therefore, at worst, if politics didn't work out for him, he could always go back to the farm much later in his life. But that looked unlikely as everything was happily going to plan. He met and fell in love with Susan, a law graduate who was on track to become a solicitor. They moved into a rented flat in Clapham and spoke openly of marriage. Alistair was twenty-four and, with hindsight, it was probably all going too well.

Things changed dramatically when his father died suddenly in a car accident near the family farm. He was hit by a speeding car whilst walking along a narrow country lane. Bloody tourists. He was just forty-eight years old when he died, leaving a widow and a wayward son with no interest in running the family business.

Alistair's mother, Geraldine Buckland, was an imposing woman who ruled the roost. She intimidated her son and nothing he did ever seemed good enough for her. His father left everything to Alistair in his will – the farm and entire Buckland estate - but it came with one very strict condition. He must immediately take over the business, working alongside his mother, and would not take sole ownership until her eventual death. If he refused, he would inherit nothing – not a single penny, ever.

Obviously, when Geraldine had convinced him to add the condition to his will, Alistair's father had no expectation of dying so young. The condition was therefore only intended as an insurance policy. Geraldine said she would otherwise have to sell up if her husband died - unless Alistair stepped up to the plate. His father hated the thought of that happening after so many generations in the family. In truth, they assumed Alistair would have eventually come around anyway, long before they died of old age. But, tragically, it all came to a head way too soon.

Alistair didn't actually care if he lost his inheritance. He was happy making his own way in the world, despite the estate being worth several million pounds. Farming just wasn't his 'thing' and it certainly wasn't Susan's. But his mother pressurised him - playing every card from loyalty to family honour, guilt to blackmail. To make matters worse, all his wider relatives took her side. How dare he desert his poor widowed mother in her hour of need and force her to sell his father's beloved farm, all because of his selfishness and personal ambition?

Eventually he agreed to give it a try, just for a while. He desperately hoped to find his mother an alternative solution - perhaps a tenant, manager or suchlike. It would have been perfectly viable if she had only seen his point of view. But she wouldn't.

He reluctantly left his job, expecting it to be only a temporary break. Susan stuck by him, but stayed in London whilst he sorted things out at home. Unsurprisingly, she lost faith after a couple of years and the relationship ended. Alistair was heartbroken but also bitter and angry, blaming his domineering mother for ending his chance of happiness. But she was a heartless woman, seeing the breakup as a positive step - further cutting his ties with the life he dearly wanted. A life that, inch by inch, was slowly ebbing away. He gradually lost the will to fight, finding it easier to just get on with running the busy farm.

To his credit, he actually did a very good job, bringing his business acumen to the task and slowly modernising the estate. It became more successful and profitable than it had ever been before, but he still hated and resenting both the farm and his mother.

Although the estate took up pretty much all of his time, he was still involved with politics. He helped the local party during elections and, if nothing else, became a very generous donor – much to his mother's clear disgust.

His love life was scarce to non-existent. He had the occasional relationship, but none of the girls ever met with his mother's approval. She saw them all as gold-diggers who couldn't possibly be interested in a loser like Alistair for himself. He felt she just hated the idea of him ever being happy.

Alistair would never wish a terminal illness on anyone but, when Geraldine contracted pancreatic cancer at the age of only sixty-eight years old, part of him was actually relieved. She survived for just six months until the summer of 2004, by which time Alistair was forty-four years old. Despite the life sentence handed down in his father's will, he had finally won time off for good behaviour. But, by then, farming had reluctantly become his life's work. He had never achieved his full potential and couldn't see how he ever could in a life spent herding and milking cattle. So, when he was duly freed from the onerous condition on Geraldine's death, he quickly put the whole Buckland Estate up for sale. It eventually sold for close to six million pounds in 2005.

Alistair was now a very rich man and moved to a luxurious penthouse in Hove. He had seen enough green fields to last a lifetime. His many years of generous donations paid dividends and he was chosen as a candidate for the local Council in 2007, representing the ward where he now lived in Hove. He duly won the seat and was re-elected at three successive elections thereafter.

He became a popular, hard-working Councillor, actively involved in all aspects of the local community. He chaired various committees and everyone said he would make a very good MP. But time was running out. Despite considerable goodwill and support within the local party, he failed to win the candidacy for any of the three Brighton seats. It was not until 2023 that he finally got his chance. But then Sarah entered the fray and that, as they say, was that.

But at least he had Gabrielle and perhaps she was his greatest achievement. His political career had only reached the heights of overseeing a seagull cull rather than advising Prime Ministers on election strategy. It looked like this was as good as it was going to get.

As he put down the empty whisky glass on the bedside table, the gentle clink disturbed Gabrielle's sleep and she slowly rolled over. She smiled at him before getting up for the bathroom. He smiled back and was actually pleased she was awake. It meant he could now go over to the mini-bar without disturbing her. He needed another drink.

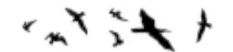

18

Bradley

TUESDAY 10 DECEMBER 2024

'Who exactly do you have to kill to get elected these days?' said Bradley.

'If you want that as a serious option' said Rod 'I'll need to make another list.' Presumably he was joking, but Bradley could never really tell.

'I know we've managed to quell the storm, for now, in terms of anyone else putting in a leadership bid' said Trevor, 'but the ship is creaking at the seams.'

'It is, yes' said Rod, 'and I have it on very good authority that the PM now wants to bring the election forward to next June. He's even being pressed to go in May, given the POG's ten-point lead, but he's a wimp and still wants to see the Council election results first. If they confirm he's on for a good win - and assuming Matthew is still limping on as OP leader at the time - then it's a pretty safe bet that he'll call a General Election straight away.'

'So, June it is?' said Peter.

'Probably.'

Bradley sighed. They were meeting at Peter's house and things were not going well. It didn't help that the media were making jokes at his expense, with headlines like '*sorry ladies, Deakin still can't get an election*' amongst others. The BBC had also 'suggested' he extend his break from '*Speakin' to Deakin*' until Easter, when they would review the situation again. Guest hosts were filling in for him whilst his political ambitions were still waiting for their flight to be called. It was all very frustrating and he was getting impatient.

'Any progress?' he said, knowing the response.

'We've offered more knighthoods than King Arthur' said Peter. 'And peerages. There's no shortage of MPs willing to step down at the next General Election - but not mid-term. It's as you said originally, Bradley. They don't want to look like the mercenaries – which they would be, of course. For some reason they've developed principles and, I have to say, we're struggling. There isn't a hint of ill health amongst them and they're all way too boring to get involved in a scandal. We're therefore setting our sites lower in terms of target seats. But the polls show that you could comfortably take pretty much anything other than a safe POG seat, so that isn't such bad news. We just need an election. *Any* bloody election.'

'Yes, the polls show you are still the man voters want' said Trevor 'and they want it to happen soon, just as much as we do.'

'We'll get there' said Rod, without any apparent grounds for saying it.

'HOW?' said Bradley in frustration. 'I can't keep living in limbo like this forever.'

'OK. In that case, I'm going to need more funds, Peter' said Rod, casually.

'More?' replied Peter in dismay, sounding like Mr Bumble from *Oliver Twist*. 'How much more?'

'£100,000' said Rod, without flinching, but the reaction implied he should justify himself. 'I've got a lot of people working off the radar, trying to find dirt that will force someone to stand down. It's not easy and its not cheap. Sorry, I *am* making headway, but it isn't without risk or overheads and it *will* produce results. I promise.'

'Bloody hell!' said Peter.

'How much do we have left in the war chest?' asked Trevor.

Many OP donors had given money specifically to support Bradley's campaign and it had paid for multiple trips around the country to garner support. In truth, nothing had touched the sides of the vast sums being donated.

'Plenty' said Peter. 'It's not that we can't afford it. It's just hard to be transparent when, half the time, even *I* don't know where all the money is going.'

'Put it through as another bonus payment to me' said Rod. 'Honestly, it's better you don't know exactly what's going on and even more important not to leave a trail.'

'This *is* all legal isn't it?' asked Bradley, looking perplexed. 'It's all being done in my name, you know.'

'Look, leave it with me' Rod said, not really answering the question, which didn't help to inspire confidence. 'Give me the hundred grand and I'll get you a by-election. Trust me.'

Bradley wasn't sure that he *did* trust him, but they had little choice but to agree. They were running out of both time and options. He just prayed that Rod could deliver on his promise.

19

Dan Billingham

WEDNESDAY 1 JANUARY 2025

Two o'clock in the morning is no time for anyone to hear the door-bell ring. Especially when their wife hasn't come home.

It can mean several things. Firstly, that she's forgotten her keys or lost the ability to use them after partying all night. On the plus side, that would at least herald her safe return – but generate a row as to why she was rocking up three hours late without answering her phone in the meantime. The second possibility might be drunken revellers thinking it fun to press random door bells on their way home. If so, Dan would give them hell if they were still within sight when he opened the door. But the third possibility didn't bear thinking about. It meant bad news – possibly the very worst – as to why his utterly reliable wife had not come home.

She had promised to leave the party at eleven, so should have been home by 11.45 at the latest. Instead she had gone off the radar. For the first hour, Dan was angry, believing she had simply lost track of time - although that seemed unlikely on an evening when everyone has a constant eye on the clock. As midnight came and went, having seen the new year in on his own, that anger was mixed with disbelief. He left three sharp phone messages saying '*Call me and let me know where the hell you are!*' But by one o'clock he was just consumed by worry and concern for her safety. Another seven phone messages now displayed an element of panic, bordering on desperation. *'Please call me as soon as you get this. Just let me know you're OK.'*

He felt helpless and wondered whether to call Alistair, who had been at the annual POG shindig as well. But he was probably tucked up in bed by now and Dan didn't want to wake him. He had pondered on who else he might call and whether they would just think he was being controlling or ridiculous. She was a grown-up - the local MP for goodness sake - and it *was* New Year's Eve. Everyone was out partying. *What's the big deal? Lighten up, she'll be home soon.*

Sarah didn't even want to go to the bloody party anyway but, as local MP, she was obliged to show her face. If their babysitter hadn't cancelled so late in the day, Dan would have been there too. But they agreed that Sarah would just go along for the dinner, say a few words and then make an early exit. Dan would stay home and look after Charlie in the meantime.

Sarah had driven herself to the party as she had been allocated a parking space – a perk of the job. She could actually have asked for a car to take her there, but didn't want to be any trouble. She never had a drink when she was driving anyway and the venue was only thirty minutes away. That was the problem. She was utterly reliable. The bell rang again. *Please let it be her. Please!*

With an increasing sense of foreboding, Dan walked into the hallway and turned on the light. He could see two shapes through the frosted glass front door and his heart instantly froze. The light reflected brightly off their high visibility jackets. They must either be builders, emergency workers . . . or the police.

He tentatively opened the door and started to shake. It was the latter. A male and a female police officer stood stern faced, clearly not there to wish him a Happy New Year. Anything but.

'Mr Dan Billingham?' said the male officer.

Dan nodded. He was ashen faced and couldn't speak.

'Are you married to Sarah Billingham?'

Same again.

'May we come in please? I'm afraid we have some very bad news about your wife.'

Dan stumbled backwards, falling against the wall to his left. The officers entered, calmly closing the door behind them.

THE POLICE HAD BEEN PIECING TOGETHER events overnight using CCTV and records from the Robo-lorry's data files. Apparently, many people on the seafront had witnessed the immediate aftermath of the accident but few had actually seen the moment of impact. Most of them, unsurprisingly, had been the worse for drink.

It was now 9 a.m. and a Family Liaison Officer was sitting with Dan in his lounge. Sarah's parents were there too, having come straight over after he'd called them with the tragic news. Reporters and TV crews were already outside the house, having arrived soon after Sarah's name was formally released at 7 a.m. He could see the bright TV lights shining through the window on a dark, overcast morning.

'From what we can tell so far,' said the officer, 'another vehicle left the scene immediately after the crash.'

She had identified herself as PC Yvette Allan but invited them to use her first name. Presumably this made bereaved relatives feel more relaxed.

Dan's own parents had also rushed over and were currently looking after little Charlie in the conservatory. He didn't yet know that his mother was dead, but he was nearly six and old enough to know something was going on. Dan's next task would be to break the news to the little lad, not knowing how to explain something he didn't even understand himself.

Sarah's father had one arm around her mother, who was resting her head on his shoulder and sobbing into a screwed-up piece of tissue. Dan wished someone would do the same for him. Preferably Sarah. He desperately needed to hug her.

'We know your wife, Sarah, left the party at 23.05 hours and reached her car at 23.10. That's all on CCTV. She then exited the car park and had to drive down West Street towards the seafront because of the New Year's Eve road closures. We know she then stopped at a red light at the T-junction and that the Robo-lorry was heading east along the seafront and had a clear road ahead. The data log shows it was doing 30 mph and had received clearance from Traffic Command that it would safely clear the green light before it changed.

Its sensors picked up Sarah's stationary car at the junction to its left, waiting at the lights and posing no perceived threat. But the dash-cam then shows her Mini suddenly shoot forward, just as the lorry approached the lights, and move straight into its path. I won't distress you with too many details but, obviously, the lorry hit her, at speed, squarely on the driver side. We're confident Sarah wouldn't have known anything about it and died instantly, if that is any comfort.'

Dan paused a while before speaking. It was no comfort at all. 'You mentioned another vehicle?' he said calmly, not really taking it all in.

'Yes, it appears that a black Range Rover Elite was seen emerging from West Street onto the seafront immediately after the crash. It drove around the lorry wreckage and headed west. Witnesses say it was missing its front bumper and had a broken headlight. Others say they saw the car hit Sarah's Mini from behind and shunt her into the lorry's path. We cannot yet determine whether it was deliberate or accidental and, of course, given who she is, we cannot rule-out terrorism.'

'Have you caught him?' said Dan.

'We identified the same vehicle on CCTV further along the seafront, doubling back northwards into the city centre. We were tracking its route when we received reports of a vehicle matching its description being spotted on the South Downs. Witnesses staying at the Belle Tout Hotel - the old converted lighthouse above the cliffs – were up in the viewing gallery at about 00.15 hours having just watched the midnight fireworks over Eastbourne. They saw the vehicle driving at speed along the Beachy Head Road, which is about four hundred yards from the hotel. The car mounted the grass verge and drove right up to the edge of the cliffs. Two figures were then seen doing something at the rear of the car, presumably placing a burning rag into the fuel tank. They pushed the car over the cliff and flames could immediately be seen as it went over. It exploded on hitting the rocks at the bottom.'

Dan listened in silence.

'The two figures ran off on foot' PC Allen continued 'but the witnesses couldn't see where they went in the darkness and were also distracted by the explosion. We've launched a massive manhunt but have found nothing so far. The wreckage will be recovered today so we'll confirm if it is the same vehicle, but it seems fairly certain. Disturbingly, the registration number was fake so we'll need to trace the car's real owner. As I say, we can't rule anything out but the random timing of the lorry's arrival, together with the lights being red when Sarah got there, make it hard to believe it was planned. Our best guess it that it was just a tragic accident involving professional car thieves who then panicked - knowing they were in a stolen car - fled the scene and destroyed the evidence. Obviously, we're ruling nothing out and both the Anti-Terrorism Squad and MI5 are also involved. I'm afraid that's all I have for you at the moment.'

Dan was listening but not really taking it all in. He suddenly felt claustrophobic and needing to get away. 'I'm . . . just going out to get some air' he said.

He stumbled into the hall and could hear Charlie playing in the conservatory. He went through to the kitchen and out into the rose garden. The cold air hit him hard and he shivered, but it brought him back to life. His lovely, warm, funny, clever, beautiful girl was gone. She had *'died instantly.'* Just like that. Her priceless life snuffed out in a heartbeat.

He could hear the wind swirling in the barren trees and either a helicopter or a drone was noisily throbbing in the sky somewhere nearby. He assumed it was either the police or the media. But the loudest sound was that of the seagulls overhead. Dozens of them, screeching and screaming as they circled above him. They all cried in unison, either panicked, distressed or frightened by something. Dan knew exactly how they felt.

20

Bradley

WEDNESDAY 1 JANUARY 2025

The theme music to *'Speakin' to Deakin'* shattered the silence and rudely awoke Bradley from a very deep sleep. It was the ringtone on his phone and frightened the life out of him. As it rang, the time lit up on the screen. *Who in God's name calls at 6 a.m. on New Year's Day?*

He and Emma had been to a neighbour's party last night. Emma had drunk enough champagne to float a battleship and Bradley's head felt like it had been used to launch the bloody thing. They had only fallen into bed about three hours ago.

Emma groaned without moving, face down like a beached whale. The groan easily translated as *'shut that bloody thing off - now!'* He wanted to ignore the call but, having seen Peter's name on the screen, decided it must be important.

'Errrroorrwww?' he said. His mouth was dry and he seemed to be using someone else's ill-fitting tongue.

'Bradley, I'm so sorry to call you this early, but I had to catch you before the press start ringing you for comment.' Peter sounded serious and very much awake.

'What's happening?' said Bradley, the power of speech quickly returning. Emma gave another aggressive growl so he crawled out of bed and into the bathroom, closing the door quietly behind him.

'Its good news tied to some truly awful news' said Peter. 'It looks like we've finally got our by-election and it's definitely a winnable seat. That's the good news.'

Bradley reserved judgement. 'And the bad news?'

'I'm afraid it's Sarah Billingham. She's the POG MP for Brighton and Hove. A lovely lady – I've met her several times. Has a dear little boy too, it's an absolute tragedy. It seems she had the most appalling car accident last night. Rod just called me. Goodness knows how he found out so soon, the police haven't even released her name yet. But anyway, it's unclear whether she jumped a red light or something else happened but, either way, a bloody great Robo-lorry hit her side on and killed her outright. I've never trusted the ruddy things, myself.'

'My God! That's . . . terrible' said Bradley, now fully awake. He'd never met Sarah but had read good things about her in the press. A rising star by all accounts and quite a cute little thing too, as he recalled.

'As soon as her name is released, the media will obviously put two and two together and see that it creates a golden opportunity for you' said Peter. 'So, they'll want to know whether you'll be standing.'

'And will I?' asked Bradley.

'I think so.' Said Peter. 'Well, I know so. She has . . . had . . . the smallest majority in the country. 173 for goodness sake, practically a tie! If it *has* to be a POG seat, then you couldn't really ask for a better one - tragedy aside, of course.'

'It seems a bit tasteless even talking about it when the poor woman's body isn't even cold' said Bradley. *Yes! Yes! This is it!*

'I know, but that's politics for you' said Peter. 'You're right, though. It's no time to appear crass and insensitive - that could easily go against us. I propose we just tell the press you'll be sending your heartfelt thoughts and prayers to her family and leave it there, for now. Let them draw their own conclusion. It's bloody obvious you'll be standing anyway. You should *Google* Sarah in the meantime and get more background. It'll look good if you can mention her husband and family by name - gives it a more personal touch. She was only elected last year, poor girl - well, I guess it's the year before last now. Happy New Year by the way.'

'Let's hope it will be' said Bradley. 'I'll send the family a personal message if you can get me an address. It does sound like a terrible waste. How very sad.'

'Yes, well…' said Peter unperturbed. 'It is, of course. And I know it sounds awful, but we *have* to be practical and start planning. First off, swot up on everything you can about Brighton. Rod will prepare you a pack. It'll take a few months to arrange an election, not least out of respect to the family, but we should push for a date in May if we possibly can. It's not our decision, sadly, because she was a POG MP. But the OP can apply some serious pressure on the PM for an early date, although that's probably the last thing he wants. Hopefully he'll not be tempted to call a General Election instead. We're so close and that would be a disaster if it happens before we can make you leader. Trouble is, I suspect his own MPs will be terrified at the thought of you saddling up your horse so they'll be pushing him to go early. But leave that to us.'

Bradley tried to take it all in. 'Brighton, you say?'

'Brighton and Hove, yes. They get funny if you leave the Hove bit off, apparently, so get used to that.'

'Fairly close to home, at least. Better than somewhere up north.'

'Look' Peter went on, 'the party will decide how we can head the PM off at the pass. Thankfully, the economic and employment figures are due out this month and I understand they're bad news for POG. We can capitalise on that. Plus, the idea of you becoming leader for real may actually cause an upturn in our own poll ratings. That will also scare him. I just don't think he'll be brave enough to call an early General Election and look like he's running scared. Never a good image for a PM. I think he will just hope to defeat you in the by-election by putting up a really good candidate. It isn't out of the question that they could win it, of course. It *is* their seat after all - even with such a tiny majority. Let's see anyway, and be positive. We're nearly there Bradley, I can feel it.'

Bradley still couldn't think clearly. He wasn't sure if he was even sober yet. He agreed to speak to Peter later in the day and crept back to bed. Emma had not moved and remained slumped across the bed like a heavily sedated warthog.

'Hoozzur frucck wazzat?' she mumbled, equally unable to use her tongue.

'Peter' he replied, calmly. He kissed her on the forehead. 'Happy New Year, Ems. Get your arse out of bed. By this time next year, you and I will in Downing Street.'

21

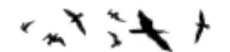

Harvey

WEDNESDAY 1 JANUARY 2025

It was 6.10 a.m. and Harvey was making coffee. He hated New Year, always had done. He couldn't be bothered with all the false bonhomie so soon after Christmas and it was also too late at night and the wrong time of year. If they would just move it to a sunny evening in June – say, around 10 pm - then he might see things differently.

But, as it was, Harvey and Claire rarely went out to celebrate. They had gone to bed as normal last night at around 10.30 and, as usual on New Year's Eve, were expecting to be woken up later by the fireworks and other midnight revelry. However, last night, Harvey had actually been disturbed a bit earlier, having heard sirens whizzing up and down the seafront at about 11.30. He continued to hear them for a good while longer before finally falling asleep at some point in the early hours of 2025.

He had woken at six as normal and tiptoed down to the kitchen, leaving Claire fast asleep in bed. He looked at the news on his tablet and was unsurprised to find little going on nationally. But the local news pages were dominated by a fatal accident on the seafront late last night, involving a car and a Robo-lorry. It didn't give many details, but Harvey guessed it was the cause of all the noise. *Some poor sod's family will be waking up to a lousy new year this morning. Presum-ably a drunk driver.*

As the kettle came to the boil, Harvey's phone rang and displayed the BBC switchboard number. They sometimes rang about this time when a scheduled newspaper reviewer had called in sick. He was always happy to help Dale out but knew his friend wasn't working today. If they wanted him to cover this morning it was therefore very annoying. He was attending the Brighton home match that was kicking off at lunchtime, and didn't want to miss it just because some unprofessional hack had woken up with a hangover.

'Hello Harvey? Its Ashley.' He was surprised. If they needed last minute cover, he wouldn't normally expect Dale's producer to call him in person.

'Hi Ashley, a Happy New Year to you' replied Harvey. 'To what do I owe the pleasure?'

'It's. . .well, really terrible news, I'm afraid' said Ashley. He didn't return the traditional new year greeting and was clearly pre-occupied. 'Really terrible. I've just called Dale to tell him. There was an awful accident last night and we've just received word that Sarah Billingham was involved. I'm afraid she died.'

Harvey was stunned. 'Oh, my word, that's terrible! What on earth happened? The news said something about a lorry?'

'We don't know yet, it's all very sketchy' said Ashley. 'I'm at the studio and it's a bit chaotic, to tell you the truth. The police are releasing her name at 7 a.m. and giving a press conference at nine. We want to do a special show this morning paying tribute to Sarah. Memories and thoughts from friends and listeners, the usual sort of thing. It's starting at ten so I need to juggle the schedule around. I've asked Dale to host it but, obviously, he's in a bit of a state. He insisted he'll only do it if you're there beside him and I think he'll need a good deal of support to tell you the truth. It'll be an emotional experience.'

'Of course, I will' said Harvey. He felt so sorry for poor Dale and decided to ring him straight after the call. But he was touched that his friend wanted him there as support. The Seagulls would just have to get by without him this afternoon - he had a job to do.

After the call, he wondered how best to break the sad news to Claire. She would be very upset too, having really taken to Sarah. They had both been delighted to receive a personalised Christmas card from the MP, which took pride of place on the mantlepiece.

Harvey stared down blankly at the kitchen table, deep in thought. A Sunday magazine was lying in front of him, with the cover uppermost. At first, it didn't register. But slowly, the page began to focus in his mind. On the front cover was a large close up photo of Bradley Deakin with the headline '*Speakin' of Deakin - will 2025 be his year?*'

The awful realisation suddenly sunk in. Bradley Deakin was desperately looking for a by-election, which could only mean one thing. He'd now be coming after Sarah's seat in Brighton.

'No, no, no!' he said aloud to the empty kitchen. 'No! Not here!'

.

22

Alistair

WEDNESDAY 1 JANUARY 2025

Alistair had enjoyed one of the best New Year's Eves he could ever remember. He usually stayed home on his own, but last night was different. Sarah had personally invited him to the POG's annual dinner dance and it then turned out that Dan couldn't be there because of some last-minute babysitter problems. She'd therefore insisted that Alistair take his place alongside her on the top table. Given that he had otherwise been assigned to a table at the back, near the toilets, the upgrade was all the more welcome.

He therefore found himself sitting with the POG's elite - Andrew McKenzie, the local Chairman, and Tom Jeffrey, the local party leader, were both there with their wives. They all treated Alistair like a VIP, complementing him on the seagull cull work and generally giving him a warm reception. The icing on the cake was when Sarah singled out *'my former colleague, mentor and dear, dear friend Alistair Buckland'* in here speech.

She left early at around eleven, so it all went a bit flat after that. Alistair was glad to have booked a taxi for 12.15 a.m., giving him a good excuse to leave as soon as the midnight ritual was over with. He then received a phone message that it was running very late as, apparently, there had been an accident on the seafront which was causing chaos. Most of the roads around the hotel were therefore cordoned off so he cancelled the cab and headed towards Churchill Square on foot, hoping to get a bus home instead. But the buses were also in a mess and packed to bursting point. He eventually walked all the way back to Hove, taking about thirty-five minutes on top of the long wait. He finally arrived home at 2.15 a.m. feeling cold and exhausted.

Even that drama had not sullied a wonderful evening and he planned to call Sarah later this morning to thank her. He hadn't slept much, if at all, and looked out to see the time. It was 6.20 a.m. so he decided to get up and make a coffee. Suddenly, out of the darkness, the phone rang. *Who on earth is ringing at this time of the morning?*

23

Harvey

WEDNESDAY 1 JANUARY 2025

'You're doing great, Dale' said Harvey. 'I'm actually in awe of how well you're doing.' For once there was no sarcasm or banter involved. He meant it.

It was 10.45 a.m. and they were mid-way through the Radio Brighton tribute programme. Ashley was not joking when he said it was chaotic. The skeleton crew had just been expecting a normal, sleepy Bank Holiday. But instead, they were scuttling around like ants, frantically contacting people who knew Sarah, political and terrorism experts, police spokesmen and anyone else who might bring something to the programme. The switchboard had been overwhelmed with more listener calls that anyone could remember.

Dale was indeed holding up incredibly well. Harvey was truly impressed at how professional and detached he was on the air when, emotionally, he must be in pieces. Sarah's death had hit him very hard but he was conducting interviews and reminiscing with distraught callers in a considered and sensitive way.

'Thanks, H,' he said, 'but please don't be nice to me. I'm only just holding it together.'

'It's so hard to believe this is happening' said Harvey. 'I heard the sirens last night but it just didn't occur to me that it could be anything like . . .'

Ashley came into the studio and interrupted. They were in the middle of playing a music track and neither of them was exactly sure what was coming next.

'Dale, mate, I need you to read this out now, if you would please' said Ashley, handing over a piece of yellow paper. He was normally quite officious but was handling Dale with great sensitivity today.

'What is it?'

'It's a statement from Councillor Alistair Buckland. He was one of Sarah's closest friends, as you know. He agreed earlier to come on the show, but now says he can't face it. Too upset. But he has emailed us this statement. The intro is at the top. Better go, song's ending.'

Ashley quickly closed the soundproof door behind him and Dale prepared to go live. He didn't have time to scan the page but Harvey knew he was experienced enough to read things straight off the bat. Dale pulled the headphones back onto his head and took a deep breath.

'That was Whitney Houston and I'm here looking back on the life of Sarah Billingham MP, who was tragically killed in a car accident very early this morning. Harvey Britten is with me and I now have a statement from Councillor Alistair Buckland who was a great friend of Sarah's and I understand was actually sitting alongside her at a party last night, shortly before the accident occurred. Gosh.' Dale paused briefly, clearly reflecting on that awful thought. 'Ahem. We were hoping to have him on the phone but, understandably, he's too upset and has instead kindly sent us a statement that I'd like to read out now if I may. It says:

'*I am shocked and devastated to hear of the tragic death of Sarah Billingham, my dearest, dearest friend. My heart goes out to her husband, Dan, and her gorgeous little boy Charlie, who I am honoured to also call my Godson. I know how much Sarah loved them both and that Charlie was....*'

Harvey could hear Dale's voice beginning to crack a little, but he carried on.

'...*was the light of her life and he will miss his mummy so very....*'

Dale was struggling, with tears filling his eyes. Instinctively, Harvey reached across and took the page from his shaking hand.

'I'll finish this shall I, Dale?' he said, scanning to find where his friend had left off.

'... *Charlie was the light of her life and he will miss his mummy so very much, as will we all. Sarah had only been our MP for twenty months but, during that time, made a huge impact, which was no surprise to me at all. Many people questioned why I stood aside for her last year but they very soon understood why I did so. Her warmth, compassion, consideration and dedication to the people of Brighton and Hove was beyond parallel. I know she justified my deci-sion a million times over and was, without doubt, one of the kindest most caring people I have ever met - or will ever meet. My heart is breaking but I know her memory will outlive us all in the city that she loved so much. God bless you Sarah. I am proud to have known you and to call you my friend.*'

Harvey paused. It was an emotional statement and even he was struggling. 'Well, powerful words' he said finally. 'So, thank you, Councillor, for sharing your memories. I think we have another record now . . . yes, this is Giselle, another good friend of Sarah's, with '*my love is yours.*'

'Thanks H' said Dale, composing himself whilst wiping tears from his face. 'I owe you one. Very unprofessional. It was just . . . talking about Charlie that did it.'

'Don't be daft' said Harvey. 'I'm amazed you got this far. Shall I do the next link whilst you take a moment?'

'Yes please, but don't get any big ideas!'

'I know my place' said Harvey, pleased that Dale could still share a joke.

HARVEY ACTUALLY DID the next ten minutes of the show on his own whilst Dale went out to compose himself. It was a turning point for Harvey. The phone lines lit up even more as listeners heaped praise on him for helping his friend. The clip from the studio webcam was later shown on all the TV news bulletins and was also shared several hundred thousand times across social media in the next few days. Reports of the incident similarly appeared in the national papers and it seemed to sum up the local - and soon national - outpouring of grief over Sarah's untimely death. As a result, people across the whole country began to know the name of Harvey Britten.

It was just the start.

24

Gabrielle

MONDAY 6 JANUARY 2025

'I'll make us a coffee' said Gabrielle, not a service her clients normally asked for.

It had been an odd evening. FG had called last week, begging to see her. He was distraught but this was the first time she was free to meet him. She wished she could have cancelled one of her other clients - knowing it was important to him - but couldn't realistically do so.

It was impossible to avoid the coverage of his friend's death last week and FG had also been in the news himself because of a moving statement that he'd written. Actually, it was more about the way some crappy local DJ had gotten all weepy whilst reading it out. Gabrielle had seen the clip of him blubbing away whilst an older guy stepped in. Everyone thought it was really emotional but, personally, she found it a bit embarrassing. Either way, they were FG's words and Gabrielle felt a little bit proud, for some reason.

She knew Sarah Billingham meant a lot to him. It was *her* who had stopped him becoming an MP a couple of years ago, much to Gabrielle's disgust. But, ironically, there was now another chance on the horizon. The accident – or maybe murder, the jury was still out – meant FG might now be asked to stand in Sarah's place. The media were speculating about him being the natural successor as POG candidate, although there was far more coverage about Bradley Deakin being favourite to actually win the seat. Even so, FG was no longer the loser she had come to believe.

Yet here he was, looking like a broken man. Obviously, she hadn't expected to see him jumping for joy when she arrived at the hotel room earlier, but she had not expected *this*. He'd opened the door and simply thrown his arms around her. Hugged her for ages, so tightly it almost crushed her. His eyes moist with tears.

They had then moved over to the bed - as they invariably did when she arrived - and she started the usual ritual. But he wasn't interested. He just wanted to hold her and, this time, he burst uncontrollably into tears. His head was on her chest, sobbing - for ages.

She held him tightly to comfort him - not something she really knew how to do. In fact, the whole experience was new to her. She realised she had never comforted *anyone* like that in her entire life, ever. It was a disturbing thought. But although it was distressing, it actually felt quite nice. Oddly comforting to be comforting someone else. She had patted him on the back - gently, soothingly - and said '*ssshh*' and *there, there*' because she thought people said that in such situations. But it just made him hold her tighter. Bizarrely, that made her feel safe for some reason. She couldn't remember anyone comforting *her* like that either. Offering *her* the reassurance he now craved and she was providing. Telling *her* that everything would be OK. There were times in her past when she would have desperately liked that, needed it even. So, who was really comforting who?

After a while he calmed down, laying back on the pillow next to her, almost exhausted. They had then spoken for an hour or more and he told her how lost he was feeling. He spewed out all his memories about Sarah, how great she was and all that. Gabrielle wondered if anyone would speak about *her* so lovingly if she suddenly died. She realised that, in reality, only FG would do so. He really was such a lovely man.

After a while she tried to cheer him up by kissing him, hoping to kick-start the ritual again. But he gently pushed her away. No-one ever did that. It was certainly a day of firsts.

'I just want to be with you' he said. 'and not feel so . . . alone.'

So, she had offered to make coffee.

'What happens now?' she said, returning to bed with two white hotel mugs. Thankfully, the room had a coffee machine rather than the disgusting powdered cat litter found in the hotel rooms they used when the Council was paying.

'They're still investigating' said FG. 'We're hoping the funeral can be held soon. Dan - that's her husband - is in a terrible state.'

'What about their little boy, what's he called again?'

'Charlie' said FG. 'Not sure he's taking it all in. He's been staying with grandparents because the house still has the media camped outside.'

She nodded gently at the thought of the poor little brat. 'The papers say there'll have to be an election at some point. They mentioned your name too - nice picture. Would you stand, possibly, do you think?'

'People are being very kind' replied FG. 'Everyone says it should be me and Sarah would have wanted it. But I'm not sure I have the appetite any more, ironic really.'

Gabrielle sighed inwardly and hoped FG didn't see her frustration. The guy needed a serious kick up the arse to motivate him. *For goodness sake, this is your chance!*

'Well, it probably *is* what Sarah would want' she said with commendable empathy. 'So, perhaps you should do it anyway - for her. You'd be a brilliant MP, you know that.' *And a very useful one too. Perhaps.*

'Thanks' he said, smiling gently. 'You've always supported my ambitions. More than I deserve and I appreciate that, I really do.' He sighed and looked so sad. 'I guess I probably will stand, if they want me to, but there's an awful lot to think about. Anyway, Bradley Deakin will probably win, so what's the point?'

'You don't know that' she replied, 'and don't put yourself down. From what I can see in the papers, people like you after hearing that statement . . . thing. You should capitalise on all this goodwill. Do it for your Sarah. Make her proud of you, just like I am.'

He looked at her. She didn't mean to say the last bit and he was clearly shocked to hear it too. He stroked her hair and thanked her. Then he leant across, kissed her and the ritual finally fired into life. It was gentle, loving almost.

NEXT MORNING, as she got ready to leave, he pulled out his wallet as normal, but she refused to accept the money. Perhaps she was going soft in her old age, but it just didn't seem right.

25

Alistair

TUESDAY 4 MARCH 2025

'I've just had a call from the PM's office and it's all good news.'

Andrew McKenzie was sitting opposite Alistair in his office and looked truly pleased. 'If you're willing to accept, then we have the all clear to offer you the candidacy. And, if I may say so, it's a bloody good choice too.'

'I'd be honoured' said Alistair politely. This ought to have been the most exciting news possible. But it had come at such a heavy price and he was still struggling to come to terms with Sarah's death.

It had been an emotional three months. The police and security services were still unable to find clear evidence of terrorism or murder. The two men seen pushing the stolen car off Beachy Head had still not been traced, despite a massive manhunt. Unsurprisingly, social media was rife with conspiracy theories, not least as the 'men in black' - as they'd become known - were clearly very professional. The Range Rover was stolen from outside a house in Manchester last December but had not appeared on any CCTV in Brighton – or anywhere else for that matter - until the crash itself. That suggested it had been moved around on a lorry and was unloaded in the road where the crash took place. Every such vehicle picked up on CCTV anywhere in Sussex during the previous few weeks had been meticulously traced and excluded.

As expected, there was not a trace of DNA or any rogue finger-prints left in the burnt-out wreckage and the two men themselves were not captured on CCTV after making their escape, either travelling on foot or by bus. This added to the conspiracy theories that someone was therefore waiting for them, meaning it was all pre-planned. But, whilst it was all very odd, it was still largely hearsay without evidence. The apparently random timing of the incident, with so many variables involved, still suggested it was just a tragic accident involving professional car thieves and, if so, Sarah was simply in the wrong place at the wrong time. Unless new evidence was discovered from the ongoing investigation to suggest otherwise, the final inquest was likely to conclude that it was accidental death.

It didn't really matter to Alistair, either way. Sarah was dead and he was still heartbroken. Now he was stepping into her shoes as POG candidate in the forthcoming by-election which looked certain to be announced for May 8th 2025. He knew he needed to start feeling enthusiastic about it, but it was hard.

The timing of the by-election had been a difficult decision politi-cally. The PM was deeply aware of Bradley Deakin hovering on the side-lines and almost certain to throw his hat into the ring. There was pressure on the PM to therefore call a General Election instead, but the *Daily Record* was baiting him about being scared of Deakin. They had mounted a campaign to call the by-election quickly, which was gaining public support. They were also making a lot of capital about the appalling economic and employment figures in January that had made the government appear weak. Their poll rating had slipped to 5% since then.

It was a dilemma either way: try to trump Deakin by calling a General Election before he could be made leader, but still risk losing – or risk such a formidable foe entering the gates of Westminster via a by-election. It was a close call, but the PM had eventually decided the latter option was safest, hoping that a good local candidate might somehow head Deakin off at the pass. That candidate was

Alistair Buckland and all hopes for the POG were therefore resting on his shoulders. It was a daunting responsibility.

'Are you sure no-one else will contest selection?' said Alistair.

'Not this time' said Andrew. 'The PM sees you as our best chance against Bradley Deakin. You've a good local profile and, above all, you can capitalise on the intense local sympathy about Sarah. The huge national outpouring of grief may have been unexpected but it's certainly caught the public's imagination. Your tribute on that radio cock-up really struck a chord and showed how close a friend you were. Being crass, that's bound to count strongly in your favour. We'll portray you as doing this for Sarah to continue her legacy. Especially after you stood aside for her two years ago. That shows you're a man of integrity. Voters will lap that up whilst Deakin will come across as a cynical opportunist, exploiting her tragic death for his own grubby ambitions. If the OP had any shred of decency, they wouldn't even be contesting the seat. That would be the normal etiquette, given the tragic circumstances.'

Alistair agreed, but wasn't entirely comfortable with the cynical way Andrew was using Sarah's death for political advantage either. But politics was politics and he was just being practical. The party was moving on and Alistair wished he could do the same.

'Now' said Andrew, leaning forward on his desk. 'There will, of course, be a selection panel, but that's now a formality. The PM has made his views clear and the local party members will not argue. The candidacy is yours. But there's one thing I *have* to ask you – something the panel will also want to know. With Deakin involved, and so much riding on it, you'll be exposed to far more media scrutiny than we've ever seen here before. The OP will be going through your dustbins to discredit you – as will the *Daily Record*.'

'So, what are you saying?' asked Alistair.

'I know you've led a blameless life, worked hard all those years as a farmer and a dedicated local Councillor. But I have to be sure – *we* have to be sure – that there are no skeletons in your cupboard that could rattle their bones during the campaign.'

'Of course,' said Alistair 'I understand. I must say it's all a bit daunting to be under the spotlight like that.'

'Be in no doubt it will be intense,' said Andrew, 'and will require the utmost care and no slip-ups.' He paused, apparently still waiting for an answer to his question, but Alistair didn't give one. 'So?'

'So, what?'

'Do you have anything lurking in the shadows that we should know about. A gay lover, perhaps? Is all your money in an illegal offshore tax scheme? Is an obscure member of your family a drug dealer, a pimp or, worse still, an OP supporter? That sort of thing.'

'No, nothing.' Alistair answered immediately. If he appeared to be thinking too long, it might imply that there was something to think about, so he tried to sound confident and decisive.

'Thought as much' said Andrew. 'One of the good guys, our Alistair. Putting us all to shame. Sorry, I had to ask, you do understand.'

'Thank you and, yes, I understand entirely.'

THEY PARTED company and Alistair walked down the familiar corridor on the way out of the Council offices. He nodded to various people along the way, but didn't stop to talk. There was only one thought in his mind - Gabrielle. Should he have mentioned her? Alistair didn't see her as a skeleton, but she was certainly a secret. His one *big* secret. He knew he could trust her implicitly and no-one really needed to know about her. They wouldn't understand anyway. Gabrielle hadn't even charged for some of their more recent sessions after Sarah died. No, their relationship wasn't something dirty or sordid. It was just . . . complicated. But neither of them was married. They were just two people in love - well, one of them was.

He also needed to protect her. A scandal would destroy her reputation as much as his. Alistair didn't want that. He had thought about it a great deal over recent weeks as the likelihood of him standing became ever more likely. Reluctantly, he would need to take a break from seeing Gabrielle - at least during the campaign. If he won, well, he didn't know what he would do. But, if he lost, it would be business as usual. So, deep down, part of him hoped he would lose. The part he was trying to suppress. The same part that had dragged him down into the darkness when Sarah died and was stifling his enthusiasm to stand. The insecure part that loved Gabrielle desperately and knew that, with Sarah no longer in his life, she was his only source of happiness. He just didn't know what he would do without her.

But he needed to fight his way out of that darkness. This was a huge opportunity and needed to be grasped with both hands, for his *own* sake and to honour Sarah's memory. He owed her that and therefore had to give the election his best shot. Focus only on winning the bloody thing and doing it in her name. That was important. '*Continuing her legacy*' as Andrew put it. He knew it would hurt like hell but it had to be done. Gabrielle would understand.

But he needed to see her just one last time before it all kicks off. He just had to.

26

Terry

WEDNESDAY 12 MARCH 2025

Investigative journalism is nothing like it's made out to be in films and TV. They never show the endless hours of surveillance with the poor sod of a hero desperately wanting the toilet. It's certainly not all action stuff and car chases. No, the reality is far more tedious and routine – and Terry was experiencing that today.

He was sitting in the foyer of the magnificent Grand Central Hotel in Mayfair, the newest and chicest hotel in London. A contact claimed to have information about wide scale football match fixing by a Chinese betting syndicate and they had arranged to meet at 4 p.m. Terry had checked into a room for the secret interview, but it was now after six and the informant was a no-show.

Terry had chosen the hotel as it had a very large and busy reception area, comfortable couches and armchairs in abundance. It was big enough to sit and wait without hotel staff noticing or caring. But he had now been there for over two hours and was starting to look conspicuous. He'd ordered, and drunk, two pots of ridiculously expensive coffee to prevent the valet staff pestering him. Hence the need to use the toilet. The luxurious - but uncomfortable - soft couch he was sitting on offered no back support whatsoever, but it did provide a clear, uninterrupted view of the main entrance doors.

The informant said he would be wearing a blue polo shirt and beige trousers but no-one matching that combination had entered so far. Terry decided to give it one more hour before calling it a day. The informant had either got cold feet, was actually a hoaxer or had been beaten to death by the people he was betraying. Terry didn't really care which. At least he was booked in for the night, so it wasn't a complete waste of time. He planned to enjoy a good meal on expenses and then watch the Arsenal game in his room. There were always positives to any situation.

As he stared blankly at the doors, a portly, grey haired man in a suit waddled in carrying an expensive looking, leather overnight bag. He made his way to the busy reception desk, joining a short queue to check in. Terry recognised him as Alistair Buckland, the Councillor who had given that tedious press conference last year in Brighton. That was four hours of his life Terry would never get back. But, more recently, he had seen his name and picture following the death of Sarah Billingham, the MP smashed up by a lorry over new year. There was talk around the *Daily Record* offices about him being the prospective POG candidate in the forthcoming by-election, but no-one seemed too bothered. Their main topic of conversation was Bradley Deakin, who would surely wipe the floor with a loser like Buckland.

Terry wondered what he was doing checking into a swanky London hotel. Perhaps there were some formalities to complete at his party's London offices. But he quickly got bored thinking about it and checked his watch again. 6.15 p.m. God, time goes slowly when you're waiting. Buckland checked in and then headed for the lifts, but didn't see Terry. He wouldn't have recognised him anyway.

Thirty-five minutes later and Terry was ready to call it a day. The elusive informant was obviously not coming and he wanted to get dinner over with before the match started at eight. Time to go.

As he gathered himself together, trying to get blood flowing back into his stiff joints, he was distracted by a woman gliding through the glass entrance doors. A beautiful woman at that. Tall, elegant and oozing class. She was probably in her mid-thirties but still looking as hot as hell. She wore a stylish coat and her hair was tied up loosely on top, with odd strands casually hanging down. On some women it would suggest they'd been dragged through a hedge backwards but, on this one, it just looked sexy. Really sexy. She was slightly aloof but with a sweet, enchanting face. She carried a large designer bag over one arm, somewhere between a handbag and an overnight bag. It was impossible to tell the difference with fashionistas nowadays. Surprisingly, she gave the reception desk a wide berth and instead walked purposefully towards the lift lobby. *Must already be a guest.* He enjoyed the view as she passed by before continuing to gather his bag and newspapers together. Mission aborted - time to enjoy his expenses paid evening of five-star luxury.

He walked to the lift-lobby and was pleasantly surprised to see the mystery beauty still waiting for a lift. With six available, he'd assumed she would have been long gone by now. She turned her head and gave him a gentle smile. She reminded him of Audrey Hepburn in that old film he was watching on Netflix the other night. Whilst her smile was gorgeous it was more her eyes that attracted him. Those eyes! Deep, dark and inviting. Terry was like a helpless puppy.

The lift arrived and Audrey stepped inside. Terry followed, pleased they'd be alone in such a small space. The waft of expensive perfume consumed him and he stood as close to her as he realistically could without looking like a pervert. The lift didn't move and Audrey started to fumble in her bag. It was the type of lift that needed a room key-card to activate it for security reasons. Terry's card was in his breast pocket so he gallantly leant across in front of Audrey to swipe the lift into action.

'Thank you, kind sir' she said and flashed the smile again. 'Mine's in here somewhere.' He smiled back, as alluring as he could but suspecting it came across as a leer. Audrey pressed the button for the second floor.

'Oh, my floor too' he said, hoping she'd believe it– as it was true – and not just think she'd acquired a stalker. She simply nodded and kept her eyes to the front.

When the doors opened, all too soon, Audrey was out and away in a flash. Annoyingly, a young couple with a baby buggy were stood in front of the doors and, by the time Terry had side-stepped them, she was nowhere to be seen. The corridor zig-zagged left and right so, when Terry emerged through the lobby doors, he couldn't tell which way she had gone. He sighed and set off towards his room. He was kidding himself that he stood a chance with her anyway and his hormones slowly settled back to manageable levels.

As he walked down the endless corridor towards yet another corner, he heard a knock on a door ahead of him. He turned the corner to see Audrey facing a bedroom door on the left, about twenty feet ahead. The door quickly opened and, facing him through the gap, was an old man. He was apparently wearing nothing but a white towelling bathrobe as his legs and feet were bare. Audrey walked straight in without speaking but Terry passed by just as the man was closing the door behind her. He recognised him instantly. It was Alistair Buckland.

INSIDE HIS OWN ROOM, the cogs in Terry's mind started whirring like an ancient timepiece. What had he just witnessed? His first thought was jealousy. What was an old git like Buckland doing with a cracker like Audrey? Surely, she can't be his girlfriend and it can't have been a business meeting. He was greeting her naked in a bathrobe for goodness sake. No-one did that anymore, not after all that #*me too* malarkey six or seven years ago.

And she had been looking for a room key in her bag, so why did she knock? But then, she couldn't realistically *have* a key for Buck-land's room anyway because he'd only just checked in. Terry realised that he had been used - victim of the oldest trick in the book to by-pass key access lifts. Just get someone else to swipe their card instead. He felt stupid. He'd been duped by a pretty face and played right into her hands. It now made sense why she had still been waiting for the lift when he got there. She needed someone else's key card - and he was the first sucker to arrive.

So why was she there anyway and who was she? To Terry's mind, only two types of person slip up to a hotel room past the security measures. Given that Buckland let her in, she can't be a thief. Which means she must be a prostitute.

But this wasn't some brass in fishnets and a red leather mini-skirt. She was one classy woman. If she *was* a hooker, she was really high end. But Buckland could afford it. There was something in his biography at the press conference about selling his family farm. Must be minted. *Dirty old man.* Thoughts of what he was probably doing to Audrey right now filled Terry with envy.

But then it hit him. This wasn't just some sad old man getting his end away with a high-class hooker. No, this was the likely POG candidate who would soon be going head to head with Bradley Deakin - the darling of the *Daily Record* and its readers. The great OP hope for future Leader of the Opposition and, eventually, Prime Minister. This had the makings of a scandal that could damage his opponent and therefore help the cause. A story that the paper's OP obsessed Editor would lap up and surely place Terry's name right on the front page as the reporter who exposed it. This was potential pay dirt.

So, what to do? Terry tried to calm his excitement. He needed evidence and opened his bag to remove the pouch containing the tools of his trade. He quickly found what he was looking for - a state-of-the-art miniature surveillance web-cam. It was the size of a walnut and contained a motion detector, a micromini-phone card and a solar powered cell. He opened the App on his phone to link it all together and then returned to the corridor outside Buckland's room. He was in luck. On the corner, where Terry had observed the couple, was a floral display. There was actually one on every corner to cheer up the stark, winding corridor. He attached the camera to the stem of a fake lily, moving a few leaves around to disguise it, and checked his phone to review the transmitted image. The door was covered perfectly.

He returned to his room and decided dinner could wait. If Audrey was indeed a hooker, then there were now two possibilities. Firstly, she would give Buckland his money's worth, get dressed and then leave immediately. Off to meet her next trick. If that was the deal, then she would be out very soon. Alternatively, Buckland may have paid for a 'deluxe executive package' meaning she'd be staying the night. In that case, Terry expected her to leave early the next morning.

The motion detector was set to ping whenever anything activated the camera. It did so almost immediately as two guests passed by on leaving a nearby room. Terry kept watch for an hour, then two, then three. He had one eye on the football match and the other watching for his phone to ping into life. He couldn't relax as he had kept his jacket and shoes on, ready for a quick move in case she suddenly came out. But nothing happened. It looked like Buckland had paid for option two – so Audrey was there for the night.

He got very little sleep, lying fully clothed on the bed with the phone pinging constantly all night. There was a seamless join between guests coming back ridiculously late and those leaving ridiculously early in the morning. Hotel staff filled the gaps in between, doing who knows what but each activated the camera.

He gave up trying to sleep at around five, so washed and shaved in preparation for Audrey's expected departure. It came at seven o'clock. The phone pinged, showing her leave the room and walking briskly towards the camera. She disappeared out of shot within ten seconds. Terry was out of the door like a rocket, heading down the corridor in hot pursuit.

When he got to the lobby, he just caught sight of her stepping into the lift. The key-card was not needed to go down. He descended the stairs as quickly as he could and was surprised to find she was not yet on the ground floor when he emerged. The lift was still on the first floor, presumably having stopped to pick someone up on the way down. Terry quickly went into the foyer and hid by the leaflet display so she wouldn't see him. A second or two later, Audrey and another guest emerged from the lobby and she headed straight for the main doors. Terry followed and worried that she would simply grab a taxi outside and be gone. Jumping into the one immediately behind and shouting *follow that cab*' may have worked in the movies fifty years ago but not in 2025 London. With heavy traffic and lights on every corner, he'd lose her even before they reached Park Lane. But he was in luck. She instead turned right and started walking.

Terry followed from a safe distance but Audrey never looked back. She turned up Park Lane, across Marble Arch and into Edgware Road. From there she turned left into Kendal Street and eventually climbed the steps into a building that Terry assumed must be her home. Bingo. It was a small but impressive mansion block with apartments spread over three floors.

Once she was safely inside, Terry wandered up to the entrance and checked the door-bell panel. Helpfully, it had names against each flat number. There were six in all - presumably two on each floor. He was in luck. He could quickly discount three names, all clearly men. Two other bells had women's names against them, but one of those was Chinese and the other Middle Eastern. That left just one likely candidate – Ms Sharon Morgan in Flat 2.

'IT'S GOOD, but we'll need more.'

Along with the *Daily Record's* Head of Investigations, Tony Monroe, Terry was sitting in the Editor's office, facing the great man himself across his cluttered desk.

After locating Sharon's home, he had quickly returned to the hotel to check out before then hot-footing it straight to the newspaper's office in Southwark. He had shown Tony the hotel corridor footage which he, in turn, thought sufficiently important to immediately show the Editor, Alan McQueen.

'I mean, well done and all that, great work' said Alan. 'But this may not be enough to completely scupper Buckland's campaign on its own. OK, he's a dirty old man but he isn't married or nothing. People aren't so bothered if they're not married. Some will probably just say *good luck to him*. She looks a bit tasty actually, though I've never heard of a prozzie with a name like Sharon before.'

'What more would we need?' said Terry, a little disappointed that he was not being lauded for the scoop of the century.

'See if you can put the squeeze on her to give up some dirt. Perhaps he's into bondage or something more sleazy. Or some juicy pillow talk. That would be good! Tell her we'll pay for her side of the story but will otherwise be publishing as is. We'll be saying she's a prostitute but, as she looks high class, she won't want to be portrayed as some backstreet whore. And tell her we'll be printing her photo too, from the CCTV footage. It will bugger up her business if all the hotels now know her boat race. But if she *co-operates* . . . say we'll black out her face and keep her name out of it. Don't worry, she'll talk to us for money. It's the nature of the beast.'

'How much can I offer?' said Terry, feeling a bit more optimistic.

'Depends what she's got' said Alan. 'I'll leave it to your judgement but you can go up to £50,000 if it looks like powerful stuff. But don't throw it around. On the off chance it's real gold dust then get back to me sharpish so we can take a view.'

'I'm on it' said Terry, getting up to leave.

'And let's keep this strictly between us three' said Alan. 'If this really looks like it could damage the POGs man in Brighton, then we need to be very crafty with the timing. The campaign hasn't even started yet. We don't want them dropping him before kick-off, if it looks like he might be a liability, so we'll need to wait until nominations close first. Then it will be too late and they'll be stuck with him for the election. With a bit of luck, if we time it right, it might just swing the vote. At the moment, the polls are not as good as we'd like for Deakin. He has a five-point lead on InstaPoll, based on the list of speculative candidates, but it's a funny old place, Brighton. Somewhere else would have been better but beggars can't be choosers. But if we can just turn a few votes away from Buckland it will be great. OK, Get what you can from this posh tart. The more dirt the better.'

Terry left with a slight spring in his step. One way or the other, he would make sure this was the scoop that made his name. If the Editor wanted dirt – then dirt he was going to get.

27

Gabrielle

FRIDAY 14 MARCH 2025

Gabrielle was watching the lunchtime news which was speculating on the date of the Brighton by-election. They were pretty convinced it would be announced for 8th May 2025. All the coverage was otherwise about Bradley Deakin, whose camp were hinting strongly that he was going to stand. He and FG would therefore be going head to head. The odds of beating a heavyweight like Deakin were probably very slim, but not impossible. By all accounts, FG was gaining a lot of local support and sympathy on the back of the MP's death.

As she watched the weather forecast after the news, the entry phone suddenly rang. It was a shock as she rarely received visitors, apart from deliveries, but hadn't ordered anything. She picked up the phone and the distorted face of a scruffy man in his thirties appeared on the viewing screen.

'Ms Morgan?' came an equally distorted voice through the speaker.

'Who is that please?' she replied.

'My name is Terry Macdonald from the *Daily Record*. I wondered if I might have a chat with you?'

Gabrielle shuddered. A journalist! No, it was worse than that. She vaguely recognised him from somewhere. This can't be good.

'What about?' she said.

'I'd really prefer not to discuss it over an entry phone' he said pompously. 'And I suspect you wouldn't either. Can I come up please?'

There was fear in the pit of her stomach as she pressed the buzzer to let him in. If, as she suspected, it was about her nocturnal activities, then he was right, she didn't want that shouted on the doorstep. The neighbours all thought she was some sort of self-employed beautician. She heard footsteps in the hallway and opened the front door.

'Terry Macdonald. Can I come in?' She stepped aside and allowed Satan into her home. Gabrielle had lived there for about a year. She tended to move every two years or so, just to be on the safe side, and always travelled light. The fixtures were clean, modern but unexciting.

'What do you want?' she said, abruptly.

'Shall we sit down?' MacDonald replied. 'I want to show you something.'

They both sat on the couch and he opened his briefcase to remove a tablet. He swung the screen towards Gabrielle and played a very short clip of a woman in a hotel corridor. Of course, she recognised it instantly. It was in 5HD quality and her face was unmistakable.

'To save time, can we just agree that this is you?' he said. The cocky little shit was enjoying himself.

'Obviously' she replied. 'But what's your point?'

'And this . . .' he continued, ignoring her question 'would be Alistair Buckland if I'm not mistaken.' He swung the screen around again to show another familiar face leaving the same room. 'That was about thirty minutes after you left, funnily enough. I observed you entering the night before so that's an impressive twelve-hour shift by my reckoning. So, I'm interested in the line of work you're involved in, Ms Morgan. Can you offer any help on that score?'

Gabrielle was horrified. She suddenly realised where she had seen him before. He was the creep in the lift who she had hood-winked into using his pass key. She didn't know what to say.

'You see . . .' he continued, 'when I saw you enter the room, our fat friend here was wearing a dressing gown and very little else, as far as I could tell. Which means that, presumably, you must know him very well, given that such a disgusting sight didn't seem to put you off. You didn't even flinch. And, as we can see, you clearly then spent the night. You like fat old men, do you, Sharon?'

'Why is that any of your business?' she said sulkily. She remem-bered hearing someone coming down the corridor when she'd knocked on FG's door the other night, so went in as soon as he opened it. That must have been MacDonald, slithering like a snake along the corridor behind her.

'Well' he continued. 'My belief is that you are − how can I put this politely − a 'lady of the night' shall we say? And Buckland was therefore paying you for sex, dirty old bugger that he is. I'm sure you know that he's the likely POG candidate for the Brighton election?'

'How dare you make such a suggestion! I'm his girlfriend' she said, indignantly.

'Come on, darlin', don't waste my time' he smirked. 'I think we can both see that's not really going to wash, is it? No luggage and both leaving separately? Blagging your way up in the lift with a pretty smile? Do you really want to use that as a defence when we splash your name and face across the front page? And, trust me, sweetheart, we will. As I see it, we've got enough here to publish a sordid little story about him seeing prostitutes. Now, that's his little problem to deal with. I'm far more interested in yours. How exactly do *you* want to be represented in all this?'

'What do you mean?' Gabrielle replied. She could see her world collapsing around her.

'Well, do you want us to portray you as some cheap little tart, complete with a nice full-face screen grab photo, or would you prefer we tell *your* side of the story. If you do, then we'd be happy to blank out your pretty little face and keep your name out of it. Only if the story's good enough, though. But if it is - we'd also pay you handsomely for it. That's a win-win to my mind, Sharon. May I call you Sharon? So, what do you think?'

Gabrielle suddenly saw a chink of daylight. 'How much?'

'Bloody 'ell, that was quick!' he replied, with a sneer. 'Up to you darlin'. How much you get from us depends on how much we get from you. What do you have on him? Any juicy gossip? Nasty little bedroom habits? Something to disgust our readers and the Brighton electorate?'

Gabrielle had a serious problem. When she had met FG the other night, he had chosen a particularly lavish hotel to break the news that he couldn't see her again, at least for a while. The sweet old sod even had a bottle of champagne on ice to let her down gently. She understood, of course, and was delighted he'd decided to stand. But when she got home, she was consumed by a strange, unexpected feeling. Guilt mainly, but something else too. She realised that she would actually miss FG and had been feeling a bit down and empty ever since. It confirmed what she already knew - that she couldn't bring herself to hurt him. So, she had been planning to delete his file at the weekend.

But, now, along comes this creep, hell bent on destroying FG's political ambitions and saying she was powerless to stop him, regardless of whether or not she co-operated. It was obvious why she was in his room and they could easily disprove any other version of events. More important to her than anything else - even FG's reputation – was that she did not want her real name and picture being made public. That would be a disaster in every way – not least where Sophia's plan was concerned.

So, did she tell them to 'publish and be damned' - and be left exposed herself - or instead turn a negative into a positive? Perhaps even make some money out of it? Possibly a great deal of money. Possibly even enough to no longer need Judgement Day. In fact, maybe this was actually a better way of launching Sophia's Plan. She would happily sell her other clients down the river if the price was right. Perhaps the paper would pay for them instead and spare FG.

Terry kept pressing her. 'Bottom line, I want to know everything about your relationship with Alistair Buckland - how long it's been going on, any evidence to support what you say and any juicy little tit-bits that might help sell my paper and bugger up his campaign at the same time.'

'He's a good man' she said, surprising herself at how quickly she tried to defend him. *But it's true. He is a good man.* 'I don't want to see him hurt.'

'Good doesn't up the price, I'm afraid' he said. 'I need *bad*...the badder the better.'

She paused for a while to think.

'I've had a lot of high-profile clients on my books in my time' she said, finally. 'There's been an England footballer, a judge, a few leading chief executives and a good few celebrities over the years. How much would you pay for them instead of Alistair Buckland?'

'Wow. Well, now we are talking. If you have a few goodies like them in your bag as well, then I'm sure we'd pay top dollar for the whole package. But I'm afraid Buckland is non-negotiable. He's going in the paper with or without your co-operation.'

It didn't come as a surprise, but it was worth trying. She knew they would never barter away what they had on FG, so he was doomed either way. It was now a matter of what was best for *her*. At the end of the day, her own future came first.

'If . . .' she said finally, still struggling with her conscience 'IF I gave you all that you want about Alistair Buckland AND the others, then what would you give me in return?'

'I'm authorised to go to £50k, but only if it's worth it' he said proudly. She wasn't impressed and showed it.

'Fifty-grand isn't going to cut it' said Gabrielle. She was disappointed. 'I'd be finished if you publish my records. I'd probably have to leave the country. My life might even be at stake. Some of my clients are . . . not very nice people.'

'What sort of records do you have?' said Terry, looking curious.

She got up to collect her tablet from a drawer and handed it to the journalist, showing him a photo. His eyes opened wide and a broad smile spread across his face. He then burst out laughing.

'Nice' he said nodding 'very nice indeed. Oh yes, fantastic!'

'I've got the same - or worse – on all of them. Plus, full records and evidence of times, dates, locations and everything they've ever told me about their lives. The sort of things they wouldn't want anyone else to know. It could even put some of them in prison. So, you'd better start adding a few extra noughts.' She may as well go for broke.

'Give me some names and let me make a call' he said, eagerly reaching for his phone. 'I think you could come out of this a very wealthy lady, Sharon.'

'Its Gabrielle' she replied. 'Please. And you get no names until we have a deal. You'll just have to trust me.'

AFTER HE LEFT, Gabrielle sat staring into space. She realised that she could actually launch Sophia's Plan in a far more spectacular way than she could ever have imagined. And without even having to use blackmail, achieving the same result but in a much cleaner fashion. It was potentially the answer to her prayers - if it wasn't for poor, sweet FG. If she went ahead - as she knew she now must - what would all this do to him and how could he ever forgive her?

Emma Deakin

THURSDAY 3 APRIL 2025

'So, with great pride and humility, I can confirm what I believe is the worst kept secret in politics. I am delighted to say that I have been selected as the official OP candidate for the Brighton and Hove by-election on May 8th'

Emma stood beside her husband on the stage of the Brighton Theatre Royal. He was standing at a lectern festooned with the OP's logo. Behind them was a huge backdrop carrying the words *'Going Forward into the Future'* in large white letters, being the slogan Bradley and his cronies had come up with for his campaign.

To Emma's right stood their son Stephen. He carried the embarrassed look of a teenager who clearly wanted to be some-where else. To Bradley's other side stood Peter Wilkinson and a few senior opposition MPs. She guessed they were all there to show their undivided loyalty early on, doubtless in the hope of securing a ministerial post in a Deakin government when the time eventually came. Making up the group was the weasel, Rod Archer. He had been selected as Bradley's Election Agent and Emma neither liked nor trusted him. But he was viewed as a good strategic organiser so the job was his.

'It is, of course, with great sadness that this election is needed at all' continued Bradley with a serious expression. 'We all know that it has resulted from the tragic death of Sarah Billingham, who served this community tirelessly as it's MP and who died way too young. Sadly, I never met Sarah, but know she was gracious, professional and dedicated herself tirelessly to her work. It is my strongest desire to honour her memory by serving this constituency with the same dedication and to lead this fantastic city forward into the future.'

Emma smiled wryly as her husband shoe-horned part of his crappy slogan into the eulogy. She didn't really want to be there any more than Stephen, but Bradley had made it very clear - to his son in particular − that they *must* show family unity. But the prize was a big one - a real chance to be 'first lady' to the Prime Minister, if all went to plan.

When she and Bradley had been interns together at Westminster all those years ago, it all seemed a long way off − a dream. Bradley desperately wanted to be an MP and Emma admired him for his ambition. His father was Chairman of a local Council and, although they didn't always share the same politics, he'd pulled a few strings to get him the internship. She had loved politics too, back then. But she'd had to fight hard to get her own place as an intern whereas, for Bradley, it had landed right in his lap. Everything always did. Other people struggle for years to be chosen as a Parliamentary candidate, where he had them queuing up to select him. He oozed self-confidence, charm, good looks and humour and the party had lapped it all up.

Even so, she'd adored him from the first time they met - the most gorgeous looking man she had ever seen. She would have followed him anywhere and was amazed that he felt the same way about her. They became inseparable − or so she thought. There were always suspicions that he was seeing other women. But he was an incorrigible flirt and girls just threw themselves at him, so it was hard to be sure. She had reassured herself over the years that, even if he *did* indulge elsewhere − which he always denied - they didn't actually mean anything to him. *She* was his only real love and soulmate. He told her that all the time.

They had married in early 2008 and she had been there beside him for his first by-election attempt later that year, exactly as she was now. But it was altogether different back then. He was still young – only twenty-five – and wet behind the ears. The opposing candidate was a former heavyweight MP who was looking for a new seat. He made mincemeat of Bradley, but he learned from the experience.

When he then won his own seat in 2010, she was again right there beside him – only this time, sharing his victory. They thought they had the whole world at their feet. The power and - let's face it - the fame too, appealed to Emma just as much as Bradley. But he was quickly distracted by his blossoming TV career. It made him, somehow, different. He loved being recognised in the street and the autographs and selfies taken with young, giggling girls. Again, she suspected he did more for them that just posing for a photo, but she could never be certain. He was always very discreet.

It was no great surprise that he lost his seat in 2015 but, for Bradley, it was devastating. He assumed re-election was a formality and didn't work hard enough to achieve it, in Emma's view. But, as ever, he landed straight back on his feet with the BBC's offer, eighteen months later. Emma hoped the huge salary would overcome her slight feeling of disillusionment but, instead, Bradley had become even more detached.

She soon had everything a woman could want - a big house, pots of money, a handsome and successful husband and an adorable young child. But she gradually began to feel empty. Bradley was never home, Stephen grew into a spoilt brat and she had to give up work - fed up with people constantly asking about her famous husband and using her as a way to meet him. She lost her own identity.

So, this life changing opportunity had initially brought new hope. She thought she had wanted it - but now she also feared it. They were not the united team they had been first time round – both in it together, side by side. The political spotlight was also very different to the showbiz one that shone on his glittering TV career. In the last few months, the media had featured *her* in some of the coverage. '*The power behind the throne?*' was a headline she approved of, but the rest were bitchy and critical. They mocked her dress sense, her hair and anything else they could pick fault with. None of it had anything to do with Bradley's ability to do the job or her right to stand beside him.

It would all have been tolerable if Bradley had been there for her. Protecting her. Telling her she looked gorgeous and to ignore the press calling her a chav. But, deep down, she knew he was only interested in how it affected *him* or damaged *his* chances. She sensed his resentment at any bad press for which she could loosely be blamed.

The phone call last year about Dixie Tart-Face had changed everything for Emma. Suddenly it was all real – knowing for certain he was sleeping around. Worse still, knowing that everyone at the BBC knew it too. The façade was shattered. She should have gone through with her threat to throw him out for good. But the idea of all *this* – the glitter and glamour of power – had foolishly clouded her judgement. Now she felt trapped. Yes, he had been faithful ever since - or so he claimed - but she knew that was only for his own benefit, not hers. He didn't want a scandal messing up his chances. She had no doubt it would start again as soon as it was safe to do so.

'I'm happy to take some questions' said Bradley. The stalls of the old theatre were filled with journalists, cameras and dazzling TV lights. He was in his element - the centre of attention, right where he always loved to be.

'Jim Myers, *Daily News*. POG have just announced Alistair Buckland as their candidate. He was a very close friend of Sarah Billingham and it looks like her husband, Dan Billingham, is to be his Election Agent. With all the emotional outpouring from the public following her death, do you think you'll actually have quite a fight on your hands?'

'Well' said Bradley, adopting his serious face again. 'I believe the POG are very worried about taking me on and, to me, this looks like a desperate, cynical attempt to exploit Sarah's death. But I'll put up a fair fight. I believe Brighton deserves better – the country deserves better – than anything this Government - or their candidate - can offer. I want to preserve Sarah's memory like everyone else, but please remember this is about looking forward. *Going* forward into the future. Together as a great city, a great party and as a great country.'

Emma bit her lip. *Oh God, I think I'm beginning to hate him.*

29

Bradley

FRIDAY 4 APRIL 2025

Bradley had got to bed late, hadn't slept very well and was dog-tired. The last thing he needed was the alarm going off at 4.30 a.m. He had spent most of the previous day doing TV and radio interviews and felt the campaign launch could not have gone better. The overnight InstaPoll ratings placed him at 42%, seven points above Buckland on 35%. There were 16% of voters classed as undecided, but he was confident of soon charming them into his camp. His lead was not as decisive as he would have liked, but pretty darned good for the first day.

The plan had been to return home this morning, but Rod insisted he do just one more local interview instead. It was to be live on BBC Radio Brighton's Breakfast Show at 7.15 a.m. In preparation, Bradley first needed to go through a briefing pack that Rod had pulled together, knowing he would be grilled on local issues. In particular, there was a consultation about culling seagulls a few months back and the Council were announcing the result this afternoon. Bradley was certain it would be the big talking point today, so he needed to swot up on the background and statistics. Especially as Buckland had chaired the review, so this might be a good opportunity to question his judgement and land a few body blows.

Whilst he had already been interviewed on BBC Brighton yesterday afternoon, Rod felt this last-minute booking was necessary because some old guy on the show had been stirring up a lot of noise against Bradley being parachuted in as OP candidate. He was very much 'Mr Local' and his comments had apparently been hitting the spot with some of the listeners.

Bradley was aware that these were the same two presenters who'd become famous for reading out Buckland's eulogy to Sarah Billingham. The clip had gone viral because the slightly camp lead presenter had burst into tears. They had a strong local following so Rod wanted to nip it in the bud early on, especially as they were both friends with Sarah as well. Since Buckland was a solid local candidate himself, Bradley's credentials needed to be established quickly. He wasn't particularly bothered about the interview. A local radio nobody and his grumpy old sidekick were hardly a match for a seasoned broadcasting pro like he was.

'SO, THE MAIN THING' said Rod as they waited to be called into the studio 'is to keep very calm and not argue. Just accept they have a point and then rationalise why *you* would still be the better option for Brighton, despite not being a local.'

'Got it' said Bradley, dismissively. 'I'll have them for breakfast which, given I've not had anything to eat this morning, will be very satisfying. What sort of hotel doesn't serve breakfast until seven?'

'We can eat on the train back to London' said Rod. 'Hello . . . we're on.'

An assistant led them through into the studio whilst a music track was playing. On one side of the desk sat a chubby, middle-aged guy wearing a Radio Brighton T-shirt. Bradley knew the radio interview would also be transmitted online via a web-cam, with clips doubtless appearing on other news media later in the day. He assumed the main presenter was therefore obediently dressed in a regulation T-Shirt to promote the station to the wider world.

'Mr Deakin, welcome and thank you so much for coming in so early' he said, extending his hand as Bradley walked in. 'Dale

Glover. Great pleasure to meet you. This is Harvey Britten, my occasional co-host.'

Bradley shook hands and gave his best showbiz smile. He turned to the other presenter who also rose to shake his hand. He was an older man, stocky with grey hair but balding slightly on top. He sported a neat moustache of equal hue and wore wire framed glasses and an open-necked blue shirt. Clearly, he had not read the dress-code memo.

'Jenny will get you settled in, then we'll be live in a couple of minutes' said Dale. *At least they're friendly. This shouldn't be too difficult.* Through the glass, Rod raised and lowered his eyebrows as a gesture of encouragement.

"Welcome back, its 7.17' said Dale Glover as the music faded. 'Well, our big story is TV talk-show host Bradley Deakin, who has formally announced that he's standing in the Brighton and Hove by-election and I'm delighted that he's here with us, live in the studio, this morning. Welcome, Bradley, sorry to get you up so early.'

'Not at all, my great pleasure to be here and meet you both.' Bradley slipped effortlessly into his smooth broadcaster persona.

'Now, the big issue we've been discussing is that you want to replace the late and great Sarah Billingham, who was born and bred in Brighton and was previously a local Councillor before becoming our MP. Your opponent is Alistair Buckland, who is also a local candidate. So, why should the people of Brighton and Hove vote for *you*, someone with no links at all to the city? Many say that this by-election is simply the first cab off the rank as an opportunity for you to get back into Parliament. Is that the case?'

'I can absolutely accept that concern' said Bradley. 'But it's not uncommon for MPs to have no initial links to the constituencies they represent. What *is* important is their desire to serve with all their strength and commitment. To embrace the issues and concerns of the local population and to represent them with passion and dedication. That's what I plan to do and I'll give it my all to make the people of Brighton as proud of me as they were of Sarah Billingham.'

"Yes, well that's all well and good' said the older one, poking his oar into proceedings. 'But it's well known that you want to become Leader of the Opposition and, ultimately, Prime Minister. I worry that, as soon as you're elected, you'll be straight off around the UK campaigning for the leadership and - assuming that works – you'll then be setting out your stall for a General Election. And if you win *that*, then . . . well . . . you'll be way too busy running the country to bother with us down here in Sussex. I therefore ask you - where does Brighton fit into all that? How can you represent *us* - putting *our* issues first and foremost - if your mind is fixed on much higher ambitions?'

'Well, again,' said Bradley 'I totally see your concern. All party leaders and senior ministers have similar problems but it always works fine. Be assured that I'll work as hard for Brighton as I would for the country, given the opportunity. I give you my word on that.'

'Do you plan to move here?' said Harvey.

'What? well, I'll certainly get a base here, of course, but . . .'

'But you'll still live in Hampstead with one eye on a little house in Downing Street too, I guess. Again, it's not the same as looking after us from here in Brighton, as Sarah did so well. Putting Brighton first, just as it should be.'

The conversation continued along similar vein for a tedious five minutes or more. The old guy chipping away whilst Bradley defended his corner.

'Obviously,' said Bradley, beginning to get bored with the line of questioning. 'If people oppose me just because I'm not a local then they are, of course, free to vote for Alistair Buckland. But I hope they'll instead trust *me* to do a much better job, given my experience on a much bigger stage than just the local Council.' *Get that one in.*

'Yes, but that's exactly my point,' said the old guy, who wouldn't let it go. 'If people don't share Buckland's politics, and instead normally support the OP, then they really have no choice in the matter. I've no objection to you personally or your policies. But I strongly believe that people who stand as an MP should have at least some inkling of the place they represent. Not just be parachuted in from who knows where, get themselves elected and then disappear until the next time they want our vote.'

'I know enough about Brighton to represent the people admirably,' said Bradley. He was trying not to sound irritated but it was proving difficult. This guy was being a real pain. 'If you care that much, perhaps you should stand yourself.'

'But *you're* the one standing, not me,' the pensioner went on, refusing to let it lie. 'So, tell us about Brighton. For example, where are the football team in the league at the moment?'

'What?' said Bradley.

'Harvey is our resident Albion fan,' said Dale. 'Everything centres around football to him, I'm afraid.'

It was getting a bit fractious and Bradley appreciated the attempt to ease the tension. He had no real interest in football and Rod had only provided details about unemployment and population figures, commercial and environmental issues. *Why don't they ask about the bloody seagull cull instead of all this trivial nonsense?* There was nothing in Rod's pack about the football team, but he had a vague idea they were having a God-awful season.

'Well,' he said. 'I can't give you their exact position, but I know they're having a pretty challenging time at the moment. I'm very confident that things will pick up soon, though, with such a professional and . . .'

'. . . they're bottom' said Harvey.

'What? Yes, well, as I say, I'm sure things will improve.'

And so it went on, with the old guy asking stupid question after stupid question about the city. How tall was the i360 tower? How old is the pier? Bradley could answer some questions, but most of them he could not. He was getting frustrated.

'Well, we'd better leave it there' said Dale finally. 'But one last question. How do you think the Seagulls will get on this evening?'

At last! 'Well, it is a difficult and emotional subject, culling birds, and . . .'

'No' said Dale. 'Sorry, not those seagulls.'

And then it happened. Bradley was tired and irritated and his train of thought was momentarily lost by the interruption. Without thinking, he said 'What? well, what other kind is there?'

Harvey Britten gave a condescending laugh. "THE Seagulls!' he said.

Bradley looked confused. What was the old fart talking about? Then he suddenly realised. If he'd only been given a chance to correct himself it would have been accepted as an honest mistake. But they didn't give him that chance.

'Brighton and Hove Albion!' shouted Britten in mock dismay. '*The* Seagulls! They're playing tonight in a crunch game against Fulham. Lose, and they're likely to be relegated! Guess you would know that if you were a local.'

'I . . .'

'Anyway, thanks for coming in' said Dale, who seemed more interested in getting some music in before the travel news. 'We really appreciate it. Back in a moment with your reaction. Meanwhile, here's Supertramp.'

'I knew that!' said Bradley 'You hoodwinked me!' But it was too late. The microphones were down and they were off the air. But he could already see the phone lines lighting up through the glass.

ROD AND BRADLEY quickly left the studio and walked back to the hotel. They hadn't taken a car to get there as Bradley thought it would be good being seen on the streets. He regretted the decision now and just wanted to get back.

'It'll be OK' said Rod. 'Easy mistake to make. The rest went fine.'

'Obnoxious old sod' said Bradley, in a huff. 'They set me up. Why didn't you put anything about the bloody football team in the dossier?'

'Sorry' said Rod. 'But, seriously, who doesn't know they're called the Seagulls?'

Bradley didn't reply. He was in a very bad mood. Above him a flock of gulls were circling and screaming in unison. To Bradley, it sounded like laughter. But he didn't feel they were laughing *with* him. They were laughing *at* him and he didn't like it one little bit.

30

Terry

FRIDAY 4 APRIL 2025

'This is brilliant stuff' said Alan. 'Absolute dynamite.'

The Editor of the *Daily Record* was leaning over the boardroom table, surveying everything Terry had obtained from the interview with Gabrielle. He scanned it all with wide-eyed excitement, like a starving man gazing on a banquet.

Terry sat opposite, alongside various lawyers and the key people who were in on the story. This was the biggest scoop they had seen on the paper since the merger two years ago. Best of all, it was Terry who had delivered it and was now the man of the moment.

'It wasn't easy' he said, milking it for all it was worth. 'But, in the end, she agreed to give us the lot. This woman keeps the most meticulous files. I think she's been planning to use them herself for blackmail, although she wouldn't admit it. But no-one keeps records like this just for admin purposes. It's not as if she's planning to file an annual tax return.'

The records were indeed extraordinary. Photos, dates, hotels, details of sexual preferences, notes on some *very* indiscreet comments – some admitting to criminal acts - and a range of other documents. It was all very incriminating and her wretched clients would struggle to dispute it. Given the profiles of those involved, the lawyers were very comfortable that it was in the public interest to publish.

'I can't believe all these names!' said Alan, placing his hand on his head in disbelief. 'Will Wilkins, England centre forward! Justice Wigmore who did the Brexit appeal and, of all people, Alexander Wheelan, the author who penned that awful biography about our owner! I can't wait to wash *his* dirty laundry in public. Sanctimonious little git.'

Terry's feathers were preening like a peacock on a promise.

'But she's absolutely clear?' said Alan, suddenly becoming serious. 'She can't breathe a *word* to Buckland before publication? If she does, she doesn't get a penny, right?'

'Right' said Terry. 'She desperately wanted to exclude him. I think she has a soft spot for him, for some reason. But I told her – he's the centre piece of all this. Without him, there's no deal. The poor slag had no-where to go - I told her we were going to publish anyway.'

'She's doing alright out of it' said Alan, dismissively. 'One million pounds is a record for any kiss and tell story - ever. She'll be able to keep her knees together for the rest of her days. But it's worth it. This is one hell of a haul. Biggest single expose in history, I reckon. And you're certain we have *everyone* on her books? She isn't keeping anyone back?'

'No' said Terry. 'I saw her computer folder and this was all of them. She did ask to confine it only to people who paid her for sex and not include old boyfriends, but that seemed fine to me. We're not interested in her life before she went on the game and she was very happy to throw the rest of them under a bus.'

'Good' said Alan, still distracted by the treasure trove. 'I love it that she files them under aliases. Buckland is *"Farmer Giles"*, Wilkins is *"Rovers Roy"*, Wigmore is *"The Gavel"* and Wheelan is *"The Mighty Sword"*. I hope to God his *mighty sword* is his pen and not his dick. I want to humiliate the bastard not boost his ego.'

'Guess the poor sods all thought she was being discreet' said Terry. 'They're in for one hell of a shock.'

'You bet!' said Alan, still sifting through the papers and stopping at one particular file. 'Ah yes, our old friend Ivan Pevlonichic! The sleazy Russian who let the PM use his yacht last year for a holiday. We'll give the POG a nice big slap over that one too. Looks like he's an even bigger crook than we thought. They're all married I assume?'

'Apart from Buckland' said Terry, trying to hide his disappointment. 'That's the annoying bit. It would have made it so much more powerful if he was playing away. The readers would hate him more as an adulterer rather than just an old sleaze.'

'Hmmm' said Alan, pensively. 'Let's go through all this stuff again. We don't just want to embarrass him, we *have* to take him down completely and clear the way for Deakin. If he's not betraying his missus then some readers will just think he's a dirty − even lucky - old man. The photo is great though. We can make him into a laughing stock. But I want to make him unelectable. Remind me what she said about him again . . .'

Terry went through his notes. "Umm . . . well, he had a very good relationship with Sarah Billingham, as we know. In fact, Gabrielle implied he adored her. He was gutted when she was killed. Then there's . . .'

'Hold it right there' said Alan interrupting. 'Do you think there was anything going on between them? Buckland and the MP?'

'She didn't say that in so many words, no' said Terry. 'But he gave up the chance to stand for Parliament for her.'

'Exactly. What idiot does that if he isn't dipping his wick?' said Alan. He mapped out a headline in the air in front of him. '*Buckland in love with Billingham. Was there a secret affair?* That will do for starters. What else?'

Terry felt slightly uncomfortable. Having sat with Gabrielle over two days conducting the interview, she hadn't suggested there was anything going on between them. But it wasn't Terry's call and he could see they needed more meat.

'OK' Terry went on, going back to his notes. 'Well, she said he wasn't himself after Sarah died. Said he's almost lost interest in sex, which is a bit weird when you're paying a sex worker. I assume they work on a pay-as-you-go basis . . .'

'Or pay-as-you-cum' said Alan. The room smirked.

'Yeah, good one, boss. Well, either way, he's apparently not been sleeping and she felt sorry for him. Even gave him some of her old sleeping pills to take home or something. Then . . .'

'I supplied Buckland with drugs, says prostitute.' Alan, mapped out another dubious headline in the air. 'Carry on.'

Terry was shifting in his seat. 'Are you sure about that?'

'It's what she said – technically. She gave them to him. Puts the suspicion out there that he may be drug dependent. We just need to sow the seeds, Terry. Start with a few facts and let people interpret them how they want. It's not like she's going to sue us for misrepresenting her words, is she?'

Terry went back to his notes. 'OK. Well on that basis, there's possibly something with his expenses . . .'

'Go on . . .' said Alan, sensing scandal.

'Well, apparently, he charged the hotel room to the Council if he was in London on business at the same time as he was seeing her. Oh, and he helped her set up her bogus beautician's business . . .'

'Buckland expenses and money laundering fraud' said Alan, miming again. 'The gentle stench of political corruption. Thank you, that'll do nicely, sir.'

Terry was struggling. He wanted the recognition but not if the story was too embellished or – as it was becoming in the Editor's hands – made into a pack of lies. The boss was spinning it like a plate on a stick.

'Right.' said Alan to the room. 'Timing. The last day to register candidates is Thursday 10th April so I vote we hold fire until Monday 21st, that's two weeks before the election. Just close enough to still be fresh in the voters' minds so Deakin can romp over the finishing line. But if we publish the stuff about all the others at the same time, that might overshadow the Buckland impact. Most of it is far more explosive. So, whilst it pains me to wait, I think we should hold back on the other toe-rags until after the election. I don't want *anything* detracting from Buckland's story. And anyway, the rest will keep our circulation going nicely during the summer.

That mean's we've got two and a half weeks to pull all this

together. But not a word in the meantime. I'll sack anyone who breathes a dicky bird outside this room. The whole package has the makings of an award-winning scoop, but Buckland is the priority. Bring him down and we can take the credit for putting Deakin into power. He'll owe us big time when he's PM one day. Terry – you write it up and ask for all the help you need. You have priority over everything and anyone and will report directly to me until we go to press. I've also thought of a code word we can use to keep it quiet....'

He printed his final headline into the sky. 'How about . . . *Pantsgate.*'

31

Tom

FRIDAY 4 APRIL 2025

For some reason, Tom had been thinking about Sharon today. It wasn't something he often did nowadays, hardly at all in fact. But he had just popped into a department store to buy an expensive bottle of perfume for his wife. Things had not been wonderful lately and he hoped it would help put the ship on an even keel.

Seen from behind, one of the girls spraying scent onto unsuspecting passers-by looked just like Sharon. Only for a second, of course, and she didn't really - once he saw her face. Anyway, it had been, what, seventeen or eighteen years? She obviously wouldn't look like that now. No, it was just the girl's similar hair, slim figure, height and poise.

But it suddenly brought the memories flooding back about what a fool he'd been back then. Had he not hedged his bets by keeping two girls on the go at the same time, he wondered if it he might now be buying perfume for Sharon - not as a peace offering but as a gesture of love.

It still annoyed him that she'd been snooping around his phone and spoilt it all. He felt sure he would have ended up with her if things had not come to such an abrupt end. She was special. It wasn't just the sex but - oh boy - she was incredible in that department. He'd never had better - before or since. No, it was everything about her. But then he'd blown it - big time.

If she had only let him explain and given him a second chance. But, instead, she had just vanished and he'd never seen or heard from her again. God knows he had tried. He'd given her time to calm down and then gone to her flat with perfume. But she had disappeared, left her job with no forwarding address. No-one had a clue where she'd gone.

He often wondered where she was now. He hoped she was alive and well and, above all, happy with her life. She deserved that. It was so ironic to have ended with *her* feeling betrayed. First time round, it was *him* who felt that way. Rightly so too. She lied to him. Boy had she lied. He had immediately ended the relationship and was angry with her for ages. Livid in fact. But then he'd bumped into her again that day and, once he saw those eyes again, that was it. She had matured into a stunning physical specimen and clearly still wanting him too. All the anger had melted away and the past was forgiven. He'd known at once that they were meant to be together. But then he'd thrown it all away. Why hadn't he just dumped his girlfriend, as soon as he knew? Why? Because he was a coward, or an idiot - or both.

So, here he was, thinking about her again, all these years later. Sitting in the back of a taxi holding a bag of perfume, just like he had that day. He'd done well for himself since. A perfect wife and family, lovely house, good job and salary. All boxes ticked. He had the ideal life and a bright future lying ahead. He was a lucky man with no real complaints. But was he really happy? As happy as he might have been with Sharon?

The last time he had seen those beautiful, haunting eyes they were filled with tears, hatred and betrayal. Doubtless, some other lucky bastard was looking into them right now and getting that look in return. Whoever he was, Tom hoped he was worthy. Making her happy and loving her as much as he had himself. Or still did himself. Maybe. His wonderful Sharon, wherever she might be.

32

Harvey

SATURDAY 5 APRIL 2025

'Happy birthday H' said Dale as Harvey opened the front door. 'You don't look a day over seventy.'

'I don't have to let you in' smiled Harvey stepping aside for Dale and David to enter. They had been invited to a small celebration at Harvey and Claire's house to commemorate yet another passing year. Sixty-two and counting.

Sam, Piers and little Phoebe were already there. They had come bearing expensive gifts as always. Piers was a wealthy fund manager with his own very successful company in the City of London. Initially, Harvey had not liked Samantha's choice of would-be husband when she'd first brought him home, some six years ago. There was a certain arrogance about him. But the main worry was that he was fifteen years older than her.

Piers had never married and came with a reputation as something of a playboy before he met Sam. He was rich, very good looking and incredibly charming, so definitely something of a 'catch'. But despite his chequered romantic past, he was now a good husband and doting father. As a family, they appeared blissfully happy, although Claire often thought it was a bit of a show. Sam had said a few things to her mother in recent months that suggested things were not all sweetness and light. There certainly seemed to be some friction when they arrived today, but the mood had eased since then.

Piers was always generous to his wife, daughter *and* his in-laws. He constantly showered Sam with expensive gifts - usually perfume, flowers or something hanging from a gold chain. Samantha joked about opening a perfumery outlet, given the number of bottles she'd accumulated on her dressing table. Claire often benefited when Sam slipped the odd unopened bottle into her mother's handbag on the way out.

At one time, Harvey suspected that his son-in-law's generosity was based on guilt and he must therefore be having an affair. But he now accepted that Piers just liked giving presents and, to be honest, he could easily afford it. In time, he had therefore won over first Claire and then, eventually, Harvey. And Sam generally seemed happy which, at the end of the day, was all that mattered to both her parents.

'So, will this be your election head-quarters?' teased Dale.

'In your dreams' said Harvey, dismissively. 'What can I get you both?'

Harvey knew Dale wasn't entirely joking. Following the interview with Bradley Deakin yesterday, things had become slightly surreal. For the rest of the programme, dozens of callers expressed outrage at Deakin's lack of knowledge about Brighton and especially the Seagulls. But a wider theme had also developed. Many callers agreed that they didn't want Deakin but, presumably as OP voters, didn't want Buckland either. In the latter case, the general reason was that *'his politics, his seagull report and his party all stink'* as one caller succinctly put it. When asked who he would therefore vote for instead, the caller replier *'Well, I do at least agree with Deakin on one thing - Harvey Britten should stand. I'd vote for him any day of the week. He's the man.'*

It caused some amusement in the studio, but the phone lines were then swamped with other listeners supporting the ridiculous suggestion. Some offering unbridled encouragement whilst others phrased it more callously - along the lines of *'either put up or shut up'.*

Harvey dismissed them all, at the time. Amongst other excuses, he claimed that the £600 deposit needed to stand for Parliament would be better spent on next year's season ticket for the Albion. But within a few hours, someone had set up a crowd-funding page to mount his campaign. Remarkably, it stood at £11,000 last time he looked.

The hashtags *#WeWantHarvey* and *#PutBrightonFirst* were trending on social media locally so he could easily raise the ten signatures needed to support a nomination were he to stand. But he had no intention of doing so.

'We've been telling him it's not such a stupid idea' said Samantha. 'I think it's a brilliant one, actually.'

'Hashtag me too' said Claire.

'There you go H' said Dale, stirring it up for all he was worth. 'You must always do what your family says on your birthday. It's the law I think, isn't it?'

'Other way round, actually' said Harvey. '*They* have to do what the Birthday Boy wants – and he wants nothing to do with it, thanks all the same.'

He handed champagne to Dale and David and took a seat. Phoebe was the only guest not giving him a hard time as she was playing quietly on the floor with a new game.

'I've told him he should have a go' said Claire. 'It'll give him something to get his teeth into and get him out from under my feet. I don't want to vote for Deakin and certainly won't be voting POG, so it would also solve my problem too. I refuse to abstain and I suspect a lot of OP supporters feel the same. And POG voters for that matter. What with the government being so appalling and Buckland stirring up controversy about culling the poor seagulls.'

'Sorry – the football team?' teased David.

'The birds!' said Claire, playfully tapping his arm.

'But if I *were* to stand' said Harvey, looking to his wife, 'let's just say, for the sake of argument, I took a lot of like-minded OP votes away from Bradley –wouldn't that just hand the election to Buckland? You'd want that even less, wouldn't you?'

'Hold on there, Dad. I don't think any of us believe you would actually make *that* much of an impact. Or even a dent' said Sam. 'No offence.'

'None taken' said Harvey.

'But you'd be making a stand for Brighton' she went on. 'Standing up for what you believe in.'

'Very noble idea, but no' said Harvey, shaking his head. 'What's the point of all the effort involved if there's no expectation of winning or even making any impact - as you so kindly point out? It's all a waste of time isn't it? I might as well put on a silly costume, like those losers you always see on stage when the results are being announced. Monster Raving whatever they are, making a mockery of the whole thing.'

'Dress up as a seagull!' said David. 'That would wind up Buckland.'

'I don't want to stifle your creative process,' said Dale to his partner, 'but I think that one's already covered. The *Brighton Argus* is reporting that some animal rights activist or other is standing in protest against the Buckland Report. He's apparently doing it dressed as a seagull.'

'You couldn't make it up' said Harvey shaking his head in despair.

'But that's my point!' said Sam, the only one not laughing. 'He *knows* he won't be elected or even save his deposit. But he's standing up for what he believes in . . .'

'. . . and to get his gob on TV' said Dale. 'Or his beak, whatever.'

'Perhaps' Sam went on. 'But, so what, if it means he can air his protest on the bigger stage? With Deakin standing, the coverage will be huge. Good for him I say.'

'You always were an idealist' said Harvey, smiling gently at his daughter. 'Perhaps you should volunteer to be his campaign manager.'

'No, I won't' she replied. 'But I *would* volunteer to be yours. Seriously. Be nice to get my mind working on something again. And you could do far worse with all my marketing background. I've had a few great ideas and we could . . .'

'Woah, hold on, there, lady' interrupted Harvey, trying to deter the job pitch. 'Thank you, sweetheart, but I'm afraid the position is currently not available. We'll keep your details on file, though.' His daughter looked disappointed. 'You're right, though, Sam – you'd be brilliant.'

'So, let her have a go, you miserable old git' said Claire.

'That's nice, on my birthday.'

'Come on mate' chipped in Piers. 'I'm sure Claire and my parents would have Phoebe whenever needed, and Sam could do a lot of the organising from home anyway. I'm all for it. Go on Harvey! Stand up for what you believe in. Britten for Brighton!'

'Actually – that's quite a good slogan' said Sam, who was getting inspired again. Harvey could see her inventive mind churning around ideas like a tumble dryer.

'And you've got all the money raised by the listeners' said Dale, adding fuel to the fire. 'It was up to £15,000 this morning, when I last looked.'

'Good God!' said Harvey. 'It's still going up, then?'

'You bet' said Dale. 'And, seriously, it wouldn't do you any harm at all, H. It would really help your profile in Brighton and the BBC will love that. Strictly between you and me, they're talking about formally making you my co-host after the summer. Properly. Not just a guest spot twice a week. It would be brilliant and I'm all for it. Putting yourself out there in such a high-profile campaign would seriously help that decision - assuming you're up for co-hosting the show with me full time, of course? You being a bumbling amateur.'

'Are you kidding? I'd love it! Of course I would' said Harvey, side-tracked at the idea.

'But you'd need to take a break during the campaign, though' said Dale. 'BBC rules I'm afraid. Just like Deakin, but on a different scale of course.'

'Well there you go, then!' replied Harvey, standing up. 'Why would I stop doing something I really love, to take part in an election that I've no desire to enter or any expectation of winning.'

'Speculate to accumulate' said Dale. 'The bigger your profile, the more money the Beeb will offer you when the time comes. And it's only for a month or two anyway. Then you can come back on the radio as the returning people's champion.'

'Horribly defeated and publicly humiliated' said Harvey.

'But having stood up for Brighton and what you really believe in' interrupted Sam. 'A real hero. MY hero. My dad.' Sam could always pull Harvey's strings.

'Come on' said Piers. 'You'll enjoy the challenge. What's the worst that could happen?'

'That I could win I suppose' said Harvey, dejectedly.

But he knew he was outnumbered, outvoted and beaten. The decision was made. The democratic process had unanimously decided against him, as it doubtless would in the much bigger contest to come.

'Oh, go on then' he said, with a sigh of resignation. 'As you say, what's the worst that could happen.'

33

Alistair

SATURDAY 5 APRIL 2025

'Well, it isn't a bad start, all things considered' said Dan.

Alistair was meeting him for a daily update, something they planned to do throughout the campaign. As it was Saturday, they were at Dan's house so he could also keep an eye on little Charlie. Sarah's parents had been priceless in providing childcare ever since the accident, but Dan liked to give them a break at the weekend. Unsurprisingly, they had taken Sarah's death very hard, but they were a stoic couple and had rallied to look after Charlie whenever Dan needed them.

Alistair was fully aware that work had been the last thing on Dan's mind over the past few arduous months. He wasn't taking on any new projects, so his finances were feeling the strain. But he needed as much time as possible with Charlie - the only source of normality in his life. Agreeing to be Alistair's Election Agent had therefore been a big, but very welcome, surprise and he had certainly not expected Dan to agree. They had become very close since Sarah's accident - kindred spirits, as Alistair saw it, offering mutual support.

'Bradley's lead is down two point overnight' Dan continued, studying the InstaPoll results. 'Just five points in it now.'

'I suspect that's down to him rather than me' said Alistair. 'That radio interview yesterday was something of an own goal.'

The papers, TV and social media were dominated by fall-out from the Radio Brighton debacle. Whilst the embarrassing clip about the Seagulls mix-up had gone viral, the sight of Deakin flouncing out of the studio afterwards had also damaged his ultra-smooth, nice-guy image. Alistair smiled to himself. He was no football fan but knew how incensed true supporters would be. He wasn't sure if the presenters had deliberately set him up, but they'd certainly given his effortless campaign a kicking. Good for them. It certainly wouldn't do Alistair any harm, being very much a local candidate himself.

'We need to capitalise on it, either way' Dan continued. 'Emphasise your local credentials compared to Deakin's. It's clearly his Achilles heel so you should start today's podcast by commending Brighton on their crucial win last night. And make sure you call them the Seagulls!'

Each candidate already had access to the official election website to post podcasts and other material. Then, once nominations close next Thursday, regular webinar press conferences would be held on the site. Dan had a web-cam set up in the dining room to cover all this activity.

'All this has overshadowed yesterday's announcement about the seagull cull, though' said Alistair, with some disappointment. He knew the decision to announce the result of the consultation during the election campaign was a cynical ploy by the POG run Council to boost Alistair's profile. Re-naming it *The Buckland Report* was a further attempt to link him to decisive local decision making. But that was a double-edged sword as a lot of animal rights supporters were campaigning against the proposed cull. Alistair had only really administered the process and acted as spokesman for the committee of qualified experts, so he didn't really like his name over the door. Being the face of the cull had already placed him on the receiving end of some vicious social media abuse and he expected that to only get worse now he was the Parliamentary candidate. To the animal rights brigade, he was now the devil incarnate.

'How are *you* doing Dan?' said Alistair, changing the subject. 'I've said before, if all this gets too much for you, just tell me. You know I appreciate your help more than you could know, but someone else can step in any time you like. The POG are pouring huge resources into this campaign anyway, so it wouldn't be difficult.'

'Thanks' said Dan. 'But it's actually a valuable distraction for me and we both know that Sarah would want me to help in any way I could. It's good to get my teeth into something that would matter to *her*, not just another pointless work project. So, don't worry, I am doing this for me as much as you.'

'Well' said Alistair. 'It means a lot, you know that.' He felt a tear welling up in his eye, something that happened a lot nowadays. But he composed himself quickly. 'I thought it was a really cheap shot for Deakin to accuse us of exploiting Sarah's death by choosing me as candidate and you as my agent. Really cheap.'

'Water off a duck's back' said Dan. 'And the statement we put out yesterday on social media has had a very positive response. It can only hurt him to start punching below the belt. Emotions are still running high in Brighton and you're riding a tide of goodwill because of your friendship with Sarah. Why shouldn't we use that? She would want us to.'

Dan was right. A huge pile of flowers had been placed on the seafront throughout January, right opposite the scene of the accident. It became the focal point of the city's grief, despite the atrocious weather, and the - surprisingly national - outpouring of grief had crossed party lines. Perhaps it was the sight of Charlie in his little black suit at the funeral, sobbing for his mother. Or perhaps it was because no-one had a single bad word to say about Sarah's vibrant personality. Either way, she had certainly won a place in people's hearts and Alistair was ideally placed to capitalise on it. The PM knew it, the party knew it and he would be fooling himself to think it was not the main reason for their finally selecting him as candidate. But he also knew that Sarah would be pleased for him. She was up there somewhere, willing him on.

'Yes, I know it's what she would want' said Alistair. 'So, let's give it our best shot and win it for her.'

He just wished he could feel as motivated as he sounded.

34

Bradley

TUESDAY 8 APRIL 2025

'Who, Grandpa Walton, off the radio? Said Bradley, in disbelief. 'For God sake! Are you really telling me he's standing because of the cock-up over his blessed football team?'

'Not just that' said Rod. 'But, don't worry about him. He's just a distraction. He'll get a bit of air time from Albion fans because he's on the radio . . .'

'. . . or *the Seagulls* as we now know they're called' interrupted Bradley, sarcastically. He blamed Rod for the oversight but, deep down, knew it was his own stupid fault. And, boy, had the media milked it. The clip had been viewed six million times and there was no question it had damaged him. *'What other kind is there?'* had become a hashtag, a T-shirt slogan and a catchphrase used against Bradley in far too many real-life situations. He always had to smile through gritted teeth and pretend to be self-deprecating about it. But inside he was fuming.

'Yes, well' said Rod 'we need you at the next home match to put this thing to bed. They're playing Leicester City on Saturday and I've got you an invite for the Director's Box. I suspect Buckland may rock up too and, obviously, Britten will be there as a loyal fan. Oh, and just to be aware, there's some bloke dressed up as a seagull who is standing in protest against Buckland's cull. Normally, that would only hurt *him* but . . . well, you know how the press are . . .'

'Indeed' said Bradley.

'So, whatever you do. You *cannot* be photographed anywhere near him. The headline writers will have a field day if you are. I'll make sure we keep you at a safe distance.'

'You do that' said Bradley. 'I don't want any more slip-ups.'

'One more thing to cheer you up' said Rod. 'They won't say what it is exactly, but Peter has heard in strict confidence from his mate, the Editor of the *Daily Record,* that they've got some serious dirt on Buckland. They're waiting for the right moment to publish, but Peter got the distinct impression that it's dynamite.'

'You reckon? Let's hope so' said Bradley. 'But he's such a boring son of a bitch I can't think what on earth it can be.'

'Guess we'll know soon enough.'

35

Gabrielle

THURSDAY 10 APRIL 2025

Gabrielle had not slept again last night. But then, she hadn't slept properly for two weeks. Her mind was a mixture of emotions. The main one was excitement at Sophia's Plan finally coming alive in a way she could never have imagined.

She had always known there were risks associated with blackmail. It was the key ingredient to the plan in its original form but was, after all, a crime. And she had planned to take her clients' money but still expose them, so there was always a risk of them going to the police afterwards - having nothing more to lose. Of course, she would be long gone by then, but the police might have been persistent where blackmail was concerned and, either way, she would have spent the rest of her life as a fugitive from justice. Whilst she could hide from her angry and vengeful clients easy enough, the police had far more resources.

So, this unexpected solution was perfect. There was no reason that her clients would receive any help from the authorities to track her down and she would retire as a very rich woman in France. Yes, she would need to keep an eye out for the taxman, but doubted they would spend too much time looking for her. She was a small fish as far as tax evasion went.

Her mind was busy planning the next few weeks before her departure. It was all happening so quickly and she needed to put the final pieces into place for her disappearance. The sleazy journalist, Terry MacDonald, said they would start serialising her story on Monday week, starting with FG. The rest would be held back until after the election but, even so, once her clients saw Gabrielle's name promoting *'more revelations to come,'* it would scare the life out of them and some would surely try to find her. Especially *Big Red*. She really feared what he might do to silence her although, if he had any sense, he would instead head for the hills to avoid his father-in-law's wrath. But he was a vicious thug and, more importantly, would do anything he could to stop his name being published.

MacDonald had been clear that she would receive complete anonymity. That would at least buy her some time as none of her clients knew who she really was or where she lived. She had been very careful about that. She always walked home from her liaisons in all weathers to avoid the risk of a taxi driver being traced and she often took a convoluted route home too, if she felt someone was following her. If only she had been more careful with MacDonald. She had been so distracted thinking about FG that she had taken her eye of the ball on the way home.

Without having her photograph printed, no past or present nosey neighbour would therefore recognise her and McDonald said the newspaper would die in a ditch before they would ever disclose a source. They may have to. Only he and the Editor actually knew her real name anyway and she felt she could trust them. They had a lot of money at stake. The million-pound payment would be transferred to her solicitor's account on the 21st April – the day of publication - and would immediately be moved to her account in Jersey. Before the day was out, it would have been split up into manageable chunks and distributed around the world using a laundering technique learned from her former client, who she called *Big Bucks* – a dubious city trader. It would then rest in various Cayman Island accounts until she was safely living in France under her new fake identity. Then it would make another complicated global journey, finally ending up in six French bank accounts under her new name.

Gabrielle had bought her gorgeous little *Gite* near Poitier, southern France, last year and it had taken nearly all of her life savings. She bought it using the fake documents, passport and back-story that had themselves cost her £50,000. But it was the best investment of her life. It was airtight. She had again drawn on the assistance of a former client – this time a retired French secret service agent. She had destroyed all records for *Big Bucks* and *Inspector Clouseau* and both had enjoyed a few freebies as an additional show of her gratitude.

She had tested out the new identity many times, travelling back and forth to France without issue. She was now fluent in French, a benefit of all the spare time that her job had provided over the years. So, the plan was to disappear via the Eurostar in two or three weeks, once she had dealt with Tom.

She would travel light. She had gradually moved all the clothes she needed to the *Gite* and could therefore walk away from her rented flat with just hand-luggage. Her mobile phone was already discarded and she was now using a temporary pay-as-you-go handset that Terry MacDonald had given her to keep in touch. In doing so, she had cut off all contact with her clients overnight, which suited her just fine. Never again would she sell herself to any man.

She had originally hoped that Sophia's Plan might raise about £500,000 in blackmail money, so the million-pound fee from the *Record* was way off the scale. Selling her story to the papers had never actually occurred to her – assuming it would expose her too. Despite many of her clients being famous, she had clearly underestimated their true value. Terry said it would shake celebrity culture to its core in terms of kiss and tell journalism. No-one would ever feel safe 'playing away from home' again.

There were so many clients in the package that it would take the paper until late summer to expose them all. From their point of view, the fee was therefore a good investment in terms of potential sales and publicity. Not that Gabrielle cared about that. She had hit the jackpot herself, except for the one element that was *really* keeping her awake at night – the betrayal of poor FG. She was still wrestling with her conscience over what she had done.

She had tried to soften the blow by saying nice, positive things about him in the hope that people would understand. She also kidded herself that he wouldn't win the election anyway - up against a heavyweight like Deakin. But she was still destroying his credibility and his reputation. Yes, she was doing that to *all* her clients, but with FG it was different. With him she actually cared. Worse still, she knew it would break his heart to know she had betrayed him. He'd hate her for it and, strangely, that troubled her most of all.

She desperately wanted to warn him, but knew it was not possible. Terry was very clear about that and the payment depended on it. So, care as she did about FG, it wasn't enough to throw away her own future. He would eventually get over it and move on - in time. The woman he thought he loved was a fantasy anyway who, very soon, would no longer even exist. She too would move on and put Alistair Buckland behind her - poor, lovestruck old fool that he was. If she could only stop thinking about him, and the pain she was about to inflict on him, she could start to enjoy thinking about the bright future that now lay ahead.

Which just left Tom as her one piece of unfinished business. The icing on her very nice little cake. The timing would be delicate, given that he, alone, knew her real name. He could therefore track her down very easily. She would therefore deal with him immediately before leaving for France and, after that, none of it would matter anymore. She would finally be free of the past that had defined her. Both Sharon and Gabrielle would disappear into the sunset, leaving an exquisite trail of destruction in their wake. Revenge may well be a dish best served cold – but it could also be very enjoyable when delivered via an Exocet missile.

36

Harvey

SATURDAY 12 APRIL 2025

The thought of hitting the streets in an election campaign filled Harvey with terror. It was therefore a gentle introduction to be starting off at Brighton's Amex Stadium where he knew he would be amongst friends. Indeed, he'd received as many messages of support from Albion fans as he had from his radio listeners.

The last week had been a whirlwind of activity and he had yet to catch a breath. The funding page had raised an amazing £112,000 and was still climbing. He was right in thinking that Sam was the perfect choice for Election Agent. She had performed miracles so far, calling in favours from old friends in the marketing industry to produce a very professional set of posters, stickers and leaflets in a ridiculously short timescale. A willing army of volunteers, drawn from his radio listeners, were also coming forward to help distribute them .

They had lodged his nomination last Tuesday – just before the deadline - and Sam had used *'Putting Brighton First'* and *'Britten For Brighton'* as his campaign slogans. The plan today was to set up camp outside the ground before the Seagull's home game against Leicester. Sam, Piers and Claire were all there in support and Dale was also putting in a personal appearance to help draw the crowds.

Harvey teased him that he was more likely to drive them away, but was actually very grateful. Phoebe was being looked after by her other grandparents.

Harvey was standing on a portable platform armed with a public address system that Sam had somehow purloined from an old business contact. His legs were literally shaking as he stepped up for the first time.

'Hi Harvey, pal! Up the Albion!' said a passing fan who he immediately recognised. The fan didn't seem to notice what Harvey was doing there. *A good start.* 'I hope I can count on your support?' he shouted as the fan headed towards the turnstiles, but he got no response.

'At least he was friendly' said Sam. 'Do your spiel now, quickly. It's getting busy.'

It was 1.45 p.m. and the crowds were indeed arriving in force. Harvey had carefully positioned himself near the home fan's entrance. He took a deep breath and spoke into the microphone. 'My name is Harvey Britten, and I'm your *Putting Brighton First* candidate in the forthcoming by-election.'

'You're the bloke off the breakfast show!' said another passing fan, presumably recognising his voice. 'We like you. Up the 'Gulls!'

Harvey carried on with his prepared speech, and the PA system attracted a small, but curious, group of people to watch. Harvey knew that his limited local fame was probably more of a draw than his political opinions, but at least no-one was throwing rotten fruit at him. In fact, it couldn't have been a better introduction. Despite some good-humoured heckling from the fans, the group soon turned into a small crowd and he managed to put his points across. Leaflets and stickers were handed out and, by 2.25 p.m. Sam and Claire felt it had all gone as well as they could have hoped. Harvey went in to watch the match with Dale whilst his small, but loyal, support team cleared up and went home.

INSIDE THE GROUND, he took his usual seat and received a warm welcome from nearby supporters. At around 2.45 p.m., an announcement was made that two candidates in the forthcoming election were inside the ground and asked that they be made welcome. Firstly, the announcer introduced TV personality and OP candidate Bradley Deakin, whose face then appeared on the big screens. The cameras picked him out in the Director's Box and he received loud applause and cheering - although a large section of the crowd made the sound of seagulls calling. Harvey had to smile. Football fans could always be relied on to bring people down to size.

'And next, lifelong Seagull's fan Harvey Britten, standing as an independent for "Putting Brighton First". Give him a big cheer!'

Harvey suddenly saw his own face appear live on the screen, viewed from a camera located in the roof. He looked shocked but the fan in the next seat nudged him and said *'stand up you idiot!* He rose and received a huge cheer and round of applause. Way more than Deakin.

A sea of blue and white flags waived around the ground and a section of the crowd behind him started chanting and clapping *"Harrr-vey-Brittt-tennn'!* He wasn't sure if they were being ironic but it was all good humoured. He was definitely amongst friends. He sat down and was unable to concentrate for the first quarter of an hour of the match.

He had just one thought in his mind. *What the bloody hell am I doing?*

37

Bradley

SATURDAY 12 APRIL 2025

Back in the hotel after the match, Bradley read through the social media feed with a frown. His appearance had not gone as well as he would have liked, nor Rod had promised.

'Why did you put me in the bloody Director's Box?' he shouted, sulkily. 'Made me look a right elitist idiot compared to Britten. And I want to lodge a complaint about that bloody announcer! He was clearly biased.'

'You're being paranoid' said Rod. 'Britten is one of their own so he's bound to receive support in the ground. Doesn't mean they'll actually vote for him. And we had to put you in the Director's Box so the camera would find you.'

'They found Britten easy enough' said Bradley, still sulking. 'You only had to tell them the bloody seat numbers for goodness sake.'

'Yes, well' replied Rod 'don't worry about it.'

'But have you *read* this stuff?' said Bradley. 'They're saying it was just a cheap publicity stunt. And as for all those bloody seagull impressions when they called my name. They were laughing at me . . .'

'Well' said Rod 'It wasn't perfect but served its purpose. This is all about being seen. I've put out a statement saying how much you enjoyed the match . . .'

'0-0 – it was boring as hell' said Bradley.

'Yes, but I said you were willing them on to get the vital points needed to be clear of relegation. There's nothing to be gained by having a go at them. We move on.'

'At least Buckland didn't show up' said Bradley. 'And we never saw the nutter in the seagull costume either. That's one thing to be grateful for.'

'Yes' said Rod, frowning. 'Buckland is trying to take the moral high ground. His feed says he was visiting the hospital, claiming he doesn't need to prove his local credentials like you do.'

'Bastard' said Bradley. 'How are the polls doing?'

'Still a two-point lead over Buckland' said Rod. 'But don't worry. Britten is just a short-term novelty act and Buckland will be dead meat within a fortnight.'

'How can you possibly know that?' said Bradley.

'Just wait and see' came the reply. 'Just wait and see.'

38

Harvey

THURSDAY 17 APRIL 2025

Harvey found the press conference podcasts a daunting proposition. There'd been four so far but he had not contributed very much in either. Just answering the odd question or chipping in where he felt strongly about a comment. Obviously, the journalists always focused on Deakin and Buckland, as the two main contenders, so Harvey's role was largely that of an observer. The same applied to the other independent candidates, and he was fairly happy with that. At least he didn't have to dress up as a seagull like the animal rights activist. All credit to him for always staying in character. It must be very hot in that costume.

The experience so far had not been as bad as Harvey expected and, to his surprise, he was actually quite enjoying himself. Getting out and about to meet people had been great fun and everyone seemed to give him an easy ride. Presumably they didn't see him as a major threat and he never received the aggressive or angry reaction both Buckland and Deakin experienced when out in public. They each carried the baggage of their parties with them which polarised opinion just as it did in any election, regardless of the personalities involved.

The big difference was Bradley's celebrity. He was drawing the sort of huge crowds that he otherwise would when opening a super-market or suchlike. From a shaky start, he now held a four-point lead over Buckland. Harvey was way behind but was proud to have an 8% poll rating – more than all the other independent no-hopers put together. His stance certainly resonated with some of the voters that he met on his travels and he clearly had some *real* supporters. Nothing like enough to make an impression, but enough to make it worth the effort.

Buckland had been wheeling out the government big guns to support him. The Foreign Secretary, Home Secretary and other front-bench politicians were all coming down for photo opportuni-ties on the hustings. Apparently, the Prime Minister himself was due to visit next Friday. Deakin too had welcomed a few big shots from the OP, but also played his trump card by inviting various celebrity friends to share a platform with him. That had clearly paid off in terms of publicity. The draw of A-list celebrities over boring politi-cians was a huge bonus in attracting large crowds.

This morning's press conference was well underway and the usual policy questions were being asked and answered. Harvey found it all a bit routine but still needed to pay attention, as a rogue question could easily come his way at any time. He had noticed that the usual correspondent from the *Daily Record* was absent today and a reporter called Terry Macdonald was standing in for him. As the paper was a rabid supporter of the OP, most of his questions were, unsurprisingly, directed at Buckland, so it was business as usual, despite the change of messenger. That was, until he surprisingly asked Harvey a question.

'Could I ask Mr Britten, as a Brighton resident, what is his view on prostitution? I understand there's a growing problem with girls propositioning people in the Lanes and under the pier late at night?'

Harvey was unaware of such a problem. 'Um, yes, well, obvi-ously it isn't good for people to be propositioned and, equally, it's a concern if girls are being exploited or victims of people trafficking and suchlike, so it does need to be addressed.' *Not bad for an off the cuff response.*

'And you Mr Deakin?' continued MacDonald 'What would you think?'

'Well I agree with Harvey. It's a disgrace that the POG Council hasn't addressed the issue and cleaned up the city. It doesn't show Brighton in a good light if pimps see Brighton as a soft touch where nothing is being done to clamp down on vice.'

'And you Mr Buckland' said the journalist, apparently doing the rounds of all the candidates. 'Where do you stand on prostitution?'

Buckland stuttered for some reason. Harvey assumed he was in a difficult position being a POG Councillor too. Anyway, it was more the Council's problem than the MP's. He nonetheless gave a similar answer but, this time, MacDonald followed up.

'Yes, but what do you think about prostitution in general' he said. 'Do you think it's a good thing, Mr Buckland?'

Buckland again stuttered. 'Well, as has been said, there's always a concern for girls forced into selling themselves for whatever reason. Many are drug dependent and vulnerable so we should always do everything we can to help them.'

'And could I ask you - since you mention drugs,' MacDonald went on. 'Are you on any prescription medication yourself?' *What an odd question.*

'Why do you ask?' said Buckland. 'I'm not sure my medical records are anyone's business. Or those of any candidate for that matter.'

'Well, you mentioned drug dependency' said MacDonald 'and people have a right to know whether their prospective MP may have drug issues. That's fair isn't it?'

Buckland seemed bemused. 'Well, perhaps. But I assure you that no-one has anything to worry about on that score with me and . . .'

'So, to be clear, you confirm that you are not on any prescription medication . . .'

'Look I . . .'

'I think this is a very odd thing to be asking' Harvey found himself saying. 'If it helps, in the spirit of openness, I can reveal that I have a regular prescription for pile ointment. Can we move on now please? I'm feeling uncomfortable sitting on this hard chair?'

There was a muttering of laughter and someone else then asked a question about the government's record on job creation. Harvey didn't know why he had stepped in but was pleased to make the journalists laugh. It did seem unnecessarily intrusive to probe into people's private medical records, though. Harvey thought Buckland may be a lot of things, but a drug addict was unlikely to be one of them.

What on earth was MacDonald getting at? Probably trying to make a name for himself whist the main correspondent was away. That must be it.

39

Alistair

MONDAY 21 APRIL 2025

Despite having taken a sleeping tablet at ten, Alistair had not slept a wink. It was 2 a.m. and his mind was in disarray. He'd got up and poured himself a brandy and was now sitting in the lounge, staring into space.

He had felt increasingly nervous since the press conference last Thursday. The off the wall questions about prostitution had sent a shiver up his spine. He prayed he was just being paranoid. Whatever his agenda, the reporter could not know about Gabrielle and the follow up questions about drug taking at least helped to relieve his concerns. The guy was clearly just fishing.

Dan had equally concluded that it was just some junior hack trying to make a name for himself. By the weekend, Alistair had almost forgotten about it, especially after the usual political correspondent for the *Daily Record* was back in harness on Friday and things seemed to return to normal.

But then, four hours ago, he had received a phone call.

'Terry MacDonald, *Daily Record,*' the caller had said coldly. 'We're publishing a piece in tomorrow's paper and wondered if you would like to comment.'

'About what?' Alistair had replied.

'About your relationship with a lady called Gabrielle.'

Alistair said nothing, struck dumb.

'Shall I take that as a *no comment?*' the cocky reporter added after a few moments silence. Again, Alistair didn't know what to say.

'OK, *no comment* it is. Thank you.' The reporter hung up.

After a few minutes, Alistair's mind began to clear. His first thought was to call Gabrielle and warn her that, somehow, the media had found out about them. But when he called the usual number, it was dead. He felt uncomfortable and wondered if he should call Dan, or even Andrew. Suddenly, he understood the question about prostitution. This was the same reporter from the press conference last week. The bastard had been trying to catch him out.

Should he wait before calling anyone? See what the paper printed? He had been constantly monitoring the *Daily Record's* website since the call but their main story was just something trivial about a predicted summer heatwave. Perhaps they had nothing, or decided not to print. But they still knew Gabrielle's name. That cannot be good.

At 4 a.m. he checked the website again and his heart fell to his stomach. The front page had suddenly changed and the headline now read *'Deakin's rival caught with his pants down.'* It filled half the page, in large type, but it was the other half that shook him even more. A photo of Alistair emerging from a bathroom wearing nothing but a large pair of baggy white underpants. How in God's name had they got that photograph? There could only be one way, or one person – Gabrielle.

He read the piece on his phone. The paper had dedicated several pages to the story and it was earth-shattering stuff. How he had been visiting a 'high class call girl' named Gabrielle for ten years and used council funds to pay for their hotel trysts. There were damning CCTV stills of them both leaving a hotel room and, whilst Gabrielle's face had been blacked out, his own had not. The story told how she had supplied him with prescription drugs, how he'd helped her set up a bogus business to launder cash and asked her advice about confidential constituency business. It included countless misrepresented anecdotes that made him sound weak, spineless and sleazy. The article then promised '*more shocking revelations to come*' in the coming days. It had a tacky '*Pantsgate*' stamp in the corner.

Alistair was shaking. He put down the phone and poured another brandy, not knowing what to do. Clearly, the story must have come from Gabrielle and he was in total shock. Surely, she wouldn't set him up like this, would she? But how else did they have a secret camera in the hotel corridor if she hadn't tipped them off? And only she could have taken that photo of him coming out of the bathroom in his hideous pants. *How could she?*

Alistair's phone buzzed as the world began to see the news. The paper had clearly used the old trick of keeping back a major story until it was too late for rival papers to change their own front-pages. But now it was out there and the wider press and social media were alive. He was receiving messages and Twitter notifications by the dozen. Social media trolls, mostly OP supporting fanatics, were pouring bucket loads of bile onto him already. *Don't these bastards ever sleep?* It was only 4.15 in the morning for goodness sake. Endless messages and emails were coming in from the media, seeking comment and interviews.

Alistair realised he must make some urgent calls, regardless of the early hour. If *he* was receiving messages then others would be receiving them too. He started to call Dan but it was too late. The phone rang in his hand. It was Andrew McKenzie, the local Party Chairman.

'I thought you might be up' snapped Andrew, his voice curt and officious. 'What the bloody hell is going on? Is all this shit true?'

'I . . . I'm so sorry Andrew' said Alistair, not knowing where else to start.

'Sorry?! SORRY?! Have you any idea how this will make me look? I recommended you for this! Stuck my neck out for you!'

It didn't surprise Alistair that Andrew's first thought was how it all affected him.

'And *this* is how you repay me? I've already had a message to call the minister urgently. The PM will be livid! This will damage the party, not just your own miserable reputation.'

It was not exactly the reassurance Alistair needed, but it was very much as he expected. It was doubtless the first of many roast-ings he would receive today.

'So, how much of it is true?' demanded Andrew.

'Well . . .' said Alistair. 'It's true, of course, that I've been seeing her for many years. But it's not as sleazy as they make out. Our rela-tionship was . . .'

'Do you pay her for sex?'

'Well, yes, but . . .'

'So that's all true then. You're visiting prostitutes.'

'*A* prostitute' said Alistair, as if it really mattered to Andrew. He always knew that no-one could possibly understand his relationship with Gabrielle. Indeed, it now looked like he didn't even understand it himself. She had sold him down the river and he'd obviously meant nothing to her after all.

'How about using Council funds to pay for your grubby little encounters?'

'That's not true' Alistair said. 'I *did* have some legitimate overnight stays in London and, yes, I did sometimes see her at the same time, but . . .'

'So that's true too, then.' Andrew was definitely not in the mood for sympathy.

'But it's all exaggerated!' said Alistair in frustration. 'They said I was bragging about it and that's just not . . .'

'And what about discussing confidential constituency business with her?'

'Again' said Alistair 'they've misrepresented it. I may have asked her opinion now and again on a few constituent's problems, but only to get a different perspective. A female perspective. Like all Council-lors probably do with their husbands or wives. I never mentioned names or anything that . . .'

'So that's true too' came the unforgiving response once again. 'And what about the drug taking?'

'Now that *is* nonsense' said Alistair angrily. He could increas-ingly see how the story had enough facts to hang him but without context to give the true picture. 'She felt sorry for me not sleeping and gave me some old sleeping pills she didn't use anymore. She was just trying to help.'

'So, are you addicted to prescription medication, like it says?'

'Of course not!' replied Alistair. 'I got a prescription for sleeping pills after Gabrielle gave me hers, just because they seemed to help, but that's all. I'm not . . .'

'Money laundering?'

'No! Look I . . .'

'Did you help her set up a business to launder cash?'

'I gave her advice on setting up a business. I thought she . . .'

'Its enough' said Andrew with a sigh. 'It's *all* enough to prevent a categorical denial.' He went quiet. He was either thinking or had nothing else to say.

'What happens now?' asked Alistair, breaking the unbearable silence. 'Should I step down as candidate?'

'You can't!' snapped Andrew. 'It's too bloody late! The bastards waited until after nominations had closed, knowing you couldn't then be dropped or step aside. Being a liability is not a legitimate reason to get rid of a useless candidate. Only an independent can withdraw and only the death of a party candidate can cause an election to be postponed. I fear we are well and truly stuck with you. Damn you, Alistair!' There was utter contempt in Andrew's voice, so different to the fawning praise he had heaped on Alistair over the past months.

'I'm sorry' said Alistair, sounding totally dejected.

Andrew sighed heavily again. 'This is going to take a lot of thought. There's the press conference podcast this morning, for God's sake! That will be a horror show.'

'Should I pull out?'

'Can't see how you can' said Andrew. 'It would look like we're running scared. You have to balls it out somehow. Think about what you're going to say and I'll get some advice from Party HQ. We're going to need the big guns from our PR team to advise on how the hell we handle this.'

'Ok' said Alistair sheepishly 'thanks.'

'One more thing' said Andrew. 'What are these *'more shocking revelations to come'* that the *Record* promises?'

'I've no idea' said Alistair. 'Honestly. There's nothing else I can think of. But they've twisted everything else to make it sound awful so I can't imagine what else they'll make up. Seriously I can't.'

'I'll call you later. Don't say a word to the press until I do.' Andrew hung up abruptly.

THINGS DIDN'T IMPROVE as daylight fully broke. It was going to be another warm sunny day but the panoramic sea view from Alistair's lounge window did nothing to gladden his heart. TV crews were already setting up camp on the Hove lawns opposite, doubtless using his mansion block as a backdrop to their report. Breakfast TV was broadcasting live by 7.30, having presumably broken the land speed record to get their news crew down from London at such short notice.

The photo of Alistair in his unflattering baggy pants was everywhere. It was already being expertly Photoshopped on social media to portray him coming out of 10 Downing Street and other famous doors. Worse still, the PM's head had also been superimposed onto Alistair's body and used to poke fun at him too. Alistair might have found some of the posts inventive and funny - had it been anyone else. But it was him and he was mortified. His reputation was being kicked around like a tin can in a school yard.

Dan was far more pragmatic and supportive than Andrew, but Alistair wasn't surprised. After what he had been through this year, nothing would ever phase him again. But then, he had far less resting on the result. By contrast, the POG *desperately* needed Alistair to win. Their majority would be all but wiped out and, more importantly, it would let the Silver Fox into the hen house. It was no secret that Deakin scared the life out of the POG hierarchy and Alistair was now handing him victory on a plate. He'd let them down badly. Sarah too, which hurt him even more. How could Gabrielle have done this to him? The woman he loved and who he thought loved him too - in some small way at least.

40

Harvey

MONDAY 21 APRIL 2025

'Morning sunshine' said Harvey, carrying a cup of tea into the bedroom. Claire yawned and stretched as she woke up. It was 7 a.m.

'Prepare to be amazed' he said, smiling.

'Ooh, Mr Britten' purred Claire. 'Can I clean my teeth first?'

Harvey laughed and handed over the tablet. Claire stared open mouthed in disbelief at what she saw.

'Oh . . . my . . . God . . !' she said, placing a hand to her mouth. 'No way!'

'Poor sod has been done up like a kipper' said Harvey. 'Whoever this woman is she's been setting him up for years. Must have been waiting for her chance - and this election is clearly it. Read it all, the guy is absolutely stuffed.'

Claire read the rest in disbelief. 'Well, it goes to show' she said finally. 'It's always the quiet ones. But those pants! You can tell he's not married. I would NEVER let you out of the house wearing those. Ever!'

'Didn't they used to call them passion killers?' said Harvey. 'Unless you're paying for your passion, I suppose. Then it probably doesn't matter.'

. . .

THEY BOTH WATCHED TV over breakfast. The story was everywhere and the general consensus was that Buckland was a dead man walking and Deakin was as good as home. The *Daily Record's* Editor was interviewed on every channel and looked as smug as they come. He wouldn't give away what further revelations were still in the offing but alluded to the paper having similar dirt about other famous figures who were on the prostitute's books. They seemed to have a major scoop on their hands.

Harvey's mind turned to the morning press conference webinar at ten. Would Buckland even turn up? If so, what on earth would he say? The wolves would be baying for blood. Sam had already called and they discussed how Harvey should play it from his own point of view. He suspected no-one would actually be interested in him today and they agreed he should just keep a dignified silence. *'Let Buckland hang himself'* as Sam put it.

AT FIVE TO TEN, Harvey was sitting in front of the webcam waiting for the press conference to start. Sam was in her usual place, just out of camera shot where she could pass him facts and figures if needed.

Buckland's face was last to appear, in a window in the top right of the screen, and he looked a dejected figure. All credit to him for even being there. This was going to be vicious.

Unsurprisingly, the first question came from the *Daily Record's* reporter. 'Mr Buckland, is it fair to say that, whilst your campaign was making little headway anyway, it could now best be described as total pants?' There was a murmur of schoolboy sniggering from the other journalists. Buckland was a sitting target.

'You may as well get your jokes out of the way early' said Buckland, slightly more aggressively than Harvey had expected. 'I'll not be commenting on this salacious, tabloid trash journalism other than to say that I am in contact with my lawyers.'

'Are you saying it's not true then? That you weren't paying prostitutes for sex at the tax payer's expense?'

'No . . . well, yes . . . but it was not like that.'

'Are you going to resign from the Council?' said a different reporter.

'Are you a drug addict? said another.

They were indeed on a feeding frenzy. Buckland ducked and parried the blows as best he could but continued to take punch after punch to the body.

'Do you still have the famous pants?' came another random question, detracting from the wider grilling. Someone must have sent their fashion correspondent. Harvey felt that Buckland's corner should throw in the towel. Their man was taking a serious beating.

'Could I just say' said Harvey, after the last question, 'that it would be nice to keep the level of questioning somewhere above the belt if possible? I think any of us here - or those of you in the media pack, for that matter – would die at the thought of seeing a photo of *us* in our underwear being spread across the newspapers. Which of us could proudly say we look good in our pants? Not me for sure. Regardless of anything else Mr Buckland has to answer for, I think publication of that photo was a cheap shot and a pretty shameful thing to do, if you ask me.'

'Hear hear' came a few unidentified mutterings from the more liberal press. 'Well said.' Harvey suspected they were just happy to pop the *Daily Record's* balloon, but it was reassuring to get a positive response. Again, he didn't know why he had interrupted, but it seemed like the right thing to do. It at least caused the hyenas to stop gorging on Buckland's battered corpse and the rest of the conference returned to normal subjects.

Deakin seemed to have adopted the same plan in keeping a dignified silence. He was clearly trying not to look over-confident, but Harvey wasn't sure he succeeded. The OP must be delighted, knowing that victory was essentially in the bag.

A STRANGE THING happened at the end of an extraordinary day. The overnight InstaPoll results showed that, unsurprisingly, Buckland had taken a big hit. His poll rating had plummeted from 40% to 23%. But it could have been far worse in Harvey's view. Strangely though, Deakin had only risen two points to 44%. The main beneficiary had instead been Harvey Britten himself. His rating was now up from 8% to 18%, putting him squarely in third place and only five points behind Buckland.

Clearly, Deakin's massive twenty-one points lead now made him the runaway favourite, but suddenly Harvey was a player in the game. Of course, there were far more *'don't knows'* than voters choosing him. But it had certainly made things interesting. He was quietly pleased and saw it as the perfect position to be in - just enough to make it worth all the effort of standing, but still with no risk whatsoever that he could actually win the thing.

41

Gabrielle

MONDAY 21 APRIL 2025

'You lied to me!' said Gabrielle, having finally got Terry MacDonald on the phone after trying all day. 'You've twisted everything! You said you just wanted to damage his campaign, not completely trash his reputation and make him into a laughing stock. How could you?' She was tearful, as much from guilt as shock.

'Sorry sweetheart' said Terry, with a patronising tone to his voice. 'Didn't we mentioned the need to destroy his credibility entirely? I'm sure it was written on the back of that massive cheque we gave you. Perhaps the size of the amount blinded you in some way.'

'But you . . .'

'*But you* nothing!' he went on, giving no ground at all. 'Listen, darlin'. *You* gave us the dirt. *You* gave us the photo. No, worse than that, you *took* the bloody photo! I don't think you wanted it for your year book, did you? Whatever mischief you had planned for him, don't tell me it wasn't something like this. Well, we saved you the trouble, sweetheart. Blackmail is an ugly business so don't take the moral high ground with me. You planned for this and now you've got it. Only difference is that you've been paid legitimately for it.

Sorry, but you can't throw a hand grenade and then complain when someone gets blown up. Anything else?'

Gabrielle knew she was wasting her time and that, deep down, he was right. She may have changed her mind about exposing Alistair but that didn't detract from her original motive. She was just as bad as the wretched paper.

'Is the money going through?' she asked, sheepishly.

'Ah yes, there we go!' said Terry, laughing. 'Showing your true colours! Don't you worry, my sweet, it's on its way as we speak. Pleasure doing business with you, goodbye.' He hung up.

Gabrielle felt utterly wretched.

42

Emma

MONDAY 21 APRIL 2025

'Someone's Christmases have all come early' said Emma, as her husband arrived home with a big smile on his face. She hadn't seen too much of Bradley over the last couple of weeks and, despite everything, was pleased to see him.

'I've opened champagne' she said 'I thought you might want to celebrate.'

'Thank you' said Bradley. 'You read my mind.'

She poured two glasses of Dom Perignon - this was definitely a time to bring out the good stuff. As she did so, he took her slightly by surprise, putting his arms tightly around her waist from behind, giving her a big hug and kissing the side of her neck. It was a very nice surprise, come to think of it.

'We're on the way, Ems,' he whispered. 'It's as good as won.'

She capitalised on the moment by turning into his arms and staring into his eyes. They were warm and bright for a change, not disapproving and empty as they so often were nowadays. Success always acted as his aphrodisiac.

. . .

'YOU HAVE to feel a *bit* sorry for him' said Emma, propping herself back up on the pillows.

'Why?' said Bradley, as he got back into bed. 'What idiot sleeps with the same hooker for ten years. Ten! Most marriages don't even last that long!'

'Well, there must have been more to it than just sex' said Emma. 'He shared a lot of stuff with her over the years so it must have felt like a relationship of some kind - to him at least. But she's really knifed him in the back. Sounds like a right bitch.'

'Let's hear it for the sisterhood!' said Bradley, realising that his glass was empty and reaching down for the champagne bottle beside the bed.

'Yes, well' said Emma. 'On the plus side, they're saying that celebrities will think long and hard in future before having a bit on the side.' She looked knowingly at her husband, who could clearly see what she was eluding to.

'Let's not go there,' he said, as he topped up her glass too. 'Its just me and you now, Ems. Onward and very much upward.'

'What time will tomorrow's papers come out?' she replied, wisely changing the subject. 'I want to see the rest of the shitstorm they're going to throw at him.'

'Not sure exactly' said Bradley. 'Either way, Buckland is dead meat. It's just a bit disappointing that his poll ratings have gone into freefall but mine are only up by a couple of points. I would have expected more. That senile old DJ seems to have picked up the bulk of it.'

'Well,' she replied, 'think about it. You said this was about winning the centre ground and getting the floating voters on your side. So, if the POG's loyal supporters are now unhappy with Buckland then, surely, they're more likely to lodge a protest vote with some neutral candidate than vote for the OP, aren't they? It would be against their religion to vote for you. Just as it would be for a die-hard OP activist to vote for Buckland if, heaven forbid, it was *you* being disgraced in the papers instead. Isn't that right?'

'True, I guess' said Bradley, nodding. She still knew a bit about politics, even if she no longer displayed any outward interest.

'And this Britten guy has got a lot of good reviews,' she continued, pleased to be having a sensible conversation with her husband for a change. 'And he's funny too. I've listened to all the press conference and I quite liked him. If I go off you, I might even vote for him myself . . .'

'You can't vote' said Bradley. 'You don't live in Brighton.'

'Oh yeah' she said. 'But neither do you, come to think of it. So, you'd better not upset your fanbase with some sleazy scandal of your own. If you can't even vote for yourself in this election, you'd probably be looking at *nil point!*'

Bradley chuckled, which was nice to see. Emma rarely made him laugh any more.

'Don't worry about me' he said, lying back with a self-satisfied smile. 'I'm an absolute saint.'

43

Alistair

TUESDAY 22 APRIL 2025

'*Buckland and Billingham – the secret affair?*'

The headline glared out from the screen as Alistair stared back in disbelief. Once again, the *Daily Record* had used a decoy story for the early editions before launching the real headline like an artillery shell, late into the night.

Alistair was staggered at the lies he was reading. The central plank was Gabrielle claiming that Alistair was madly in love with Sarah. The question mark at the end of the headline showed it to be speculation, but the words came across squarely as fact. The story recalled how he had stepped aside to allow her to stand as an MP, which Gabrielle said was '*the greatest act of love he could possibly make.*'

The story took that idea and ran with it like Usain Bolt chasing after a bus, speculating that there must have been an affair as a result. How they came to that conclusion is anyone's guess, but it was clearly a cynical ploy to discredit him. There were photos of Sarah and Alistair laughing and joking as he looked lovingly at her. But the photos had all been carefully cropped and taken out of context. They appeared to be alone when, in reality, they were at public events with other people close by. Alistair even recognised one photo where Dan was actually sitting alongside them, but he

had been cynically cropped from the shot. It was malicious speculation bordering on libel, in Alistair's view.

He nursed a glass of brandy as dawn broke on a potentially
awful day ahead. He wasn't sure whether he could take another one
like yesterday. He had been attacked by all sides of the party,
making it clear that he was a liability and single-handedly threatening the government's future. He had been advised not to give any
interviews after the roasting he received in the press conference,
despite countless invitations to put his own side of the story. The PR
gurus were deciding on the best way to do that, if and when the
time came. For now, they'd decided to wait until all the revelations
had come out before committing to an interview. That was looking
like a wise move if this morning's nonsense was anything to go by.

All visits by senior cabinet ministers to support his campaign
had been abruptly suspended including, unsurprisingly, the scheduled visit by the Prime Minister. He was apparently apoplectic with
rage, believing his own chances of keeping Deakin at bay would
now go down with Alistair's ship in Brighton. All in all, Alistair was
public enemy number one within his own party. He'd never felt so
alone and isolated.

In the past, his first instinct would be to see Gabrielle - his
source of comfort and reassurance during any storm. But no longer.
It was *she* who had whipped up this particular hurricane and that
very fact was causing him the most despair. It was more than just a
betrayal. She had stuck a sword right through his very soul. He'd
always kidded himself that they could be together one day. Even if
she didn't feel the same love for him as he did for her, he thought
she at least cared about him – loving him in some small way. Everything she said or did indicated that. How could it all have been an
act? A cynical long game, setting him up for whenever the time was
right? Was that really why she was so encouraging about his ambitions to stand as an MP?

He sipped his brandy, sighed deeply and shook his head in
despair. It was 4.30 a.m. The madness would start again soon as the
trolls saw the news and loaded up with fresh ammunition. Today's
story would certainly un-leash the hounds. Being accused of an

affair with a married woman who had just left a widower and young child behind her. *Oh God! How can I face Dan?*

HE CALLED AT SIX O'CLOCK, having taken that long to pluck up the courage. At least Dan answered, which was an encouraging sign.

'It's all lies Dan' Alistair said immediately. 'You know that don't you? A total, filthy pack of lies.'

'I suspected as much' came the reply. It wasn't quite the empathy Dan had shown yesterday.

'You know I loved her,' he said, 'but . . . not like that. She was like a daughter to me. I'm Charlie's Godfather for goodness sake! I love all of you. You're like a family to me and I value that more than anything. This is just twisted mischief-making to sell papers. Dirty speculation. When would she ever have had time for an affair, for goodness sake?'

Dan was silent, but then sighed. 'I know' he said finally. 'Of course, I do. It's just that . . . I hate her name being dragged into all this. People will believe it of *you* after yesterday so that means they'll believe it of her.'

Alistair had to agree, which broke his heart too. Sarah's memory was sacred and these scumbags were trampling on her grave. Yes, he had once harboured a dream of something more than friendship, but that was all it was – a dream. It was long ago and he had never told Gabrielle anything to suggest otherwise. Although, with hindsight, perhaps that was why he started seeing her in the first place - unfulfilled romantic dreams elsewhere. But his friendship with Sarah had been one of the most treasured things in his life, as was the relationship that later developed with Dan and Charlie too. He'd been to Christmas lunches, shared big events in their mutual lives and they had gradually become the loving family he'd never really had himself. Tarnishing that relationship was pure evil and hurt him to his very core.

'We have to put out a denial quickly' said Dan. 'A strong one. Both of us. I won't have this festering away in people's minds for a second longer than it needs to. We'll call an emergency press conference podcast today to rebuke the accusations and then walk out in disgust. The press are parasites.'

Alistair agreed. The party had demanded media silence from him but this was different. The paper had overstepped the mark this time and must be put in their place.

AT TEN O'CLOCK Alistair was sitting at the webcam with Dan right alongside him, fully in camera shot. Both they, Andrew and the PR team felt it vital to show solidarity. Thankfully, none of them had believed the story. That created at least some level of sympathy, as well as a need for damage limitation. All the other candidates were sitting in on the press conference as well.

Alistair started with a prepared statement. 'As you can see, Dan Billingham, Sarah's loving husband, my good friend and Election Agent, is here beside me to refute the foul and wholly unsubstantiated claims made in today's *Daily Record*. Not only are they untrue but they are defamatory to both myself and, more importantly, to Sarah's memory. A wonderful woman who is no longer here to defend herself and, if she were, would be just as incensed as we both are at such a disgusting slur against a wife, mother and dedicated politician. I cannot put into words how despicable these accusations are or refute them enough as being a pack of evil lies. Again, my lawyers will be looking into this vile newspaper's conduct and I will also be reporting this matter to the Press Complaints Commission.'

Alistair felt better having said it and there was initially and embarrassed silence from the press pack.

'But were you in love with her?' came a question. It was the *Daily Record*.

'I'm giving no more time to this story other than to deny categorically that there was anything inappropriate in my friendship and relationship with Sarah. That is the end of the matter.'

'But were you in love with her?' came the same question again. Alistair bit his lip and decided to take Dan's advice.

'That's it!' he said theatrically. 'I've had enough of this nonsense!

I'll not be taking part in any more press conferences until I receive a formal apology and retraction from the *Daily Record* for these cynical smears. They are clearly intended to scupper my campaign like the bunch of Opposition poodles they are. Good day to you.' He clicked off his live feed and the window went blank. But Alistair continued watching to see what happened next.

'Well done' said Dan, which meant a lot.

On the screen, Alistair was not surprised to see Harvey Britten step in again.

'I would like to voice my support for Mr Buckland's comments. Not for him personally, but for Sarah Billingham. My wife and I had the pleasure of knowing Sarah briefly, whilst my brilliant radio colleague Dale Glover was a lifelong friend. She was a wonderful lady and it is, indeed, scandalous to claim she was anything other than a loving wife and mother. It's depressing to see the media stoop so low and spread what appears to be nothing more than malicious speculation. We all loved Sarah Billingham in Brighton – and she loved this city back. I think, out of respect to her, we should all reflect on the cynical motives behind this story and remember which party – or candidate – is behind it. I, too, think we should end it there.' To Alistair's surprise, Britten then turned off his live feed too. Bradley Deakin looked a bit exposed.

'Well' he said finally. 'Of course, I can state, categorically, that I had nothing to do with this being published. But, given tempers are obviously running high today, let's call it a day there shall we?'

AS THE DAY WENT ON, the media were divided. There was actually considerable sympathy for Alistair, notably from those desperate to discredit the *Daily Record's* scoop that had been stealing all the limelight. But social media was less forgiving. There was no middle ground in the twisted minds of internet trolls. No smoke without fire. Like piranha fish swarming around a blooded piece of flesh, the feeding frenzy began again. For some, there was no disease or method of death that was inappropriate for his sins. It was painful and nauseating to read. He had no idea what sort of people could say such things but it added to his despair.

The overnight InstaPoll showed a further drop in his ratings, but less than he feared. Deakin was unchanged at 44%, but his lead over Alistair was now up to twenty-three points, a rise of two percent. It was, again, Harvey Britten who had benefited from the day's events, rising by four percent since yesterday. It was either Alistair's own disenchanted supporters changing allegiance or previous 'don't knows' having now decided who to vote for.

Alistair had actually been impressed by Harvey Britten's unexpected support and didn't begrudge him benefiting from his own misfortunes. But it did create a worrying situation. Britten was now ahead of Alistair by one clear point on 22% so was officially in second place. The party would not be at all pleased that his own campaign was clearly in free-fall. But, equally, perhaps Britten might be his salvation. If Alistair couldn't win himself, then an independent just might be the POG's best chance of keeping Deakin outside the castle walls.

Alistair was about to go to bed, in a futile attempt to sleep, when the phone rang. It was Dan.

'Sorry to ring you so late' he said. He sounded stressed. 'I've just had a call from the police. They want to see me tomorrow morning at 9 a.m. and I asked if you could be there too. Can you come over then?'

'Of course. What's going on?' asked Alistair.

Dan, was clearly distraught. 'They want to update me on the investigation into Sarah's death. Alistair, they now say they have evidence to suggest she was murdered.'

44

Alistair

WEDNESDAY 23 APRIL 2025

Alistair arrived at Dan's house just as a police car approached from the other direction. Two officers from Special Branch, DI Williams and DS Crawley, got out. They had apparently taken over the investigation after the Anti-Terrorism Squad gave the all clear last month. From their point of view, any self-respecting terrorist would *not* have made Sarah's death look like an accident and they would also have claimed responsibility by now. As a result, the investigation had been transferred back to the police to investigate as a possible crime.

'Thank you for seeing us at such short notice' said DI Williams. 'We promised to keep you informed of any developments so I wanted to speak to you before we hold a press conference at lunchtime.'

'I thought it was being scaled back after the initial inquest' said Dan. 'What happened?'

'Two things' said DI Williams, getting straight to the point. 'You'll recall that the Range Rover was found to have been cleaned and stripped of any identifying numbers and data. It was a very thorough and professional job and, of course, that's not uncommon with professional car thieves. But we still didn't like it. Normally, you would expect them to steal it, clean it and then smuggle the car overseas as soon as possible - not drive it around Brighton on New Year's Eve.'

'So, what have you found?' asked Alistair.

'One solitary finger print. Well, most of it, anyway,' said the DS. 'But enough. It was behind the false number plate. We only found it whilst going over the car again in the hope that we had missed something first time round. We got lucky as it turns out we have a match for the print to someone on our files.'

'Who?'

'Can't say a name for obvious reasons' said the officer. 'But it belonged to a garage owner who we have previously charged with handling stolen goods. That was a good few years back and he has since given the appearance of going straight, setting himself up as an apparently legitimate mechanic. But this, of course, suggests otherwise. He's being brought in for questioning as I speak and we'll see what comes of that.'

'But even if that proves he was involved in stealing or cleansing the car – why does it make you think Sarah was murdered' asked Alistair.

'Yes, why?' Dan piped up. 'You said there were two things.'

'Indeed. Well, we've also been meticulously exploring ways that such an incident could possibly be fabricated. There were too many random elements, which is why the provisional inquest leaned towards it being an accident. Even if the plan *was* to deliberately ram her car, how would they know the lights would be on red, just when she got there, and how did they know that a juggernaut would be passing by, just at that exact moment that she was waiting on her own? Were they just lucky? Would they otherwise have followed her to find a better opportunity? But if they had done, we would then have CCTV of them trailing her and it would have been realised straight away that it was deliberate. This lot seem to have gone to an awful lot of trouble to make it look like an accident - an awful lot.'

'So, wasn't it?'

'We no longer think so, no. We've been working with Traffic Command in Brighton. They have data from every traffic light in the city and we've examined the records for that particular unit. The normal overnight sequence is set for thirty seconds on green and forty-five on red, being as its a side road off the busy seafront. It's always that sequence, and it had been running that way all night. Until the accident. Then it was on red for a full two minutes.'

'What?'

'Indeed. and the question is therefore why and how? The first part is easy - so they could keep Sarah at the lights until something big came along, like the supermarket Robo-lorry. The second bit is less straightforward and took us some time, but now we've got there. The lights were removed for forensic testing and we found a slight tweak to the software had been made. Very sophisticated and very hard to spot. Traffic Command say there had been no work done on those lights for six months before the accident. But when we interviewed the local residents again, one remembered seeing workmen there a week or two before Christmas.'

'So, what was the software change?' asked Dan.

'It looks like it acted as a remote-control beacon.'

'No!'

'I'm afraid so,' said Williams. 'So, we reviewed the dash-cam footage from the Robo-Lorry again. There were many people on the seafront as you know, given that it was new year, and we'd already identified and spoken to those who came forward as witnesses. But when we looked closely, there appears to be one figure standing back from the kerb but right opposite the turning. We traced a few other automated lorries that had passed along the seafront in the previous thirty minutes and he appears to have been there for at least that amount of time. It may even have been longer. But he has never come forward. We suspect it was *him* controlling the lights and waiting for an appropriate vehicle to come along. It looks like pure co-incidence – and good-luck on his part – that the huge Robo-lorry happened to pass by when it did because, if it hadn't, he may have chosen another large vehicle instead that may actually have been manned. We would then have been looking at more casualties. Once he saw it approaching from a suitable distance, he simply had to alert the Range Rover to head down the street at full speed and shunt Sarah into its path.'

'Have you been able to identify him?' asked Alistair, shocked at the appallingly callous image of someone deliberately orchestrating, and then watching, Sarah being killed.

'Sadly not' replied the DI. 'He, too, was dressed all in black with a hooded jacket. We're putting out stills from CCTV at the press conference today in an appeal for witnesses, but they are not at all clear in terms of identifying a face.'

'Shame' said Alistair. 'So, you think the Range Rover was parked up and waiting?'

'Yes, if we now assume that the accident was indeed planned, then it explains why it was a large, strong SUV. They needed a vehicle that could withstand the impact and still drive away after-wards. We were always unclear on the exact route the car took to Brighton as it doesn't appear on any CCTV before the accident. We now think it was delivered by truck directly to West Street and left to lie in wait. We have identified a recovery truck in the area at around nine-thirty with what could well be a covered vehicle on the back. That truck also had false plates and we've yet to trace it. Chances are that passers-by would have seen the car being unloaded but thought it was just an innocent breakdown recovery. Again, we're appealing for witnesses today based on this new theory, using a still CCTV shot of the truck.'

'But they didn't follow her from the hotel, did they?' asked Dan. 'So, how did they know exactly when she would get there so they were ready to . . . you know. If I had been with her as planned, we would have stayed for another couple of hours. They can't have known she would leave as early as eleven. Could they?'

'Logically no' said the DS. 'So, the theory we are now looking at is that they got into their positions early, to catch her whatever time she left, but I'm afraid it then looks increasingly like there was a *fourth* person watching the hotel who then tipped them off exactly when she left. It is just a theory and we haven't identified anyone. But they could have been in the car park or anywhere *en-route*. We just think they must have known in advance – not just waited to spot her when she turned into West Street. The guy operating the lights would have needed to keep them on green until the very last minute to ensure no-one else got there ahead of Sarah. She *had* to be first in the queue for it to work. We also think the Range Rover may have pulled out just after she passed them so they could then wait in the road to ensure no-one else came up behind her. They just waited until the driver got the cue to put his foot down and hit her from behind. But we can't prove any of that as there is no CCTV in West Street.'

'My God' said Dan, 'How many of these bastards were there?'

'Well, if we are right about this, then it certainly looks like a conspiracy' said Williams. 'And if it's not terrorists – then it can only mean it's a complex and very well organised murder plot.'

'Deakin!' said Alistair.

'Well, we obviously can't speculate on who might be behind it,' said the DS.

'Deakin!' said Alistair again, angrily. 'It must be!'

45

Bradley

WEDNESDAY 23 APRIL 2025

Churchill Square, in the centre of Brighton's shopping district, is one of the busiest pedestrian areas in the city. It sits alongside the main bus terminus and forms the external concourse to Brighton's principal shopping mall. The busy square was therefore the perfect place for campaigning or, in Bradley's case, making a public appearance. Rod had ensured that the event was well publicised in advance and, as a result, they had drawn an even bigger crowd than expected. People were standing fifty-deep, encircling the small platform being used to broadcast Bradley's words of wisdom to the masses.

For those photographers wanting a quirky shot, Bradley had just bought a Cornish pasty from a small kiosk in the square. Whilst it was an awful cliché, politicians doing something that 'ordinary' people also did – like buying fast food or ice-cream – always went down well, so he was happy to oblige. As long as he was never photographed actually trying to eat a messy or ungainly takeaway meal - perhaps with the risk of bacon or sauce dripping from his mouth - then everyone got what they wanted.

With the pasty humanely disposed of, Bradley then gave the adoring crowd another variation of his standard campaign speech.

He spoke about change and how he offered a bright new future for both Brighton and the country. He had the crowd in the palm of his hand, laughing heartily at his carefully prepared ad-lib jokes and queuing for selfies afterwards. He was never really sure if he was talking to the party faithful or just star-struck fans wanting to see him in the flesh. But all that mattered was that they were there in huge numbers as he gladly moved amongst them like the star he was. It offered the perfect visual image for the TV news. *Look, our man is the Messiah! See how the crowds worship him!*

Afterwards, Bradley, Rod and Peter made their way back to OP head-quarters for their *real* lunch - pasties not being on the menu. Their luxury Mercedes SUV set off with Bradley waving royally to the crowds from the back seats.

'Good work' said Peter, as they pulled away. 'A few more of these will do the trick. Buckland couldn't even draw that sort of crowd for his public hanging – with or without his comedy pants!'

They all laughed.

'Talking of which, it was a bit of an anti-climax in the paper today' said Bradley. After all the revelations about Buckland over the last two day, there had been no new allegations in the *Record* this morning.

'Well' said Peter. 'Given the allegations about an affair with Sarah Billingham backfired so badly yesterday, my info is that they're taking a short break. But I understand there's still more to come and they're just waiting until nearer the election. So, *stay tuned*, as they say. They're also holding back on the hooker's other punters – or should I say 'victims.' Apparently, there's some really hot stuff involved and they're worried it might overshadow Buckland's escapades. They don't want to move the agenda away from him and nor do we. The public need to keep the idea of him and his God-awful pants in their minds.'

'Horrible image to conjure up before lunch, though' chuckled Bradley. 'We certainly owe the *Record* a favour.' He thought Peter's friendship with the Editor of the *Daily Record* was certainly paying dividends.

Rod shook his head. 'They're not doing it *all* for us. They'll use the time to get new online subscribers and, anyway, the other revelations will keep them busy for months.'

'So, should I be worried about Britten?' said Bradley, changing the subject. He didn't really care how well the paper did out of it. 'I know he's essentially just a safe harbour for Buckland protest votes, but even so . . .'

'Yes, that's *exactly* what he is' said Rod dismissively. 'Look, the POG's core voters wouldn't vote for the OP if Mother Theresa was standing. Trust me, there's nothing to worry about. Let him have his moment in the sun. He can't possibly win and Buckland's dead on the ground. Everything's playing nicely into our hands.'

'He looks dead, but can Buckland come back from this?' Bradley asked. 'There was certainly some sympathy for him yesterday.'

'No chance' said Rod. 'The damage was already done on Monday. Rumour has it the Council has suspended him pending investigation about the misuse of expenses. Accusations of corruption are going down as badly with voters as him sleeping with the whore. Bit of an own goal on their part in terms of damaging his campaign. Makes it look like they are distancing themselves from him already. Bizarre thing to do.'

'Did you see that some of the papers are running fashion pieces about men's underwear?' said Peter, chuckling to himself and clearly not worried about their two rival candidates either. 'The photo of him in those hideous, saggy pants has gone international with some classic spoofs on line. My favourite is the picture of a bowling ball in a string bag, asking who it reminds you of. Classic. I've got it on my phone here somewhere . . .' He started searching.

'So, we're as good as home,' said Rod. 'I've got more public appearances like today's booked in and plenty of celebs are coming down to be seen schmoozing with you next week. All fairly routine, but it will see us over the line. By this time next month, Bradley, you'll be taking your seat in the House of Commons and then the fun can really start.'

'Thanks Rod' said Bradley as the car approached the local Party HQ. As it pulled up, a group of reporters were waiting outside, but Bradley was not unduly concerned - they followed him everywhere.

'Sorry if I've doubted you at all, Rod' he said, as they prepared to get out. 'This is all very stressful for me, but you really are doing a grand job organising everything and I really do appreciate it.'

But Rod didn't answer. He was studying his phone and looking ashen. 'Shit' he said.

Before they could question him, the car door had been wrenched opened from outside so Bradley got out. The scrum immediately surged towards the car, with microphones thrust into his face and cameras flashing like a firework display.

'Do you have any comment on the police statement just now?'

Bradley looked at Peter, who appeared as bemused as he was. They both looked at Rod, who was himself looking a bit shocked.

'I'm sorry' said Bradley, deciding it was easiest to be honest. 'I've been campaigning all day and haven't heard any news. What police statement?'

'Saying that Sarah Billingham was murdered. Do you have any comment?'

'Goodness me, no' said Bradley, walking the short distance into the building. 'Obviously, I need to see it first, but it would be shocking if that's what they're saying. I'll comment later when I've caught up. Thank you.'

They broke free from the crowd and were rushed through the main door. Bradley wondered why they had not known in advance about the police statement. As they went in, he heard one last question that stood out from the rest.

'Did you arrange her murder Mr Deakin? Surely, *you* stood to benefit most.' He turned around but was quickly ushered inside and the door shut behind him.

'What on earth is going on?' said Bradley, perplexed.

'I'm on it' said Rod, who clearly was not. He was frantically reading his phone to catch up on the press conference that had apparently taken place just thirty minutes before.

'And, what's more' said Bradley, who was now livid, 'why are they asking whether I did it, for Christ's sake?'

'It's just lazy speculation' said Rod. 'Trust me, I'm on it. Leave it to me.' He left them standing in the hallway and scurried away.

. . .

THE NEWS SITES had the police press conference as their main story for the rest of the day, overshadowing the election and doubtless giving Buckland some respite. As well as reporting on new evidence found by police, some websites were asking the same question as Bradley had heard outside. *Who would want to kill Sarah Billingham and why? Who would benefit most from seeing her dead?* Unjustly, in his view, some were shining the spotlight brightly on both Bradley and the OP. He knew it was just mischief making by sections of the POG supporting press, trying desperately to pull back support for Buckland by heaping suspicion on Bradley. But he still didn't like it. Something Rod had said as he left bothered him - *'Leave it to me.'*

It suddenly reminded Bradley of a previous time Rod had said the same thing. It was last December. *'Leave it with me. Give me a hundred grand and I'll get you a by-election. Trust me.'* Two weeks later Sarah was dead and now the police were saying it was a highly organised murder conspiracy. Bradley didn't want to put two and two together, but could not stop the thought entering his mind. *Trust me,* Rod had said. Bradley really hoped that he could.

46

Gabrielle

THURSDAY 24 APRIL 2025

Gabrielle was watching the news on breakfast TV, which was dominated by yesterday's police announcement. They were discussing how social media was awash with conspiracy theories, all centred on either Bradley Deakin, his supporters or the OP itself.

Everyone seemed to agree that it was Bradley who had benefited most from Sarah Billingham's death. One minute he was looking for an elusive by-election and then, suddenly − surprise, surprise −one falls right into his lap. In the absence of a safe OP seat to contest, the speculation was that Brighton - with the smallest majority in the country − was seen as the next best thing. A highly winnable seat for a popular figure like Bradley Deakin. Two plus two had very easily added up to five.

Gabrielle watched it all with moderate interest and amusement. At least it took some of the heat off FG. She hadn't actually said that he was in love with Sarah or, at least, she didn't think she had. But she'd spoken to Terry MacDonald for hours and said so much. It was therapeutic to get it all off her chest once she got going. Whilst she couldn't remember exactly what she *had* said, it was naïve and stupid to think they wouldn't twist her words to suit their needs.

Either way, the net result was that she had thrown Alistair Buckland under a bus. At least all the murder conspiracies today were making Deakin look even worse than FG was, so there may still be a chance to make amends.

The good news was that the money had duly come through. All one million pounds of it was now safely ensconced in the Cayman Islands. She had one last thing to do. Today she would contact the rival *Daily News* to offer up her story about Tom. She was under strict instructions not to speak to other media organisations until the dirt on her full list of clients had been published by the *Daily Record*. But she was safe speaking about Tom - he was not on the list of clients. And even if the *Record* did try to sue her for breach of contract, they would never get a penny back. By the time the story came out, she would be long gone. So good luck with that. She hoped the *Daily News* might publish next week, which would be perfect. Then her work here would be through.

She didn't care how badly it would harm Tom. She now only cared about FG. She knew that ship had sailed – and probably sunk – but there was just one last chance of a salvage operation. Her plan had always been to tell Tom's wife about their affair so she would realise that he'd married her on the rebound. That was the main thrust of Plan A, with the aim of simply destroying his perfect marriage by showing its foundations were built of clay. To beef it up a little more, she was also going to claim that she had given birth to Tom's child after they broke up and was forced to give it up for adoption whilst she, herself, was driven into a life of prostitution. It was mischief making and would destroy Tom's happy home life. The one that should have been hers.

But there was also an alternative Plan B. She only ever considered it on sleepless nights when she was feeling particularly bitter and resentful towards Tom. She had never planned to use it because, in the cold light of day, she knew it was just plain evil. But sometimes it made her feel better to think about ways to completely destroy Tom himself, not just his perfect marriage. However, things had now changed. She was desperate to repair the damage she had done to FG and this looked like the only way she could put things right. So, Plan B it would be instead - and God help Tom when it hit him.

47

Harvey

THURSDAY 24 APRIL 2025

14 days to go

'. . . So, its *Murdering Scumbag* in the lead as they approach the final straight, but coming up fast on the rails is *Hero Harvey*! Look at him go as he gains ground with every stride! Pulling away from *Pantsgate Boy* - sagging a bit at the back - then it's *Stupid Birdy-Man* from . . .'

'Yes . . . thank you' said Harvey, pretending to be unimpressed by Piers's horse racing commentary but, in fact, it was making them all laugh. Piers had arrived with Sam unexpectedly this morning because he had a day off work. They had brought little Phoebe with them too, which would normally have been a nice surprise for her grand-parents. But today, Harvey was slightly annoyed by the distraction. He and Sam had work to do, preparing for the webinar press conference at ten o'clock. That was in just under two hours, so the whole family, including Claire, were having a quick cup of tea in the lounge before they got started.

'You're playing a blinder' said Piers returning to his normal voice. 'Everyone I talk to says you're doing great. We're really proud of you.'

'Thanks' said Harvey 'but I think all I'm doing is just stepping over the bodies. A bit like Foinavon, since you're on a horse racing theme.'

'Who?' said Piers. Sam looked equally bemused.

'Too young, damn you' said Harvey. 'Famous Grand National winner back in the mid 1960's. Bit of a donkey running at 100-1 and trundling along at the back. Then there was a pile up at one of the final fences – a loose horse was running in the way, as I recall – so everyone in front of him either fell down or pulled up. Foinavon just stepped through the carnage and trotted on to win. I now know how he felt - not that I'm going to win of course. There's a pretty impressive stallion who is still on his feet and galloping along, way ahead, regardless of the murder conspiracy. Thank goodness for that I say.'

'Still looking at a podium finish, though' said Piers. 'And he's only in the lead for now. He's slowing up. Down two points overnight – close enough to see his tail twitching in fear.'

'I'm not sure a twenty-point lead is what you'd call *close*, Piers' said Harvey. 'It's a classic case of trial by media. There's no evidence to suggest either he or the OP had anything to do with Sarah's death. People are just speculating and drawing their own conclusions.'

'Dirt sticks' said Piers. 'Look at your mate Buckland. All that guff about an affair with Sarah Billingham. You know it's complete nonsense but people believe it.'

'Yes, well' said Harvey.

'How are the "hustings" actually going, anyway?' asked Piers, being serious again. 'It would frighten the life out of me, I can tell you.'

'He's doing brilliantly' interrupted Sam. Harvey felt himself slightly blush. 'Seriously, like a duck to water. Chatting away to people, it's no wonder they're all turning to him instead of the other two losers.'

'Or the bloke dressed as a seagull' said Harvey. 'Let's not forget him. This is all very bizarre. Suddenly, the media want to speak to *me* and hear what *I* have to say. I still don't feel I belong in all this and yet, somehow, instead of fighting it out for last place with the seagull guy, I'm in second place, for goodness sake. I'm struggling to understand what happened . . .'

'Well' said Claire 'people saw and heard you on those press conference things and decided you're the only honest and decent person on the ballot. That's what's happening.' Harvey was certainly feeling loved today. 'Everyone at the hospital is behind you and it's not all protest votes either. They want someone local to represent them too and agree with everything you've been saying about not seeing Deakin for dust once he wins. Don't put yourself down, Harvey. You're doing really well because of *you*, not them.'

Harvey didn't agree but appreciated the sentiment. He was actually enjoying the campaigning, having spent every afternoon with Sam, travelling around shopping centres, local parks, pitched in front of the pier or anywhere else that might attract a modest crowd. But suddenly, the TV and press were indeed following him around - filming his speeches and reporting his appearances as if he really was a serious player. He was David in a David and Goliath election - the kind of underdog that the media love. But his nagging concern was that David actually ended up winning – although at least that couldn't happen here, thankfully. Not unless a set of Range Rover keys and a road map of Brighton were found hidden in Deakin's attic.

AS THEY WAITED for the press conference to start, Harvey was feeling far more nervous than normal. This was the first webinar since he had moved up into second place – or rather, Buckland had fallen into third. When he was just the best of the also-rans, he was always fairly relaxed. But now the media was portraying him as the voice of reason, decency and common sense - and the electorate seemed to be responding. He had received so many messages of support. They started in single figures - mostly football or radio fans - but were now pouring in by the thousand from all quarters. It was all very surreal.

He studied the faces of the other candidates on the screen. The *'Stop the Cull'* idiot dressed as a seagull always appeared in full costume. The sight of his head and shoulders – if that's what seagulls have – provided some light relief in the bottom corner of the screen. To date, he hadn't said a word and, unsurprisingly, had not been asked for his views. But Harvey always found it strangely comforting to see him there. It put some perspective on this nonsense. At the end of the day, it was all just a fancy-dress show. A beauty-pageant.

Buckland's face was at the top left of the screen and Deakin was in the top right. Harvey's face was now positioned between them, in the middle. Presumably it reflecting their poll ratings. The other boxes contained the remaining independent candidates, who were either standing to make a nuanced political point or just wanting to get their mugs on TV. Who knows what motivates people to stand for Parliament when they have no chance of winning? God knows what had motivated Harvey himself.

Buckland looked drained, his face staring down at nothing in particular. It was a face of utter dejection.

'We're ready for the first question' said the facilitator, bringing Harvey back into the room. 'Yes, Bill from the *Daily Record.*' Harvey suspected Deakin was about to have a nice easy question teed up for him.

'Thank you' came the reporter's voice. 'Mr Deakin, do you have anything to say about the false allegations circulating about you – apparently without any evidence – claiming that you and the OP were behind Sarah Billingham's death?' Harvey was right. *Over to you Bradley with an open goal to say your piece.*

'Yes, I do' said Deakin, with a serious tone to his voice. The same tone Harvey had often heard him use on *'Speakin' to Deakin'* when introducing a guest with a tragic story to tell. Harvey suspected he could turn it on and off like a tap. 'I'm obviously disgusted at these accusations which, as you kindly point out, are entirely without evidence or substance. I guess I should now wait for Mr Britten to step in– as he usually does about now - to stoically defend one of his beleaguered opponents!'

The was a ripple of laughter. Harvey was a little taken aback. He wasn't sure if Deakin was mocking him or just using him as a foil to detract attention. Was it gentle joshing or deliberate mockery? He also wasn't sure if he was now expected to speak. Thankfully, another reporter stepped in and solved his dilemma, whilst also wiping the smile from Deakin's face. It was the *Daily News* correspondent.

'Amusing as you clearly find Sarah Billingham's murder, Mr Deakin' he said pompously, 'how can you be so sure that *no-one* in your team, your party or any of your fanatical supporters, was responsible for her death? Surely, it's not impossible that some misguided OP supporters were responsible, even if you didn't know about it yourself? This was clearly a well organised, well financed and professional hit without any other apparent motive. No-one else would benefit from her tragic death. No-one but *you*, Mr Deakin. It does therefore beg the legitimate question, doesn't it: why would someone – anyone - else want to murder Sarah Billingham?'

Deakin glanced off camera. Presumably he had his own aides sitting nearby, just as Harvey had Sam. But there were no facts or figures that would help him on this one.

'I can only say again' Deakin replied, returning to his serious voice. 'There is absolutely *no* substance to these vile accusations and that is the end of it.'

'Now you know how I feel' said Buckland, interrupting. He didn't move or look up, which prompted an uncomfortable silence, but he continued. 'For those of us who knew and loved Sarah, this talk of murder is distressing beyond belief. I agree that only someone motivated by a sickening desire to help Deakin in his naked ambition for power would have done this to our wonderful Sarah.' Harvey realised that Buckland was getting tearful. 'And it was so well organised' he went on, 'so well financed, that it can't possibly have been some random fanatical supporter. People have been very quick to believe the shit printed about me, but there's far more here. So, print this headline, you bastards: *do people really want a murderer for their MP?* I sure as hell don't.'

The embarrassed silence returned. Buckland had said his entire piece looking blankly into space rather than at the camera. His accusations, and bad language, had come as a shock and his speech was slightly slurred. Harvey, and doubtless others too, suspected Buckland was drunk - at 10 a.m. in the morning.

'Excuse me!' said Deakin, who now looked, and sounded, indignant and angry. 'This is *not* a kangaroo court and I'm *not* going to take that sort of accusation from someone like Alistair Buckland. A womaniser, a fraud and - I think we can now all see - a drunk. I really don't . . .'

'Oh, this is all very embarrassing,' said Harvey, who found himself stepping in, yet again.

'Oh, look, here he is – right on cue!' said Deakin, sneering.

'Well,' Harvey went on, undeterred. 'This is supposed to be an election for someone to fill Sarah Billingham's enormous shoes. A lady who loved Brighton as much as I do. Who believed in it as a city, as a community and a way of life. But the manner in which my two opponents have dragged this contest into the gutter is an insult to her name, her memory and her legacy. Can we please just stop all this nonsense and focus on the *real* issues that affect Brighton, and stop indulging in accusations and petty point scoring.'

'Well, there's an opportunist party political broadcast if ever I heard one!' said Deakin, now using his sarcastic voice. 'I really must protest . . .'

It would doubtless have gone on, with mud flying in all directions, except that Buckland suddenly stood up and disappeared from the screen. It stopped Deakin in his tracks. Harvey wasn't sure if he would ever come back. The man seemed to be on the verge of a nervous breakdown, unless it was just the drink talking. But Harvey had a disturbing feeling that, whatever the reason, his own poll ratings was likely to go up still further as a result.

48

Derek Walters

THURSDAY 24 APRIL 2025

14 days to go

Derek Walters, Editor of the *Daily News*, stared out of his office window whilst sipping a cup of coffee. The late afternoon sunshine was beaming across the room and he was deep in thought. There was a slight smile on his face, something that had been visibly missing during the early part of the week. This had certainly been an interesting day.

It had been a terrible week for the paper – no question about that. The *Daily Record*'s sensational scoop had sent shock waves throughout the industry and caught its main rival completely off guard. How they had kept the secret beforehand was a mystery to Derek. Whilst he resented their success, he also had a secret admiration for their achievement. He knew the thrill of getting such an exclusive and the nightmare of keeping it quiet until publication. The *Record* had handled it masterfully. Like Alistair Buckland, the *Daily News* had truly been caught with their trousers down.

The paper's owners had, unsurprisingly, giving Derek a hard time about the notable increase in sales and subscriptions being enjoyed over at the *Record*. But Derek knew they would never have allowed *him* to publish the story. The paper was just as loyal a mouthpiece for the POG as the *Record* was for the OP. No way could he have published a story discrediting the POG's candidate and risk handing Bradley Deakin a victory that was now his for the taking. Derek had been desperately encouraging the rumours about the OP being behind the murder conspiracy, but it was all very speculative. He needed something stronger to reign in Deakin's lead, and now looked like he had it. Yes, today was a wonderful day.

HE HAD HEARD a tap on his office door at 9.55 a.m., just as the Brighton press conference was about to start. He'd normally have sent the caller away with a flea in their ear. But it was Toby Shinton, head of the paper's investigations team and a close friend as well as a colleague.

'It had better be quick and bloody important' he'd snapped. 'Looking at Buckland sitting there like a limp lettuce, this is not going to be pretty.'

'Sorry, but I think we've got something big' said Toby. 'We've had another call from someone claiming to be this Gabrielle woman.'

'Oh, God! Tell me its more than that, for Christ's sake!' Derek threw his head back in despair. 'How many does that make this week? Twelve already? All wannabees trying to make a name for themselves - and all fake. Leave me alone!' He waved his hand dismissively and returned his attention to the large media screen on his office wall.

'I know' said Toby, unfazed by the rebuff. 'But I really think this one is the real thing. I'd stake my reputation on it.'

Derek immediately changed his demeanour from contempt to fascination. Toby was the best journalist on his books and didn't make such claims lightly. 'Go on then. What makes you think that?'

'She isn't like the rest' said Toby. 'And I don't think Gabrielle is either. Look, all the kiss and tell merchants we've ever known always have three key objectives - money, self-publicity and . . . money again. We know Gabrielle was paid a mint by the *Daily Record* for sure, but she was unusually keen to keep her identity private. Normally, they're main aim is to become famous . . .'

'. . . infamous' said Derek, cutting in. 'And I believe that's only because she feared for her safety, given the dangerous pondlife apparently included on her list.'

'Well, either way, I don't think she's a chancer like the rest.'

'Your point being?' said Derek who was getting impatient again. The press conference was due to begin any second.

'For a start, all the others sounded too young and – well, like tarts. Not high-class call girl material. Their first question was always the same - how much would we pay for some sleaze or other. But this one was different. Said she'd withheld one story from the *Record* and didn't want any payment from us to publish it.'

'Yea, right' said Derek, cynically. 'What's the catch? Presumably not worth a bean anyway. Or just some disgruntled chancer wanting revenge on an ex-lover.'

'No, it is worth it, trust me.' Toby went on. There was an excitement in his tone that Derek didn't see very often. 'She described how Terry MacDonald followed her home and caught her out. Details no-one else would know.'

'Still speculative' said Derek, unconvinced. 'Could have just made that up to sound more convincing.'

'But they never do, do they?' said Toby. 'And more than that, she spoke affectionately about Buckland. Said she'd been horribly misrepresented and wanted our assurances that, if she gave us this story, we must promise to also redress the lies published about him.'

'Chance would be a fine thing' said Derek. 'It still doesn't prove its her.'

'She said MacDonald just laughed when she complained about him twisting her words. Told her to count her money and forget about it. I just don't see a hoax caller going there, do you? She wouldn't give a number and just said she'd ring back at eleven to speak to you and no-one else. Said if you didn't take the call she'd go elsewhere. I don't know, Del, there was just something about her that rang true. I think you need to talk to her. Please.'

'OK' said Derek. 'Just say I agree, only as a favour to you. Who is it that she so desperately wants to dump on, free of charge?'

49

Bradley

THURSDAY 24 APRIL 2025

14 days to go

'That was outrageous!' said Bradley, as he muted the live feed from his hotel room after the press conference had ended. 'He can't just call me a murderer to my face, can he?'

'I suspect he damaged himself more than he did you' said Peter, who was there with Bradley and Rod. 'He's shown himself to be a drunk. He's washed up. You owe this Gabrielle woman a bunch of flowers, trust me.'

'But he called me a murderer?'

'It's no more than is being said online and elsewhere' said Peter, dismissively. 'Especially on social media.'

Rod looked up from his phone. 'Yes, and the press are already reporting Buckland's performance as a car crash. Sorry, unfortunate analogy. They're focusing on him having a drunken rant. Look.'

He handed his phone to Bradley. It was as Rod described, all negative about Buckland being drunk and little about what he had actually said. But it gave Bradley little comfort.

'Yes, but look' he said, handing back the phone. 'It's also going on about the sainted Harvey Britten being the voice of reason, yet again. I told you he's a threat. This is going to benefit him not me. You mark my words.'

'You're still walking it' said Rod. 'Don't worry. There's no evidence to implicate us in Sarah Billingham's death. Nothing.'

'That's an odd way to put it' said Bradley.

'How'd you mean?' replied Rod.

'*There's no evidence to implicate us.* Rather than, *its nonsense, we had nothing to do with it.* Don't you think?'

Rod looked sulky and uncomfortable, as he had been all day. 'Well, there isn't and we didn't' he said finally. 'It's all bollocks.'

'Are we REALLY certain nobody in this party - or associated with it - had anything to do with her murder?' asked Bradley, looking directly at Rod. 'They're right. It does look like a well-organised and well-funded professional hit, meticulously planned to look like an accident. And it only leaves us – me – who had a motive. She's been projected as an angel with no enemies. Rod – tell me to my face that we had nothing to do with this. That YOU had nothing to do with it.'

Rod actually looked hurt. 'Do you *really* think I would?' he said, suddenly sounding angry. 'That I'd risk prison and my own reputation just to get you elected? Its important to me, yes, but not that important.'

'So, what does *leave it to me* mean?' said Bradley. Whist the cards were out on the table, he may as well give all his concerns an airing.

'What?' said Rod, patronisingly.

'It's what you said when you left the room back in December. Our last meeting before Sarah died.'

Rod sighed, impatiently. 'I told you then that I was finding dirt on MPs who might stand down and . . . well, then she died, so it didn't matter anymore. I resent all this, you know. Deeply resent it.'

'Where's the money?' asked Bradley.

'What?'

'You asked for - and we paid you - £100,000 to get me a by-election. As you say, Sarah then died two weeks later, meaning you didn't need to do anything. So . . . where is the money.'

Rod was getting very frustrated. 'Look, I had a team of very expensive investigators running all over the country digging up dirt. You don't want to know how. That's why it was under the radar. They hadn't been paid yet so the money covered their outstanding bills - not necessarily new ones. It's all gone. Sorry, and you don't want to know where. But I utterly resent these accusations after all I've done for you and this party. You have no idea . . .'

'Well, I'm sorry' said Bradley, still not entirely convinced. 'But you now know what its like to be me - wrongly accused of who knows what.'

'Let's all calm down' said Peter who'd been watching in silence. Bradley knew he shared exactly the same concerns because they had spoken about it yesterday. He was therefore disappointed that his friend had left Bradley to be the bad cop. 'We may never know who did it, but if that is the sworn assurance Rod is now giving us, then at least we know that the OP wasn't involved, nor anyone in this room. So, let's talk about more important things.'

Bradley was not convinced but knew there was little point in throwing accusations around without evidence. There were enough people doing that elsewhere. Whatever his concerns, he needed Rod on side.

'You're right' he said. 'I'm sorry Rod. I just needed to be sure. I'm going to be grilled about this a lot and, well . . .'

'Let's forget about it' said Rod. 'Now, Harvey Britten. As I say, He's nothing. But do you want me to dig around and see if there's any dirt about him that might come in handy? Just in case?'

'Yes, do it' said Bradley. 'Get anything you can. Even saints have secrets.'

50

Alistair

THURSDAY 24 APRIL 2025

14 days to go

'Well, that's it then' said Andrew. 'We may as well call it a day. No-one's going to vote for you now. What the bloody hell were you playing at Alistair? Look at the state of you!'

Andrew had arrived at Alistair's flat just after the press conference ended. Too late. He had been caught up in traffic and Dan was also late because Charlie had been unwell. As a result, Alistair was entirely on his own for the disastrous press conference. Both of them would have stopped him participating if they had arrived in time, seeing how drunk he was before kick-off.

Yet again, Alistair had been awake all night and had drunk a few brandies to calm himself down. He had fallen asleep around four o'clock and then awoken at eight, still slumped on the coach. He didn't feel drunk when he took part in the call - certainly not as bad as he sounded on camera. But he was now all too aware that he had looked and acted like a walking disaster. The bigger problem was that part of him really didn't care anymore. The greater part, in fact.

'Well? Speak to me for God's sake!'

It was fair to say that Andrew was not a happy man. Alistair knew he had gone from hero to zero in under a fortnight and had now slumped still further in the polls. He was a complete liability in Andrew's eyes and no doubt everyone at the centre too.

'I'm sorry' he said, without being able to look Andrew in the eyes. 'I just lost my temper. Its obvious they did it. They must have. Yet they'll get away with it and then that . . . monster will win Sarah's seat. It's wrong, just wrong.'

'So, turning up pissed looking like an unmade bed will convince people of that will it?' snapped Andrew, not in a sympathetic mood. 'I had a call to confirm that no more ministers will be coming down to support you, Definitely not the PM. We've been told to make encouraging noises about Harvey Britten as the only alternative to handing the election to Deakin in a gift-wrapped box. You've turned the government into a laughing stock and this is *not* going to end well for you. You're finished with this party once this election is over with. Finished!'

'So, what can I do?' said Alistair, who looked both lost and defeated. 'I can't withdraw but I can't go on like this. I just feel so . . .'

'You know what Alistair?' said Andrew sharply 'I really don't give a toss how you feel. You lied to me! To my face. You said you had no skeletons in your closet when it had more bones than a butcher's dustbin! And now you're making drunken, murder accusations against your opponent. Yes, I agree they look dodgy, but we can't prove it so you can't just go around accusing rival candidates of murder without a shred of evidence! What is it with you, Alistair? One minute you're Mr Reliable and now you're a basket case.'

'What can I *do*?' said Alistair again. He'd never felt more worthless.

'You can't do *anything*! That's the bloody point!' shouted Andrew. 'We're buggered. Just keep out of the way unless we tell you otherwise and let's hope our core voters will either hold their noses and still vote for the POG – *despite* you, not because of you – or at least defect to Britten. It still won't make much difference. Deakin is knocking on the door of Number 10 and the PM may as well start booking the furniture van.'

AFTER ANDREW LEFT, Alistair felt even more despondent. He poured himself a brandy, using a glass that was still on the coffee table from last night. It was nearly lunchtime and he needed it. Something to mask the constant and endless torment churning in his mind. He wished it would all end and everyone would just leave him in peace.

51

Gabrielle

FRIDAY 25 APRIL 2025

13 days to go

Gabrielle closed the front door behind her and fell back against it. It was done. She had told her Plan B story about Tom to the *Daily News* and handed over the damning evidence to confirm it.

Earlier, she had agreed to meet a journalist called Toby Shinton in a Mayfair hotel room. It felt somehow fitting, given that was her normal environment for meeting men. Toby said it had been hard work convincing his Editor that she really was Gabrielle. Apparently, all sorts of opportunists had been claiming to be her - stupid girls. They had no idea how dangerous it was being her at the moment. The likes of *Big Red* could easily harm an imposter just to send her a message. But, thankfully, none of the girls were good enough liars. Toby said they had all sounded too common. She quite liked him, compared to that other little shit, Terry MacDonald. She believed he would at least print her story as told and not make up their own version, as the *Record* had done.

Toby said he needed to cross-check a few facts and dates but was otherwise delighted. The paper also wanted her to swear an affidavit with a solicitor. She planned to do that on Monday, using the same brief who had handled the payment from the *Daily Record*. He couldn't tell the paper without breaching client confidentiality and, anyway, their deal only covered men who had *paid* her for sex. She did that deliberately, knowing Tom would then fall outside of the condition.

The *Daily News* wanted to pay her for the story but Gabrielle wasn't interested. She was doing it for the right reasons this time - although the million pounds from the *Daily Record* did make it easier to take the moral high ground. The paper was publishing the story next Wednesday - a week before the election - so Gabrielle had booked a Eurostar ticket to France first thing that morning. She wanted to see the reaction but not be around to risk Tom tracking her down, or any of her other client for that matter. He would surely reveal her true identity to the media, meaning *Big Red* and his ilk would be on her case in a heartbeat. She had therefore booked into a hotel at St Pancras Station on Tuesday night, just to be on the safe side.

Sharon had first met Tom in February 1999. She was not old enough to drink alcohol at the time but had befriended Jessica, a girl who lived in a flat down the hall. She was seventeen and they'd first met at the bus stop going to their respective schools. Jess seemed to feel sorry for Sharon, knowing of her mother and the life she led. By contrast, Jess had a settled home life, but never really appreciated it. She was a classic rebel teenager - smoking, drinking and with the suspicion of soft drug use in there somewhere too - but her new best friend was Sharon's passport away from the losers in her own age group.

Because Sharon looked older than her years, especially once Jess helped to perfect her hair and make-up, she had no trouble getting into the pubs and clubs around Uxbridge. Door security rarely turned down a pretty face and, on occasions, the two girls even hit the town in London. Jess was an attractive girl too and they never wanted for male attention. They always had drinks bought for them and, sometimes, Sharon went home alone if Jess got lucky with some lad or other. Sharon never wanted for offers herself, but always said no. She loved the attention but none of the slobbering clowns were ever worth the effort. Until she met Tom.

He had travelled over from Ruislip with friends to celebrate a mate's birthday. He was tall, athletic and he too looked older than his age, never being questioned when buying drinks. He entered the club whilst Sharon and Jess were standing at the bar and she was immediately attracted to the good-looking boy with a gorgeous smile who seemed to ooze self-confidence.

She caught Tom's eye just as quickly as he caught hers. She gave him her 'look,' which was still in development, but worked its magic even then. He found an excuse to come over and they were soon chatting as if they'd known each other forever.

They lived five miles apart but neither had their own transport, so it was not going to be an easy relationship to manage whilst both were still at school. But they spoke on the phone over the next week and hooked up again the following Saturday when Tom came over by bus. They met at the same club and engaged in what her juvenile school friends would call 'serious snogging.' But that was as far as it could go without a venue - or vehicle - in which to do anything more. Sharon did not want to invite a classy boy like Tom back to her mother's grotty flat.

It was Tom's birthday the following Saturday so they planned to go out to celebrate, but he called her on Friday to say that his parents had just rushed off to Birmingham for the weekend. Apparently, his grandmother had suffered a major heart attack or something. It meant he now had the family house to himself, which was way too tempting an offer. Sharon pretended to have a sleep-over with a school friend and packed a bag for the night. Not that her mother cared.

She caught the bus to Ruislip where Tom laid on the full seduction package. Low level lighting, cheap wine, pungent after-shave and Barry White on the CD player. It was cheesy and laughable, but it worked - and would have done if he'd made no effort at all. They slept in his parent's bed.

As she lay in his arms in the half-light, with a second empty bottle of wine beside them, she spotted an odd shaped box on his mother's dressing table. He got up and returned with what turned out to be a Polaroid camera. He had no idea that his parents owned one and they laughed drunkenly at the hideous thought of them engaging in amateur porno shoots.

Selfies were a long way from being commonplace back then, this being eight years before the smartphone was invented. But Tom held the camera at arms-length as they lay on the bed and hit the button. Being taken blind, the resulting photo was slightly off centre but not a bad attempt. Sharon looked a bit confused - not knowing what he was doing and being taken by surprise - whist Tom was smiling like the cat who'd got the cream. He'd drunk far more than Sharon and they both fell asleep shortly afterwards.

Next morning, whilst Tom was taking a shower, Sharon was packing for the trip home when she noticed the Polaroid snap on the bedside table. She smiled at the memory of last night. As far as she was concerned, Tom was 'the one,' the boy of her dreams, straight out of a teenage magazine. She was madly in love and this was a photo of their *'first time'*, something they would one day look at nostalgically whilst their grandchildren played in the garden. She picked up a pen and wrote the date across the white space at the bottom of the Polaroid– February 6th 1999. She intended to treasure the date, the photo and the memory. The day that her blissfully happy life with Tom first began.

The following Thursday, Sharon got off the school bus and was walking back to her block of flats when she saw him. He had bunked off school and come to surprise her with a bunch of flowers as an early Valentine's Day gift. She was in school uniform after an afternoon of netball and looked very much her true age. He was shocked.

When they first met in the club two weeks earlier, she had told him that she was fifteen and would be sixteen in a couple of months. She told all the boys the same thing. Of course, they had celebrated his own sixteenth birthday on that magical night last weekend. But in truth, she was only just approaching her *thirteenth* birthday in April. He was both horrified and angry that she had lied to him. But she had to. He would never have given her the time of day otherwise and, by the end of that first evening, they were getting on so well that it was impossible to tell him the truth. She desperately wanted to see him again and knew he wouldn't agree if she admitted being only twelve at the time.

He had thrown the flowers on the grass and run off. She shouted after him but he just threw his arms in the air dismissively and didn't look back. He wouldn't answer her calls and she didn't see him again until that chance meeting in the department store eight years later. Had he not been buying perfume that fateful day, life might then have been so different. But, instead, he had come back into her life, rekindled the flames into an inferno and she had fallen hopelessly in love with him once again.

But this time it was real, passionate and grown up, not the puppy love of a teenager. Deep and committed love that grew over eight wonderful months. The teenage Sharon, despite her tender age, had actually been right - he was indeed 'the one' who she wanted to spend the rest of her life with. But then he had betrayed her. He was actually living with some girl who she later found out he had gone on to marry. That made it even worse. She both loved and hated him with equal measure, but the latter emotion won the day and she swore to have her revenge. He had driven her to the life she now led - a life wasted when it could have been perfection, with Tom.

Now she was enacting that bitter revenge, eighteen years later. She had handed in her story about Tom to the newspaper - well, a twisted version of it, anyway. It would still serve to destroy his marriage but Plan B went a good deal further and would hopefully repair the harm caused to FG as well. Suddenly, the need to help *him* was far more important than anything else. Far more important than even the truth. So, the die had been irrevocably cast and, for Thomas Bradley Deakin, it would truly be the Judgement Day to end all Judgement Days.

52

Bradley

TUESDAY 29 APRIL 2025

9 days to go

Bradley awoke from a nightmare that involved a flock of angry seagulls swarming around him like an Alfred Hitchcock movie. There were thousands of them, pecking and screaming as he ran for his life, desperately fighting them off. He was relieved to awake and find himself safely tucked up in his Brighton hotel, but unnerved to hear seagulls somewhere in the distance - the downside of booking a sea-view room.

The day started moderately well. The polls had stabilised and he was now sitting on a steady 40% with Harvey Britten on 30% - a ten-point lead that would translate into a comfortable majority at next week's election. Alistair Buckland had slipped to 18% and was no longer a threat. The *Record's* hatchet job, enhanced by his own self-destructive actions, had seen to that. Bradley was amazed that Buckland could still count on even that level of support.

The conspiracy theories about Sarah's murder had rumbled on over the weekend but, thankfully, there was no tangible evidence to directly associate either Bradley or the OP to the alleged crime. But, annoyingly, the story wouldn't entirely go away and, to many on social media, there was no smoke without fire. But Bradley decided not to let it worry him. He got up, dressed and headed off to the station. He needed to be back in London by ten.

IT WAS eleven o'clock when the first salvo of explosive shells landed behind Bradley's lines. He was meeting Rod and the OP marketing team when his phone rang. It was Derek Walters, Editor of the *Daily News*. Bradley had known him for years and they often dined together. He considered him to be a friend.

'Morning Derek, how are you today?' Bradley was careful to always sound upbeat and positive with any journalist.

'Good, thank you, Brad' came the reply, although Derek sounded serious. 'Afraid I have some very bad news for you. We've got a story that we intend to publish about you tomorrow and I need a formal response, if possible. Given its nature.'

Bradley frowned and wondered what further nonsense the POG had dragged up. He beckoned Rod into the next room, where he switched the phone onto speaker. 'I appreciate that consideration' he said, feeling it best to maintain a level of courtesy. 'What's it all about?'

'We've received an allegation of historic sex abuse against you' said Derek. The devastating phrase was left hanging in the air, presumably to gauge his immediate response. Bradley was shell-shocked but managed to keep his composure. He sighed audibly. It must be some long-forgotten fling - another wannabee on a quest for fame by making false allegations. The trouble was, whilst it would obviously prove to be nonsense, even *talk* of some kind of inappropriate fling would be damaging.

'This had better be good' he said, not sure of the best approach.

'You're aware of the woman involved in the Pantsgate saga in the *Daily Record?*' said Derek. 'The lady exotically named Gabrielle?'

'Of course,' Bradley replied. 'But if she's saying I've ever worn underwear like Buckland's, then I'll sue.' He tried to make light of the situation, and felt slightly reassured. He had never paid for sex in his life, so this must all be a misunderstanding.

'No' said Derek, without changing his tone. 'Nothing like that. She's approached us with a story of how you raped her when she was a child. Back then, she was known as Sharon Morgan.'

'WHAT THE BLOODY hell is this all about?' said Peter, via a video conference link. It was thirty minutes after the devastating call from Derek. Peter had only been given the basic details – but enough to get him straight on the phone. 'Tell me it isn't true.'

'Of course it isn't true!' said Bradley, running his hand through his hair in despair. 'It's lies! I can't believe she could say all that.'

'But you did know her when she was a girl?'

'Yes, well . . . briefly, but it wasn't anything like she is saying.' Bradley was in shock. 'Look. I met her in a night-club. I was nearly sixteen and she said she was two months' younger than I was. Honestly. And she actually looked older. She was with a friend who looked about twenty so it didn't cross my mind that it wasn't true. She was mature and almost world weary. We got on well and, yes, we slept together - once. Consensually. Then about a week later I discovered she was only twelve - well, nearly thirteen. But, either way, she lied and tricked me. I was livid and dropped her like a stone. And that was it. No way was it against her will and it abso-lutely was *not* rape.'

'How old were you when you slept with her?'

'It was my sixteenth birthday.'

'And she was only twelve at the time?'

'Nearly thirteen. Just a couple of months away from her birthday in April.' But Bradley knew how it looked.

'Statutory rape applied for anyone under thirteen, consensual or otherwise' said Peter, coldly.

'But it . . . it wasn't like that!' said Bradley, exasperated. 'We were both kids. She claims I invited her to the house, pretending there was a big party, and then forcibly raped her when she got there. That's not how it was at all. She brought an overnight bag with her, for goodness sake! If she'd been fifteen like she told me she was, I believe we'd have gone on to become a real item. I know it. She was . . . special.'

It's her word against yours' said Peter, his mind clearly working on a solution. 'You said they have some photo or you both?'

'I took a Polaroid after we . . .' said Bradley. 'I forgot all about it - even at the time. We were both drunk. She must have taken it home with her, but it was harmless. It seems she has since written the date on the bottom for some reason. God! She was setting me up all along, just like she did with Buckland. Even then, scheming little bitch! Playing the long-game.'

'She's saying Bradley raped her and then took the photo as a trophy' said Rod, quite calmly, given the devastating words he was saying. 'She claims to have stolen it before she got away, was too scared to tell her mother and that Bradley said no-one would believe her anyway. She never told anyone, but wrote the date on the photo to remind her. Worse still, she's saying that it so damaged her that it led to her becoming a prostitute.'

'For God's sake!' said Peter.

'But that's simply not *true!*' shouted Bradley. 'It just wasn't like that! For a start, we met by chance about eight years later when she was working in a department store in Oxford Street. We had a relationship for about eight months! So, she wasn't a hooker then, was she? And we were in love. Really in love. I'd probably be married to her now if she hadn't . . .'

'Hadn't what? Said Rod.

'Found out I was living with Emma. We broke up and . . .'

'Christ!' exclaimed Peter again, wiping his hand across his face as if trying to wash the sorry mess from his mind. 'Can you at least prove you had an affair with her then? It would certainly help to dispute you attacking her as a kid.'

'I don't think so' said Bradley, trying desperately to think.

'Photos?' said Rod. 'There must be photos of you together over those eight months? You were happy enough snapping away when she was a child.'

'No' said Bradley, who resented the jibe. 'If there were, I'm afraid they're long gone. I was . . . discreet, because of Emma.'

'And did Emma know?' said Rod. 'Could she at least confirm you were being unfaithful behind her back with this . . . prostitute?'

'No. And I told you, she was *not* a prostitute!' said Bradley.

'She says she went on the game at eighteen.'

'She . . . wasn't' said Bradley, putting his head in his hands. 'She was selling perfume when I met her. I bumped into her and she was thrilled to see me. I was too. We had a connection . . .'

'Ok' said Peter, sounding more positive. 'First off, let's try and delay the story and buy some time. I'll get the legal team to seek an emergency injunction today. It's salacious, speculative and deliberately intended to damage your campaign, without decisive evidence to support it. Hopefully she looks sixteen or more in the photo, which might at least support your side of the story - a little, although rape is rape at any age. Or we can say she invented the date now to discredit your campaign and make some more money.'

'Apparently she isn't getting paid for it' said Rod. 'She just wants the truth to finally come out, according to Derek.'

'Oh, for fu . . .'

'I'm done for, aren't I?' said Bradley, his head slumped downwards. 'Dirt like this . . . it sticks. History is littered with the broken careers of celebrities hit by historic sex allegations, even if they weren't proven. It's guilty until proven innocent nowadays. The suspicion never goes away. Burying the story is only a short-term solution, especially with the internet. It will still get out there. We *have* to get her to admit that she lied about her age, made up the attack story and crucially had an affair with me later I wasn't to blame. Honestly I wasn't.'

'How can she be taking it to the *Daily News* anyway?' asked Peter. 'I thought the *Record* had her handcuffed to an exclusive deal?'

'Derek said that agreement only covers people who paid her for sex' said Rod. 'Their lawyers are satisfied that this falls outside. Although, the *Record* still won't be happy.'

'She must be easy enough to find' said Bradley. 'She wanted the

Record to keep her name secret, which means she *must* still use it in real life. Her punters may only know her as Gabrielle, but we know who she *really* is. Get someone to trace her address. I want to see her.'

53

Gabrielle

TUESDAY 29 APRIL 2025

9 days to go

Gabrielle put down the phone and was now feeling very nervous - and angry. Derek Walters had just told her that they were obliged to let Tom know about the allegations on the eve of publication so they could include a comment. But it looked like they had told him way too early. They had given Tom enough time to seek an injunction but, worse than that, he had been given a head start in finding her. On the plus side, the injunction had just been refused, so the story would go ahead tomorrow as planned. But that made it even more certain that Tom would now be looking for her. She had to leave for the hotel, straight away. He alone knew her real name, which she still used for bank accounts, Council tax and other formalities. It never really mattered, until now. She was Gabrielle as far as her clients were concerned. But Tom would be looking for Sharon Morgan, and it wouldn't take him long to trace her, especially with the big OP machine behind him.

She quickly packed the rest of her hand luggage so she could leave for the hotel in St Pancras immediately. All the clothes she was leaving behind were too warm for the wonderful climate in the

South of France anyway. Everything she needed was already there waiting for her.

It had apparently been five hours since Tom was contacted. *Five hours!* Derek had left her really vulnerable by not letting her know earlier. She was livid and told him as much on the phone. She didn't think Tom would physically harm her, but couldn't take the chance. She really had no idea how he would react.

She still referred to him as Tom, despite everyone else now knowing him as Bradley. But that was how she knew him and the name of the man who betrayed her. He had started using his middle name in 2009 so Gabrielle had no idea that he'd gone on to become a public figure until about ten years ago. She rarely watched current affairs programmes back then so had not seen him as one of the *Three Amigos*. They were always on TV when she was either working or asleep, anyway.

It was only in the 2015 General Election that she stumbled on him by chance, whilst watching breakfast TV before going to bed after a long night. They were summarising the big Election Night shocks and, suddenly, there was Tom's face. They announced that he had lost his seat and spoke about his TV career. They even showed a clip of the result being announced. 'Thomas Bradley Deakin' stood glum faced as his humiliating defeat received loud cheers. She remembered staring at the screen in shock, shivering at the sight of him after nearly ten years. Older now, and more distinguished than when she had last seen him. But still breathtakingly handsome. She didn't know what to think.

She had immediately *Googled* him to find masses of information. She had never looked him up before and would not have expected to find anything anyway. Yet, there he now was, in all his glory. Idle curiosity was quickly replaced by pure horror. It revealed that he had married this Emma, the brassy looking girl pictured on his phone that day. They even had a son. It was then that jealously consumed her and she first became hell bent on destroying their cosy little marriage. It should have been her, not this smug looking bitch.

She discovered why he had changed his name. Apparently, he'd first stood for Parliament in 2008, a year after their affair. He was still young and was up against a veteran former MP as his opponent. He was apparently an arrogant sod who had given Tom a really hard time - treating him like some little upstart, snapping around his noble heels. During a public debate, he had condescendingly sneered that *'it appears that they'll allow any Tom, Deakin Harry to stand for Parliament nowadays'*. The audience had all laughed and, whenever Tom was then out campaigning, people shouted it at him in the street. As a result, he had started using his middle name in time for the General election in 2010 and had been formally known as Bradley ever since.

After rediscovering him, she started following his career with mixed emotions and increasing animosity. She resented his success, his beautiful wife, cute young son, gorgeous house and huge BBC salary. She knew it should have been *her* reclining beside him in the glossy magazine spreads, beautifully groomed and dressed in designer clothes. His wife was way too chavvy for her liking. Gabrielle would have carried it off with much more class and knew he would have been proud of her. She resented him, hated both him and his tarty wife and often cried herself to sleep over what might have been. It was on nights like these that Plan B was first conceived.

Any thoughts of reconciliation were certainly long behind her. Especially now that she had told lies about him. She hadn't originally intended to. She could have broken up his marriage using Plan A at any time she wanted during the ten years since she rediscovered him. But doing so risked exposing her own identity long before she was ready to launch Sophia's Plan. He was now very famous, so his marriage breakup would inevitably be well publicised. It was sadly far more important to keep her real name safe from her other clients for the time being, so, she instead factored Tom's demise into Sophia's Plan. A bomb that would explode under his perfect marriage as her final act of retribution before she disappeared to safety.

But things had changed and she had now upped the stakes dramatically in the hope of repairing the harm done to FG. Plan B was so explosive that it might even swing the election back in his favour. Of course, it could be too late. But she needed to tell the world that Alistair Buckland was actually the good guy and his rival was the real villain. She justified her actions by convincing herself that Tom deserved nothing less. But she did feel a twinge of guilt, it was one hell of an accusation.

As she was zipping up her bag to leave, the door buzzer suddenly sounded, making her jump. She ignored it but it rang again, longer this time. She went to the entry phone fearing the worst - and was right. A familiar face was staring back from the screen. Too late. It was Tom.

54

Bradley

TUESDAY 29 APRIL 2025

9 days to go

Bradley's day had gone from bad to worse. The final blow had been hearing that the emergency injunction had been refused. The judge concluded that publication was in the public interest, given that his accuser had sworn an affidavit yesterday and the photographic evidence was felt to be compelling.

Bradley was looking at the damning Polaroid on his tablet now. It was the first time he had seen it in some twenty-six years. Even at the time, he didn't really remember taking it. He wasn't good at holding his drink at that age and was trying to impress Sharon. The photo showed him beaming into the camera with a stupid, smug grin on his face. The face of a teenage lad who had just got laid on his birthday.

He also looked pissed, which he was. But his own appearance wasn't really the problem. It was Sharon. She looked serious and stern faced, which he knew was only because she had been caught by surprise. A brief moment of confusion caught on film forever, just before she burst out laughing. But to anyone looking at it today, in the context of the evil story she had now concocted, it was possibly a look of fear or even intimidation. A scared little girl alongside a boy with the look of a predator. Above all, Sharon looked young. Way more than he remembered at the time. But then, he was young too. Teenagers look old to each other but young to their parent's generation, whilst middle-aged people look young to each other and absolutely ancient to youngsters. He was now forty-two - not sixteen - and she looked bloody young. But not twelve for goodness sake! Not even thirteen. Fifteen? Perhaps, at a push, but certainly not seventeen or eighteen, as he'd thought at the time. Bloody idiot.

Back then, he was just a horny lad who had met a gorgeous, confident girl of around his own age and who was well up for sleeping with him. But now she looked like a pretty young kid - wide eyed and innocent. Or was he just looking at it with the same jaundiced view that everyone else now would - after Sharon had so horribly distorted the real truth.

He didn't remember much about the actual night but knew for a fact that he hadn't forced himself onto her. She was all over him and, next morning, they were like two lovebirds. Just as they were on the phone over the next few days. He'd been mortified when he found out how young she really was. She'd screamed after him, pleading for him not to leave her and saying that she was sorry. Begging him and grabbing his arm in the street. He'd had to shake her off to get away. Would she have done all that if he had forcibly raped her as she now claimed? No, it was a lie. A filthy, evil lie. She must have taken the photo home as a souvenir and added the date as a reminder of their first time. The date now staring back at him from the screen. In that child-like handwriting. *Oh God!*

He really couldn't understand why she was doing this to him. They'd been so happy when they met again, eight years later, and the past was instantly forgotten. She was 21 and absolutely *not* a prostitute. No way. They would still be happy now if it wasn't for his stupidity and that bloody I-Phone. So, what was she up to - twisting the truth like this? Was she now a POG activist? Was she planning to press charges? He could go to prison for goodness sake! Rod suddenly rushed in.

'We've tracked her down' he said, excitedly. 'There are twenty-four Sharon Morgans registered in London for council tax or on the electoral roll, and we've looked into them all. Once you discount those who are married or the wrong age, it comes down to three. Two have social media accounts and their histories don't match - which leaves just one. She lives in Paddington, is thirty-eight and there's very little known about her. Which makes it even more likely to be her. I'm 99% certain it's our girl.'

'Brilliant. I think I should see her in person.'

'Quite right' said Rod. 'But we don't have a phone number anyway. It will be harder to lie if she's staring you in the face. Get her to call the paper in front of you if you can. Just do whatever you have to. Charm the pants off her – literally if you must.'

Bradley was not sure how he would play it after all these years. Being civil to someone who was trying to ruin his life would be difficult, leaving aside all the emotion and history between them. This would need every ounce of his diplomacy.

'OK. Tell me the address' he said.

'You can get it in the car' said Peter. 'There's one outside waiting to take you there. Good luck, Bradley. Do whatever it takes. Just get her to put a stop to this.'

HE PAUSED for a moment on the doorstep. He hadn't seen Sharon for some eighteen years and had no idea how she would react. He feared she wouldn't even open the door but, either way, he felt strangely nervous. Scared even. There was so much resting on this going well. He hit the buzzer for Flat 2, waited a while and got no reply. Was she in? Rod believed she would be. Laying low and certainly not working. He hit the buzzer again. Longer this time. Suddenly – unexpectedly – the speaker crackled into life.

'I don't want to see you' came the voice. He knew it was Sharon, despite the distortion.

'Please' he said, turning on the charm, with his voice as calm as he could make it. 'I just want to talk. Quietly, between the two of us, just to sort this out. I think you owe me that, at least, don't you? Sharon?'

It went quiet again, for what seemed like a lifetime, and then the door burst noisily into life. He pressed against it, hard, with his shoulder - not wanting to miss the chance and have to buzz again. Once inside, he jogged up the stairs rather than take the lift. There were only two doors on the first-floor landing, one either side of the central staircase. The door to Flat 2 remained closed, at first, but then opened very slightly - clearly on a chain. Through the narrow gap he could see her - Sharon Morgan. Those eyes still as big and bright as they always were, but now looking different. More world weary. Frightened.

'Hi, stranger' he said, the charm cranked up to the max and a fake smile forced onto his face. It was his showbiz smile, used to disguise his true feelings in any situation. 'Don't be scared, I'm not going to hurt you Sharon. I promise. You know I couldn't *ever* do that, don't you? I just want to talk – to clear all this up. Please?'

She shut the door, which could have gone two ways, but went the right one. He heard her dislodge the chain before opening the door fully. She still looked gorgeous, despite the hate he felt for her at that moment. Still the beautiful girl he had fallen in love with all those years ago. Only now she was a mature woman. A few laughter-lines stretched from the sides of each eye, but he suspected laughing hadn't caused them. Apart from that, she was unblemished.

She turned and walked the few steps into her lounge, which was neat and bright but lacking any character. There were no photographs, trinket or other personal possessions to speak of. Nothing to give a hint of her own personality. 'Soulless' was the best way to describe it.

'I'm in a hurry so make it quick' she said finally, a cold edge to her voice. She didn't offer him a seat, but Bradley sat on the couch anyway. Almost reluctantly, she took the armchair opposite him.

'Thank you for seeing me' he said. 'Truly. It's been a long time and, believe it or not, I'm actually pleased to see you. I never really got the chance to apologise for being such a complete tosser, back then.'

She didn't move a muscle in her face, simply looking at him - or through him.

'I know its ancient history but . . .'

'It is' she said.

'. . . but I really did love you, Sharon. I honestly planned to leave Emma for you. I came around to tell you . . . explain and make up . . . but you'd gone. I searched everywhere. I never forgot you or stopped regretting how stupid I was. I know I must have hurt you because I know how much I hurt myself . . .'

She looked slightly uncomfortable, finally breaking her stare and looking towards the window. He wondered if she, perhaps, had a tear in her eye and didn't want him to see. He was actually telling the truth. Up until this morning, he had often dreamed of having this conversation. Of even getting back together with her, sometimes. But things had changed since then and now he was definitely *not* looking for a reconciliation. The woman must now be deranged.

'You broke my heart' she said finally, looking down into her lap. Hopefully there was regret in there somewhere.

'I broke my own too' he said, keeping to the same theme, as it seemed to be working. 'I'd do anything to turn back the clock. But I can't. I made a *huge* mistake and have lived with it ever since. But I just don't understand why you're doing this to me now. You know its not true, Sharon. That it wasn't anything like how you've told it to the newspaper?'

'I was twelve!' she said, still not looking him in the eye. 'By law it counts as statutory rape. I've looked it up. You were sixteen and took advantage of me.'

'You know that's not true!' he said, slightly raising his voice but pulling back, just in time. 'You told me you were fifteen and you looked every day of it. Well, when you were dressed up to go out you did. I'd never have . . .'

'Yeah, well, whatever' she said, shrugging her shoulders.

'But why make it sound so . . .' he tried to find the words. 'And why are you denying that we had a relationship later? If it meant so much to you - broke your heart as you say – why are you are denying that those wonderful months ever happened? Just to give credibility to the lies about when you were . . . twelve? I really don't see what this is all about, Sharon. Please, help me understand. You know what it will do to me if this is published don't you? I'll be finished. Not just this election, but my whole TV career too - everything. People believe these allegations regardless of whether . . .'

'I was twelve!' she said again, but with less emotion. 'It's not an allegation, it's a fact.'

'But not like you told it!' He took a deep breath to keep his tone calm. 'I did not force myself on you like you are saying. I never conned you into coming over by saying it was a party. None of that is true is it? So why say it? We had a magical night until . . .'

She said nothing for a while until muttering 'you hurt me' again, under her breath.

'When are we talking about now? When you were twelve or twenty-one?'

'Both' she said. 'I . . . loved you.'

At last! A breakthrough. She admitted that they'd known each other later. He wished he was recording this. *Damn.*

'And I loved you too' he said. 'Until this morning I'd . . . still have . . . but . . .'

She looked at him. He felt she was checking his face to see if was true. Perhaps she was hoping it *was* true. From hope might come regret.

'Still have what?' she said.

'Would have left my wife and started over with you. If you'd wanted to. But not now . . .'

'You turned me into what I am' she said, as if not wanting to hear it. 'I loved you and you broke my heart and my soul. That's why I do what I do. You made me a whore! You made me feel worthless and hate myself. Whilst *you* had it all. SHE had it all. The money, the fame, the house, the . . . family. It should have been me! But no . . . *this* is me!' She pointed to herself and he now knew what this was all about. She was jealous. A festering jealousy that had taken eighteen years to explode.

'Look' he said. 'I see that I hurt you even more than even I realised. But, like I said, I'd have preferred it to be you beside me. Not Emma. But I can't change the past, I can only apologise for it. But *you* can change the future. Do you *really* hate me – and resent Emma – so much that you'd destroy my whole life with these lies? Please, Sharon, I'm begging you. Call the paper and tell them the truth. I'm not the first man to screw up the chance of happiness through his own stupidity, and won't be the last. I've paid for it already - dearly - by not having you in my life. But do I really deserve *this*? Please don't destroy me.'

She looked at him, expressionless. *What is she thinking?*

'OK' she said, slowly, and with a big sigh. 'But if I call them, I want you to leave and then I never want to see you again.'

'That I can do' he said, trying to mask his utter relief. 'I'm so sorry it came to this. If I'd only met you again at some other time in my life . . .' She picked up her mobile and dialled a number. 'Thank you so much, Sharon' he said. 'If there's anything I can do . . .'

She looked at him with those eyes and he tried not to think about them. They were hypnotic, but the moment broke as she looked away, presumably because someone answered the phone.

'I need to speak to Derek Walters' she said formally. 'Urgently, please. Yes . . . its Sharon Morgan. He'll know what it's about. Thank you.' She listened and then her shoulders slumped. 'OK, but can you please tell him to call me back urgently? He has my number. Yes, thank you.' She hung up. 'He's on a conference call to New York but she'll get him to call me back as soon as he's finished. But I think you should leave now.'

'Yes, of course' said Bradley, leaping to his feet. He would have preferred to hear her sort it out in front of him but, even so, he felt confident she was now on side. He had dodged a bullet.

'Thank you, Sharon. It was . . . really good to see you again, despite everything. You look after yourself. And like I say, if there's *anything* I can do to help you in *any* way, just . . .'

She said nothing and led him to the front door. As he stepped outside, he looked back. But the door shut behind him before he had chance to say another word. She was obviously a disturbed woman.

Had he really done that to her? That beautiful, fragile, but genuinely wonderful girl he had known and loved all those years ago? He tried not to think about it. He walked down the stairs, taking out his phone on the way to call Rod with the good news.

As he opened the front door, a man in a black leather jacket was coming in. Distracted by the call, he thought nothing of it and let the man pass. In doing so, he unknowingly ripped up his '*get out of jail free*' card.

55

Gabrielle

TUESDAY 29 APRIL 2025

9 days to go

Gabrielle shut the front door and started shaking, not knowing how she had managed to keep it together. The sight of Tom after so many years sent all sorts of emotions screaming around her body. Anger, love, hatred, fear . . . love.

She had not wanted to let him in. She feared he would grab her by the throat or something. Why wouldn't he? But, instead, he'd been polite, considerate - caring even. But then, he needed something from her. The two options were to use either threats or charm to get it - and he had chosen the latter approach. He hadn't exactly grovelled in the way she would have liked. Down on his knees, begging her forgiveness - in tears. That's how she had always imagined it would be. How it *should* have been.

She wondered if he was sincere in what he said. Had she perhaps been too hard on him? Should she have given him another chance, all those years ago, rather than run away? She wasn't lying when she said his betrayal had steered the whole direction of her life. But, why did she throw it all away so easily? Was that down to him, or her? Who was the bigger fool?

Either way, it was done. Whilst she felt *some* sympathy and regret, it was more important to help FG than dwell on what might have been with Tom. FG had *never* betrayed her like Tom had done. Instead, she had betrayed *him*. The only way to turn that around was to destroy Tom. She had no choice. Things were no longer in her control. And it was too late to go back anyway. How could she tell Derek that it was all a pack of lies? She had just sworn an affidavit. They would just say Tom had intimidated her and she was scared. It was in their own interest – in their candidate's interest – for it all to be true.

She had pretended to call the paper but, instead, had dialled her messaging service. She had to get Tom out of the flat and it seemed to be the easiest way. There would be no return call from Derek. No retraction. So, she had to get the hell out of the country before Tom found out the truth. It was time to turn a new page – start a new life. Forget the past and everyone in it – Tom, FG, all of them. Starting right now.

There was a knock on the door. It took her by surprise as no-one had buzzed from outside, so she assumed it must be Tom again. She felt anxious. Had he forgotten something? Perhaps a coat or his phone? She glanced around, but there was nothing. She really didn't want to let him in again, but there was another knock - not aggressive, but certainly impatient. She had no choice but to answer. She didn't want to make him suspicious, but she wouldn't let him in this time. She would see what he wanted and then get rid of him as soon as possible. She opened the front door but, this time, fatally, did so without the chain.

56

Bradley

TUESDAY 29 APRIL 2025

9 days to go

Bradley was with Peter and Rod in a wine bar just off Trafalgar Square. He felt more relieved than he could ever remember. It was nearly 7 p.m. but, whilst their spirits were high, there was not quite a celebratory mood. Rod was constantly checking his phone and didn't look entirely comfortable. He was paranoid that someone at the *Daily News* would leak the story anyway and, worryingly, they had yet to receive confirmation that the paper had spiked it. But Bradley believed Sharon and was sure that all was well. He had seen that look in her eyes. It was still there, that special bond between them.

'Should we call them?' asked Peter. 'I'd feel better knowing for certain.'

'We can't let them know that Bradley spoke to her' said Rod. 'They'd think he must have forced her to retract under duress – meaning it might still be true. She did swear that bloody affidavit after all, so they'll take some convincing. Thank God they didn't pay her.'

Right on cue Bradley's phone rang. It was Derek from the *News*.

'Hi Derek, thank you for calling back,' answered Bradley, slipping effortlessly into charming politician / broadcaster mode.

'Have you got that comment for me now, Bradley?' came the cold reply. 'We agreed seven o'clock was the deadline before we print the story without one.'

Bradley's jaw fell open. 'Sorry? You mean you're still going to publish?'

'Of course,' said Derek. 'The injunction failed. You know that, and . . .'

'But she called you!' Bradley saw Rod's face tense, but he had no choice but to say.

'Sorry, what?'

'I . . . I spoke to her. Met her, just to clear this all up. It's all lies. She called your office in front of me at about 4.15 or so. You were on a conference call to New York and . . .'

'I haven't had a conference call all day - New York or otherwise. I've been right here at my desk. She neither called me or left a message. Now, do you have a comment or not?'

Bradley was shaking. He covered the mouthpiece and told the others what he'd just heard.

'Stall him' said Rod. 'Tell him we need an hour. Let's get over to see the bitch.'

'Can you give me one more hour, Derek? Please? I swear I'm telling the truth. Come on, we're mates. I swear on my son's life that she admitted it was not true and promised to call you . . .'

There was a brief pause. 'OK, one more hour, but that's it I'm afraid. We're then putting you down as a *no comment.*'

'At the very least it is a *categorically denied all the allegations!*' Bradley retorted, but then took a deep breath. 'OK, thank you, Derek. Sincerely, I owe you. I'll call you at eight o'clock sharp - if not sooner.'

THEY GRABBED a taxi and headed for Sharon's flat. The traffic was heavy around Trafalgar Square and it took an age to go anywhere as the West End was gridlocked. Perhaps they should have taken the tube. Bradley checked his watch almost every minute. At 7.35 they were still dodging around the back streets of Mayfair to avoid Park Lane.

It was another ten minutes before they reached Kendal Street. Bradley was tense, irritable and sweating. He only had fifteen minutes to turn this around, but the traffic was even at a stand-still in this stupid little side road. He threw open the car door.

'I'll go on foot!' he said, and was gone before they could answer. He started to run alongside the row of stationary cars, dodging pedestrians and moving as fast as he could. Then his heart stopped dead as Sharon's block came into view. There were three police cars in the road outside, all with blue lights flashing. They were strewn across the road, which explained the traffic queue. He just stared open mouthed at the scene - now a crime scene, judging by the blue tape strung across the pavement either side of Sharon's front door. He turned in despair and trudged back towards the taxi. Peter and Rod were jogging towards him and met him half way.

'What's going on?' said Peter.

'It's over.' Bradley replied.

57

Harvey

WEDNESDAY 30 APRIL 2025

8 days to go

'Bloody hell!' said Harvey as he watched the TV screen. 'Claire! Come quick!'

He was making breakfast and, unusually, Claire was up early too, having been woken by the birds singing in the garden. She came through to the kitchen, looking concerned.

'It's Bradley Deakin . . . look!' said Harvey, trying to hear what was being said whilst updating his wife at the same time. He decided he should do the latter first.

'Apparently, that prostitute who did the dirty on Buckland is now accusing Deakin of raping her when she was twelve! There's a photo of them together at the time. The bastard took it as some form of trophy, apparently.'

'No!' said Claire.

'Then it looks like he went to shut her up yesterday, and now she's gone missing. There's blood in her flat and it's a right mess. The police fear for her safety and are apparently questioning him. Jesus! What *is* going on with this bloody election!'

Claire said nothing and stared at the TV screen in disbelief. The kettle boiled and switched itself off - tea could wait. The TV flashed a still shot of the *Daily News* front page with the banner headline: '*Deakin's child rape shock*' above a grainy photograph of Bradley - young but clearly still him - smiling arrogantly at the lens. The photo was taken at a forty-five-degree angle and, alongside Deakin's head, was the face of a young girl. It was hard to tell her exact age or whether she looked serious, frightened, curious or all three. But, apparently, the date on the photo confirmed she was only twelve when it was taken - on his sixteenth birthday. The fading ink had apparently been analysed and was definitely written at least twenty years ago. But no-one seemed to be doubting the authenticity of the photo or the date and, therefore, the story itself.

Deakin had apparently spoken to the *Daily News* last night and admitted trying to see Gabrielle yesterday afternoon, claiming she had then retracted the story. When told by the *News* that she had not done so, he became angry and they worried he was going to harm her. They called the police who then found the door open with signs of a struggle. There was blood splattered on a wall and they also found Gabrielle's passport in her real name, Sharon Morgan. Police are appealing for witnesses, fearing for her safety.

'Bloody hell' Claire said finally. 'I don't like him but I didn't have him down as a paedophile.'

'Just like the rest,' said Harvey. So many of their TV heroes from the seventies and eighties had fallen from grace, exposed for various historic sex offences. Whilst the flow had died down in recent years, he wondered if another generation was still to face the music. *What is it with these people?*

'So, what'll happen now?' said Claire. 'If he's charged, presumably the election can't go ahead, can it?'

'I'm not sure' said Harvey. 'I really hope not. If it does, it could be a disaster.'

'Why?' said Claire.

'Because, at this rate, I might end up winning the bloody thing, that's why.'

58

Bradley

THURSDAY 1 MAY 2025

7 days to go

If Tuesday had been the worst day of Bradley's life, he realised it was actually only the warm-up act for Wednesday. That really *was* the worst day, being largely spent in the police station and various crisis meetings.

After they left Kendal Street on Tuesday night, Peter insisted that they all return to Party HQ and set up a crisis centre. The traffic had not eased and it took them another forty minutes to reach the offices in Pimlico. Bradley had called Derek from the car at eight o'clock and he didn't sound surprised that the police were at Sharon's flat. As he later found out, it was Derek who actually called them. Some friend he was. Bradley suspected it was just a way to twist the sizeable knife that the *Daily News* had plunged between his shoulder blades.

The police arrived at Party HQ at around 11 p.m. having called an hour beforehand to arrange it. Bradley had willingly gone with them to Paddington Green Police Station and, thankfully, there were no press outside to photograph him being loaded into the car. At least he hadn't been taken away in handcuffs.

At the station, he was questioned under caution by a DS Gordon and DS Mohammed. The interview was taped and Bradley declined a solicitor. Peter felt that was a mistake, but Bradley didn't want to look as if he had anything to hide. He hoped that he'd made the right choice and – given he was later released without charge – it looked like he had. But they had only questioned him about Sharon's disappearance, not the rape allegations. For now.

He had given the police details about his movements on Tuesday. Records from the original driverless taxi confirmed the trip to Sharon's flat and, thirty minutes later, CCTV showed him hailing a cab on the busy Edgware Road to come back. Payment records confirmed taking Bradley to the bar in Trafalgar Square, so he could at least prove that he had not personally abducted Sharon in the afternoon. That was one positive.

The wine bar's CCTV confirmed that he was there with Rod and Peter until seven and the timescale between then and the police arriving at Sharon's flat at 7.20 p.m. proved he could not have got there before them. But there were no CCTV cameras in Kendal Street, nor in or around Sharon's block of flats. Nothing to show who was responsible for the attack or what had then happened to her. Unsurprisingly, social media trolls were drawing their own conclusions. Bradley must have used a highly trained team of thugs to do his dirty work for him. After all, he'd used them to kill Sarah so must have sent the same boys round to attack poor Sharon too. Throw in the accusations of child rape and he was now the embodiment of Satan.

It was unbelievable how judgemental people can be without any understanding of the facts. He began to feel some sympathy for Alistair Buckland who had been through the same ringer himself in recent weeks. No wonder the guy had hit the bottle afterwards.

In the eyes of the law, at least, the police had said publicly that Bradley was not currently a suspect in Sharon's disappearance. 'Currently' was not the complete vindication he would have liked - but it would have to do. And there was also the small matter of being accused of child rape. For now, given that Sharon had not lodged a formal complaint with the police – only a newspaper –

they intended to hold fire with any investigation until they could speak to her in person. Again, it was not the vindication Bradley would have liked but at least he was a free man. Again, for now.

Meanwhile, Sharon was still nowhere to be seen. Her clothes, passport and handbag were still in the flat. It did not appear that she had simply moved out, especially as the blood found on the wall was her group. The splatter pattern suggested she had been struck in the face, further raising concern for her fate.

None of her neighbours heard anything and said she generally kept herself to herself. There was no blood or other evidence or witnesses to suggest that a body had somehow been removed via the front door or rear fire escape, especially in broad daylight on a fairly busy street. It suggested that she must either have been abducted or left of her own free will. For now, the police were treating it as a kidnapping and looking for the man in black leather who Bradley had passed on the way out. The fact that 'men in black' were again involved further added to the online conspiracy theories.

The impact on the overnight InstaPoll was depressing but not unexpected. Bradley's rating had taken a serious hit. His previous 40% polling had halved to 20% - falling off a cliff even faster than the car that hit Sarah. But he saw it as a blessing that he'd even clung on to 20%. Just as he'd marvelled at Buckland retaining a similar level of support after all the allegations levied against him, now one in five OP supporters were *still* willing to vote for an alleged paedophile rapist and double murderer. If he had not been directly involved himself, he thought this would make an interesting debate on his show – what exactly *would* it take to stop party loyalists, on either side, from voting for their candidate? But that could wait. For now, it was all too real and too personal.

Thankfully, most of the OP voters who *had* turned away from him, appeared to be identifying themselves as 'don't knows' rather than choosing another candidate. For now. Bradley knew they would never turn to Alistair Buckland so there was only one likely recipient - Harvey Britten. But *his* rating had only increased by seven points. Still enough to now place him in the lead, but offering some hope that loyal OP supporters were not exactly organising buses over to his camp - yet.

He wondered whether he could get them back in time, especially with only a week until the election. He was kidding himself to think that would be easy. In fact, it looked impossible. The rumours would continue to circulate unless, or until, Sharon turned up safe and well. Only *she* could clear him of both the abduction and rape accusations. *Where the hell was she?*

He was not facing imminent prosecution on either front for now so, after frantic consultation with the Electoral Commission, the Acting Returning Officer in Brighton, Lionel Montague, decided that the election must therefore proceed. That despite *both* the two main party candidates being badly holed below the waterline and looking for a way out. Ironically, when the POG sought to have the election declared void last week, the OP had successfully objected – something Bradley now regretted. But worse than that, even if he lost the election and decided to then forget all about politics, he wasn't sure whether his TV career would now survive. Child rape was the worst possible accusation and the public were unforgiving. The BBC had yet to comment, only saying that they were 'monitoring events.' It did not bode well.

And if all that wasn't enough, there was then the small matter of Emma to deal with. In order to defend the rape accusations in public, he would have to tell her about the affair with Sharon in 2007. It was a matter of public record that he was engaged to Emma at the time and that they married six months later. Emma would not like that revelation one little bit. She would think that he only married her on the rebound. And perhaps he had. He would speak to her tonight. The perfect end to a perfect day.

59

Alistair

SATURDAY 3 MAY 2025

5 days to go

'Is that a seagull or a flying pig, up there over the Channel?' said Andrew, looking out of the window with an air of disbelief in his voice. 'Alistair, believe it or not, you could still win this! The POG's internal polling suggests that people's attitude towards you is mellowing, what with Deakin's exposure as a nonce and possible kidnapper. Suddenly, Gabrielle is a victim and that makes you more palatable too. She did you a *huge* favour before she . . .'

Alistair knew what he meant. Despite her betraying everything that he held dear – being their relationship – he still worried about her safety. On the plus side, the *Daily News* story had painted an entirely different picture of Alistair to the smears published in the *Daily Record*. Gabrielle portrayed him as a thoroughly decent man who deserved to win the election. She claimed to have come forward only because she felt it wrong for Deakin to triumph, given his own heinous crimes. That was more the Gabrielle that Alistair knew. Perhaps she had actually been forced to expose him by that slime-ball at the *Daily Record*, who had then twisted her words to make him look bad. That *was* the whole purpose of the exercise after all.

But where was she now? The hospitals, airports and Channel ports had shown no trace. Was she being kept prisoner? Or worse, had she been shut up for good? And was Deakin – or at least his party – behind it all, just as they were behind Sarah's murder?

'Hopefully, she'll turn up' said Dan, interrupting Alistair's train of thought. But he didn't sound convinced. 'And Andrew's right, Gabrielle may well have saved your skin. On balance, POG voters seem to be warming to the idea that you are not as bad as you've been portrayed. That you had a *real* relationship with Gabrielle, not just a sleazy sex scandal. If you could just . . .'

'. . . get your bloody act together and put some fight back in you' said Andrew.

Alistair had not looked at either of them throughout the conversation. Andrew and Dan had come to his house for an urgent meeting. It was the first time Alistair had seen Andrew all week. The party had dropped him like a hot potato. He was an embarrassment and they had written him off as a lost cause. But suddenly, there was a chance of turning it all around. Now, here he was, just as if nothing had happened. But it had.

'So' said Alistair 'you're saying my name's not a dirty word around Westminster any more. Is that right?'

He was still looking at the floor. It was ten o'clock in the morning and he had a monster headache, having drunk himself to sleep again last night. He knew it was wrong, but he didn't care anymore. He had actually stopped looking at social media. It was like self-flagellation to read the filth people were still firing at him. But he'd become immune to the abuse and death threats. He almost wished someone would carry them out.

'You were a loser pitted against a winner, before this' said Andrew, damning him with false praise. 'Now you're a loser pitted against an even bigger loser. Worse than that - against a murdering paedo loser. Your crimes pale into insignificance by comparison to Deakin's. The feedback we're getting from the polls now is that - *OK, so he slept with a prostitute and fiddled his expenses a bit – but at least he didn't kill or rape anyone.* Yes, I know that's a depressing way to select an MP, essentially picking the least-worst candidate. But even so, your poll rating has shown a slight improvement and now you're in second place to Harvey Britten. If we could only bring him down too . . .'

'Hang on' said Dan. 'Last week you were looking to shepherd disgruntled POG voters into Britten's camp as a safe haven from Bradley Deakin. Now you want to discredit him too?'

'Politics' said Andrew, shamelessly. 'We got some dirt on him a while ago, in case we ever needed to use it. And now we do.'

'Being what?' said Alistair, finally making eye contact.

'We put out a call, locally, to see if there was anything on him' said Andrew, again without any sign of shame. 'It wasn't easy. The guy seems to lead a fairly boring life. But one of our local activists came up trumps and the *News* is going to publish it in their Sunday edition tomorrow.'

'What is it?' said Alistair, again. He actually didn't like the idea of attacking Britten. He seemed a decent enough man and his wife was friendly with Sarah. If Alistair couldn't win the seat himself, then Britten was still a good alternative, in his book, and he was sure Sarah would agree.

'Wait and see' said Andrew. 'There's something more important that I need to discuss with you, anyway.' Alistair looked back at the floor. 'You recall that the Public Affairs guys were trying to arrange an interview for you to put your side of the story, once the *Daily Record* had finished with you? But then you had your drunken rant so it all looked like it would be a waste of time - and the TV companies weren't interested anyway.'

'So?' said Alistair.

'Well, after the revelations about Deakin hit the fan, the OP has asked for a chance to put *his* case and the TV companies want to do it. But it means they will have to give equal time to the other main candidates too. They have proposed a prime time, live BBC interview with all three of you on Tuesday. It's a great opportunity to rehabilitate you Alistair. Huge.'

'Three candidates?' said Alistair.

'Sadly yes.' Said Andrew. 'Obviously, Deakin is the one they all want but, in the interest of balance, they have to give equal billing to you and Harvey Britten as well. He's got to be there too, sadly, given that he's now ahead in the polls. But he'll have some humble pie to eat himself, after tomorrow's revelations. He just doesn't know it yet!' Andrew laughed. It was all a game to him.

'So' he went on, calming down and suddenly adopting a serious face. 'We've got to get you fully match fit within four days. The PR guys are on the way over to prepare you. We're setting up a dummy interview to put you through your paces. This is the most important moment of your life and you *cannot* blow it Alistair. Do you hear me? It's a long shot, but you could still pull this out of the fire at the eleventh hour.'

Alistair continued to sit motionless. The fight had gone out of him just as the party now wanted to re-ignite it. He had no choice but to go through with the charade, but the idea unnerved him. 'Just tell me what you want me to do' he replied. There was no point arguing.

'First off' said Andrew 'someone needs to stay with you between now and Tuesday to keep an eye on you. No drinking, plenty of rest and tidy yourself up. We're also getting you some help to sort out your . . . mental issues. I'm sorry Alistair. All this can't have been easy for you and perhaps we haven't been as supportive as we could have been.'

Alistair looked up and gave the nearest thing to a smile for two weeks. But there was no pleasure behind it. It was a wry, contemptuous smile. The party had abandoned him in disgust and were now back on the case as if nothing had happened. Business as usual – no hard feelings.

'But that's all behind us now' Andrew continued, clearly embarrassed. 'We go forward. Deakin's a dead duck, no matter what he says on Tuesday. Its too late to change people's minds at such short notice. Even if the jury is still out about his involvement in Sarah's death, they certainly think he's done something to Gabrielle, regardless of what the police say. Provided she doesn't turn up before Tuesday and give him a defence, of course. Let's hope she doesn't.'

Alistair could not believe Andrew was being so callous. 'But even if she does' Andrew went on 'it won't change the stigma of a rape allegation. That's what will do for him.'

'So, you want Alistair to focus on Harvey Britten, presumably?' asked Dan.

'Yes' said Andrew. 'Put yourself back in the frame as the best local candidate for Brighton. Britten's a one trick pony and has nothing to offer other than being a local boy. But so are you, Alistair. We need to milk that more than anything.'

'So, it will all just go away if I turn up in a blue and white Seagulls' scarf carrying a stick of Brighton rock. Is that the case?' said Alistair, sarcastically.

'Well, of course you'll need to defend yourself against the Pantsgate stuff' said Andrew. 'But the association with Gabrielle will be easier now. Gloss over paying her for sex – just focus on the strengths of your relationship. God, my marriage didn't last as long as you did with her! And pound for pound the divorce probably cost me more! Perhaps you're not such an idiot seeing prostitutes after all.'

Alistair couldn't be bothered to correct the mistaken plural again. If Andrew was trying to cheer him up, then it certainly wasn't working.

'*I'll* stay with him' said Dan, getting back to the plan. 'My parents will happily have Charlie until Tuesday. I think Alistair needs a friend to support him - not psychologists and minders. I'll make sure he's a good boy and I'll be sure to guard the drinks cabinet.'

'OK' said Andrew. 'He's yours at night. But for the rest of the time it's all hands to the pumps. We'll need a lot of help to get him match fit by Tuesday. I understand that each candidate will have exactly thirty minutes for their individual interviews. No audience – not enough time to organise it – so it will just be you and the interviewer in a studio at BBC Broadcasting House. They want Deakin top of the bill, but the Electoral Commission won't allow any favouritism or commercial influences. You'll all draw lots on the night for the order of service. Hopefully, we'll be last on so the others won't have chance to rubbish what you say.'

'OK. I'll do my best' said Alistair.

'Your best isn't good enough' said Andrew curtly. 'You'll have to do better than that. *Everything* rests on this. Absolutely everything.'

60

Harvey

SUNDAY 4 MAY 2025

4 days to go

Harvey read the *News on Sunday's* main headline with horror. '*Racist Britten*' stared back at him in bold letters. '*Banker sacked ethnic minority workers in favour of white employees.*' He then read the full piece with increasing dismay.

One of his former employees at his branch in North Street, Brighton, had given an account of the time, three years ago, when the SS&I Bank had a major downsizing in staffing levels. It was the first step towards the inevitable closure that followed last year.

At the time, the directive from on high was that 25% of his workforce must be relocated to other branches and another 25% made redundant to save cost. It was a stressful time and contributed in no small way to his decision to take early retirement only eight months later. Making redundancy decisions that would so dramatically affect his co-worker's lives was a horrible experience. But it was a decision largely made by his Area Manager. The redundancy criteria were a brutal '*last in first out*' for the lower grades and '*whichever one is paid highest*' for management. Individual talent – and certainly race - did not come into it.

Deepak Singh had a chip on his shoulder from the day he started and had taken his redundancy badly. He was a twenty-one-year old junior support officer who'd only worked at the bank for ten months. Harvey never liked the cocky young lad's attitude. He was born and raised in Brighton, of Indian parents, and had a much higher opinion of himself than he merited. But he was claiming that his redundancy was racially motivated and that 80% of all the redundancies were also black or Asian employees.

Harvey recalled that Deepak was heavily into politics and a POG activist. He felt sure that the party was trying to discredit Harvey as a threat to their own candidate's fortunes. Perhaps they saw some hope after the current fun and games with Bradley Deakin. Whatever their motivation, they had clearly been in too much of a hurry to bother with such trivial matters as checking the facts. Harvey had not even been asked for a comment.

'Have you seen this Claire?' he said, handing the tablet to his wife.

'I guess we shouldn't be surprised' she replied, far more upbeat than he felt himself. We've had sex, drugs, adultery, child abuse, rape and alcoholism. . . I guess someone was always going to play the race card at some point. You've had a pretty easy ride of it so far and they were bound to turn their guns on you sometime. Especially now you're the front runner.'

Harvey was in no doubt she was right. The *News on Sunday* said he was not only a racist but an OP candidate in disguise. They cited Claire's history as an OP activist in her youth and having stood as a Counsellor in their name. This was all getting too personal.

'I know' he said with a sigh. 'But this is just such nonsense. Utter . . .'

'Of course it is' said Claire. 'And I imagine the other two said the same thing when reading the stuff printed about them too. But that's the name of the game.'

Harvey did not answer. It was not an excuse and he was still angry.

. . .

IT WAS a Bank Holiday weekend and Harvey was taking a brief respite from campaigning. In any event, he didn't think voters would be very interested today, anyway. Unlike normal Bank Holidays, where it rains solidly until people go back to work on Tuesday, the forecast was for a very warm and pleasant weekend. People would therefore be flocking to the beaches and politics would be the last thing on their minds. But, in fact, the revelations about Bradley, the disappearance of Gabrielle (or Sharon Morgan as she had now been re-named in the press), and the whole *Pantsgate* saga had made this little by-election into a national talking point. Every newspaper, TV news channel or other media outlet was focusing on little else. If the tide had begun to ebb slightly over the weekend, today's revelations about Harvey would doubtless send it back up the beach like a tsunami.

After Harvey had moved into second place in the polls – albeit still by a distance - he had experienced far more media attention than he'd ever expected. The press loved the 'David and Goliath' aspect of his story. He was a retired bank manager (or, for the purposes of media stereo-typing, a 'pensioner') – taking on a mighty TV celebrity destined for national leadership. But the story still remained a novelty, with Deakin expected to win with a comfortable majority. But that had all changed dramatically last week when Deakin's lead had completely evaporated. He currently sat on just 18% this morning.

Oddly enough, Buckland's popularity had rallied on the back of his opponent's misfortunes. He was now narrowly ahead of Deakin with 20%. But Harvey had clearly benefited from the troubles heaped on both candidates. He held an extraordinary rating of 27%, giving him a seven-point lead. It was not enormous and there were still a massive 33% of voters languishing in the 'don't know' category. Experts predicted a high number of abstentions which, combined with normal voter apathy in any by-election, suggested another record low turn-out was on the cards.

There had been the usual noble rallying calls from all sides supporting democracy as a concept - *Just get out there and vote on Thursday, whoever you decide to vote for.*' But, for once, that wasn't as easy as it sounded. Lifelong supporters of both parties were suffering a terrible moral dilemma. Clouds hung over both candidates so protest votes or abstentions were the only real alternatives. In that case, Harvey was the best choice. The student dressed as a seagull was still polling badly, which slightly disappointed Harvey. With all the madness going on, it seemed somehow fitting that an idiot in fancy dress might emerge as the eventual victor.

But regardless of how he got there, Harvey was now the front runner, which dramatically changed the way he was perceived. He was no longer just a novelty. He was a serious contender - the likely next Member of Parliament for Brighton and Hove. Harvey Britten MP. He just couldn't get his head around such a preposterous idea.

LATER IN THE MORNING, the press were camped outside Harvey's front gate. Sam, Piers and Phoebe had stayed overnight so, thankfully, didn't have to run the gauntlet when they arrived. All the family were currently in the lounge discussing how to respond to today's allegations, except for Phoebe who was busy drawing pictures in the corner of the room.

'This is *not* what I signed up for!' said Harvey.

'It's just mischief making, Dad' said Sam, trying to calm him down. 'It will be easy to defend from what you've said. If you're a racist then I'm an astronaut - and you know I don't like heights.'

Harvey smiled at his lovely daughter.

'It'll be fine – you can balls it out' Piers chipped in, more bluntly. He was as upbeat as ever. 'Why don't we just all go out there and face them - as a family? That would show everyone it's all nonsense.'

'Not a chance' said Harvey. 'That old cliché of a disgraced politician standing by his front gates with his loyal family beside him. No way! It always looks utterly contrived.'

'So, my honourable friend now sees himself as a *politician*, does he?' said Claire, teasing her husband with a reassuring pat on his arm.

'You know what I mean' he replied, dejectedly.

'Yes, well' said Sam. 'That clichéd photo is normally needed when a sleazy politician is caught sleeping with an intern. That's not the case here - and Piers has a point. If we were just to . . .'

'No!' said Harvey, firmly. 'I'm not having my family paraded in the papers like a circus act. If I'm going to keep going with this then I'm going to do it properly. I'll just tell them the truth.'

'What do you mean – *if I'm going to keep going*?' said Claire gently, the only one to pick up on the point. 'You're not thinking of giving up, are you?'

'It *has* crossed my mind' said Harvey. He'd actually been thinking about nothing else for two days, even before today's twist. 'Look, this was all supposed to be a bit of harmless fun. Well, not fun exactly . . . but making a point. You said I'd be like the guy in the seagull costume - standing up for what I believe in but without dressing up like a prat. I didn't want to win, I never intended to win and, as you all told me – fairly bluntly as I recall – I didn't have a cat in hell's chance of winning anyway. So, I reluctantly went through with it and, to an extent, have enjoyed the experience. It's been nice meeting lots of people and sharing all the banter. And I've enjoyed knocking on doors - even though it scared the life out of me at first. Everyone has been really friendly. It restored my faith in ordinary people as decent, civilised human beings just trying to get on with their lives. The quiet majority - not the noisy lot who shout loudest on Twitter and claim to speak for everyone. I now know for sure that they don't - and it's been great. But, this is now getting serious. I could bloody win this, for goodness sake, and it terrifies me!'

'You'd be a brilliant MP' said Piers. 'I know what we said at the start but, think about it. The reason people are supporting you is because you come across as the very sort of person you've just described. Ordinary, decent and honest. Just like the people you'd be representing. A beacon of light shining out from a pile of . . . fertilizer.'

'Thank you for cleaning that up in front of Phoebe' said Harvey, looking bemused at his son-in-law. 'But it's all turning to . . . fertil-izer. Look where we are now. One guy is drinking himself into oblivion with a string of accusations about prostitutes, expenses fraud and drugs hanging over him. Yes, I never thought he was suitable as an MP – a lousy Councillor who'd make a lousy MP, to my mind. But I don't think he really deserves the bucket load that has fallen onto him with all this Pantsgate business. The poor man is clearly on the verge of a nervous breakdown. Then there's the other guy – the great hope for Western civilization and our would-be next Prime Minister. Look at him! Facing accusations of child rape and murder! How bad a candidate can you possibly get?'

'So, that's all the more reason for you to step up to the plate' said Piers.

'But I don't *want* to be an MP!' said Harvey in frustration. 'I just want to enjoy my life here with my family, my football and my little spot on the radio. I don't want all the crap that goes with being in Parliament – the all-night sittings, lobbying, political back-stabbing and doubtless a shed load of paperwork. I'm retired for goodness sake!'

'I don't think they pull all-nighters any more' said Sam.

'Well, there's one thing to be grateful for, I guess' said Harvey. 'But really, I just wish I hadn't started all this. I blame you lot.'

'So, who *should* be our MP, then?' said Claire. 'If not you, then . . . who? *Someone* has to win. If you pull out now, it will be one of the other two, regardless of how repulsive they both are. That's not what you want is it?' She was speaking calmly but there was a resilience in her voice.

'Our MP should be someone Brighton can be proud of' said Harvey. 'I agree that neither of those two comedians fit the bill, but why me instead? I'm not qualified. I wouldn't know where to start. Its not just about being nice or decent. You must be able to do the job too. I haven't got a clue how to be an MP. Really I don't.'

The more Harvey thought about it the more he just wanted to run away. Forget the whole charade had ever happened. He had checked the rules and, as an independent, he could withdraw without the election being affected. And he wanted to do just that, right now. It was all a horrible mistake. He wasn't cut out to be a politician but, somehow, the planets were aligning to make him win. Deep down inside he was scared. Really scared. And he was even more terrified about being interviewed live on national television in two-day's time. He felt unprepared and hopelessly out of his depth. If that wasn't bad enough, now he would also have to answer these awful race allegations.

'So, do you think Sarah knew how to be an MP when she won?' said Claire. 'She said it frightened the life out of her too. But she just got on with it and turned out to be brilliant. Brighton was proud of her and they would be proud of you too.'

'And let's face it, Harvey' said Piers. 'There could be a General Election at any time. You might only be there for a few months. No offence, but these two guys won't be on the ballot paper next time around, so . . .'

'Well, thank you for your vote of confidence' said Harvey, pretending to be offended. 'So, what you're saying is that, once both main parties put up a *proper* candidate, I'd be out the door in a flash!'

'Or . . . the voters may actually see you as the best MP they've ever had and want to vote for you again, next time around' said Claire, which actually didn't help. Overall, Harvey preferred the scenario Piers had painted. *Serve your time and you'll be out in a few months.*

'Look' said Sam. 'You want someone Brighton can be proud of. Well, that's *you*, Dad. Whether you like it or not, *you* are up for election and *you* are going to win. If you step down now, the election will still go on without you. You owe it to the city of Brighton not to desert its people just when they need you. Face the responsibility head on and give them your best. Sarah Billingham would be bloody proud if you took over from her. And I'd be proud of you too. My dad, MP for Brighton -the city he loves, with the football team he loves and the people he loves. You could finally be in a position to help change this place for the better.'

'Sounds like *you* should be the one standing, Sam' said Harvey. 'You're so much better at it than me.' He thought for a moment. 'Anyway, Sarah would have wanted her mate Buckland to win. Not me.' But he knew he was just making excuses. Sam did make a compelling case for going on.

'She may have done at one time, yes' Sam replied. 'But I don't think she would now. She would want what's best for Brighton too. And I'm afraid that's you, Dad.'

He nodded reluctantly. 'So, just say I *do* go on. What do we do between now and Tuesday about that lot camped outside?' He looked through the window at the press gathered in the road. A bright light was pointing at an ITV reporter who he vaguely recognised. If they turned on the TV now, they would see his weather-beaten rhododendron bush displayed to the nation. All the neighbours must be having a field day watching the spectacle from their windows.

Just at that moment, little Phoebe ran across the room, laughing at something she had drawn, and leapt onto her granddad's lap to show him. It bought a beaming smile to Harvey's face as the two of them giggled at each other. He touched noses with her and made a silly noise, making her laugh even more. Sam instinctively reached for her phone and snapped a few photos of the idyllic family scene.

Harvey reluctantly accepted the compromise proposed by his daughter, which Piers also agreed was the perfect solution. Within an hour, Sam had posted the best photo from the set onto Harvey's election web page and social media feeds. It carried the simple caption – '*Enjoying some well-earned time off with my beautiful grand-daughter on a glorious Bank Holiday weekend.*' Tomorrow, the photo would be on the front pages of all the papers and, by mid-afternoon, it was trending on social media, having been shared some 50,000 times.

Of course, Harvey knew the people who post judgemental comments would never admit to being wrong. Nor of having jumped to an ill-informed conclusion. But some, more reasonable, people were circulating the photo as evidence that the *News on Sunday* story might just be contradicted by reality.

Even so, the more fanatical and intransigent trolls still maintained their lofty stance. '*Just because he's got a black granddaughter doesn't mean he's not a racist*' being the gist of their argument. To their eyes, someone who shared their fanatical political views, especially expressed in a newspaper that endorsed them, could never make up or distort the truth. Their truth. Only supporters of the other party did that. No, this story must be true if it came from one of their own. So, here you go, Harvey, have another death threat on us, just to be on the safe side.

Harvey despaired at the nonsense he read. He knew he should stop looking at social media, but it was hypnotic. No matter how awful it was - vile even - he had a natural desire to see what people were saying about him. Even so, just as her parents had anticipated, the image of his gorgeous, mixed-race granddaughter sitting on her granddad's lap *did* send a subtle message to the wider world. Any broader defence of the unjustified accusations of racism could wait until the TV interview on Tuesday. He was not in the mood to face the media today. He was enjoying a day with his family. That was all that really mattered in his life right now. Or ever.

61

Emma

SUNDAY 4 MAY 2025

4 days to go

Emma was alone at her parent's house. Bradley's party machine had been working overtime to distance him from the murder conspiracy and he was beginning to weather the storm. But then came the rape accusations and it had all imploded. That was in an entirely different league.

Emma poured a glass of wine and took the bottle through to the lounge. She slumped on the sofa and sat in silence, contemplating her own future as the evening wore on. Bradley had been livid about the claims and denied them emphatically. Emma spoke to him on Tuesday whilst he was running around London trying to get them withdrawn. All he had said was that it was nonsense. They were just two teenagers in love. He was sixteen at the time – but it was on his birthday. If it had happened the day before, then he would have been fifteen. Yes, the girl was, technically, twelve but was only two months away from being thirteen. A bit of creative mathematics and there were only two years between them. But he swore she had lied to him about her age, saying she was fifteen when they met. He was also adamant that he had not forced himself onto her and it was a pre-arranged consensual triste whilst his parents were away.

Put like that, it sounded viable but Emma was still uncomfortable. The two-month gap to her thirteenth birthday was crucial. It meant she was still legally a child. *Everything* was his word against hers and the world was an unforgiving place when accusations like this arise nowadays. Presumptions of guilt were the norm unless they could be proven false beyond any doubt. Even then, it could take months or years to clear someone's name. Bradley had just four days before it would no longer matter. Or, at least as far as his political ambitions were concerned. There might still be time to save his television career.

The big question in Emma's mind was - why? Why would the hooker make such an appalling accusation unless it was true? She didn't seem to be politically motivated, other than having a soft spot for Alistair Buckland and his enormous pants. But would she really come up with such a distorted lie just to help him? And why would she keep that photo for twenty-five years or more if it was just a teenage fling that ended as quickly as it started? Emma worried there was more to this that Bradley was letting on. And there was. He sheepishly told her on Thursday evening - the last time she saw him.

'EMMA, I've got something to tell you' he said, as she was pouring a drink. 'Its important, can we sit down?'

He was about to go into London, so the timing was curious. He looked exhausted and deflated but suddenly needed to talk, just as he was about to leave. She knew her husband well and, deep down, he was a coward. He would now reveal some bad news and then run off before she had time to process it. He had done that before, many times.

'What is it?' she said.

'It's . . . about Sharon.'

'Go on.'

'She lied about so many things, but she's got that photo proving we slept together. And I've never denied it. But you know my side of the story is that it was nothing like she says.'

'She lied about her age and you didn't attack her. Yes, I know' said Emma. 'Don't tell me she's telling the truth?'

'God no!' he said, looking startled. 'Nothing like that. No, she's lying. I can prove it, but . . . it's difficult.'

'Just say it.'

'OK'. He took a huge breath. Emma knew she wasn't going to like what was coming. 'It's just that, well, what she failed to mention is that we met again, quite by chance, a few years later. She was twenty-one by then and working in a department store in Oxford Street selling perfume. I happened to pass by and we . . . started having a relationship. We were together for eight months. It proves that I can't have forced myself onto her first time round. Why would she have a relationship with me, years later, if I'd raped her?'

'Well, that's great news - isn't it? Can you prove it?' Emma had not yet done the maths.

'I'm trying, but it's difficult. I don't have any photos or anything. But it proves this is all about revenge. Not for when we were teenagers but because of what happened when we were going out together later.'

Emma had finally made the calculation whilst he spoke. 'So, why would she be so vengeful? How did it end?' She knew, but wanted the little shit to tell her himself. He shuffled on the spot like a naughty schoolboy.

'Look' he said. 'There's no easy way to say it. You and I were living together at the time. It was 2007.'

'The year before we got married.'

'Yes' he said, taking another slow breath. 'The year before we got married. So only whilst we were engaged.'

'Oh, that's alright then!' Emma replied, sarcasm slipping into her voice. 'Gosh, for a minute I thought you'd done something wrong!'

'I know' he said. 'And I'm sorry. It just . . . happened. She was special, even when we were kids. I broke it off then because she lied about her age. But when we met again, she had grown into this beautiful . . .'

'Aren't they all' she said, dismissively. 'Doubtless ticked all your usual boxes.'

'No, it . . .' He was struggling - and so he should. 'Look. There was something between us. It was good. Special. But she found out about . . . well, you. That was the end of it and I never saw her again.'

So, if she *hadn't* found out . . . what would have happened then?' Emma was gradually putting things into place and didn't like the picture being formed.

'I don't know. Really.' He seemed to be speaking honestly for a change, without thinking about the repercussions. 'But it ended, so it's not worth speculating. As it was, I came back to you and committed to *us*. We got married and I like to think it was the right choice. We've been happy ever since, haven't we?'

'Woah, woah, woah, hang on a bit' she replied, ignoring his question. 'You *like to think it was the right choice?*' He was not glossing over the details that easily. 'What the hell does that mean? Not *I definitely made the right choice*. No, its *'I like to think. . .'*

'I didn't mean it like that. Of course it was the right choice.'

'It isn't a glowing endorsement is it? You wanted *her* but got stuck with *me!*'

'No!' he said, looking frustrated. 'I loved you then and . . . I love you now. It was just a silly fling . . .'

'. . . which, if she hadn't found out about me, might have carried on. Perhaps it would now be *me* exposing you in the papers as being the bag of bollocks that you are, instead of her. She'd be your wife! Honestly!'

He looked at his watch. *Here we go.* 'Look, I'm sorry. I've got to go. We'll talk later. I know it stinks but it was years ago. We need to look at who we are *now* and what's happened since. All we have - and have had - together. I made the right choice.'

'She made it for you!'

'No!' He sighed and took a deep breath. 'Honestly, that's not true. But, look, I have to talk about this in public. It's my only defence. These are bloody serious accusations, Ems. My whole life's at stake here! I just needed you to know first before it comes out.'

'Oh great!' she replied in dismay. 'So, the fact that you had a grubby affair and then tricked me into marrying you will now be all over the TV. Thanks a lot.'

'I didn't trick you! I . . .'

'You made me believe I was *everything* to you. That we were an inseparable team. When all the time you'd been shagging her for months and only married me because she dumped you. I was second best but would have to do. You were looking to get elected and needed a nice little wifey alongside you. Was that it?'

He didn't answer. 'I've got to go' he said, walking away. She stumbled to find words and ended up saying nothing. Instead, she threw the wine bottle after him, which chipped the paintwork on the door and smashed into pieces on the tiles. It didn't help.

SHE POURED a glass from a fresh bottle and felt the tears welling up. She had been here before and knew she would be again if she didn't do something drastic. This time it was on a different level. It wasn't about private suspicions. She would be humiliated in public as the truth came out and the papers did the maths. She was a trophy wife not a partner. The woman he had *really* loved – and lost - was Sharon Morgan. Emma Deakin was just the consolation prize.

Had he now killed Sharon or made her disappear? Was he capable of that? She didn't think so. He was ruthless in his career but wouldn't know how to start organising a professional hit . . . sorry, two professional hits. There was the small matter of assassinating an MP to defend as well. It was so hard to keep up sometimes.

He was never going to be Prime Minister now. The allegations would hang around forever like the smell of a dead rat under the floor boards. He didn't have enough evidence to prove they were unfounded, not least because part of it was true. The bottom line was that he had slept with a twelve-year old girl, no matter what the mitigating circumstances had been. He was finished. The girl was younger than Stephen is now!

Emma suddenly felt disgust move in alongside the anger and hurt. She downed the rest of her glass in one gulp and stood up, unsteadily, having risen too fast. She paused to gain her balance, put down the wine glass and went to find the details of a good divorce lawyer.

62

Bradley

MONDAY 5 MAY 2025

3 days to go

'We've had a breakthrough' said Rod, rushing in whilst Bradley and Peter were going through a dummy interview with the Public Relations team.

'Make it good' said Bradley, not wishing to get his hopes up.

'We've been trying to track down old school friends for Gabri-Sharon, whatever' said Rod, enthusiastically.

'Go on' said Peter.

'Well, apparently she wasn't the virginal little angel she claims. We've found a party worker in Uxbridge who went to school with her. Said she was the girl the others all wanted to be like – confident, sexually mature and looking older than her years.'

'Yes! That's right, she was!' said Bradley.

'Anyway' Rod went on. 'This woman, Lynn Freeman, well remembers some lad bragging about having it away with Sharon round the back of the bike sheds or wherever, and she then made a complete fool of him in the dining hall. Made the girls admire her even more. But the point being, she was only twelve at the time, and so was the lad, I guess. But Lynn says Sharon *always* hung out with older boys after that. The other girls thought she was just so . . . grown up.'

'Will she give a statement or go public, this . . . Lynn?' Peter asked.

'Yes' said Rod, unable to hide his excitement. 'She'd be delighted. Better that that, she's still in contact with some of her old school friends and will ask if they'll come forward too. They'll all remember Sharon Morgan, apparently. She certainly wasn't some shrinking violet sitting at the back of the class, studying to be a nun.'

Bradley frowned. 'What's wrong?' said Rod, looking visibly disappointed.

'Anything from later?' asked Bradley. 'When we were together as adults? I just worry that rubbishing her as a child won't do it. People will still say she was just a kid and not responsible for her actions. Which is true. Saying she was actually a little minx won't make this go away. And it doesn't answer the accusation that I attacked her – tart or angel. We need something from later, when she was twenty-one.'

'Well, like I said, it's a breakthrough' said Rod, visibly dejected. 'Its more than we had before and something to build on. We're trying to find people who worked with her in Oxford Street, but it's hard. The store can't help. Bloody data protection means staff records from back then have all been destroyed. But they're going to ask around just in case someone remembers her. Bit of a long shot though. Are you *sure* there's no-one you spoke to about her at the time?'

'No' said Bradley. 'I was keeping her quiet from my friends, obviously. I imagine she would have been telling people about me, though. She didn't have any reason to be secretive. But I never met her friends or work colleagues. It wasn't that sort of relationship.'

Peter looked disapprovingly and Bradley knew why. His friend had always liked Emma and wouldn't approve of how Bradley had treated her. His loyalty was being severely strained and Bradley felt Peter was becoming despondent. It was hardly surprising. He really believed Bradley offered a bright new future for the OP and had worked hard to get the party on side. Now he may not even win this by-election, let alone go on to become leader. The implications for the party that Peter loved were immense. He appeared to be losing heart and Bradley knew he had let his friend down badly.

'Let's get on with the dummy interview' said Peter without further comment. 'We've a lot to do.' Bradley watched him move away, feeling his ambitions of leading the OP were probably walking away with him.

He turned to Rod and said quietly, 'thanks mate, good work. But please keep digging. I'm going to need a hell of a lot more if we're going to pull this out of the fire.'

63

Harvey

TUESDAY 6 MAY 2025

2 days to go

Harvey was as nervous as he had ever been in his life. A hollow feeling filled his chest and stomach as the black BMW negotiated London's Portland Place, heading towards BBC Broadcasting House.

The car had picked up Sam and himself from Victoria Station where they had arrived right on time at 4.23 p.m. The driver was waiting at the platform, holding up a tablet with Harvey's name on it. Being given the star treatment didn't necessarily help Harvey's nerves. It just highlighted that he was way out of his depth. He would soon be interviewed live on national TV to an audience of goodness knows how many millions.

Harvey had never liked Drew McKinley, the formidable interviewer who he would be facing tonight. He considered him rude and opinionated. The only good thing was that his two opponents were likely to offer much more meat to satisfy his carnivorous appetite. They must be feeling equally apprehensive about their own interviews. There was far more riding on it for both of them than there was for Harvey.

'You OK, Dad?' said Sam, touching his hand in the back of the car. He was pleased she was there and wished Claire could have been too. But this was not a social event and they had to be professional. Sam was there as his Election Agent, advisor and – thankfully – his loving and supportive daughter as well. He felt that he was in safe hands.

'I guess so' he replied, not entirely convinced. 'I'll just be glad when it's over with.'

'You'll be great' she said, sounding like she meant it. 'It's not as if you are a stranger to the microphone. Just treat it like you do on the radio. Relax, speak slowly and carefully and always think about what you're saying before you say it.'

'That's actually the opposite of what I do on the radio' said Harvey. 'I just rattle away with the first thing that comes into my head. I can usually just focus on one person listening at the other end – mostly your mother or some friendly face making breakfast for the kids. But with all the lights and cameramen milling around, I just don't know what I'll be like.'

'Well, you were great yesterday with Dale so just put your head in the same place' said Sam. 'I know it's difficult, but at least you're not Deakin or Buckland having to answer the difficult questions they'll get. Just put it into perspective. What's the worst that can happen?'

Sam was right. The test run had gone well yesterday. Harvey was sure that his opponents would have used the most experienced media experts to help with their own test interviews. They would have done them in specially hired TV studios, designed to look just like the real thing. The experts would have raked over every answer, each facial expression, choosing the perfect sitting position and posture to convey confidence and assertiveness.

By contrast, Harvey was an amateur. He knew it before and was even more certain of it now. Ironically, he would have benefited most from such intense media training but, instead, only had Dale to conduct his dummy interview, which took place in his friend's dining room. It had gone as well as it could have done but, by his own admission, Dale was no Drew McKinley. He had tried to mimic the veteran broadcaster's style and Scottish accent but that only made them both break down in gales of nervous laughter. It made it more enjoyable, but Harvey now felt horribly under-prepared. He was being driven into the gladiators' arena with neither a sword or a shield to protect him. He fully expected to be torn to shreds.

His nerves didn't improve as the car turned into the concourse of Broadcasting House. As they paused for the security bollards to be lowered, Harvey could see people, cameras and lights gathered around the front entrance. The driver must have sensed his anxiety in the rear-view mirror.

'Don't worry. It's not a lynch mob' he said. 'That'll be the press, mainly, and the Beeb are probably filming as each of you arrive. Part of the introduction shots for the programme I expect - adds a bit of drama, apparently.'

'Thanks' said Harvey who felt slightly sick.

The car pulled up at the entrance and both rear doors opened from the outside to let Harvey and Sam get out. Cameras flashed and Harvey stood briefly by the car door like a rabbit caught in a lorry's headlights. There were a few members of the public standing nearby, either curious passers-by or, more likely, fans waiting to catch a glimpse of Bradley Deakin when he arrived. Harvey sensed their disappointment as his little-known face emerged from the car instead.

A couple of BBC dignitaries introduced themselves and led him through the entrance. A young assistant called Davina then took Harvey through to make-up. She told him that each candidate would have their own dressing room, both to prepare and observe their rival's performances with their teams. Harvey wondered what sort of entourage the other two would bring with them. He felt even more inadequate, being just him and Sam on his team.

His balding head was dabbed with copious amounts of powder before Harvey was shown to his dressing room, where Sam was already waiting. It was only small and he imagined Bradley Deakin probably had a much bigger room. One with a big star on the door.

The producer, Shirley Nolan, popped in to explain the format.

The draw for the batting order would take place in the presence of the three Election Agents about ninety minutes before the 7.30 kick-off. That was in about half an hour's time. Harvey was first to arrive but the other two were apparently now on site too. He sat down with Sam on the two-seater sofa and they spread their papers across the coffee table in front of them. He tried to both concentrate and relax, but found he could do neither.

JUST BEFORE SIX O'CLOCK, Sam was called away for the draw. Harvey stayed in his room and turned on the TV to distract him. It didn't help, because the upcoming interviews were the main story on the news. Suddenly, there he was on screen, emerging from the car as a backdrop to the commentary. He looked terrified. By contrast, Bradley Deakin was shown smiling broadly as he arrived and was greeted by the same nameless VIPs. Finally, Alistair Buckland was shown arriving. Harvey took some comfort that Buckland looked just as nervous and apprehensive as he had done himself.

His phone pinged with a text from Claire. *'Relax, you'll be fine'* it said. He assumed she was watching the news at home, which just confirmed that he must have looked as scared as he thought. It made her feel a long way away.

The door opened and Sam hurried in.

'Well?' said Harvey, eager to know the outcome of the draw.

'Guess what?' said Sam. 'You're top of the bill! On last!'

'Oh my!' Harvey replied, not knowing what to think. It was probably good news, but all he could think was that it meant an extra hour before his ordeal was over.

'Deakin's lot were not happy at all' Sam went on. 'He's on first, with Buckland in the middle. I think the producer wasn't too happy either. No offence, Dad, but I got the feeling they wanted Bradley on last to stop people turning over to *Crash Team* straight after his interview.'

'I can see their point' said Harvey. 'I'm happy to swop if they like?'

'Doesn't work that way, Dad' said Sam, shaking her head

sympathetically. 'The draw was done with the Electoral Commission present to ensure fair play, so I'm afraid it has to stay as it is. And anyway, it's good for us. We can see what the others say before you go on so you'll then have a chance to respond. And, to be honest, it's absolutely the right running order. You're leading in the polls and Deakin is third. They may not like it but you are the main event. Not just tonight, but on Thursday too. Its good news, Dad, honestly. Be positive.'

Harvey was trying, but felt like he was swirling around in violent seas as the tide carried him away.

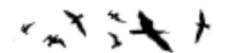

64

Bradley

TUESDAY 6 MAY 2025

2 days to go

Bradley kicked the chair in frustration when Rod told him the news. He had been waiting in Dressing Room One, the spacious accommodation reserved for top stars and where he was always based when recording *Speakin' to Deakin*. He wasn't sure who'd allocated the rooms today, but was pleased to still have friends at the BBC. At least *someone* still saw him as one of their own. He might need his old job back soon, so took some comfort in that.

'It's ridiculous!' he said, sulking. 'It will kill the ratings. People might watch to see if Buckland delivers another car crash, but they'll all have turned off before Britten comes on last. Can't they do it again?'

'The producer was as hacked off as you are, Brad' said Rod. 'But a draw is a draw and that's how it has to be.'

Bradley felt particularly worried. He knew he'd get the worst of the questions from Drew. Their encounter on the *Today* programme proved he could no longer rely on their friendship for an easy run. Drew would relish giving him a hard time on live TV.

'And anyway' said Rod. 'The discovery today may be our trump card. It should put McKinley off his stride.'

'I bloody hope so.'

BRADLEY HEARD the title music play as the broadcast went live at 7.30. It was some imposing stock orchestral piece, presumably intended to set a sinister mood. *'This is serious stuff'* it was saying. *'Put down your phones and tell the kids to shut up. The gladiators are about to enter the arena.'*

Drew's over-dramatic, pre-recorded voice-over boomed out as the screen behind him showed a montage of the candidate's faces. Shots of them getting out of the cars and other images of Big Ben were thrown in to add some gravitas. As an opening title sequence, Bradley could see its merits. But he was not interested in the TV technicalities. He felt very anxious and wanted to get on with it. The title music finished with a dramatic kettle drum roll as the camera swung round in front of Drew. He was standing centre stage in front of two lonely chairs on a raised platform.

'Good evening' he said. 'It's the by-election in Brighton that many are calling the most important in the history of politics. An election with everything at stake. A possible Prime Minister in waiting for the OP - the BBC's own Bradley Deakin – seeking to win the Parliamentary seat that he so desperately needs. But he's faced with damaging allegations of child rape, the abduction of his accuser and even involvement in a murder plot.

His challenger for the POG is a highly respected local Council-lor, Alistair Buckland, who himself has been exposed for paying a prostitute for sex over some ten years, sometimes charging the hotel room to the local tax payer. He's also facing allegations of drug-taking, drunkenness and even having an affair with the previous MP, Sarah Billingham, despite her husband, Dan, being his Election Agent. And if that wasn't bad enough, his choice of underwear has also raised a few eyebrows.

And to complete the line-up of our three principle candidates, we have local pensioner, part-time radio presenter and retired bank manager, Harvey Britten. He started by making a stand against Bradley Deakin being parachuted into his beloved Brighton, but is no longer just an also-ran independent. Instead, he finds himself leading the polls, perhaps as a result of his opponents' misfortunes. But even *he* hasn't been immune to media allegations. This weekend he faced accusations of racism in the Sunday papers. Truly, you couldn't make it up.

Well, they're all here tonight to defend themselves and convince voters in Brighton that they are the best choice for their next MP. So, this is truly a unique television event - the first time that candidates in a local by-election have faced a live, national TV interview in a format more akin to a General Election. I have the honour of putting the questions to them tonight so - let's make a start, shall we?'

Bradley, braced himself to be introduced. A studio assistant stood beside him waiting for the cue to push him forward into the arena. As if he needed any help - he was a pro.

'Before the broadcast' Drew went on 'all three candidates drew lots for the running order and, first up – either with the long or short straw, depending on how you look at it - is Bradley Deakin.'

The main theme music rang out again to cover up the absence of an audience clapping. Bradley suspected the TV audience at home would not have been expecting to see him as the warm up act. He walked confidently into the spotlights, smiling broadly and holding out his hand to Drew as if meeting a long-lost friend.

'So, Bradley' said Drew as they both took their seats. The set was stark and minimalist so they looked small and isolated in the middle of the vast empty space. 'An odd experience for you, I suspect, sitting in the interviewee's chair tonight for a change?' He was presumably trying to soften his prey before taking a bite out of his jugular.

'Yes, it certainly is, Drew' Bradley replied, trying to adopt a light tone, which he did easily. *Get the TV audience relaxed and on side early*. 'Very odd. But I'm sure you'll be gentle with me.' He flashed a knowing look at the camera, just as he often did on his show.

'Well, don't count on it' said Drew. 'So, let's start working down the long list of accusations lobbied against you and hope we have time to fit them all in.'

'Yes' said Bradley, sensing more than a hint of sarcasm in the host's voice. 'And I'm very pleased for the opportunity to show what a pack of lies they all are. You may well find it amusing, Drew, but having your reputation attacked in such a despicable way, without any evidence, is something I wouldn't wish on my worst enemy. So, yes, please do fire away.' *That put the smarmy git in his place.*

'OK' said Drew, indignantly. 'Let's start with the allegation that seems to have at least *some* evidence to support it, despite what you say. The alleged rape of Sharon Morgan – a.k.a. the prostitute Gabrielle. She claims you raped her whilst she was still a child of twelve years old. Now, you have denied this, many times. But perhaps you can clarify why - given there is a photograph allegedly taken by you on the night in question, clearly dated to confirm your respective ages at the time. What is your defence against those allegations?'

The cold way that Drew put the case for the prosecution sounded pretty damning.

'Well,' Bradley replied, taking a deep breath. 'Clearly, I've never denied that we slept together that night, but I strongly refute the circumstances. I'm disgusted that the paper did not print my side of the story alongside such defamatory claims, but it's clear that publication has far more to do with politics than anything else. However, that said, I'm pleased to say that we have now uncovered evidence in the last couple of days which helps prove Sharon's version of events is totally fabricated.'

'And where *is* this evidence?' Drew interrupted, looking surprised.

'I'll come to it in a moment' Bradley went on, refusing to be rushed. It was important to lay this out in the way he had practiced with his team. 'I've said that Sharon Morgan was not an innocent child as the *Daily News* claims. We originally met in a night club in Uxbridge two weeks before. Now, this was a place with a strict over-18 entry policy so, even if you allow for very lax door security, the idea that a twelve-year old child could get in without looking much older is clearly implausible. I think that adds some weight to my claim that she looked much older than twelve and lied by telling me that she was fifteen.'

'But they let you in – and you were fifteen yourself?' said Drew.

'Well, yes' said Bradley, realising it devalued his argument a little. 'But I looked old for my age too'

'And, did you check her age?' asked Drew.

'What?' said Bradley. 'No. Fifteen-year old boys didn't ask for photo ID back then, and I doubt they do even now. I had no reason to doubt she was telling the truth. We talked about the school she went to, what exams she was taking and so on. It was all plausible and, what with her being fully made up and dressed to kill, I assure you, she didn't look like some twelve-year old kid in pig-tails.'

'But' said Drew, 'she claims that you forced yourself on her, so it's largely irrelevant how old she looked. Rape is rape.'

'I absolutely did not rape her.' said Bradley. He described their night of drunken – but consensual - passion, how the photo ended up being taken and how he'd discovered her true age a week later, causing him to end the relationship.

'So why would she say it was rape, so many years later, if it was just love's young dream?' said Drew. 'Some would say she is a brave to come forward now, knowing she would be doubted, especially given her current profession. Did she deserve to be raped?'

'I say again, I did not rape her.' Bradley was getting frustrated that Drew was ignoring his answers. 'I know what she's saying makes it sound like I did. But, crucially, she left out what happened later, when she was twenty-one. That was when I bumped into her in a department store in London. We got together and had a lovely relationship for eight months. She was the love of my life and she thought the same about me. When it ended, well, that clearly hurt her very badly and I believe *that* is why she is taking her revenge now. She bore a serious grudge. Boy, was it serious! One that has lasted eighteen years. But, crucially, she denies ever seeing me again after the alleged rape, because it otherwise entirely undermines her accusation. But what I am telling you now is true and I can prove it.'

'So, how did this *relationship* end to make her so vengeful?' said Drew, condescendingly.

'She found out I was . . . living with the woman who went on to be my wife. Emma.'

'So, you were seeing Sharon whilst you were engaged to your now wife?'

'Yes' said Bradley. 'I was being unfaithful to her. But only because Sharon was so special. I would have left Emma for her and, in fact, I was intending to. I know that sounds awful now but, at the time, I loved Sharon more than anything, or anyone, in the world. It was my own stupidity that led to us breaking up and I've regretted it ever since.'

Bradley's mouth went dry. There, he'd said it - live on TV. But it was cathartic to tell the truth, regardless of the repercussions. 'I'm saying all this now, probably to the detriment of my marriage, because I need to show you that Sharon was hurt, angry and bitter about what happened when she was twenty-one - not twelve going on twenty.'

'Hell hath no fury . . .' said Drew.

'Clearly' said Bradley. 'I beg people to please believe me. If I had raped her as a child and turned her to prostitution, then we wouldn't have had that magical time together later. I threw it all away when we were grown-ups, not children. The story about . . . rape and child abuse. It's all vile and untrue. I didn't realise how much I must have hurt her to do this.'

'And . . .' said Drew. 'You mentioned you had evidence?'

'Yes' said Bradley. 'Finally, I can prove it. At least to some extent. A former colleague at the department store, someone who miraculously still works there, came forward yesterday because she remembers Sharon well. They were friends, of sorts, and she recalls Sharon being in love with a man called Tom. That's me. Apparently, she spoke about me all the time but the friend remembers her leaving very suddenly after we broke up. She recalls Sharon being heartbroken and just not turning up for work one day. She just vanished. I know, because I went looking for her after a few weeks. It proves Sharon lied when she said we never saw each other after the alleged rape and that, in turn, proves she was lying about the rape itself. There was none. Just two young kids getting it together as thousands are probably doing as I speak.'

Drew shuffled his papers. Bradley's team had deliberately kept this discovery quiet to put Drew off his stroke. 'Well' the gruff interviewer said finally. 'People will take a view on that. But the poor lassie has now disappeared and you were the last person to see her alive before she vanished. Why were you there?'

'To try and make her see sense' said Bradley. 'She tricked me into believing she was going to call off the dogs, so I left.'

'Perhaps she was frightened of you?' asked Drew.

'I don't believe that' replied Bradley. 'And, as I've told the police, I passed a man in a black leather jacket as I left the building.'

'Ah yes, you let him in I understand' said Drew, perking up. 'Convenient, some would say, if you didn't want to get your own hands dirty. If you wanted your own revenge against someone about to destroy your chances of becoming Prime Minister, would you not let your accomplice do the dirty work for you?'

'No!' said Bradley. 'I don't know who he was, or even whether he had anything to do with it. But I assure you he was not sent by me. Remember, the *Daily Record* intends to expose *all* of her clients. I understand there are some high-profile characters involved and some are not nice people at all and will be a queuing up for revenge. The police are looking at them all.'

'Well' said Drew 'as we're on the subject of sinister men in a black, there are another couple linked to the most serious accusations levied against you - murder?'

Bradley knew this was the big one. 'Look, I needed a by-election, everyone knows that. But if the only way to get one was to bump off a sitting MP, then would I really choose a marginal seat held by the POG? A seat that could go either way? No, if I really was the cynical, murderous monster that some people on Twitter now see me as then, surely, I'd have taken out an Opposition MP with a big fat majority, wouldn't I? A seat with a 100% certain chance of winning and therefore worth organising a murder for. Why choose one with only a 50/50 chance of victory at best?'

'Less obvious perhaps?' asked Drew.

'No' said Bradley. 'A majority of just 173 would not be worth the risk, in my view. I've never planned a murder but I'm sure I'd take a bit more care to ensure that I was certain of getting what I wanted out of it.'

'Perhaps' said Drew. 'But are you certain that no-one *else* in your campaign might not be as cold and calculating as you and, instead, just went for it? Or perhaps killing one of their own offended them in some way. Are you convinced that no-one close to you was involved?'

'Categorically, yes.'

'Then, who *did* kill her?' asked Drew.

'I really have no idea, but I have faith that law enforcement agencies will find and bring them to justice. But the OP would never dream of committing such a hideous act.'

'Well, time will tell whether that is true' said Drew, clearly not convinced. 'As it is, I'm afraid we've run out of time so, Bradley Deakin, thank you.'

Bradley was annoyed not to have more time but, overall, felt it had gone as well as it could. He left the stage on the opposite side to where he'd come in. He was directed there to avoid passing Alistair Buckland, who was waiting to come on. Bradley immediately met Rod behind the set.

'Well done' he said, patting Bradley on the back as they returned to the dressing room, led by another studio assistant. 'Let's see how it goes down on social media whilst we watch that clown sink without trace!'

Bradley, looked back across the set, where Drew was giving the next introduction. He could see Buckland standing behind the screen opposite - stern faced, clearly nervous. Having just been there himself, Bradley actually felt sympathy for his opponent.

"Let's hope it did the trick' he said.

At the far end of the corridor to his dressing room, Bradley could see a group of people gathered around the door. One was a uniformed BBC security officer, looking stressed and uncomfortable. Another was wearing a suit and talking to him. But it was the third visitor who particularly caught his eye. She was clearly a uniformed police constable, complete with stab vest and assorted weaponry attached to her uniform.

Bradley's heart sunk. What did they want with him *now*? Whatever it was, he was angry that they felt the need to approach him – or God forbid, arrest him –at the BBC, especially tonight of all nights. Would it have made such a difference to wait until he was back home?

As they got nearer, the suited man - presumably a plain-clothes detective - stopped talking and turned towards them. The other two stiffened in anticipation.

'What is it *now*, for goodness sake?' said Bradley, more aggressively than was perhaps advisable. But he was livid. He was about to say something else when he realised that none of the group were actually looking at him. Their eyes were instead on Rod.

'Rodney James Archer?' the plain-clothes officer asked. Rod nodded, looking nervous. 'I'm arresting you on suspicion of conspiracy to commit murder.'

65

Alistair

TUESDAY 6 MAY 2025

2 days to go

Alistair watched Deakin's interview from behind the set. He no longer knew what to believe in terms of the rape. Alistair had once thought that he knew Gabrielle, but could no longer be sure.

When she had first made the rape allegations, it all appeared to make sense. She had never explained why she had turned to prostitution - albeit at the lucrative high end of the market – despite Alistair asking her many times. He had seen this as a viable explanation - a poor child perverted by an arrogant thug, who had so cruelly stolen both her innocence and her future. Destroying her self-esteem and creating an inner self-loathing that drove her along such a treacherous path.

But now Deakin was putting another side to the story. She was later working as a respectable sales assistant and telling friends about her love for Tom Deakin. Whilst her broken heart on the second occasion may, itself, have prompted her career change, it was an entirely different set of circumstances.

The studio assistant standing beside him was a talkative soul who could not wait to tell him about the police officers rumoured to be here to arrest Bradley Deakin. The place was apparently buzzing with gossip. The word was that they had wanted to arrest him before he went on for his interview, but had been persuaded to wait. Although that may not be true. There were a lot of rumours flying around and Alistair suspected the young assistant was doing her fair share of spreading them. Either way, the police were definitely on site and waiting for Deakin to return to his dressing room. Then all hell would break loose.

'NEXT UP' said Drew 'we have POG candidate Alistair Buckland. He's the longest serving local Councillor in Brighton, highly respected and co-author of a controversial report into the potential cull of the city's seagull population. He was also a good friend of Sarah Billingham MP and, indeed, her husband is now running his election campaign. Two years ago, Buckland actually stood aside to allow Mrs Billingham to stand as Brighton's MP, which some say was a selfless act of friendship. However, others - notably the *Daily Record* - claim it was symptomatic of a much closer, illicit relationship.

Either way, his fortunes in this election have been badly marred by revelations that he had been paying prostitute Sharon Morgan, a.k.a. Gabrielle, for some ten years and sharing sensitive constituent information with her. He is also accused of claiming expenses for their encounters and having an alcohol and drug dependency. One thing we *do* know for certain is that he has highly dubious taste in underwear. Lots to contend with then, and he's here to defend all of those allegations tonight. Please welcome, Alistair Buckland.'

Alistair was nudged forward into the spotlight as the same sinister music played again. He walked towards the outstretched hand of Drew McKinley, feeling like a man taking a one-way trip to the gallows. He shook hands, trying to smile as he did do.

'So, Mr Buckland' said Drew, as they sat down, sounding like a stern headmaster, addressing a schoolboy he'd caught smoking. 'Let's start with the woman you knew as Gabrielle, shall we? Someone we now know to be Sharon Morgan. What led you to start paying her for sex way back in 2015?' *Go straight for the throat, why don't you.*

'You make it sound dirty' Alistair replied.

'Well, wasn't it? A vulnerable woman selling her body for sex. Did you not feel you were exploiting her for your own carnal pleasures, even if you *were* paying her?'

'No!' said Alistair. He took a breath and felt tense. But he composed himself immediately, realising that getting angry would not help him. 'She wasn't some cheap tart that I picked up from a card in a phone box.'

'Does that makes exploiting her OK, then?' Drew interrupted, not letting him get into his stride.

'Of course not' replied Alistair, dismissively. 'I'd never used a prostitute before in my life or ever planned to do so. It was just that . . . well . . . we met in a bar at the party conference and got on really well. I didn't realise she was a . . .well, you know . . . until later and, by then, it was too late. I was smitten.'

'So, you were consumed by lust – smitten as you call it – and then paid money to sleep with her for ten years. Unusual behaviour, don't you think?'

'I . . .' Alistair was struggling to make it all sound as innocent as it was. 'Maybe I should have resisted, but I didn't. But I wasn't married or anything. It's my business what I do with my money. I was lonely and she was – is – a wonderful, kind, warm person.'

'Who secretly photographed you in your generous underwear and later sold the story to the papers. Is that right?'

'Yes, well' said Alistair. 'I don't know why she did that. But I believe she was coerced into doing it by the *Daily Record.*'

'…and by a significant sum of money too, so I understand.'

'No, it wasn't like . . .' Alistair could not get his words together with the barrage or interruptions. 'I believe they twisted what she said or, at least, what they printed. The story in the *Daily News* was more reflective of how she really felt about me. More like her own words.'

'That would be the story Bradley Deakin has just dismissed as a pack of lies' said Drew. 'Or was that just the bits about him? You can see why people are struggling to find the truth in all of this, don't you Mr Buckland?'

'Yes' Alistair replied. 'But all I know is that she was special to me. That's why I kept seeing her . . .'

'. . . and paying her?'

'Yes, but I felt I was just helping her out financially. Not. . . paying for sex like you make it sound. Sometimes she didn't even charge - towards the end.'

'Perhaps you had a loyalty card?' said Drew. The patronising windbag was taunting him - urging him to lose his temper. Alistair could sense the hostility. 'Very kind of you to help the poor girl out. I assume she wasn't selling her body to you for fun. Either way, can you shed some light on whether you shared confidential information with her about your constituents?'

'That was nothing' said Alistair, dismissively. 'I just asked her advice sometimes - as a woman. I never named names or identified the constituents in any way. It was just bouncing off ideas to get the solution clear in my head. There's not a single Councillor – or an MP for that matter – who hasn't done the same with their own partner or a close friend. It's not sharing confidential information. It's just trying to find the best way to help someone by seeking another person's point of view.'

'Yes, perhaps,' said Drew. 'But bouncing ideas off a wife, husband or partner is a bit different to sharing them with a prostitute who still has her meter running, is it not?'

'The end result is the same' said Alistair. 'I valued her opinion, and it did help.'

'Well' Drew went on, looking at the tablet in front of him as a prompt. 'You're also alleged to have paid for your tristes with Gabrielle, using expenses paid for by the local tax payer. But, given you now say you were discussing Council business at these *brain storming* sessions, then perhaps they shouldn't have minded quite so much. But was that really a correct way to behave?'

Drew was twisting everything to sound like Alistair was a sleazy wretch with his nose in the trough. 'It wasn't how you imply. I had Council business in London – legitimate business – and was entitled to book an overnight hotel. The fact that I sometimes saw Gabrielle at the same time doesn't mean that . . .'

'. . . but you claimed for a bottle of champagne on one occasion? Did you drink that all yourself? We know you like a little drink.'

It was the fateful day that the *Daily Record* had caught them. Alistair had arranged to tell Gabrielle that he couldn't see her for a while and the champagne was to make it special. Next morning, he paid the bill in a hurry without checking it. It was an honest oversight as he was upset, not knowing if he was saying goodbye to Gabrielle for the last time.

'I didn't realise' he said sheepishly.

'You didn't realise!' Drew carried on, slowly twisting the knife. 'Or perhaps you were still under the influence of the champagne. We all remember you storming off the press conference the other week, clearly the worse for drink – or drugs. How do you explain that?'

'I was under a lot of pressure' Alistair replied, feeling dejected. 'I had just heard that Sarah was murdered and . . .'

'Ah yes' said Drew 'let's move on to your relationship with Sarah Billingham.' It sounded like he was simply reloading with fresh ammunition. 'Now, it's claimed you were more than just friends, were you not?'

'She was an extraordinary woman' Alistair replied. 'I was proud - honoured - to know her and I was heartbroken at her death - devastated. Still am. But there was no sordid affair. Those people who need to know – especially Dan, her husband and my friend – *do* know it. Everyone else can think what they like. But it's just more of the twisted lies peddled by the media to discredit me. I *did* love her, of course I did. But as a friend. Almost as a father. I miss her every day, but no-one should tread on her grave with such a filthy misrepresentation of the truth. You should all be ashamed.'

'Well, we're running out of time' said Drew. 'So, let's get on to Sarah's tragic death. You've been very vocal in claiming that Bradley Deakin was behind it. But we've just heard him tonight stressing - very forcefully - that neither he, nor anyone associated with him, had anything to do with it. Do you now accept that?'

'No, I don't' said Alistair. 'Nothing will ever convince me otherwise. And since the police are here tonight - arresting him as we speak - I suspect they don't believe him either.'

Drew looked surprised and uncomfortable. Alistair wondered whether he should have just blurted out the rumours live on national TV.

'Umm, well, I don't think we can comment . . . if it's true' said Drew, clearly with someone shouting into his ear piece 'I'm not aware of that and we must be careful about . . .'

'Well, I'm sure we'll find out very shortly' Alistair interrupted.

. 'I suppose we will' said the host. 'But let's wait to hear it from the police rather than speculate, shall we?' Drew had a slightly pleading look on his face.

'As you wish' Alistair replied. 'But if it suggests that Sarah's murder - and, by association, Gabrielle's disappearance - are linked to the Deakin campaign, then the man is clearly a disgrace.'

'Well' said Drew. 'I think we should probably leave it there. Time is up, but thank you for talking to us. Alistair Buckland.' Drew was clearly being told to cut the interview short before the lawyers were all over them.

Alistair didn't care what reaction he received or whether he had overstepped the mark. The police were at Deakin's door. That was enough.

66

Harvey

TUESDAY 6 MAY 2025

2 days to go

'Bloody hell!' said Harvey to the studio assistant beside him. 'I'm supposed to go out there after *that*! Everyone will be switching over to the news channels now to see what's going on backstage.'

'You'll be fine' said the assistant, who was clearly receiving instructions through her headset. 'But they're saying you must *not* mention anything about . . . well . . . you know. So, please don't.'

Harvey nodded. His legs were physically shaking.

'Well' said Drew, sending a further chill up Harvey's spine. 'On to our final candidate. A retired bank manager and part time football pundit on BBC Radio Brighton, Harvey Britten has been the dark horse of this extraordinary by-election. Standing in protest at Bradley Deakin being parachuted into his city, Britten has stepped over the bodies of his rivals as each succumbed to the allegations we've heard about tonight. He's been lauded as a beacon of common sense and decency amongst all the chaos and, as a result, accumulated a seven-point lead in the polls – at least he had until allegations of racism emerged in the *News on Sunday.* That reduced his lead to just four points, but he, too, is here to answer those allegations. So please welcome - Harvey Britten.'

Harvey walked across the stage towards Drew. They had met only briefly beforehand when the host popped his head around the dressing room door to say hello.

'So, Mr Britten' Drew began, as they took their seats. 'I imagine this has all been a bit of a whirlwind for you, has it not?' Harvey was pleased to be thrown a soft question to start with.

'It certainly hasn't gone the way I'd expected' replied Harvey. 'I guess I should have read the small print when I signed up.'

'Yes, indeed' said Drew. 'I'm assuming you had no expectation of leading the polls when you set out. Does that mean the idea of actually winning now worries you?'

'It's a daunting prospect, I can't lie about that' he replied, trying to sound like a serious politician, but feeling nothing of the sort. 'But now the position has changed, I feel ready for the challenge. It truly scares me, but I believe strongly in the city that is in my blood. I think, as you've seen tonight, whilst both candidates may have their own qualities, neither of them, in my view, deserves to step into Sarah Billingham's shoes. If the good people of Brighton therefore elect me instead – be that as a protest or because they share my belief in the city – then I'll represent them to the best of my ability.'

Harvey could see Sam off stage behind Drew's head, nodding approvingly and smiling. He began to relax.

'That's good to hear, I'm sure' said Drew. 'But there have been allegations that you are perhaps not ideally suited *yourself* to represent such a diverse city as Brighton, given the serious accusations of racism against you. What do you have to say about them, Mr Britten?'

'Well' said Harvey, taking a deep breath as Dale had told him to do. *Focus, choose your words and take your time.* 'It was a huge shock to read such rubbish and I now sympathise with my fellow candidates. If the papers can print such palpable lies about me, then I wonder whether anything printed about *them* can really be trusted either. In my case, I suspect the papers – or the POG, whoever prompted it – were desperate to discredit me in the hope of reining in my lead.'

'So, you think Alistair Buckland is behind these allegations?'

'Not personally, no' Harvey went on. 'But his party? Yes, without doubt. The chap who made the allegations was – and I assume still is – a POG activist and I'm sure that was his key motivation. But I can categorically say that his allegations could not be further from the truth.'

'So, you didn't sack him because he was Asian?'

'Of course not' said Harvey. 'Most of my employees in the branch were from diverse ethnic backgrounds. Therefore, it stands to reason that the greater proportion of redundancies would obviously be from their number. But it's important to point out that I had total control over recruitment so, if I was racist, why would I have employed them in the first place? If he had instead tried to claim that, in a diverse city like Brighton, I had turned down loads of black or Asian people for no good reason then, fine, say I'm racist. But I employed sixty people in my time and, by my reckoning, forty-five were from one ethnic group or other. I had a brilliant cashier who always wore a hijab, my mortgage advisor was born in Antigua and my Assistant Manager was from Jaipur. Excuse me, but I struggle to see where my white supremacist credentials fit into all that.'

'Well, that's as maybe' said Drew. 'But the claim is that you chose to retain your white staff when making redundancies.' Harvey got the impression that Drew wasn't fully engaged and was just going through the motions. He certainly seemed distracted, doubtless by the firestorm going on in his earpiece following Buckland's loose talk.

'Look' said Harvey. 'Since he's throwing false accusations at me, I don't need to be diplomatic. He was useless at his job and - since he was last one in - then whatever colour, creed or sexual persuasion he was, I'm afraid he was always going to be first out. But playing the race card is nonsense and I don't think the paper spent very much time researching such ridiculous claims.'

'Well' said Drew 'the people of Brighton will doubtless make their own minds up, so let's move on. You say all this started because you disapproved of Bradley Deakin being parachuted in, but your wife is a lifelong member of the OP and a former activist herself. Is not - as has been claimed - a vote for you just a vote for the Opposition by another name? So, anyone disillusioned by Alistair Buckland would actually be voting for the OP by choosing you instead, would they not?'

'My wife has her own politics' said Harvey, annoyed that Claire was being dragged into the conversation. 'Yes, I confess that me standing was, in part, prompted by her not liking the idea of Deakin either. But I actually voted for Sarah Billingham last time round. I don't believe people should always vote for the same party regardless of who they put up as candidate. In my time, I have voted for all the major parties. I vote on merit and that's exactly what I would do in Parliament. Doing what is best at the time. If I win, I'll neither be an OP poodle or a POG stooge. I'll be my own man, making my own choices. That's the purpose of an independent MP isn't it? And it ought to be the purpose of *all* MPs in my view, doing what is right for their constituents, not following like sheep. I'll therefore represent *all* the people of Brighton and Hove. I don't care which party they support, I'll be there for them.'

Harvey could see Sam pretending to cheer. Perhaps he was becoming a politician after all.

67

Rod Archer

TUESDAY 6 MAY 2025

2 days to go

It had been four hours since Rod suffered the indignity and humiliation of being arrested at the BBC. It was now approaching midnight and he was alone in an interview room at Paddington Green Police Station, waiting for his solicitor to arrive before the interrogation could start.

Being arrested was a bit of a blur. He remembered Bradley remonstrating with them and making various threats as Rod was led away in handcuffs, demanding to know who Rod was accused of conspiring to murder. Rod could see the irony in that. Such was the way Bradley's campaign had unravelled, it wasn't enough that he was being accused of murder. The candidate had a choice of two victims.

As he left the BBC, there were flashlights aplenty. Photos that would surely be all over the news media by now. The police could have chosen a less public place or, alternatively, used a side entrance. But, instead, they had pulled up out front where the press and public were still gathered. Yes, they knew exactly what they were doing. Maximum humiliation and maximum damage to Bradley's campaign. Even with the party machine applying damage limitation measures to the story, it was not looking good.

Bradley had done well in the interview. Probably enough to swing a few votes back. But Rod knew his arrest would undo all that good work. The rumour mill would now be going into overdrive. *If Rod was involved, then surely his boss must be too?*

He wasn't sure if he would be charged but, if he was, it would be game over. He needed to keep his cool. He knew how to play this and was sure it would work.

The door suddenly opened and a police officer entered with Mark Denver, Rod's solicitor. He was very experienced – and expensive – and had been Peter's lawyer for ten years. Rod had never needed a solicitor before - other than for conveyancing - and he'd only met Mark once. But he would need the very best there was to get him out of this mess.

'Thank you, I need to speak to my client now, if I may' said Mark to the officer, who duly left the room without comment, closing the door behind him.

'So, Rod' he said, too brightly by far. Rod assumed this was a common approach - make the client believe they are in safe hands. 'You should know we've lodged formal complaints against the police, the BBC *and* Alistair Buckland. It's outrageous the way they handled this. Outrageous.'

'Buckland?' said Rod.

'Ah yes, sorry' Mark replied. 'Of course, you were a bit busy when he outed you in his interview – or rather Bradley. Naked politics. Outrageous! Never fear, they won't get away with it. We're seeking to have the election postponed. There's no way it can be considered a fair contest with these smears going on.'

'Yes, well' said Rod. 'That's good to hear, but I need your help myself.'

'Of course you do, dear boy' said Mark 'Forgive me. We'll get this overturned, no problem. What have they said so far?'

'Not much' said Rod 'I asked for you straight away. Was that the right thing to do?'

'Always' said Mark, slightly pompously. 'Never worry about

calling your brief straight off the bat. The police know the score. Did you say anything else?'

'Nothing' said Rod.

'Good. Now, what's all this about?'

DETECTIVE INSPECTOR WILLIAMS and Detective Sergeant Crawley returned about thirty minutes later, accompanied by a uniformed officer to man the door. The four sat opposite each other and DI Williams started the audio recording. Rod assumed it was being filmed too.

'So, Rod' said Williams 'now we're all nice and cosy, we need to ask you a few questions about the death of Sarah Billingham.'

'I know nothing about it' said Rod.

'For the record, could you tell me where you were on the night of 31st December 2024 please?'

'Yes' said Rod. 'It was New Year's Eve, obviously. I went to a party at a friend's house. About fifty people can confirm that, if you check.'

'I'm sure' said Williams, who was thumbing through some paperwork. 'And where were you when you heard about Mrs Billingham's death?'

'It was the next day' said Rod. 'Well, about three-thirty in the morning actually. I got a call from a colleague who'd heard rumours that it was her in the accident. It was not until about five o'clock that we knew for sure.'

'And how did you feel about that?' said DS Crawley.

'Being honest?' said Rod.

'That's the general idea, yes.'

'I felt sorry for her, of course, but my first thought was - well, great, there we go. A by-election.'

'Bit callous, don't you think?'

'Possibly' said Rod. 'But I didn't know her personally. We needed an election and this was an opportunity. So yes, sorry, but to me it wasn't all bad news.'

'My client is entitled to see things from a practical perspective' said Mark, looking uncomfortable at Rod's frankness. 'It doesn't mean he was involved and I'd like to know where this is going. It's after midnight and my client has suffered the indignity of being arrested on national TV. You have not yet told him why he's here, so please either do so or let him go home.'

'In good time' said Williams, who appeared unphased. Rod wondered what exactly they had on him.

'Tell me, Rod' he went on. 'Have you ever met a man called Walter Coogan?' Rod tried not to show any sign of emotion.

'Yes' he said, calmly. 'We were in the army together. What about him?'

'You were indeed' said Williams. 'You served together in the same regiment, the Royal Engineers. Very good friends at the time, so we believe.'

'Yes' said Rod, trying to appear un-phased. 'But it was ten years ago. All the guys were mates, but I haven't seen most of them in years. Although I do see Walter now and again. Why do you ask?'

'Because we believe he is directly involved in Mrs Billingham's death.'

Rod could feel sweat on his brow and hoped it didn't show.

'Again' said Mark 'where's this going please? Who or what has any of this to do with my client?'

'OK' said Williams. 'You're right. It's getting late and I want to get home too. So why don't we put all our cards on the table, shall we? Rod, you'll remember that Mrs Billingham died as a result of being shunted by a Range Rover into the path of a Robo-lorry on the morning of January 1st 2025 on Brighton seafront.'

'Yes, of course.'

'And that Range Rover was driven by two men, known colloquially as the *men in black*, who were later seen setting the car alight and pushing it over Beachy Head. The car, as you may have heard, exploded and was badly burnt out. You may know from our press conference that we eventually found one partial fingerprint behind a false number plate. I can now reveal that it belonged to our mutual friend Mr Coogan. But I suspect you knew that already, didn't you?'

'Why would I?' said Rod, innocently.

'Why indeed' Williams replied, sounding like he was enjoying himself. 'Coogan appeared to be living a blameless life after his little episode handling stolen goods a few years back. He now runs a car repair service in Deptford and keeps his nose clean, by all accounts. Or, rather, he has been hiding it a lot better nowadays, until this little problem came to light. We pulled him in, obviously, and he denied it at first, but finger-prints don't lie. I think he was actually quite pleased to get it all off his chest, especially when he heard about the lengthy jail term that he's facing for conspiracy to commit murder. He was very keen to explain that no-one told him that the car was going to be used to kill Mrs Billingham. Naughty of him not to ask, really.

Anyway, his job was to sanitise the stolen Range Rover, wipe it clear of all identifying evidence and data, remove all tracking devices and stick on some false plates. It arrived inside a truck on the 12th December and left the same way five days later. Two guys dropped it off and collected it, leaving him with ten-grand in cash for his trouble. Nice little earner. But then he heard about the acci-dent over New Year. Says he was horrified but didn't feel he could say anything, so just kept quiet.'

'Well, it's a big shock to find he was involved, obviously. Always seemed a decent guy. But I'm very pleased you caught him' said Rod. 'Well done.'

'And the point being....' said Mark, rolling his hand to encourage the officer to get on with it.

'Well, the point being, have you seen or spoken to Mr Coogan lately, Mr Archer?' Williams was suddenly using a formal title.

'Not for a while, no' said Rod.

'How odd' said Williams. 'Because, it seems that Mr Coogan uses a large number of pay-as-you-go phones. We found a drawer full of them when we raided his premises. Like a small branch of Carphone Warehouse, it was. But one in particular had a call logged from you at 3.20 p.m. on Monday December 9th 2024. Ring any bells? Sorry, excuse the pun.'

'Umm' said Rod, stroking his chin and pretending to scan his memory. He wasn't sure that denying everything was the right approach.

'Actually, yes. Sorry' he said, appearing to suddenly remember. 'He sometimes repairs my car and I was having trouble starting it in the cold weather. I gave him a call to see if he could take a look. He came out but I didn't actually need him in the end. Got it started myself before he arrived. That was probably around the end of last year now I come to think of it so, yes, that would account for the call.'

Both officers stared at him, smirking, as if they didn't believe a word. It was unnerving but Rod kept his cool, on the surface at least.

'I thought you drove a nice, shiny 2024 Series 10 BMW convertible, Mr Archer. Presumably, that's under the dealer's guarantee, rather than you needing a backstreet garage in the East End to repair it?'

'No, it was my other car' said Rod. 'A classic MG sports car. I was moving it undercover for the winter and it wouldn't start. It's hard to get the parts but Walt is pretty good with that.'

'So, did you call him to cancel,' said Williams.

'No' said Rod. 'As I say, he came over but I didn't need him. As I recall he wanted me to pay his call-out charge but I wouldn't do so. Sorry. It was a busy time so I'd forgotten about it.'

Ah, I see' said Williams. 'Well, all very good, but that's not how our friend remembers the call. Not like that at all, in fact.'

What has the bastard said?!

'As I say, facing jail time does focus the mind a little. Hope it will with you too, Mr Archer. Let's stop messing about, shall we? Walter says you asked him to do the business with a car that would arrive in a few days. Presumably it hadn't been stolen at the time. You made clear there was nothing to worry about. Just some political skulduggery you needed to go under the radar. That's what made him angry, it seems. You lying and getting him involved in something much bigger and dirtier. I think that's why he was so willing to give up your name.'

'This is all well and good' said Mark 'but it seems to be the word of a criminal who my client has not denied knowing. He is very clear that he simply spoke to Mr Coogan about repairing his vintage car. It's perfectly reasonable to call a garage without knowing they have a criminal side line. Are you arresting all his innocent customers who happened to call him in December as well? You need evidence to suggest my client was involved. Not just a dodgy mechanic looking for someone to take the heat off him.'

'Well, you called him on a phone that only had one number it in, Mr Archer. Yours. Just as all the other phones in his drawer only had one number in each of them too. Some interesting people at the other end of those, mostly villains already on our books. All his *legitimate* customers use his advertised number rather than have their own direct line. There were multiple calls logged between you on that phone over the last two years. I wonder what other *skulduggery* you arranged with him?'

'I must protest!' said Mark. 'My client has freely admitted that he used Mr Coogan to repair his car, so any such calls are perfectly legitimate. Equally, it's not for *him* to know about the phone number he'd been given. Have you any evidence that my client did anything other than speak to an old friend who repaired his car? Or that he knew about his unusual habit of keeping multiple phones? And, whilst we're on the subject, criminals who use such phones tend to do so at both ends, don't they? That's the general idea - so both parties are untraceable. But my client called on his *own* phone, proving he had nothing to hide.'

'Unless that was a clever ploy' said Williams, unphased. 'If we'd caught you with a dodgy phone too, you'd be banged to rights, wouldn't you?'

'Well you didn't' Mark went on, now in full flow. 'So, can you prove they discussed anything other than a possible car repair – especially something so appalling? Unless you've evidence that my client was involved in a car theft or whatever else Mr Coogan then did to the vehicle, then you have no grounds to hold him. Is there anything more?' He started to shuffle his papers theatrically, as if preparing to leave.

'Well, surprisingly, yes' said Williams, not at all riled by the posturing solicitor. 'Mr Archer, the phone records for that mobile – and your own phone records – show some twenty missed calls from Mr Coogan to yourself on Thursday 2nd January 2025. The first was ten minutes after the car's registration number was announced. The others were spread over the next six hours. He seemed very keen to wish you a Happy New Year, didn't he?'

'It was a very busy day as you can imagine.' Rod replied. 'I was tied up with a lot of important calls about the possible by-election opportunity.'

'Hmm. Interesting' said Williams. 'But you were certainly aware of these calls as they only stopped when you blocked Mr Coogan's number later the same day. Why would that have been, Mr Archer? Blocking an old army chum who, it appears, was the only person trusted with your precious MG? Any thoughts?'

Rod said nothing, but the detective didn't wait for an answer anyway, he was on a roll.

'Could it be – as Mr Coogan claims – that he had just heard the registration number being announced and realised what you had dragged him into? We were still treating it as a possible hit and run at the time, but Mr Coogan instinctively knew something must either have gone horribly wrong or that it wasn't an accident at all. Given who was killed and the impact on your candidate's fortunes, it seems he concluded the latter. He was desperately trying to call you to vent his anger.'

'No, I assumed he was just following up on me not paying his call-out bill.' said Rod. '£150, which was ludicrous. His calls were getting in the way of important business so I blocked him.'

'But he didn't leave a single message. Not the best way to chase payment, is it? No, his story sounds far more credible and, I'm afraid, yours does not. More holes that a Swiss cheese.'

'But that assessment seems to be based entirely on your desire to believe Mr Coogan's word over my client, doesn't it?' Mark said. 'You've no evidence to disprove the innocent explanation my client has just given to you. Why Mr Coogan should try to drag a former army colleague into his dirty crimes is anyone's guess. But I suspect he has heard the conspiracy theories about the OP being involved, so decided to deflect attention from having to name his *real* co-conspirators. Set up my client as a fall guy, given his known links to the OP. I fear you'll need far more than the word of a criminal, trying to save his own skin by implicating a man with an unblemished record and high pubic profile. Very old trick I'm afraid. Imply a much bigger fish is involved rather than admit it was just him and his low-life car thieving chums.'

'We have a warrant and are currently searching your home, Mr Archer' said the officer, suddenly applying a threatening tone. 'We expect to find you linked to the money paid to Coogan, the two men who stole the car and therefore linking you to a conspiracy to commit murder. We believe they all acted on your instruction. As soon as we find those links – and we will – I'm afraid the game will be over.'

'Good luck with that' said Rod, relaxing slightly. They wouldn't find a thing. If this was all they had then Rod knew they would find nothing more. The £100,000 paid to him for dirty tricks had all been laundered through outwardly legitimate private detectives across the country, just as he had told Peter and Bradley. The fact they had then returned 50% of their hefty fee – money for actually doing nothing at all – and did so in cash, meant there was no link to the money he'd retained himself. A good brief like Mark would soon get him off with little effort involved. He knew he would be home by morning.

But that didn't solve the bigger problem. He would no doubt remain a suspect for some time to come and had been arrested in a very public way. The polls opened in just thirty-one hours and rumours would, by now, be flying around like a plague of locusts. If Rod was a suspect in the eyes of the world - then Bradley would be too.

68

Bradley

WEDNESDAY 7 MAY 2025

1 day to go

It was 3 a.m. and Bradley was still at the OP head-quarters in London. He had gone there straight after Rod's arrest, using a rear exit at the BBC. But that had not stopped him being photographed. It at least proved it was not *him* who had been arrested, as Buckland had said on live TV.

Bradley had not seen that interview but had since heard what was said. The OP machine had taken over with threats of legal action against anyone and everyone involved. But it was all fairly pointless. The damage had been done and the media were now making up their own stories.

Social media went further, as always, with assumptions and speculation being treated as irrefutable fact. *'Bradley is in it up to his neck. We told you so. He arranged the murder of Sarah Billingham, the disappearance (and likely murder) of Sharon Morgan and also drove the car over a cliff. Probably.'*

'Any news?' Bradley said, as Peter came into the conference room. It had taken on the appearance of a war room, full of people speaking into phones, scanning computers and gathered into small groups with serious expressions on tired faces.

'He's being held overnight' Peter replied. He looked just as serious and tired. 'It's a bloody disaster. The BBC swear they knew nothing about it in advance and the police just rocked up demanding to see Rod. They wouldn't wait and could hardly be stopped.'

'So, what are they questioning him about?' said Bradley. 'Is it Sarah? Please tell me it isn't Sarah. I've just been on national TV to swear that no-one associated with me had anything to do with her death. He assured me that was true. Why would he do . . .'

'We don't know what he did, or didn't do' said Peter. 'The police won't say a word about why he's being questioned. But they're issuing a statement at 8 a.m. this morning. I'm hoping to speak to Mark before then, but the timing is appalling. Twenty-four hours until the polls open. Twenty-four hours to make this all go away and convince the world that it's just a horrible misunderstanding.'

'And is it?' asked Bradley, not entirely sure of his Agent's innocence.

'I hope to God it is,' Peter continued. 'It's so frustrating. You did well last night in the interview. It might even have turned the tide. And now . . . this.'

'I'm screwed, aren't I?' said Bradley, still in shock.

'It's not over 'til it's over' said Peter. 'But if Rod really did have anything to do with this, then, yes. I fear you could be. And so is the party.'

'*I CAN CONFIRM that a 34-year old man, Walter James Coogan, will appear in court this morning charged with offences under the Vehicle Licence and Registration Act 1994 in relation to the theft of a car on 12th December 2024.*'

The face of Detective Inspector Williams filled the TV on the war room's wall whilst Bradley, Peter and the rest stood transfixed. Most of them had been there for ten hours. Others arrived in time for the 8 a.m. police statement, now being broadcast live on every TV and radio breakfast programme.

'I can also confirm that a 33-year old male was arrested last night and is currently being questioned in relation to the same offence. Questioning is ongoing and I cannot therefore give any further details.'

'Shit' said Peter. 'He must have done it.' Bradley stared at the screen, watching all their hopes and dreams evaporate with every word.

'Is it Rod Archer?'

'Is it the car used to murder Sarah Billingham?'

'Will you be questioning Bradley Deakin?'

The assembled journalists fired questions at the officer from all sides, but he clearly didn't intend to answer any of them.

'We'll give you a further update as and when there is some news to report and we ask that the media does not speculate about this case in the meantime.'

He turned back into the police station, followed by the two anonymous officers who had been standing beside him. As a piece of dramatic broadcasting - one that had been eagerly anticipated all night - it was a bit of a non-event. But it was enough. Within an hour Walter Coogan had been identified by the media as a former army officer, now running a garage in East London. Rod's past army life was researched after his arrest and his association with the same regiment led to an easy conclusion that the two men must know each other.

Rod was in the frame for the theft of a car which, by any amateur sleuth's deductions, must be the one used to kill Sarah Billingham. Since petty car theft is an unlikely hobby for a high-profile Public Affairs consultant, logic dictates that he instead ordered the theft and − by default − therefore ordered the murder. And if Rod − the Election Agent of the OP's candidate could do such a terrible thing to orchestrate a by-election, then how dirty were Bradley Deakin's hands? Or the OP itself? Was he acting alone? Impossible. They must all have been in on it. Ordered it. Committed the crime.

Social media − and even some of the mainstream news organisations - had unilaterally decided. The judges scores were in: *Bradley Deakin − murdering bastard.*

69

Alistair

WEDNESDAY 7 MAY 2025

1 day to go

Alistair awoke to a knock on his hotel room door. It was 7.30 a.m. He had stayed in London overnight after the interview and remembered going to bed very late. Possibly after two. There'd been a lot of late-night activity at POG headquarters to confirm if Deakin had indeed been arrested. He had not.

Overall, Alistair had been pleased with his performance. Feedback was fairly positive but, the trouble was, Harvey Britten had done even better. At best, Alistair had pulled further ahead of Deakin, but the election still looked to be beyond his grasp.

The knock came again and Alistair crawled out of bed. He grabbed the white hotel bath robe and lumbered to the door, yawning. He looked through the spy-hole to see Dan outside, so opened it. He rushed in, carrying a newspaper.

'Has something happened?' said Alistair, closing the door. Dan was already across the room and standing by the window, pulling open the curtains. The sun streamed in, dazzling Alistair as it hit him full in in the face.

'Oh yes, you could say that' said Dan. He gestured to the newspaper which he had thrown down on the bed on the way in. It was the *Daily Record*, which made Alistair's heart sink. He picked it up and read the headline: *'Buckland – the Seagull has landed'*. He tried to get his eyes to focus.

'All the other media are leading on Rod Archer's arrest' said Dan. 'But not this lot. Oh no. Can't bring themselves to rubbish their own man or miss a chance to have a go at you.'

'What's it about?' said Alistair, thinking it might be quicker to get an abridged version.

'Look!' said Dan, who presumably didn't feel inclined to explain. 'Its bloody obvious!'

Alistair studied the paper and, sure enough, it was. Beside the vast headline was a grainy photo taken in the dark. On closer inspection it was the street outside his apartment in Hove. The photo showed a large mass propped up against a lamp-post on a deserted street. Only it wasn't a large mass. It was Alistair.

The story explained that, two weeks ago, *'Boozer Buckland'* was picked up by a neighbour's security camera staggering down the road late at night. He had been carrying a bag in his arms before falling sideways onto the pavement. The bag burst and scattered two bottles into the gutter, one of which broke. Apparently, the full video could be viewed online, in all its horror, via a convenient link.

The front page claimed that this incident put the lie to Alistair not having a drink problem. He was clearly steaming drunk and unable to stand. *'And this man wants to represent the people of Brighton as their MP!'* concluded the article. *'Somehow, we don't see Brighton's electorate raising a glass to his victory any time soon.'*

Alistair looked bemused. He had no recollection of the incident, but *did* remember waking up with a large bruise on his hip a couple of weeks ago and not knowing where it came from. Dan assisted by pulling up the link on his phone. The silent footage carried the *Daily Record's* logo in the corner and was taken from a fixed camera over a door further down the seafront. He didn't know who lived there but assumed they were loyal OP supporters.

The footage showed an empty street as Alistair slowly staggered into shot from the top of the screen. As he approached, a seagull took off from a dustbin and passed in front of him. Presumably taken by surprise, Alistair stepped back and lost his balance. The bag hit the deck and one bottle rolled out. The other took the full force and disgorged its contents into the gutter. Alistair recognised the label as his favourite brandy. He was shown rolling about to collect the intact bottle and then propping himself against the lamp-post before hauling himself to his feet. A freeze frame of that moment was used as the cover photo to suggest he was lying drunk in the street. The embarrassing footage continued as he slowly staggered out of shot at the bottom of the screen. His face was clear and there was no doubt it was him.

'Why didn't you tell me about this?' said Dan.

'Because I don't remember it' said Alistair, concerned that it didn't register, even after watching the video. 'I must have gone down to the off-licence but . . . I've no recollection.'

'Well, it looks appalling' said Dan, clearly disgusted and angry. 'After all the good work you did last night, this is . . .' he let out a long, slow sigh and shook his head. Words were not necessary. 'On the plus side, Deakin is looking dead in the water. Rod Archer's arrest is going down like the Titanic and social media trolls are already jumping to their own conclusions. But you shouldn't have accused Deakin of being arrested for murder. The Electoral Commission is looking into that and the OP are taking legal action.'

'What will happen with the Commission?' said Alistair.

'At worst they could suspend the election' said Dan, 'but the party doesn't think that will happen. The confusion was addressed almost immediately so what you said didn't sway opinion in itself. Deakin has a much harder job explaining why his sidekick has been arrested. The police are making a statement at eight.'

Alistair slumped down on the bed and finished reading the article. 'I've made a right mess of everything' he said. 'They're saying I've soiled Sarah's memory. That really hurts, because it's true.'

Dan came over and sat beside him. 'She'd understand' he said quietly. 'She wouldn't blame you for all the rubbish that's been thrown at you by the media and by . . . your friend.'

Alistair dropped the paper and leaned forwards, resting his elbows on his knees. He held his head in his hands and rubbed his hair aggressively. 'I'm so sorry Dan' he said. 'So, so sorry.' The tears began to roll down his face and he sobbed uncontrollably.

70

Harvey

WEDNESDAY 7 MAY 2025

1 day to go

'I think you should start preparing an acceptance speech' said Sam. 'The other two are toast. You have to start believing you're going to win.'

Harvey sat in his hotel room with Sam, watching breakfast TV. The police statement outwardly said very little – whilst saying an awful lot at the same time. Bradley Deakin would have a devil of a job explaining how the arrest didn't implicate him in Sarah Billingham's murder too – or at least throw a cloud of suspicion over him.

At the same time, the *Daily Record* carried a disturbing image of Buckland lying drunk in the street. His two main rivals were imploding. They seemed to be doing everything possible to wave Harvey past, like an aging tortoise lumbering towards the finishing line as the two competing hares lay gasping by the side of the road.

'How are the polls?' he said, once the TV presenters were back on screen.

'An interesting night' said Sam. 'The impact of Rod Archer's arrest probably hasn't fully kicked in yet, but people seem to be settling into your camp after the interviews. You played a blinder last night Dad, really you did. I was so proud of you. Have you spoken to Mum?'

'Yes, briefly' said Harvey. 'An hour ago.' Claire had watched the interview at home and shared Sam's glowing review. 'What are the poll ratings, exactly?'

'Sorry' said Sam. She scrolled on her tablet. 'Deakin is on 20% but, as I say, the full implication of the arrest won't fully be reflected in these figures. The InstaPoll was apparently taken immediately after the interviews finished. Buckland shot up to 25%, but, again, that was before this morning's headline. He'll fall like a stone today. You, Daddy dearest, are on . . .' She paused dramatically.

'Come on, it's not the bloody X-Factor' said Harvey.

'. . . 33%! An eight-point lead even before Buckland's press coverage today. Only 12% are still *don't knows*. Dad, I really think you are home and dry.'

Harvey said nothing. He stood up and walked to the hotel window, some ten floors up and with good views over London. In the gaps between buildings, he could just about see the edge of Big Ben. The Palace of Westminster. The idea that such a famous and iconic building could soon become his workplace made no sense whatsoever. It was all madness.

'Still twenty-four hours to go' he said. 'At this rate, anything could happen by then. Come on, let's pack up and get back home to your mother.'

71

Bradley

WEDNESDAY 7 MAY 2025

1 day to go

Bradley stood on stage at the Brighton Hippodrome theatre, waiting for the journalists and broadcasters to settle down before the hastily arranged press conference could start. He had rushed back to Brighton on the 9.15 train that morning and was currently functioning on exhaust fumes. He hadn't slept for thirty-three hours and it was now 3 p.m. He was about to throw the last roll of the dice.

He wasn't quite dead yet. The body was still twitching. The *Daily Record* had worked it's magic by revealing the CCTV images of Alistair Buckland this morning. They had apparently held onto the footage for over a week but were waiting for the right moment to release it. They could not have known just how good their timing would be. If Rod's arrest had damaged Bradley's campaign, this story had caused a similar amount of damage to Buckland's fragile reputation. The media were awash with talk and chatter about how clearly unsuitable he was as an MP.

But it wasn't all spiteful or vindictive coverage. Most actually sympathised on a human level. They felt he was a man in dire need of help and support for his drink problem, not the weight of Parliamentary responsibility. Despite their political differences, Bradley tended to agree. Buckland was a hopeless drunk who'd suffered enormous stress and grief over the last few months. The worst thing that could happen to him personally would be to win the election.

So, the main – and now sizeable – threat was Harvey Britten, whose trump card was decency and his local credentials. The media had largely dismissed the racism allegations after last night's interview, and the public seemed to agree. Bradley needed time, the one thing he didn't have. It looked very unlikely that the election would be postponed and this press conference was therefore the last chance to throw himself on the mercy of the electorate.

He stood under the bright lights on a stage laid out as a set for the play *"Hobson's Choice"* which was running at the theatre that week. The OP had been lucky to get hold of the venue at such short notice, so couldn't complain about the stage props. But it meant Bradley appeared to be standing in a northern family kitchen dating from the early nineteen-hundreds.

'Can we start please?' he said, trying to quieten down the crowd. He was eager to get it done so that his defence could be reported as soon as possible.

'Thank you' he said, walking to the front of the stage with a microphone in his hand. There was no-one else with him. He would desperately have liked Emma and Stephen there beside him like last time. But they were gone.

'OK' he said, trying to appear positive. 'Thank you for coming and to the Hippodrome for letting us use this magnificent theatre at such short notice. I know many of you will be writing your own headlines, based on the name of the excellent play being staged here this week. But I dearly hope that voters in Brighton are not seeing themselves as only having a *Hobson's Choice* themselves. Harvey Britten may look like the only credible candidate left, given the firestorm of bad press that myself and Alistair Buckland have received overnight. But let me tell you this. Harvey is clearly an honest, decent, well intentioned man who has the interests of Brighton firmly in his heart and his mind. But the same can be said of me. He is also a good family man. And, believe me, so am I.

Like me, you will all have been shocked to hear the news that my Election Agent, Rod Archer, was arrested last night. Whilst the police, quite rightly, will not disclose the offences that he's being questioned about, I think too many people have drawn their own conclusions. More importantly, they've applied guilt by association and assumed that, whatever Rod is alleged to have done, then I too must be responsible for those same alleged crimes.

Well, that's just not true. I don't know – in all honesty – what he's alleged to have done with the garage owner, Walter Coogan. The police haven't told me and – perhaps tellingly – haven't seen fit to question me on the subject either. I think that says a lot about me being a co-conspirator.

I, like you, can therefore only speculate. What I do know is that, IF – and it's a very big if – IF he's done whatever he's alleged to have done, then I swear on my son's life that I knew nothing about it. If, like you, I assume it has something to do with the death of Sarah Billingham, then I can only reiterate what I said last night. I did not, would not and could not have anything to do with murdering *anyone*, especially a kind, hard working wife, mother and politician like Sarah. I just couldn't!

So, please, think what you will about my politics or me as a person. But, believe me when I say this – I was not involved in her death in any way, whatsoever. If Rod was involved – and I dearly hope he wasn't – then it was entirely of his own doing, not mine.

I therefore ask you to look at where we are with this extraordinary campaign. I'm standing in this election because I felt that people in this country - this city - believed in me. They seemed to trust me, have faith in me and wanted me to lead them. Without that belief, I would have turned down the offer and stuck to the successful TV career that I love. But I felt there was a higher calling and I should therefore rise to that challenge. And I did. The main thing I therefore ask people to remember when they go to the polls tomorrow, is this – *I am the same person.* Nothing has changed. Amongst all the chatter and noise, allegations, media speculation, wild social media claims and tragic events that have marred this election – I have not changed one bit from the man you all know.

The only thing that I *have* done - when you cut through all that noise - is to have slept with a girl, younger than she claimed to be at the time, when I was little more than a child myself. I then had an affair with her years later when I was seeing someone else. But Emma was not my wife at the time - please remember that. I felt I was in a transition between one relationship and the next. Just like hundreds, if not thousands, of people are doing right now as I speak, before they finally settle down.

But it is *not* a crime. I am not proud of myself, but I should not be judged for what my twenty-four-year old self did eighteen years ago. I love my wife, my son, my family. I love them more than anything. I'm a good husband and father, just like Harvey Britten. Please, don't judge me on hearsay, rumour or speculation. Judge me as the man you know and who I actually am. I didn't kill anyone, abduct anyone or rape anyone. I simply fell in love, twice, many years ago, with two wonderful women at the same time.

As for representing Brighton, this is a terrific city. I've come to know and respect it's people as warm, diverse and good. Yes, I wasn't born and raised here like Harvey Britten, nor do I have the lifelong passion that he has for the city and its football team – the Seagulls, yes, I *do* know.

But I would sink my heart and soul into representing its people better than anyone else. I have the experience, the profile and the will to stand up for this city and make its voice heard. Much lounder than an independent candidate ever could in the Westminster cauldron. Please, trust me with your vote. I'm not the man I've been painted to be. I'm the man you know, who's had the privilege of being welcomed into your home countless times on TV. So, please, have faith in me. Make your own choice by all means but, please, do not be swayed by hearsay and hype.'

'You seem to be asking voters to take an awful lot on trust' shouted one journalist from the back. Bradley could not see who it was. A gradual murmur spread around the assembled media. They had been sitting in silence, holding microphones before them or otherwise typing into their tablets. Bradley took a deep breath. He felt that he'd said his piece as well as he could. He looked off stage to where Peter was standing. He nodded back approvingly.

'Yes, I am' said Bradley. 'I accept that. But it is all I can do. OK, I promised to take some questions and that I'll answer them honestly.' He looked around at the sea of raised hands as the crowd shouted. 'Yes, Julia from ITV news next, please.'

'Are you still living with your wife, Emma?'

Bradley looked pensive. 'I'm afraid she took the news about the historic affair with Sharon very badly so, for the moment, she is staying with family. I hope to convince her to come back, once she's had time to digest it all. But, no, I fear we're living apart for now and have been since the weekend.'

'Have you seen the statement she's just put out?' asked the reporter. Bradley looked confused. 'She's just posted it on social media.'

'Sorry, then no, obviously not' said Bradley, worried what Emma had said. He hoped it wouldn't unravel the good work he had just put in.

'Shall I read it?' said Julia. She obviously intended to do so anyway, and didn't wait for a reply.

'I *would like to clarify that my husband is not a good family man as he has just claimed. The affair with the hooker, eighteen years ago, was just one of many during our marriage. He is a lifelong womaniser and I've now left him, taking our son with me, with no intention of coming back. If you want an example of the sort of sleaze ball he is, then ask . . .*'

Julia paused, presumably wondering whether to name names. She obviously decided it would be fine.

'*. . . ask him about Dixie Chandler.*'

'So, Mr Deakin, do you have any comment about Dixie Chandler as your wife asks?'

Bradley's blood ran cold. *Emma, you bitch.* He composed himself and tried not to look as angry and rattled as he was.

'Well' he said 'I don't believe this is the time or place to go into details about my marriage. I'll need to talk to Emma in private and, with respect, I've no wish to wash our dirty laundry in public. Everything I said before stands - I love my wife, my son and my family more than anything. That's all that matters. Now, if you don't mind, I'm afraid I must leave it there as I have to attend a pre-arranged campaign event. Thank you all so much for coming.'

The press pack exploded into a cacophony of noise, firing questions at Bradley as he walked off stage. He had no intention of answering them. So much for total honesty, but what could he do? Emma had sold him down the river. He just prayed that everything he had already said would do the trick. There would be no further opportunities to explain himself and Emma has stolen the last word. *Damn the woman.*

72

Harvey

THURSDAY 8 MAY 2025

Election Day

Harvey was not used to election day etiquette as a candidate. He knew he wasn't allowed to speak to anyone or make any political statements. But what he *was* supposed to do with himself, to pass the fifteen hours of voting time, was never fully explained. 'Keep a low profile' seemed the best advice.

He assumed the big-boys would be huddled together with their huge party machines working hard on constituents who had previously indicated their support but had not yet voted today. On that note, there was one task he certainly had to do, which was vote himself. He would not normally expect that to be particularly newsworthy. However, things had changed. He was now the front-runner in the polls, so the media saw the simple act of voting as a classic photo opportunity. It was tradition that the main candidates went to vote early, alongside their partner or spouse, and that the event be captured by the media. The aim was to encourage the great unwashed to similarly get out and vote.

The task had been stage managed to avoid the media having to simultaneously hang around all three Polling Stations at the same time, waiting for each candidate to rock up in their own good time. Instead, Sam had negotiated exactly when and where Harvey would be voting and the media co-ordinated the timing with Deakin and Buckland's people. Deakin's team had insisted on being first to the polls – choosing 7.30 a.m. – but he would apparently be doing so on his own. The absence of his wife would doubtless distract from the occasion.

Buckland's people had asked for 10 a.m. Sam joked that this was to give him time to sober up. As a result, Harvey and Claire were scheduled for 9 a.m. and they had walked down to the local school hall right on cue. They had been amazed that at least ten photographers, reporters and TV crews had accompanied them all the way there - walking in front, beside and behind them. It took ten minutes to make the two-minute walk and Harvey managed to avoid answering any questions on the way. They media then disappeared, presumably to rush over to Buckland's Polling Station, so Harvey and Claire had been able to walk home in peace.

It was now twelve o'clock and the media were clearly upset that Alistair Buckland had not been quite so accommodating. Reports were materialising that he had 'gone missing' – based entirely on him not turning up to vote. Harvey wondered what he would do in Buckland's shoes. The media had been camped outside his apartment block since the previous morning. But he had not been seen there and his car was missing.

Sam was due to arrive shortly. She had stayed at home overnight to vote herself and was due to arrive with Phoebe any time now. Piers was coming down later and would then look after the excited child overnight whilst the rest of them went to the results announcement sometime around 10 p.m.

'Have you written your acceptance speech?' said Claire, who'd been watching her husband pacing the floor all morning. 'Sam keeps telling you to.'

'No' Harvey replied. 'I think it's bad luck and a waste of time anyway. I still don't really expect to win. And I can't think of anything to say. On the off-chance I do win - I think I'll just wing it.'

'You'll win' said Claire. 'The other two spent all yesterday finding new and exciting ways to kibosh their own chances. So, it's yours to lose.'

Polls were not permitted on election day so the impact of yesterday's developments was, as yet, unknown. There was only one poll that mattered today. But would POG or OP die-hard supporters really vote for Harvey with so much resting on the result for both parties? Harvey still believed that they – and the mass of *don't knows* –would ultimately hold their proverbial noses and vote along party lines when it actually came to the crunch. If they did, then Harvey's lead would disappear as quickly as it had arrived.

In his view, either of the other two might still end up stealing it from him on the night. They were wholly unsuitable as MPs but, so what? As Sarah had once said, numerous unsuitable rogues currently sit as MPs simply because people vote for their party rather than the candidate. On that basis, are there any womanisers or those who use prostitutes in the House? Ahem, pretty safe bet. Alcoholics or drug users? Probably. MPs who take liberties with their expenses claims? Please form an orderly queue. Accused of a murder conspiracy? *The prosecution would refer m'lud to the Crown versus Jeremy Thorpe MP.*

So, whatever sins his opponents were accused of, it may ultimately make little difference to the final result with so much resting on the outcome for both parties. Expert opinion was therefore divided. No-one wanted to stick their neck out and get their prediction wrong, but Harvey was still the bookies' favourite.

The whole nation was now gripped by the contest. It was the gift that kept on giving. Just when it looked to be all over, along came Deakin's alleged infidelity with a soap star, Buckland lying drunk in the street and Archer's arrest. Either story would normally be enough to fill the papers for a week. Harvey now wondered if *he* would be the main story in the papers tomorrow– Harvey Britten, the new MP for Brighton and Hove. Surely not.

Or was there still one further headline to come?

73

Bradley

THURSDAY 8 MAY 2025

Election Day

Bradley was with Peter and assorted officials in the Brighton OP offices. They were small with only basic facilities. They were really only suitable for MP surgeries and day-to-day administration, not running a major election campaign on behalf of a would-be future Prime Minister. Although that seemed a million miles away at the moment.

He didn't need overnight Insta-Polls to know that Emma had further damaged his chances. Whilst the mainstream media were sworn to radio silence, social media maintained its self-imposed immunity to any form of restraint. But it wasn't clear how badly it had really harmed him. Some sympathised with his wider plight and claimed that his private life had nothing to do with his ability to be an MP or world leader. Bradley appreciated the sentiment but knew they were in the minority. The rest were having a field day.

Instead of being trolled as a hopeless drunk, Alistair Buckland was receiving some sympathy and attacking him was being seen as akin to kicking an injured puppy. Would that translate into votes? Bradley couldn't see how it could.

Many of Emma friends were showing solidarity with his wife by telling Bradley exactly what they thought of him. He despaired at how the standard of spelling and grammar has gone to the dogs in this country. Even the 'C' word had been spelt with a 'K' by one of Emma's dopey friends.

Peter was on the phone, pacing up and down in the corridor. He'd been trying to get news about Rod, but there was still radio silence. Even Mark was unable to give anything more than to say that Rod was still at the station whilst they searched his home and office. Peter hung up and walked back. His poker face could have been hiding either good or bad news. It was impossible to tell.

'They've just let him go – for now at least' he said. There was no sign of any relief or jubilation in his tone. 'He's going to video-con us as soon as he gets back to Party HQ.'

They both moved into the only private office available and waited for Rod's call. It came a few minutes later and Peter put it up on screen. The face of their colleague appeared and he looked like death. A man who had not slept for two days, was unshaven and had dishevelled hair.

'What the hell's going on?' said Peter, in lieu of an enquiry about his health. 'Have you any bloody idea how much damage you've caused? What *have* you done?'

'Nothing' said Rod, without any show of emotion. Bradley assumed it was down to exhaustion. 'They've got nothing. Its all circumstantial.'

Peter managed to slowly squeeze as many details as he could out of Rod about the allegations he was facing. Bradley felt that an entirely innocent man would be far more passionate in his defence. Instead, Rod kept emphasising that the police couldn't prove his involvement - rather than actually denying it. Bradley had heard enough.

'Rod' he said, interrupting. 'I just want to know one thing. Cut all the crap about circumstantial evidence and legal technicalities. Did you, or did you not, have anything to do with Sarah Billing-ham's murder?'

Rod sighed and said nothing.

'It's not a difficult question for God sake!' said Peter, showing his frustration too.

'What do you want me to say?' asked Rod.

'Just . . . yes or no, if that's not too difficult.'

'Look' said Rod, still showing no emotion. 'What's the point? If I said no, you wouldn't believe me. If I said yes, you'd go to the police. So why bother committing one way or the other?'

'Because . . .' Bradley couldn't find the words. It was obvious.

'For goodness sake!' said Peter. 'Why would you do it? *Why?*' Peter had obviously reached his own verdict of 'guilty'.

Rod shrugged his shoulders. Bradley was unsure if he was worried about incriminating himself on a potentially recorded call or if he really didn't care. Then he finally spoke. 'I believed in you, Bradley. Really, I did. I put myself on the line for you. But if you've lost this bloody election - don't try and pin it on me. It was all set up for you to win – to go on and lead the party back to greatness. It was *you* with your paedo past and constant womanising that brought you down. Not me. I've got nothing to be ashamed of and I will *not* be convicted of anything.'

Bradley realised they were not going to get anywhere and hung up the call.

'He did it. Sure as seagulls fly.'

'I just can't believe it' said Peter. 'What the hell did he think he was doing?'

'What happens next?' Bradley replied. 'Will his release help us today? It's better than being charged, surely?' He turned on the BBC news channel. The ticker tape across the bottom of the screen was showing 'breaking news' that Rod had been released pending further enquiries.

'Not exactly saying it was a miscarriage of justice' said Peter, dryly.

The news reader spoke over footage of Rod being manhandled into a car outside the police station whilst a pack of photographers and reporters encircled him. But that was it. Rod had been released pending further enquiries. End of story. Now over to the sport's desk.

Bradley slumped back on the uncomfortable plastic office chair.

'I'm stuffed, aren't I?' he said.

'It's not over until the result is announced' said Peter.

'But your honest opinion?'

'You're stuffed.'

74

Lionel Montague

THURSDAY 8 MAY 2025

Election Night

'Well, where the hell *is* he? Someone must know.'

As Acting Returning Officer, Lionel Montague had thought the worst was over in an election that he dearly wanted to forget. Just get through the day, hope no-one else is arrested and then announce the result. That was the plan. Then go back to the office tomorrow and resign from post to ensure this onerous responsibility never fell on his shoulders again. But, no. One of the main candidates had now gone missing, with the announcement only a couple of hours away.

Lionel was overseeing his third Parliamentary election in four years, surely a record in anyone's book. They were supposed to only take place every five years. He had no objection initially - enjoying both the responsibility and the challenge - until this debacle unfolded. It would have tried the patience of a saint.

From day-one it had been testing. Having a major TV personality involved was always going to turn it into a media circus. He could cope with that, it was all part of the brief. But then all the allegations, revelations and potential criminal charges appeared, bringing an almost daily challenge from either one party or the other, each seeking to have the election postponed. Lionel had been in such regular contact with the Electoral Commission that he thought he should get an invite to their Christmas party. He still wasn't entirely convinced that the result would stand, even now. There were multiple lawyers involved and Lionel suspected that, whichever party lost, his announcement would not bring an end to the legal wrangling.

Now he had another dilemma. Where on God's earth was Alistair Buckland? It was 10.15 and the polls shut a quarter of an hour ago. The agreement was that all candidates would arrive at the count by ten. The venue was a large sport's hall, seconded specially in anticipation of a large number of press expected to attend. It was one of Lionel's better decisions. The place was packed and the main TV stations had even constructed their own little studios at the back of the hall. They were using the hastily assembled stage as a backdrop.

Arriving a few minutes late would not normally be an issue. The result was unlikely until about 12.30 – later if a recount was needed. But Buckland had not been seen or heard from all day. On returning from London yesterday, he had apparently been taken to his Election Agent's house to collect his car. Dan Billingham then looked after him there for the rest of the day as he said Buckland was distressed. The POG candidate had then insisted on driving home in the evening and hadn't been seen since. He'd not returned to his flat, his phone was turned off and his car didn't have its tracking device activated.

It was a difficult dilemma for Lionel. What if he was dead? Given his state of mind, it was not out of the question that they'd find him lying in a hedge surrounded by pills or hanging from a tree on the Downs. Lionel had confirmed the rules with his new best friend at the Electoral Commission. If Buckland was indeed dead, and Lionel found out before the result was announced, then the election would be postponed, even if polling had ended. But if his death was not discovered until *after* the announcement, then the decision would stand. Of course, if Buckland had miraculously won, his corpse would not be expected to take its seat in Parliament, so another election would then be required. Otherwise, the winner would be confirmed as the new MP. However, Lionel was not sure what should happen if a key candidate simply vanishes into thin air. Had Buckland just washed his hands of the whole affair and flown off to Spain to get away from it all? Who knows?

'Get his Election Agent over here again.' Lionel shouted to his assistant.

Dan approached, looking concerned.

'I'm sorry for . . .' Lionel was not sure how best to put it. 'But I really need to know where Mr Buckland is and whether he's OK. Doesn't anyone have *any* idea where he is?'

'I've been trying all day' said Dan. 'I'm really worried about him. When I left him last night, he was . . . distressed. The police only started to take his disappearance seriously late this afternoon. They tracked his car on CCTV as far as East Dean last night, heading across the South Downs. Then they ran out of cameras. The car never made it to Eastbourne so he is presumably still up there, somewhere. They've been searching this evening but with no luck.'

'It can't be that difficult to find a car up there, surely' said Lionel. The Downs were a designated area of natural beauty, largely made up of green fields and hills leading to the wonderful white chalk cliffs of the Seven Sisters and Beachy Head.

'And they're sure he hasn't . . .' Lionel made a gesture to indicate a car going over a cliff as diplomatically as he could - but knew it still looked callous. It was an awful proposition to consider, but not out of the question.

'Definitely not. They've checked' said Dan.

'Well, find him. Please. You've got two hours before I need to make a decision.'

75

Alistair

THURSDAY 8 MAY 2025

Election Night

Alistair had not slept all night, despite nesting in a pile of old, stale straw. He had left Dan yesterday evening after assuring him he'd be alright. His friend had spent several hours listening and counselling him during the day, encouraging him to seek help for his problems – the drinking and what they both concluded was bordering on depression.

It had all been brewing for a while, perhaps ever since Sarah died. Certainly, once the security of his relationship with Gabrielle had imploded. He had always liked a drink - probably too much. Living alone, he had never seen it as a problem - and perhaps it wasn't, until his life began to unravel less than a month ago. Now it was his only comfort - the only way to make it all go away, even briefly, and allow him to sleep. The sleeping pills helped a bit, but he needed the alcohol to wash them down and really make them work. But, last night, he'd had nothing to drink in deference to Dan and their conversation.

In the past six weeks he had descended from respected local politician to a figure of national ridicule. From there, he'd reached rock bottom as a pathetic drunk lying in the street with the last shreds of his dignity running into the gutter. Oddly, that had earned him sympathy rather than mockery. But he didn't want people's sympathy. That just confirmed him to be an utter loser, which he knew he was.

Certainly, he wouldn't be elected as MP for Brighton and Hove today. He had let everyone down, especially himself. The inevitable humiliation would probably come to a head when he found himself being beaten by a student dressed as a seagull. That's how far he had fallen. Who in their right mind would vote for him? He wouldn't even vote for himself.

The media wanted to cover him casting his vote this morning but he had no intention of doing so. What was the point? Instead, he had driven to Beachy Head from Dan's house last night and walked along the cliffs to clear his head. The sea was still and calm – almost inviting. Seagulls were flying overhead, sounding like they were laughing at him. The noisy choir echoed inside his head, taunting him - '*Loser, Loser, Loser, Hark, Hark, Ha Ha.*'

He had resisted the temptation to jump, more out of fear than a will to live. Instead, he had walked back to the car and programmed it to drive to Buckland Farm. Well, it wasn't called that now, of course. It was the '*Organic and Sustainable Crop Centre*'. He'd sold it to a couple of young ex-bankers in 2005 who had given up their decadent lifestyle in Islington to live off the land in Sussex. They'd got rid of the cattle herds – or 'liberated' them, as they put it – and turned over the whole farm to growing super foods. Alistair had no idea if their business model was working, but they were still there nearly twenty years later. He didn't really care either way. The fools had paid the full asking price and he'd just wanted shot of the place at the time.

As the car navigated the familiar lanes around the farm, he realised that his time as a farmer was, perhaps, not so awful after all. It was a simpler life - fresh air and green fields. Yes, it was stressful trying to make the farm profitable with annual battles against weather, crop failures, animal diseases and government bureaucracy. But, all in all, it hadn't been such a bad life. The grass is always greener on the other side. His thwarted political ambitions, the awful relationship with his mother and his lifetime of resentment had clouded the good that was actually right there in front of him. All that he had actually achieved with the farm. His greatest success.

He switched the car over to manual and turned off the road when he saw the old gate in the lane. The entrance was overgrown as it had been many years since it was last used to herd cattle. He opened the gate and drove through, before heading slowly down the track to the old barn that had originally been one of the milking sheds, but was now empty and deserted. The new owners had stripped out and sold all the equipment and used the barn to store crops until about two years ago, but had now let it fall into decay.

Alistair was not surprised to find it unlocked. There was nothing left to steal inside, just a vast empty space with the smell of the stale straw bales, lying around the edges. He drove the car inside and the silence of the barn was beautiful. He didn't shut the doors behind him which allowed the moonlight to beam in. It felt peaceful. Almost the first time he had been able to breath for weeks. He'd climbed between the old, decaying hay bales and tried unsuccessfully to sleep overnight.

In the morning, he had contemplated his life, his missed opportunities and his many failure, whilst working his way through a bottle of vintage malt whisky. Unknown to Dan, it had been packed in his suitcase in the boot of the car. Dan wouldn't be happy, but it didn't really matter anymore. His packet of sleeping pills lay beside him and, occasionally, he stared at them. He was either trying to pluck up the courage to take them or was checking they were still there for when he finally did. He wasn't sure which.

At around 11 a.m. - he wasn't sure when exactly - he fell asleep. Whether it was the silence, the alcohol or the sense of relief in knowing that the madness would soon be over, he had just drifted off. To his surprise, he didn't wake again until seven in the evening. It was the best sleep he'd had for ages. Ironic really. Finally, he was at peace with himself.

His neck, back and shoulders were stiff and painful having slept in the same, awkward position for so long. He badly needed the toilet and dragged himself up, relieving himself against the walls of the barn. The smell of urine filled the air. It was probably 70% proof.

He actually felt sober and wandered over to the doors. The low evening sunshine made his eyes squint for a moment and it was still warm outside. Birds chirped pleasingly – a complete contrast to the angry, mocking seagulls last night. They sounded welcoming, friendly even. *Good to have you home, boss, we missed you.* He had missed them too.

He felt hungry but had not brought anything to eat. He walked over to an old, rusty bench, sat down and let the sun shine on his face. He closed his eyes and his head fell back as he absorbed the warmth on his skin, as if drawing on the solar power to recharge his batteries.

What to do? He felt calmer now and the idea of taking pills to bring it all to an end was no longer as clear a solution as it had been this morning. A good sleep had momentarily changed his perspective. He thought of Dan and little Charlie. They would miss him and he felt sad, knowing he would never see the dear little boy grow up. How would Dan explain to the child that, once again, someone else he loved was suddenly gone from his young life forever? It seemed cruel, if not heartless. He didn't want to cause any more hurt to that sweet, innocent child.

So, he walked back to the car, leaving the boxes of pills in the corner of the barn alongside the empty whisky bottle. He decided to face his demons, go back to the real world and rebuild his life. Charlie was the inspiration and strength he needed to get him through the darkness. If he could just get past tonight and the election result.

He programmed the Auto Drive for the sports hall near Preston Park where the election result was being announced later. It was still early - only 7.30 p.m. No-one would be there yet. Perhaps he should go home first? Or maybe wait just a bit longer. Enjoy the peace, silence and tranquillity for just a couple more blissful hours before re-joining the madness of his real life.

He rummaged through the glove compartment, hoping to find a

chocolate bar or something to eat. Nothing, but a half-bottle of whisky. He could not remember putting it there or how long ago he had bought it. It was unopened, so he undid the screw top. It would keep him focused whilst he enjoyed the peace and tranquillity. Then he would head back.

IT WAS NOW 9.30 p.m. and the bottle was completely empty. But Alistair still felt fine. His mind was fixed on living. He started the car, reversed out of the barn and drove back down to the lane. He was in no fit state to drive, but it didn't matter. Once the car was through the gate, he switched over to Auto Drive which he knew would get him there safely. He was just a glorified passenger.

During the journey, Alistair's mind focussed again on what lay ahead. Dozens of cameras, TV reporters and journalists staring at him on the stage as the results were announced. At home, viewers watching like the crowd at the Roman Coliseum. Judging him. Laughing at the pathetic number of votes he would receive. Savouring his demise and humiliation.

The car swung out onto the A259 and headed west towards Brighton. He winced as approaching car headlights dazzled him as they sped past. Onward along the coast road, through Seaford and Peacehaven and on towards the traumatic spectacle that lay ahead. He started to feel anxious again. All the calmness of the countryside evaporated with the setting sun, diminishing as each passing mile took him further away from the farm.

He passed through Rottingdean as the blurred Auto Drive display showed his arrival time at the sports hall would be in twenty-one minutes. He began to shake and his stomach churned. What was he doing? He had decided on a way out and now he was heading back into the jaws of hell.

He could see the lights of a truck coming over the brow of the hill about half a mile ahead. As it got closer, he saw the branding was for the same supermarket as the lorry that killed Sarah. How fitting. The massive Robo-Lorry got nearer, heading east, presumably to replenish one of the stores in Eastbourne or Newhaven. The lights got brighter and he gripped the steering wheel, hitting the Auto Drive's override button with his foot. He suddenly saw Sarah's face in the piercing headlights, which began to fill the windscreen like the sun. She was smiling, gently, serenely, and holding out her arms. He felt calm again. At peace. He turned the wheel and drove into the light.

76

Harvey

THURSDAY 8 MAY 2025

Election Night

'Good to see you' said Harvey, as Dale approached him in the sports hall.

'Only here in a professional capacity' Dale replied. 'Wouldn't be out this late if they weren't paying me.' He smiled, but Harvey knew his friend was only joking. Dale would be there even if he wasn't co-hosting the election night coverage for BBC Brighton. Someone else was anchoring back in the studio, but the producer thought it a good idea to have Dale there on-site, given that his sparring partner had a very strong chance of winning.

'How you feeling, H?' said Dale. 'Nervous?'

'To be honest, I don't know what to feel' replied Harvey. 'And, anyway, there's a bit of a distraction, what with Alistair Buckland having gone AWOL. The powers that be are getting nervous.'

'Yes, I heard' said Dale. 'Guess he'll turn up somewhere. I've just been trying to get a feel for how it's all going from the hand count.'

'And?'

'Hard to tell exactly. Looks like you're slightly ahead on the paper votes, but the electronic result is where it will be decided and the adjudicators aren't saying anything yet. But the exit poll suggests it may be closer than expected.'

'Incredible' said Harvey. 'The seagull guy has more integrity than both of them put together.'

He pointed at the student dressed in the enormous, homemade seagull costume. It was all consuming, with his skinny, stockinged legs sticking out the bottom with a pair of big yellow flippers on his feet. There was a small hole just beneath the large beak to enable the occupant to see where he was going. He seemed to be sweating under the bright TV lights.

Claire came over to join them, having been talking to a friend from the local OP who had volunteered as one of the marshals tonight.

'Janet just told me the police are here' she said.

'To arrest Deakin do you think?' said Dale. Harvey wasn't sure if he was asking as a curious friend or a radio reporter. He suspected both.

'She thinks not' said Claire. 'The guy covering the front door said they wanted to see the Acting Returning Officer and Dan Billingham. Seems they're all in the office right now.'

With that, Lionel Montague entered the hall looking flustered. He spoke to a group of officials and one of them started dialling on their phone. Dan Billingham was not far behind and looked equally disturbed and agitated. He spoke to Lionel, who nodded, and Dan then hurried towards the main doors. Lionel caught Harvey's eye and beckoned him over.

'Better go' said Harvey. 'I'll let you know what's going on.' Lionel met him half way.

'Can you find your Election Agent please, Mr Britten? Then, please come into the office with me. Soon as you can, and don't speak to anyone. Excuse me, I need to tell the other candidates.'

Lionel rushed off and Harvey wondered what was going on. He could see Sam in the press area, talking to reporters, and gestured for her to come over.

'What is it?' she said as she got to her father. 'Not the result already, surely?'

'Something's up' said Harvey.

HARVEY and the other candidates crammed into the office with their Election Agents. There were fourteen of them altogether and, not least because one of them was dressed as a seagull, there was very little space to move. Harvey stood near the front alongside Bradley Deakin. Everyone knew that his own Election Agent was indisposed, so the guy with him was presumably standing in.

Lionel finally spoke, once the door was squeezed shut.

'I'm afraid I have some very bad news' he said, sombrely. 'I'm informed that Alistair Buckland was involved in a very serious traffic accident a couple of hours ago on the way here. He's been taken to Brighton Hospital with severe injuries and is currently undergoing emergency surgery as I speak. I don't have any more details, but I understand his injuries are extremely serious. However – at the moment – he's still alive.'

'What happens with the election result?' asked Deakin. Harvey thought it was a bit callous to be asking.

'Well' said Lionel. 'The rules are clear that the election would be declared void if I were informed that an official party candidate had died before the result is announced. That is, unless the candidate is an independent, in which case it would continue. Now, in this sad case, I'm pleased to say that Mr Buckland is still alive, so the result can proceed and will stand - assuming we don't hear of any adverse change to his condition in the meantime.'

'And when do you expect the announcement to take place?' asked one of the other independents.

'I think we'll have a result within the hour' Lionel replied.

'Shouldn't you delay it until the position is clearer?' asked Deakin. Harvey assumed his opponent saw a glimmer of hope that the result might be annulled at the very last minute. That would give his team time to re-group with a fresh campaign.

'That's not necessary within the rules' said Lionel. 'Once the result is known, I'm obliged to announce it as soon as practically possible. Therefore, – and, for his sake, I really hope it is the case –

as long as Mr Buckland is still alive when the result is decided, then I will announce as planned. Once I've done so, it will then legally stand - whatever happens with his health afterwards.'

'But how will you know whether he's alive or dead at the exact time you make the announcement?' said Deakin, who could clearly smell blood. 'What if the time of death was, say, two minutes before you announce? Surely it would be better to wait until tomorrow when the position is clearer?'

'Well' said Lionel, patiently. 'In your example, I would not have known at the time of the announcement - so it would stand. Look, Dan Billingham has gone to the hospital and we've agreed that I'll call him just before I'm ready to announce. He'll check with the doctors and if, hopefully, Mr Buckland is still with us - in whatever state - at that time, then I will proceed. Now, please go back outside and do not discuss this with the media until I brief them myself. All queries should be addressed to me.'

Harvey and Sam returned to the hall. For now, Dale was classed as 'the media' - placing them both in a difficult situation. They decided to keep out of his way, just for the time being.

'Just when you think things couldn't get any more bizarre with this bloody election . . .' said Sam. Harvey had to agree.

77

Bradley

FRIDAY 9 MAY 2025

Election Night

'This is a potential miracle!' said Peter.

Bradley felt a sense of guilt at effectively wishing a man dead, but had to agree. If Buckland had deliberately driven into the path of a Robo-lorry as the TV news was saying - and was now as near to death as he must be, going by the state of the car wreckage - then he'd be doing everyone a favour by shuffling off his mortal coil as soon as possible.

'Have we confirmed if Lionel is right about all this?' asked Bradley. It had been an hour since they had all been called into the office and time was running out. It was nearly midnight and, unless an unlikely re-count was required, the result must surely be imminent.

'Afraid he's spot-on' said Peter. 'The legal team confirm that Buckland needs to die any time now for the election to be called off. Once Lionel hits the stage and calls it, the result will stand. We've got our own people at the hospital to agree Buckland's condition before kick-off, so it won't just be down to Dan Billingham's assessment. But the POG actually has as much to gain by binning this as we do.'

'Can't someone turn off his life support?' said Bradley, but immediately realised it was the wrong thing to say. 'Sorry. How is he anyway?'

'He's still in surgery' said Peter. 'Pretty beaten up by all accounts. He's got massive internal injuries as you can imagine. I don't wish ill on the man, really, but if he were to die a few minutes *after* the announcement, it would just be so . . .'

'. . . frustrating? Yes, I know' said Bradley. 'Any chance it doesn't actually matter and I've won?'

'I believe it's closer than we could have hoped, given Rod's situation. But never underestimate the resolve and dedication of the OP's loyal core vote. I doubt it will be enough, though. But I really don't know. Britten still has to be favourite.'

They looked around the packed hall. An odd mood had descended since news of the accident broke. Obviously, everyone from the POG looked sombre and miserable, although they hadn't looked much happier beforehand. The paper count had finished, but most people now voted on-line. Bradley longed for the old-fashioned paper-only system. The result would have taken a good three or four hours longer, buying them more time. But electronic votes are now calculated at the press of a button, so it would all be over by 1 a.m. latest.

'Either way, we're still trying to force a delay in the announcement' said Peter 'regardless of what the rule book says. This is a unique situation and should be treated as such. Our lawyers are arguing it out with Lionel now.'

'Good' said Bradley 'but I'd hate to force an adjournment only to find I'd actually won.'

'Well' said Peter. 'On the plus side, the result would never be known if they called it off' said Peter. 'We would all start from scratch.'

'A thought to cherish' said Bradley, sarcastically. He wasn't sure if he had the stomach to do it all over again.

78

Lionel

FRIDAY 9 MAY 2025

Election Night

Lionel ended the phone call. He was back in the office with the remaining candidates but, this time, without their agents, to provide a bit more space. It was half past one. He had known the result for over an hour but the OP lawyers had been trying to delay the announcement ever since. Getting expert legal opinion so late at night had been difficult but they had finally supported Lionel's interpretation. He *had* to announce the result.

'He's out of surgery' he said 'but still critical in Intensive Care. However, all parties confirm that he's alive and the doctors don't expect that position to change in the immediate future. So, shall we proceed?'

'I guess so' said Deakin, looking forlorn.

'In that case. I have called you in because it's customary to tell you the result before we go on stage to give you chance to digest it beforehand. So, no fist pumping or swearing when I formally announce it to the world. This is British democracy in action and I expect you to act with dignity, humility and good sportsmanship. Are we all agreed? Right.'

. . .

AS HE REACHED THE LECTERN, front and centre on the stage, Lionel looked back to ensure that all the candidates were lined up in position. They were, except for the buffoon dressed as a seagull. He was still negotiating the stairs, waddling from side to side in his flippers and at serious risk of tipping over. Finally, he negotiated the top step and stumbled like an inebriated duck to his assigned spot on the stage. Once they were all in place, it was time.

THE NEW MP shook hands with his vanquished opponents who, as instructed, smiled and shook hands with equal enthusiasm. Anyone would think they had voted for him themselves. Lionel gestured to the winner, prompting him to give his victory speech. He walked to the podium and, having gone through the formalities of thanking Lionel and his team, began to address the crowd and the cameras.

"I'm both humbled and amazed to be standing here as the new MP for Brighton and Hove. It's a huge honour and I really cannot express what it means to me. I offer every single person in this constituency my solemn word – whether you voted for me or not – to work tirelessly, night and day, week in week out, to serve your interests to the very best of my ability. Above everything else that has gone on over these past few traumatic weeks, you - and the interests of Brighton and Hove - remain the single most important consideration. I will *not* let you down.

There is no question that this contest has been divisive and has brought out the very worst in the public, press and social media in passing instant comment and judgements without seeing all the evidence. Assassinating the good character of honourable people, either by manipulating the truth or – in some cases – accepting down-right lies as irrefutable fact. All to further the cause of their own favoured candidate or political beliefs.

In so many ways, it has been a disgraceful episode, symptomatic of the world we now live in. A world where both mainstream and social media have the power to create their own truth and feed it to their followers - fuelling their prejudices and pre-conceptions. I pray things will now change. That this episode might encourage people to think again about believing the worst of people first or in only listening to opinion that mirrors their own intransigent views.

As I speak, a good man lies in hospital fighting for his life. Regardless of whether you agree with his politics, his lifestyle choices or anything else about him that doesn't fit with your own utopian ideal of utter perfection, we should all say a prayer for him tonight and hope that he recovers from his terrible injuries.

All he sought to do was serve this community, just like the rest of us. As did my predecessor as MP for this constituency, Sarah Billingham. We still do not know the true circumstances of her death and speculation has, again, been too quickly taken as fact. But if she really did lose her life at the hands of misguided fanatics who believe that their political ideals must prevail at any cost, then we should all hang our heads in shame that the world has come to such a place.

I will work tirelessly to follow in her footsteps to honour her reputation for fairness and justice. Her lifelong desire was to make Brighton and Hove as good as it can possibly be for the wonderful people who live there. Hers are big shoes, but I will do my very best to fill them. This city deserves nothing less. Thank you all.'

The audience applauded enthusiastically, more than they'd done when Lionel had actually announced the result. He reflected on the speech he'd just heard. The irony was that any one of them could have given an identical address themselves. After the firestorm that had engulfed this election, and the fall-out that would doubtless continue long after tonight, deep down, they were all the same. Flawed human beings, each with just a slightly different slant on the world. Any one of them could realistically have done the job and, with such political uncertainty at Westminster and a General Election possibly on the horizon, it might all count for nothing anyway. They could, very easily, be doing it all over again very soon. Lionel asked himself the big question - was it really worth it?

Westminster

THURSDAY 18 SEPTEMBER 2025

As he stood on the terrace of the House of Commons, looking out across the River Thames towards Westminster Bridge, the new MP for Brighton and Hove took a deep breath. It was a late summer day and still quite warm, with no breeze to spoil the occasion.

The endless refurbishment of the Houses of Parliament was finally reaching an end and the terrace had not long re-opened. Other MPs were spread along its full length, either socialising or engaged in impromptu meetings. There were far worse places to be and Harvey felt the same sense of privilege that he had when visiting as Sarah's guest, some eighteen months before. How things had changed since then.

Today he was giving his maiden speech and was taking a few quiet moments beforehand to gather his thoughts. It was a daunting occasion for any fledgling MP and he was absolutely terrified. On the positive side, he knew that everyone in the House had been through the same terror themselves at some point in their Parliamentary careers, so it was rare to get anything other than polite encouragement from both sides. Being shouted down in a hail of abuse would come later. If there was a later.

It was by no means certain how long he would enjoy the privilege of being an MP. The Prime Minister had doubtless breathed a huge sigh of relief that Bradley Deakin had not been elected. Unsurprisingly, the OP finally lost faith in their leader, Matthew Draper, very soon after the election failed to bring the new Messiah into their midst. A leadership contest would be taking place at the Party Conference next month, but the list of faceless hopefuls was as uninspiring as ever.

On the other side, the Prime Minister was still battling on. Many of his MPs felt he should have called a General Election for June or October, before the Opposition had chance to regroup. But he still had only a very narrow lead in the polls. So-called experts still believed he might go for next May, but no-one really knows anything in politics. If the speculation did turn out to be true, then Harvey's tenure as MP would last exactly a year. He was under no illusions that both main parties would field strong candidates next time round and, as an independent, his chances of retaining the seat would be slim. He would not be too disappointed. He had fulfilled the promise made in his acceptance speech to work hard for his constituents, and had done so since day one. But it was often frustrating and a complete reversal of his retirement plans. He was hardly ever home and spent too many nights in a small rented flat in Clapham, where Claire joined him as often as she could.

He had won with a majority of 3,254 over Bradley Deakin. Alistair Buckland had clung to life for two days but, sadly, succumbed to his injuries without regaining consciousness. Harvey had gone to his funeral, which was very well attended. Dan Billingham had given a very moving eulogy and, as the MP, Harvey had said a few words too.

Deakin had largely fallen out of favour with his party and they had no plans to put him forward as a candidate again. The only real winners in the whole episode were the lawyers. Legal action was still flying in all directions. The BBC had decided to axe Deakin's show during the summer so he was suing for breach of contract. He was expected to win a hefty pay-off, but so-called media experts said he was now a 'toxic' brand. No charges had been brought against him but suspicion carries its own sentence.

To make matters worse, his wife's divorce lawyer was currently playing hard ball and it was going to be an expensive and acrimonious split.

Each of Sharon Morgan's other clients could also afford expensive lawyers and had all lodged injunctions and lawsuits to prevent publication of their involvement with her. Some had succeeded, although their names still found their way onto social media. Divorce lawyers were having a field day there too, the biggest being a Russian oligarch called Ivan Pevlonichic, although he had mysteriously disappeared. The papers said his father-in-law was urgently looking for him, saying he was concerned for his safety.

But whilst none of her clients could argue that they had been seeing a prostitute, publication of all the other documents and alleged pillow talk had hit legal problems. Sharon's honesty had been discredited over the rape claim. If she had lied about the rape and the affair with Deakin in her twenties, then the publication of anything else she said was struggling to get past the lawyers. On legal advice, the *Daily Record* had eventually decided not to publish *any* allegations and had spiked the whole package. It must have been a very hard decision, given the enormous fee they had paid Sharon. Ultimately, they had paid a million pounds just to discredit a local Councillor which had, in many people's eyes, then driven him to suicide. It was no surprise that they no longer had the stomach for it, nor that both Terry Macdonald and the *Daily Record's* Editor had quietly been asked to resign.

It remained a mystery as to where Sharon – or her body – was now. Accusations hung around Bradley Deakin like a bad smell but her more unpleasant clients could also not be ruled out. The 'man in leather' was still the prime suspect but had never been traced, just like the other two men in black. Rod Archer had similarly not been charged. But he had not been formally ruled out of the police enquiry either and remained in a state of limbo, clouded by suspicion. He too had lawyers trying to sue the police, the BBC and Walter Coogan for defamation of character. But he would get nowhere unless some new evidence turned up to clear his name beyond doubt. His career was effectively over. But at the end of the day, no-one knew who had killed Sarah and - the way things were going - never would.

So, Harvey leant on the terrace barrier, looking out across the River Thames and watching the tourist boats pass by. He could well understand why there was such a lack of good political leaders coming up through the ranks. Who in their right mind would choose a life in politics nowadays? The constant press scrutiny and social media abuse would test the resolve of even the most dedicated would-be Prime Minister from an early age. Harvey wondered if we therefore get the politicians we deserve.

He was suddenly distracted by the familiar sound of seagulls cawing overhead. He had never realised that the birds lived in London too, but had soon come to realise that the city, notably the river and its estuary out towards the sea, had plenty to attract them. So, seeing seagulls over Westminster was not unusual, but their familiar sound was more often than not drowned out by heavy traffic noise.

Harvey watched them circle overhead, kidding himself that these had actually flown up from Brighton to wish him well on his big day. Their cousins at home in East Sussex were at least safe for now. The Council had delayed the cull following Buckland's tragic death. It was not known when, or if, it would be revisited. The student in the Seagull costume had – just like the other independent candidates - lost his deposit. But, in many ways, Harvey believed he had actually been the only real winner. He, alone, had achieved what he'd set out to do when deciding to stand in the election – simply wanting to prevent the seagull cull. So, who really were the fools?

He looked at his watch and realised it was time to go in for his speech. As he did so, he heard a light pitter-patter on his shoulder. He knew instantly what it was. He twisted his head to see a telling, white dribble on his suit lapel. He stared up at the gulls who continued to circle and caw loudly above him. For the first time in his life, they'd got him. He should have been angry, but instead just gave a wry smile. A couple of POG MPs, who'd witnessed the incident, came over with serviettes to help him mop up the mess.

'People say it's lucky' said one. 'But I've never known why. Bloody things drive you mad. I suppose you're well used to it.'

'Yes' said Harvey, 'I think my feathered constituents are just making sure I keep my feet firmly on the ground.'

He knew he needed to, with or without their reminder. The David and Goliath aspect of his victory had captured the public imagination and he was being offered countless appearances on television and radio. Many said he was a natural and, following an appearance on *'Look – Drew's Talking'* (the show that had replaced Deakin's programme, hosted by Drew McKinley), the producer said he would seriously like to offer him his own talk show one day - should the political career not work out. Harvey didn't actually say no. Stranger things had happened.

Epilogue - Part 1
WEDNESDAY - 29 APRIL 2026

The spring sunshine was pleasantly warm so she chose a garden sun-lounger for her usual mid-morning coffee and croissant.

Today, she was browsing through the BBC website, something she now did only occasionally, just to keep an eye on things back in England. Normally, she preferred to read the French papers, being more relevant to her new life. But today was the first anniversary of her disappearance and she was checking that the story wasn't being revisited or, more specifically, that no-one was getting any closer to finding her. There was some limited coverage, but the general tone seemed to be that she was long dead at the hands of persons unknown, so the world had moved on. The police had not entirely closed the case but had certainly downgraded it, pending any new evidence turning up. There was nothing to implicate anyone directly and all concerned had watertight alibis. The trail seemed to have gone cold, which suited Sharon perfectly.

She was happy in her gorgeous little *gite* in southern France. It provided both a sanctuary from her old life and the springboard into her new one. So far, it was everything she had always dreamed of - providing the idyllic country hideaway normally only found in travel brochures. She was finally home.

It would have been easy to leave a clue that the man in leather was actually one of *Big Red's* henchmen, sent to strong-arm her into withdrawing the revelations about him. She had no idea how he had traced her, but believed it must have been an insider at the *Daily Record*. Either way, Ivan's thug had forced his way into the flat and pinned her to the wall by her throat. He made it quite clear what would happen if a word about Ivan ever appeared in the papers and emphasised his point by slapping her hard across the face, sending a splatter of blood across the wall. He then threw her to the floor, breaking a coffee table and bruising her ribs.

Once he'd left, she realised this was actually not all bad news and Ivan's heavy-handed approach had instead played right into her hands. She messed up the flat even more to accentuate the disturbance and then donned the wig and sun-glasses that were the final touch of the scruffy clothes she was wearing for the trip. She set off on foot to St Pancras Station, using a CCTV-free route that she had carefully plotted out over several weeks beforehand.

Sharon had then immediately become Dominique Resseaux, a wealthy Parisian beauty therapist who had retired to the countryside to get away from the rat race. Any hint of an English accent was explained by her mother being English and the family having lived in Surrey until Dominique was around ten years old. But her story was never questioned, not least because her pronunciation was almost flawless. People in her little village were not suspicious anyway and welcomed her into their small community like an old friend.

The plan worked well as the police immediately suspected foul play. Slipping away quietly was one thing, but being able to convincingly fake her own death was an added bonus, thanks to *Big Red's* clumsy intervention. She could easily have left a trail of clues to his door, but this level of uncertainty suited her much better. No prime suspect to question meant there was less chance of anyone finding out she was still very much alive.

As the months wore on, Gabrielle and Sharon's names fell out of the public consciousness and Dominique grew stronger from the embers of their sad lives. She had integrated herself into the community and been enjoying her new, peaceful life. She had been offered the chance to run a small beautician's franchise in the local hairdresser's shop as Elizabet, the owner, was keen to use her services. Whilst that would give her an interest, she was in no hurry. For now, the idea of having absolutely no ties or obligations was blissful.

She had spent a considerable amount of time reflecting on her life and those involved in it. The process had been cathartic and helped make peace with her demons. For too long she had been driven by anger, hatred and resentment, either of Tom or men in general. It had eaten away at her soul and clouded any sense of reason or judgement. It had led her to only see the bad in people, especially her clients. Even poor FG. Alistair Buckland was a good, honest, caring and sensitive man and she'd thrown him to the dogs. His death – and her possible involvement in motivating it - had been the source of endless nights of anguish during her time in France. She quickly changed her background story to one where her move from Paris was actually due to the recent death of her beloved husband Michel. It helped explain her air of sadness and why she often burst into tears. As an unintended side-benefit, it also kept any potential male suitors at bay and better explained why a humble beautician had so much disposable income.

She would have done anything to turn back the clock. She wasn't sure if, realistically, she could ever have made a life with Alistair. But she could have kept him as a true friend – with or without benefits. Instead, she had betrayed him in the most callous way possible. Was it for the money? Was it because that sleazy journalist had left her no choice? Was it because, deep down, like all her clients, she subconsciously wanted to cause him harm?

It was probably all of those reasons. But she had since learned to understand her own weaknesses - to conquer her anger and animosity towards men and the world in general. But she could never forgive herself. Whether or not it was suicide or drunk driving didn't really matter. He was dead and she had set him off on that tragic path. She had allowed the world to see their relationship as something tacky and worthless when it was actually nothing of the sort. It was the most precious thing in her life. If only she had realised it at the time.

She had also reconciled her thoughts about Tom. A lifetime of resentment, hatred and bitterness had perhaps killed every other feeling she had about him - beyond revenge. But for what? He wasn't a monster. He'd been seeing her whilst also having a girl-friend. Was that so different to any number of other people? If what he'd said in that TV interview was true, he had simply made a mistake. One that he had regretted ever since. If she'd only kept her cool, he might have left Emma and come back to her. Instead, she had just run off without even giving him chance to explain.

Her whole life – and the direction it had taken – was based on assumptions, born from the man she loved – the only man she had ever loved – betraying her. Yet, when he had come to see her, the spark was still there. On both sides. She tried to hide it and thought he did too. He should have been angry at what she was doing. Lying about him when, in reality, he'd acted honourably when they were teenagers. It was *her* who lied and he ended their fledgling relation-ship because of it. But she used it against him as cheap revenge, deliberately trying to hurt him. Making out that he was some kind of paedo child rapist – the worst possible accusation that anyone could throw at him.

Despite her story later being questioned by the evidence of so-called school friends and work mates, she had still destroyed his TV and political career. The suspicion of murdering the MP didn't help, of course – although she didn't believe he was involved. But people always decide there's no smoke without fire. At the end of the day, he'd had sex with a twelve year old girl, even though he was little more than a boy himself and she was a very willing partner. His family-friendly image was shattered.

Part of her wished she could make it right. Whether it was guilt or trying to reconcile her own feelings, her hatred had certainly mellowed. Like FG, she realised that she had thrown away a golden opportunity for love and happiness. The thought still haunted her. Sometimes she dreamed that Tom was there with her in France and that they were blissfully happy - her life complete. But then, dark storm clouds would suddenly appear and he'd crumble to dust in front of her eyes before she awoke.

As always during periods of reflection, she decided to consign it all to history and focus on the future. But she had been worrying lately about being watched. Nothing solid, just a feeling. A man standing at the bus stop when she came out of the Patisserie. Was that the same man she'd seen two days earlier at the petrol station? Probably a co-incidence. But she never lost the fear that, one day, they would find her.

She took a sip of coffee and looked up at a flock of seagulls cawing noisily overhead as they flew by. It was a curious sight so far inland and she wondered where they were going - or where they had come from.

She was suddenly startled by the heavy iron knocker banging three times on the front door. It was a confident, assertive knock. Not the embarrassed tap of a neighbour. She felt fear for no apparent reason. It could be anyone. She crept back into the cottage and along the short hallway to the front door. If only she could have installed a spy-hole like she always did in London, but the solid oak door was too thick. She took a breath and opened it. A familiar face stood before her. She felt scared, but he smiled. It was a warm, sincere smile. The one that always used to melt her heart, long ago.

'Hello Sharon' he said, softly.

'Hello Tom.'

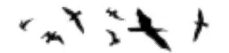

Epilogue - Part 2
WEDNESDAY - 29 APRIL 2026

He knew she was in. The investigative team had spent the best part of a year tracking her down and they were not about to lose her now. Their surveillance had followed her to the Patisserie this morning and then back home, around half an hour ago. There was no exit route at the rear, other than across fields, and they had that covered anyway. A couple dressed as hikers were monitoring from a safe distance through binoculars.

He was wondering whether to knock again, when the door slowly opened. And there she was. He wasn't surprised to see her now blond with a short bob haircut, replacing the luxurious dark hair she had last year. He had seen a recent photograph of her when they'd asked him to confirm they had the right person. She was coming out of a shop, looking relaxed and with a contented smile on her face. There was no doubt in his mind it was Sharon.

'I don't want to upset you' he said. 'I imagine you're not too happy to see me – or anyone else from the past for that matter, I guess. But can I come in, please? I just want to talk. Honestly, I come in peace!'

She paused for a few seconds and then raised a nonchalant

eyebrow, which he took as agreement to enter. She walked back inside, leaving the door open, which was also a good sign.

He closed the thick, wooden door behind him and followed her through to the kitchen. The cottage interior was traditional, like stepping back a century or more. He was slightly surprised. He'd have expected that– like most people – she would have kept the quaint exterior but then gutted the inside in favour of modern décor and fittings. But the furniture couldn't have been more in keeping with its heritage. Bradley wondered if she was simply conforming to a long held ideal of how a dream cottage should look. She was now living that dream.

'Coffee?' she said, with her back turned towards him as she filled the machine.

'Thank you' he replied. It was hard to sense her mood, but he imagined it was mostly shock. She wouldn't have expected – or certainly wanted – to be located.

'How did you find me?' she said, finally turning to look at him. She took off her sunglasses and revealed those eyes.

'I can't take all the credit' he said, trying to keep upbeat and light. 'Well, any of it really. A TV production company has spent the best part of a year trying to track you down.'

'Why?' she replied, still largely expressionless.

'Fascination I guess,' he went on. 'Seeing an opportunity for a good story if they ever found you and . . . then got you to speak to them.'

'And why would I want to do that?'

'They suspected you wouldn't. That's probably where I come in. They asked if I would like to present the documentary about how they found you and . . . do the interview.'

She turned away, an air of contempt clear in her demeanour. He could see why.

'Don't get me wrong' he said quickly. 'That's not why I took them up on the offer. Honestly. I ought to want to kill you after what you . . . sorry. Wrong choice of words given the accusations I've had to face. No, I ought to want to . . .'

'I know' she said. 'And I probably deserve it. I'm sorry. But . . .'

'Look' he said, pleased she was at least talking and, indeed, showing some remorse. 'What I'm trying to say is that I'm not here just to get an interview. I've given it a lot of thought over the past year. Goodness knows I've had time. My TV career fell off a cliff faster than my political ambitions. No-one will touch me. My wife's divorcing me and I've only started seeing my son again recently after the court made her. Even then, my relationship with him is, at best, fractious. He's fifteen and . . .'

'Same age as you when we first met' she interrupted. 'Does he have a girlfriend?'

'Actually, he does.' Bradley knew where Sharon was going. 'She's fifteen too, and . . . well. . . I don't know if they . . .'

'Hope he asked for a birth certificate' she said, with a wry smile. Her eyes sparkled just slightly and he felt a touch of their power. She had made a little joke, that can only be good.

'Different times' he said. 'They're all on social media nowadays so their lives are laid out for all to see.' She shrugged. 'Anyway, what I mean is, I've every reason to hate you and never want to see you again. When you disappeared, and people said you must be dead, well, I probably should have been pleased. But I wasn't.'

'Not even a little bit?'

'No. I was angry after I saw you and then, of course, I had to defend all your lies *and* prove I wasn't behind your disappearance. It didn't allow much time to think about anything else. But after all the election thing went away, I found myself feeling sorry. About a lot of things really - but especially you. I realised how much I'd hurt you back then and God knows I've paid the price. Not just . . . you know, now, but for all my life since we split up. You really were the girl of my dreams, Sharon. I know that now. I knew it back then too, but you never gave me chance to explain. Emma was always second best and, yes, it's true, I married her on the rebound. I paid for that decision dearly − and I don't just mean the divorce. We were never really happy. It was great at the start until I stumbled on you again, but then I realised that it was you I needed.'

'So why are you telling me this now?' she replied. She looked slightly tearful, but was holding it back.

'Because when I thought you were dead . . . I began to realise all of that. I desperately wished . . . hoped . . . prayed that you were OK. Then, when the TV company approached me, it was just the biggest relief of my life to know you were alive and well. It was silly but . . . I was just really happy. Nuts isn't it?'

She didn't say anything but was definitely softening.

'So, I know what you did was awful. Cruel even. But I want you to know I forgive you. I understand why you did it and part of me thinks I deserved it. So, this is just an opportunity to see you and say – in the cold light of day - that I'm just so sorry for everything. You were – are - the only woman I ever loved. I think I spent the rest of my life trying to find someone who matched you. I'm not a woman-iser like they say – like Emma says. Really, I'm not. It was always about you. Finding someone who could replace you, but no-one ever did.'

She was staring at him in a way that he liked. A spark of affection perhaps? Then she turned away, changing the subject.

'You didn't explain. How did you . . . they . . . find me?'

'Oh, I don't know' he replied, slightly annoyed to be getting off the point. 'An indiscreet former intern from your solicitors who helped you buy this place bore them a grudge and apparently took the silver shilling to give up a few leads. A documentary about money laundering where, by chance, they interviewed a former city trader - who's now in prison - about the various schemes people use. He hinted about being involved in something with you and . . . to be honest, I'm not entirely sure. I just know it was a meticulous operation with a bit of luck thrown in here and there. Either way, I'm here. And the point is, yes, I'm here in part to see if you would agree to an interview - to give your side of the story and put the record straight about me. I think you owe me that.'

'And the other part?' she said, still calmly.

'What?'

'You said you were partially here for an interview. What was the other part?'

'Well' he said 'Its like I was saying. I've come to realise that . . .'

'You want *us* to get back together?' she said, apparently in disbelief. 'Is that it?'

'No . . . yes. I don't know, really' he replied. He'd hoped she would be less dismissive. 'Is it really such a stupid thought, though? I guess it is.'

'Its been a *very* long time' she said, with a more conciliatory tone. 'A hell of a lot of water under the bridge. Forgive me if I'm more than a little cynical.'

'Of course,' he said, feeling more encouraged. 'Look, I guess it isn't something that can be rushed. But the TV documentary could be good for both of us. Do you really want to run for the rest of your life? You haven't committed a crime – well, maybe travelling under a false passport and a bit of tax avoidance, but that isn't major. A good lawyer would get you off with a fine. You didn't exactly fake your own death, people just assumed it. And what you said about me . . . well, that's where you can explain yourself. I can help, by being seen to forgive you and ensuring the documentary shows you in the best possible light.

But it would help me too, I guess. This documentary is the first bit of TV work I've had since it all blew up. If you told the truth, it would help clear my name. You probably owe me that. And the world needs to know about our love, not think it was based on a horrible rape.

But, honestly, all that is unimportant. I know it's stupid, perhaps mad. But I've given it such a lot of thought over the past twelve months. Those lonely days and nights, I came to the conclusion that I was a bloody fool and if I ever . . . ever . . . got the chance again . . . If it turned out that you were alive . . . then I'd bite the bullet and just . . . try to go back to how it was, or should have been. Rebuild what we had way back then . . . and would have now if I hadn't been such an idiot.'

She walked to the window and looked out without saying a word. The silence seemed to go on forever. He knew it had to be her move, but was getting impatient.

'If . . .' she said, finally. 'If we gave it a chance - and I'm not saying we should - how would it work? I love it here. Really, this is where I want to be.'

'I could live here too,' he said. 'I can see the appeal and there's an airport at Poitiers, so it's not as if the UK is a long way away. It has to be worth a try.'

'And the interview?'

'What do you think?' he asked. 'I won't do it if you really don't want to, it's your choice entirely. But, to be honest, they'll make the documentary anyway - with or without me and you - given the work that's gone into it. But if I did it *with* you . . . if we did it together . . . told our story, it could clear the slate clean to start all over again. With everything. What do you think?'

She was still staring out of the window, but then slowly turned. She walked towards him and her eyes were alight. It was a long time since he'd received the full power of that look. There was a slight sense of trepidation in her eyes, but also excitement. Love? Possibly. She stood before him and put her arms around the back of his neck. Instinctively he put his own around her waist and pulled her close. Her head fell against his shoulder and their mutual grip tightened.

'You swear you're not just saying this so I'll co-operate?' she whispered.

'On my son's life.'

He pulled his head back and looked into her eyes. They were now like lasers into his soul. He kissed her. It seemed to go on for hours and it felt good.

'It feels like coming home' she said, smiling.

'Close the front door behind you' he joked. She put her head back on his shoulder.

He smiled to himself. Job done. She would do the interview, just as he convinced the producer she would do, if they would just let him ask first. BBC, ITV, Sky, Amazon – they would all be fighting for a prime-time airing of the documentary. The documentary that would finally clear his name. After a year in the wilderness his reha-bilitation could then finally begin.

Bradley Deakin was back in the game.

Author's Notes

Firstly, a big thank you for reading this book and I really hope you enjoyed it. Please leave a rating and feedback on Amazon as I'd love to hear what you think.

Just a bit of background on the story. Firstly, you will have noticed my (clumsy) way of not associating any character to an identifiable real party. The story is primarily about the people involved so I didn't want them judged (or, rather, pre-judged), liked or disliked on the basis of the reader's politics. You shouldn't even deduce that the parties are automatically Labour and Conservative. To me, it really doesn't matter – apart from the 'Stop the Cull' Party – and I truly have no idea myself which is which. The backgrounds of the characters are deliberately obtuse so, please, don't even try to work it out.

There are, of course, risks in setting a book in the near future because time and reality will eventually overtake it. If you are reading this in 2024 or later and, by then, one political party or other is actually enjoying a huge majority, I would still wager that the Opposition Party of the day is looking for a charismatic leader to turn their fortunes around. Nothing really changes.

Not knowing exactly what the future will look like is actually a great way to cover up technical inaccuracies. If you have an intimate knowledge of anything mentioned in this book that is not accurately portrayed according to the way it looks, or is done, in 2018 – when I wrote the book - then I apologise. However, I offer an all-embracing excuse that everything will have changed to the way I describe by 2024. Probably.

Speaking of which, you will notice that - apart from driverless vehicles and a few minor electronic developments - my version of the world in 2024 does not look too much different to 2018. That is because I looked back six years to 2012 and realised that, apart from a few major changes in technology, our day to day lives are actually pretty much the same. I therefore assumed the same will apply in another six years. However, if you are instead reading this book in 2024 whilst living on Mars then, sorry, I must have got that wrong too.

Whichever way the real world looks in 2024, I really hope that we are not still arguing about Brexit by then. It is a subject I have consciously avoided in the book because *no-one* can predict where all that will end up. Perhaps that's why you are living on Mars!

Either way, I really hope you enjoyed this book, regardless of how the world looks when real life catches up. As Harvey Britten says, what's the worst that could happen?

About the Author

Like Harvey Britten, Richard Wade took early retirement at the age of sixty from his work as a Compliance Director. He now spends his time writing the books that he wished he'd had the time to write years ago.

He lives with his wife Trish in Ealing, West London, but they spend a great deal of their time in Seaford, on the East Sussex coast, where they gained their love for the city of Brighton.

Having grown up in Yeovil, Somerset, Richard shares Harvey's inbuilt loyalty to the football team he has supported for over fifty years, Yeovil Town, but has adopted the Seagulls as his second team – not least because they win more often.

twitter.com/@wadecomply

instagram.com/@wadecomp

Acknowledgments

My thanks to all my friends and former work colleagues at the Rank Group Plc who so kindly paid for the laptop used to write this book as a retirement present.

Thanks also to Sheila Edwards for proof reading, help and very sound advice.

And to my wife, Trish, for her incredible patience and support whilst I was writing this book when there were jobs needing to be done.

39087721R00226

Printed in Poland
by Amazon Fulfillment
Poland Sp. z o.o., Wrocław